THE
LIGHT

*"Superb! Adventure and intrigue, action and insight—
THE LIGHT is vintage Storm."*

*—**Randall Murphree**, AFA Journal Editor, Former Judge
at Christy Awards for Excellence in Christian Fiction*

BUCK STORM

HUMPHREY HOUSE BOOKS

THE LIGHT by Buck Storm

Published by Humphrey House Books
www.humphreyhouse.co

ISBN-978-1-7347351-0-9

Cover design by Sarah Storm

Available in print from your local bookstore, online, or from the publisher at:
humphreyhouse.co

For more information on this book and the author please visit:
buckstorm.com

Brought to you by MSPC and the creative team at Humphrey House Books.

Library of Congress Cataloging-in-Publication Data
Storm, Buck
The Light / Buck Storm 1st ed.

1st printing April 2020
Printed in the United States of America

For those precious, nameless ones who wander the valley dark

Look to the east, the sky is graying

And the sun will soon break free of the hills

What a glorious day it will be

From the Author

So many requests. So many loyal readers and friends. This is for you. A continuation of the story that began with THE LIST. But, whether you came along on that first adventure or not, I trust you'll make some new and good friends in the following pages. Maybe an enemy or two as well. After all, the darker the night the brighter the dawn.

This foray into Biblical fiction has been a step off the usual path for me. I've had to ask a lot of questions, both of myself and others—there are a lot of smart people out there! Some of the things I've held onto since Sunday school have been challenged and shifted in the honest light of scripture and historical context. I've had to repaint a few pictures in my mind so I could paint them accurately for you.

And it's been good.

Because, in my experience, when I find myself in a season of shifting unbalance, that's where I can finally end and let God begin.

THE LIGHT walks the streets of Jerusalem during a dark, confusing, and brutal time—the fifty days between Christ's resurrection and Pentecost. And what a time! It's the stuff of wonder, almost science fiction. Scripture, as well as history, shows us amazing and otherworldly events. We see a time where the line between life and death blurs. We see the pride and cunning of the Jewish elite arm in arm with the bloody brutality of Rome. Yes, the tomb is empty, but where now is the promised King? What must those first believers have been thinking? What was their experience? What did they suffer? What glories were theirs?

The beautiful thing is, even on the very darkest of roads, God has a plan. One that's been in place from the foundation of the world. There is a miraculous and beautiful thread that stitches together the fabric of scripture—redemption for the *least of these*. That thread is the foundation of the Christian faith. It's our lifeline and the very song of God. I hope it's also the thread that binds together these books.

I believe the Word of God.

I believe He alone offers hope to the hopeless. He alone brings LIGHT.

Most of all, I believe deeply in the Star of this story.

I hope you will too.

– Buck Storm

1

Black.
He blinked his eyes, opened them wide, staring into the ink.
Nothing.

Thick, heavy, black nothing.

He lifted a hand in front of his face and strained in vain to
see it. Touched fingers to his eyes. How could anyplace be so
utterly devoid of light?

Flat on his back on a hard surface, that much he could
ascertain. He moved his hands outward. Stone, cold and rough.

Where am I? How did I get here?

With careful deliberation he searched his mind, his memory,
but could find no event leading to this nightmare.

His own voice startled. "Hello?"

No reply. He tried again, louder this time.

Concentrate. Focus. What's happened?

But the more he tried, the more tangled his mind became.
His thoughts like fish in a fast-moving stream and nothing but
bare hands to grab them with. Every time he got close to one, it
twisted and shot back to the murky depths of his subconscious.

It came to him with a rush that he might be dead. But how?
When? He had no memory of dying. But, then again, did anyone

remember life's final exit? How could he know? Shocked by the possibility, he tried to sit up, but brutal throbbing in his head dropped him, sick and dizzy, to his back again.

He tried to still himself by counting his breaths, but he lost track easily and had to keep starting over. How long he did this, he didn't know. Did it matter? What's time when you're dead?

At length, he managed to count a hundred consecutive breaths, then tried calling out again. "What is this place? What's happening here? Where am I?" No answer save the sharp slap-back of his own voice.

He started counting another hundred but lost consciousness somewhere in the sixties. He woke sometime later, sweat-soaked and cold to the bone. Panic rose in his chest.

He shouted until he lost his voice and even then continued on in a ragged whisper. Never in life had he been so thirsty. He tried to swallow but couldn't. He shivered and pulled himself into a fetal position. If he was dead, this was surely Hades. Nothing but black. No sun, no moon, no stars… And no sound save the wild gallop of his heart.

Until there was.

He might have been sleeping, he couldn't be sure, but then the sound was there. Footsteps, heavy and uneven, some distance away but coming closer. Pushing against the stone with both hands and feet, he scooted himself away from the sound, imagining in an instant a hundred kinds of devils. "Who's there?" he rasped.

The steps stopped. A thump, a scrape, something heavy moved and a hundred suns swung a blacksmith's hammer into his aching head. He lifted both hands to shield his face from the onslaught of light. "What's happening? What do you want?"

"Good, you're awake." A man's voice.

He lowered his hands with care, squinted into the assault, trying to let his eyes acclimate. Not a hundred suns; only a single torch throwing uncertain light across the stone walls of…what? A cave? A cell?

The speaker moved farther into the room, the flame revealing his form. Gaunt, stooped, and thick-browed, he wore the heavy cloak and turban of a Pharisee, robes pulled tight against the chill. His fingers were long and work hardened. He held the torch a bit higher, peering down with large, obsidian eyes. "Hmm, you've looked better, I'm sure. They tell me you're a rich man."

"What is this place?"

"For you? The deepest part of Hades, I'm afraid."

"I thought I was dead."

"You may well be, that remains to be seen. The way things stand, if I were a betting man, that's certainly where I'd place my shekels."

"Are you a betting man?"

"No."

"What do you want from me? Why am I here?"

"Ah, that's the question isn't it, Joseph of Arimathea?"

Joseph of Arimathea. Yes. Thoughts aligned. Memories returned with a rush. But still no concept of how he'd come to be here. "Ariella. Where is my wife?"

The man shrugged. "Somewhere, I'm sure. Trust me, at the moment she isn't your most immediate concern."

Joseph forced himself to sit. His stomach lurched but he ignored it. "What's happening here?"

"Yes. That's the question, isn't it? Get up. Time to go."

"Go where? Where am I? What is this place?"

"Get up."

"No. Not until you—"

The kick came from nowhere, and there was steel behind it. Joseph dropped back, stars dancing in his brain.

The man moved forward and squatted. "I think I need to explain the rules here, Joseph of Arimathea. And since there is really only one rule, it's easy to remember. Are you ready?" Joseph's vision tunneled and his head dipped. A sharp slap sent lights dancing across his vision. "Come back now, no time for naps." The man gripped Joseph's face with his free hand. "Are you in there? Can you hear me? Good. Now, rule number one— in this place, I am the rule. You obey because you have no choice. Now, again…get up."

2

One day earlier

Joseph of Arimathea stood on the rooftop patio of his expansive Mount Zion home looking out at a view unparalleled on earth—Jerusalem, in all its magnificence. Across the deep Valley of the Cheesemakers, God's Temple stood unflinching sentinel atop Mount Moriah, reflecting light-diamonds into the bright morning. A hundred cubits high, another hundred wide, white Jerusalem stone overlaid with pure gold, the greatest wonder in the world. How many mornings had he taken in this view? He leaned forward, resting his forearms on the patio wall. To the right of the Temple Mount, past the hippodrome and the City of David, sheep dotted the Mount of Olives, white ants from this distance. Three stories beneath him, the wide boulevards of Jerusalem's wealthy Upper City lay nearly deserted in the early hour. In the clear, spring air, the sound of splashing fountains accompanied the whistled tune of a bread vendor and the creaking wheels of the cart he pushed. A woman stepped out through a courtyard wall doorway and called to him, waving a coin.

White stone, broad streets, lush vegetation spilling over walls—here was the Upper City in all its glory, the Jerusalem of the affluent. Of the rich and the powerful. On the western edge of the district, the four towers of King Herod's palace rose high above its sprawling grounds, an edifice of magnificence and luxury unparalleled outside Rome itself. Just south and east of Joseph's perch, the great theater threw a deep shadow across homes and shops. Beyond the theater, dust climbed from the hippodrome as trainers put the chariot horses through an early morning workout.

A perfectly beautiful, perfectly ordinary Jerusalem day. Soon, the streets would fill. Business would ensue. People would get busy with their lives. Every one of them completely unaware of the tempest of sorrow and confusion roaring in Joseph's heart.

A breeze tugged his robe and his fists clenched. He wanted to ride. He needed to feel speed. Let the wind whip his body and mind and wash the pain of these last days from his soul. But in his heart he knew riding wouldn't help. Nothing would help. Yeshua, Son of God, Savior of Israel, would still be dead at the hands of the Romans. Brutally beaten and nailed to a cross, a ragged horror of blood and bare bone hanging open to the sky and sun and flies while the Sanhedrin mocked. The Sanhedrin! The elite of Israel. The very governing body he, Joseph, was a part of. Or at least had been a part of until Yeshua had pressed into his world. Yeshua had changed everything. Yeshua offered a man no quarter. *Yeshua* with his words and whips and eyes that held universes. Yeshua with his miracles and laughter and sun-browned hands. Yeshua with his love. Yeshua, rejected and killed by the very ones he'd come to save.

Oh, God, what have we done!

Joseph let his eyes wander past the Kidron Valley and out over the wilderness, his memory pulled to that nighttime ride when it had all begun. *The shepherd and his song...* More than three years ago now, but so fresh in his mind he remembered every detail. The campfire, the quiet rustle of sheep on the dark hills, the strong bite of country liquor on his tongue... And the old man's story of an infant. Thirty years, the old shepherd had said—thirty years since he'd seen the angels. Thirty years since he'd seen the child, the Promised One of Israel. The birth of the great Messiah who would deliver his people from their suffering. At the time, Joseph had scoffed. "And what's this Messiah's name?" He'd pressed the old man with good-natured sarcasm.

But the shepherd had only smiled across the flame, dark eyes dancing. "I think you'll hear it soon enough. I think you'll hear his name so often you'll have no choice but to curse it or to bend a knee…" Later, as Joseph rode away that night, the shepherd had begun to sing, calling his sheep from the hills, gathering, comforting. Joseph hadn't known why at the time, but that gentle, haunting melody had brought tears to his eyes as tender fingers of beauty and ancient melody touched something deep and broken in him.

And the song had continued, long after he'd ridden on.

For days and weeks and then years, the song echoed his dreams and demanded his waking hours. It whispered through morning Council meetings. It flickered lamplight as Joseph poured over midnight scrolls. It whipped along beneath his feet as he walked Jerusalem streets. But on those night rides, unfettered by voices of men and life's monotonous press, that's when the song boomed. Wild and lifting, joyous it raced, howling across the desert, pounding the canyons, rattling the stars.

The song had whispered and moaned that horrible night in the garden when they'd taken Yeshua.

"I Am," Yeshua had said. "I Am."

The song…haunting, drawing, insisting.

Always the song.

I am He…

True to the old shepherd's prophecy, Joseph had bent his knee that night in the garden. He would never scoff again. Never.

"Your mind is far away this morning." Ariella appeared at his elbow.

"And you move quietly for such a waddling, pregnant wife."

Her smile touched her eyes and lifted his spirit. Morning sun reflected on the dark hair framing her face. Her smooth skin flushed and radiant. "I hardly waddle, husband. I'm not even showing yet. Far from it. And let me tell you something, even if I carried an elephant inside me, I would never waddle."

Joseph laughed. "No, you wouldn't, would you?" He pulled her into his arms and held her, enjoying the warmth of her body, her breath against his chest. "Look at the sky. The sun rises, but it's a new and different world it looks down on today."

Her delicate shoulders lifted. "We've made a stand. And it's the right stand. Whatever happens, we can know that. You've honored God and truth. And I'm proud to be your wife."

"They'll try to take everything."

"Try?"

"I'm not without resources. And I won't run away with my tail between my legs. Whatever they do, I'll fight them. They'll have to work for what they steal from us."

"Joseph, nothing is more important than our family. They can have the rest."

"I agree totally. Keeping our family together is everything. As for what they can have? I've worked too hard."

The bread vendor in the street below began his work in earnest, his calls melodious, lifting and echoing off the walls.

Joseph peered down. "Tuvia's in rare form this morning."

"He became a grandfather last night. A baby boy. He told Yaffa when she bought the breakfast bread."

"Ah, good for him. Speaking of Yaffa and breakfast, we should probably go down."

Ariella pulled out of Joseph's embrace with a sigh. "She's been overly protective lately. She scolds me like I'm a little girl if I so much as move."

"Well, she's more than a head housekeeper. More like the mother you never had. And I'm glad of it. I worry about you."

Ariella smiled. "You needn't. The woman worries enough for all of us."

"Excuse me, sir?" Avner, Joseph's head man and Yaffa's husband, stood at the stairwell landing.

Joseph nodded. "Yes, I know. Breakfast. Please tell Yaffa we're on our way."

"It's not that, sir. A message just arrived. Your presence is requested at the Sanhedrin."

Joseph frowned. "The Council? At this hour?"

"It seems so, sir."

"Fine, Avner. Thank you. I'll be down in just a minute. Please have a cloak ready."

The servant dipped his head and retreated down the stairwell.

Joseph looked out toward the Temple. "It's happening then. I'd hoped we might have a little more time."

"They'll move against you? So soon?"

"It must be that. Yeshua isn't cold in his grave and your father is already settling scores."

Ariella's face tightened. "My father is a plague. I wish he would leave our lives and never return."

"I'll echo that with my whole heart. You deserve more. He's been no father to you at all. Men like him can't see past their desire for power. But he's still Vice President of the Council. He has the ear of Caiaphas and I have to deal with him, at least for now, like it or not."

"You go, I'll pray," Ariella said. "You've done the right thing. God will have His way in this."

He hugged her again. "It will be hard for us. I'm sorry."

"We'll be together. I don't care about anything else."

They descended the four stories from the rooftop. The house, with its thick, stone walls cool, almost cold. There was no time for Joseph to visit his private *mikveh* for a ceremonial bath. But even had he been able to, he still would be considered unclean for seven days after touching Yeshua's corpse. There was no helping it. Surprisingly, he found the thought affected him little. He'd pulled Yeshua's bloody body from the Roman cross, carried it in his arms and, with the help of Nicodemus, laid it in his own tomb. And he'd do it again. Without hesitation and without question.

In the entry hall, Ariella hugged him. "Remember what's important. I don't care about the things. But I need you with me and safe."

He pushed her back gently. Hands on her shoulders, he met her eyes. "I've handled your father before and I will this time. Caiaphas as well. And we stand with God. Even when things seem hopeless, there is no greater position of strength. My apologies to Yaffa about breakfast." He pulled her close again and kissed her forehead before releasing her.

Avner appeared with the cloak and held it out while Joseph stepped into it.

"How long do you think you'll be gone?" Ariella said.

Joseph shrugged. "I don't know. They'll make quick work of it, I suspect. But with the Sanhedrin you can't tell. They love the sound of their own voices. Don't worry about me."

"We'll trust God, sir. All will be well," Avner said.

Joseph put a hand on the man's shoulder, an unusual display of familiarity. But, since Yeshua, what was normal anymore? "We will. But many of our fathers trusted as well and difficulties still came. I'm afraid it will be the same for us."

"Whatever happens, my family will stand with you," Avner said.

The man's devotion touched. Joseph smiled. "I appreciate it, my friend. But I also won't hold you to it. This will get worse before it gets better, and you have your own to think of. Still, we'll do what we can. And it blesses me to have you by my side."

The servant reached up and patted Joseph's hand. "God is God. He will provide."

"And we're not God, eh? Yes. All right. We'll trust." With a last kiss for Ariella, Joseph exited and took the landing at a trot. At the bottom of the wide outer stairs he paused at the fountain and splashed his face. A fresh wave of trepidation rolled through him. He'd kept a brave face with Ariella, but the life of luxury and ease they'd known in Jerusalem was finished, of that he was certain. One way or another, the Sanhedrin would strip them of everything. They would make outcasts of anyone at all associated with Yeshua. The only possible way he could think of to save his livelihood and household would be to deny Yeshua. But he might as well deny the sunrise. Or the tides. Or his own breath. Because Yeshua, even in his death, had shown Joseph life.

"No you don't." The familiar, gravel-edged voice pulled Joseph's attention. Davi, Joseph's longtime friend and right-hand man, stepped from the doorway of the stable.

"No I don't what?" Joseph said.

"You're not going to face that pack of jackals without me. Not with everything that's happening."

"And how did you know I was going to the Council?"

Davi grinned. "Because I'm me. What don't I know? How long have you known me now? I'm surprised you'd even ask."

Davi was a compact man. One who could be hard as stone one second and draw smiles from everyone within his periphery the next. His face, weathered and creased with wind, sun, and life, had a deep scar running from the left corner of his mouth to his earlobe, courtesy of time spent as a hired mercenary with the trade-route caravans. He'd been Joseph's closest friend since they'd met as boys on the village streets of Arimathea, north of Jerusalem. In those early days, both orphans, they'd formed their own two-person family—brothers in spirit if not blood. Davi had wandered as adulthood approached, finding work as a mercenary—an occupation perfectly suited to his steel-and-rawhide approach to life, not to mention his quick temper. Life had hardened Joseph as well, but he'd chosen a different path. He'd started his rise to wealth on street corners, selling sweet wine he pressed and fermented from cast-off grapes to housewives and farmhands. A shrewd mind and bold spirit had taken him far. Joseph's miles of private vineyards now supplied most of the wine in Israel. It had been years now since Davi had reappeared in Joseph's life. His old friend had asked for nothing, and he'd proven himself not only loyal but invaluable more times than Joseph could count.

Joseph shook water off his hands and finished drying them on his robe. "They've summoned me. I've made my stand and now I'm afraid we'll all pay for it."

Davi grunted a laugh. "So? I told you from the day we came to Jeruselem they were nothing but a bunch of braying donkeys. You're well rid of the headache."

"A place on the Sanhedrin solidified our position here, Davi. But now they'll move to take everything. They won't stand for insurrection from me or anyone else." Joseph paused. "Look what they did to Yeshua. That father-in-law of mine would like nothing better than to see us all on the street. To see me begging. Or worse."

"I've seen you down many times, Joseph, but I've never seen you beg. We'll weather this."

"From your lips to God's ears."

"Look, we'll fight, yes? Whatever that old goat Beryl gets, he'll have to bleed for, believe me."

"Fight or not, in the end we can't win against their power. We have to prepare for the fact."

Davi grinned. "But we'll have had the fight. And the un-winnable fights have a way of surprising a man. And if they take everything, so? We've had nothing before. You knew the risk when you made the choice for Yeshua. Whatever happens, you'll still have Ariella and the child. And don't forget about my beautiful face."

Joseph couldn't help but smile. "How could I? You won't let me. But tell me, what will you do for shekels if I can no longer support my household?"

"Get by like I always have. Like we always have. I may not always be the best Jew in Israel, but I have faith. Where is yours?"

Joseph exhaled a long breath. "You're right. I think I'm just mentally preparing for the battle."

"Let me tell you something an old soldier told me once. Don't pull your sword until you see an enemy. Battles will always come, but don't watch the horizon. Enjoy the sun on your face and the wind in your hair instead. And at night, sleep well. It may be the last chance you have for a while."

Joseph sighed. "My warrior-philosopher friend. All right, we stand on faith and on God. But you can't come."

"Joseph, don't start—"

"Listen, the Sanhedrin is moving against us. And that means Beryl. Davi, I need you here. Without you, Ariella and the staff are unprotected. Don't argue with me about this."

Davi looked up at the house, then back. He scratched he cheek, frowning. "I understand. You're right, of course. Beryl is a snake. But I hate to let you go alone."

"I wish you could be in two places at once, I really do. But I don't go alone, my friend. I go with God. And with the knowledge that we act in righteousness."

"Still, be careful. God gave you those eyes and ears. He won't begrudge you keeping them open."

"Thank you, my friend. It eases my mind knowing you'll be here."

Out on the street, the morning hung soft and sun drenched, at direct odds with Joseph's mind and heart. As he headed for the

Zion Bridge, his thoughts wandered to the tomb in the garden, cold and dark. And to that lifeless, linen-wrapped form. Davi was right. Where was faith? Then again, with Yeshua dead, was faith worth anything anymore? For those who had stood with and for Yeshua, what was life now? Who were they anymore? They had lost.

How could God honor a nation who had crucified His own Son? A people who had spat on and beaten His Holy Gift and shoved it back in His face, bloody and broken? Surely He would turn His back on Israel. What choice had they left Him?

And when God turns His face, what hope remains for a man?

The towering Zion Bridge cast a deep shadow as he approached. The bridge, offering the city's elite an unimpeded route to the Temple Mount, began at Herod's grand palace on the western edge of Jerusalem, crossed Mount Zion's Upper City, spanned the Valley of the Cheesemakers, and united with the Temple complex more than twenty stories above the valley floor. It was a trek Joseph had made a thousand times before. One he usually enjoyed. This morning, every step felt like walking through water.

The sun had climbed two fingers above the Mount of Olives by the time he exited the bridge and stepped into the cool recess of Solomon's Porch. Still early and between festivals, the Mount platform—the largest such outside of Rome—lay still and peaceful. Only a few dozen people, most of them men, strolled the stone. Pigeons cooed and rattled against the ceiling high above. A lone rabbi's recitation echoed across stone. Out in the center of the expanse, the Temple itself rose to a dizzying height into the cloudless sky.

Yachiel, captain of the Temple Guard and overseer of the Levitical Patrol, stood rigid next to an intricately carved pillar it would have taken five men to reach around. He frowned at Joseph's approach. "You took long enough. They're waiting in the Stoa."

"Not the Hall?" Joseph said.

"You're unclean."

"I'm familiar with the Levitical Law."

Yachiel shrugged. "I'd thought maybe you'd forgotten. The way you went groveling after the Nazarene, who knows what you're thinking? I'm to escort you. Follow me."

The man's condescension rankled. "I'm still a member of the Sanhedrin. I won't be led like a child. By you or anyone else."

A muscle worked in Yachiel's jaw. "Sanhedrin or not, I answer to the High Priest alone. I have my orders and I'll follow them."

Joseph willed himself calm. Better to get it over with. There were more important battles ahead than Yachiel's arrogance. And the man's words were true—on this mountain, the Captain of the Temple Guard was second only to Caiaphas. "Fine. Let's just get this over with."

Yachiel nodded, turned, and started down the length of the Porch without another word. Joseph followed. While Solomon's Porch, the columned portico towering along the north, east, and west sides of the Temple Platform, inspired awe in its grandeur, the Royal Stoa, stretching the length of the remaining southern end, was a true and magnificent wonder. The massive edifice served not only as one of the main entrances to the Temple Mount but as a central gathering place for the people of Jerusalem. With more than a hundred and sixty pillars supporting its immensity, the multi-storied basilica was, by square footage, the largest structure on the Mount. Though the citizens under his rule rarely had a good word to say about Herod the Great, they were admittedly proud of his monumental building projects and, next to the Temple itself, especially the Stoa. Under its arches, rabbis preached to their disciples, scribes conducted classes, and doctrinal debate raged. In its deep and shaded recesses, political deals were struck, gossip exchanged, and information bought and sold.

And this morning it seemed the Royal Stoa would be the site of the Sanhedrin stripping everything Joseph had given a lifetime of sweat and work to achieve.

They'd gathered at the eastern end, a tight collection of Sadducees, Pharisees, priests, and scribes. As tradition mandated, the seventy-one member body formed a large semicircle, centered by the *Nasi*, or President, and the *Av Beit Din*, Vice President—Caiaphas, the High Priest, and Beryl,

Joseph's father-in-law, respectively. The group quieted as Joseph approached. Stern frowns greeted. He searched the faces briefly for Nicodemus but didn't find his friend present. *No doubt already disciplined and banished.* Anger rose and he let it, knowing he might need it in the coming minutes. Nicodemus was an upright man. A seeker of truth, no matter the cost. He'd tried his best to warn the Council of their folly, to show iron-clad prophecy after prophecy proving Yeshua was indeed God's promised Messiah. But to no avail. The men gathered here were prideful fools, insistent on turning their backs to the truth right in front of their eyes.

"Joseph of Arimathea." Caiaphas' voice pulled Joseph to the immediate.

Joseph squared his shoulders. "I'm here, as you can well see. Say what you have to say. Do what you have to do."

Caiaphas raised a ring-adorned hand and pointed at Joseph. "The first thing I have to say is that you will respect the Council. We speak, you don't, unless directed. Do you understand?"

"I'm surprised he's here at all," Beryl said. "I would have thought he'd be hiding in some rat crack like the rest of the Nazarene's people."

"I think you know me better than that, Beryl," Joseph said.

"I said, you will not speak unless so directed," Caiaphas glanced over at Beryl and raised an eyebrow. "Although he's right. You should know him better than that."

Beryl's face remained neutral. "Joseph of Arimathea blatantly opposed the decisions of the Sanhedrin. He's disrupted legal proceedings in an attempt to save the Nazarene's life. He's spread vile and malicious gossip. He's—"

"What gossip have I spread?" Joseph said. "Unlike you, the only words that have come from my mouth are words of truth." Joseph looked out across the gathering. "Something I used to believe this body cared about."

"Enough!" Caiaphas said. "Quiet, both of you! How many times must I repeat myself?"

"Why not let Joseph speak?" someone said. "Not all of us agreed with killing the Nazarene."

"That's right," said another.

Caiaphas gave an exaggerated sigh. "He will have his chance. You would think that death would have rendered the Nazarene a moot point. Yet here he is again, it seems, strutting into another Council meeting. I don't remember voting him in, yet, even as a ghost, the man always shows up."

"And here he will be for all time," Joseph said. "His death is your legacy, Caiaphas. Yours too, Beryl. Generations will remember your act for what it was—spitting in the face of God."

At this, the assembly erupted, their shouts roaring through the Stoa, turning heads across the Court of the Gentiles and beyond. Beryl stood and approached Joseph, the twisted light of victory in his eyes. He spoke over the continuing shouts of the Council members, leaning in, close to Joseph's face. "You blaspheme, son-in-law. You know that when you speak against the High Priest you speak against God. We are His voice among men. We are his instrument of judgment."

Joseph shook his head. "Beryl, it's terrifying to think you actually believe that."

Beryl turned a slow circle, lifting his hands, signaling for order. It took more than a minute for the mayhem to abate enough for him to make himself heard. "We'll waste no more time here. I'm sure you all have other business to attend to." He turned back to Joseph. "What have you to say?"

Joseph lifted an eyebrow. "What have I to say? I believe I've said it. Yeshua, who you killed, was the Son of God, the Promised One, the Messiah the prophets spoke of. The scripture couldn't be more clear. Nicodemus tried to tell you, but in your pride you wouldn't listen. You took the Hope of Israel—the only Hope of Israel—and nailed him to a cross."

Shouts rose but died as Joseph moved forward, forcing Beryl to back step. "I heard your own words in front of Pilate, *Av Beit Din*. And they still echo through my memory as they will no doubt echo through eternity." He turned to the group. "And how many of you followed this man's lead? To your own peril! Do you still hear his words as I do? *His blood be upon us and our children!* Isn't that what he said? What you all said? What you demanded? Well, now his blood is upon you! To your shame and the shame of all Israel!" Joseph's words left no room for anything but silence. They hung there, heavy in the warm spring morning. A breeze shifted through the columns and across the floor. It tugged the men's robes, bringing with it the smell of sheep dung from the valley below.

All eyes upon him, Beryl's face remained calm, but his fists clenched, knuckles white. When he finally spoke, his words sounded formal and rehearsed. "A sad day today indeed, Joseph of Arimathea. To think so many here once venerated you, thinking you wise and admiring your success. But to those who climb high, the fall is far, isn't that the old idiom? You've said your piece. You make no defense. What else can be done?"

Joseph nodded. "I have. Now, since this Council no longer has a claim on my time or loyalty, I'll take my leave and return to my family."

"Don't you dare turn your back on me!" Beryl said. "I will not be disrespected. Of course you've been discharged from the Sanhedrin, that's a given, but you will now stand and answer!"

Joseph shook his head "What are you spouting about, Beryl? I defended Yeshua. Spoke for him and stood with him. I'm dismissed, banished—fine and good! I make no defense and no excuse. I want none of this anymore, anyway."

"Answer!" Beryl shouted.

"Answer what? You haven't asked me anything! Have you lost your senses?"

"Do I really need to say it? Why on earth do you think you're here?"

"To be dismissed from the Council, of course! Outside that, I have no idea what you're talking about. Either state your question or let me get back to my life."

Beryl barked an incredulous laugh. "And still you lie! Where is it, Joseph? Do you really think you can fool the Great Sanhedrin of Jerusalem with some trick? Fool all of Israel? All of Rome while you're at it?"

"Are you completely mad, father-in-law? What under heaven are you talking about? Where is what?"

Beryl stepped forward. "Where is *the body*, Joseph? What have you done with the Nazarene?"

3

Beryl paced, thinking.

Caiaphas' private room on the Temple Mount was well appointed. Rugs imported from Persia softened the polished stone floor. Tapestries commissioned from the finest weavers in Judea covered the walls, depicting glorious events in Israel's history. Candles burned, throwing shimmering fingers of light. Incense filled the room with the sweet aroma of jasmine.

Caiaphas reclined next to a low table tracking Beryl's back-and-forth progress with hooded eyes, dipping bread in wine and slurping soggy chunks of the mush through purple-stained lips. "I warned you of this very thing, you know."

"Warned me of what?" Beryl's reply sharper than he'd intended.

"Of conniving against your son-in-law. I sat in this very spot and warned you. Three years ago. And many times since. Joseph is a stubborn man. One not to be pushed. And now he's made things intolerable."

"I don't recall any warning."

"Of course you do. And despite my instruction, you not only pushed, you shoved."

"Who remembers three years ago?"

"You do, Beryl. Your selective memory is tiresome."

"Fine, you warned me. It makes little difference at this point, don't you think? What's done is done."

"I'm just saying, if you'd listened then, you wouldn't be giving me a sore neck now. Sit down, would you?"

With a grunt, Beryl eased himself onto a pillow opposite the High Priest. "The cross should have ended it. Joseph is trying to stick a knife in me by stealing the body."

"Maybe, maybe not. He might simply be trying to perpetuate the myth. Everyone knows the Nazarene claimed he would rise from the dead on the third day. That's why we requested the guards. To stop this very thing from happening."

"Well, the guards failed."

Caiaphas lifted his cup, took a long drink, and belched. Crumbs of bread residue clung to his mustache. It turned Beryl's stomach. He had to look away.

"So we control the damage," Beryl said. "It's a simple game of Dogs and Jackals. Strategy. Yeshua's followers make a move, we counter it. The guards took the money we offered, and they'll say what we told them to say. As far as the general population is concerned, the Nazarene's disciples stole the body when the guards were sleeping."

Caiaphas shook his head. "It's not enough. A Roman guard sleeping on watch is punishable by death. When they're not killed, suspicion will arise. Everyone will know there must have been back-room dealings. And, secondly, they're Gentiles. How can we trust them? What happens when they drink and gamble the money away and come back wanting more? Do we just keep paying them? Threaten them? Eventually the truth will leak, it has to."

Beryl shrugged "We told them we'd smooth things with their superiors. We didn't say when. Who knows? We're busy men. It may take some time before we get around to it."

Caiaphas gave a thoughtful nod. "Simply let them be executed. It answers any questions that asise. The thought does have merit."

"Two fewer Roman dogs in Jerusalem? We'd be doing the people a favor."

A drop of condensation slid down the side of a silver pitcher on the table. Caiaphas wiped at it with his finger. "It would still help if we could find the body. Then we would control the situation completely." He turned his cup upside down and watched as a single drop of wine splashed the table. With a sigh, he picked up a chunk of bread and dipped it into the goblet Beryl held. Beryl eyed the cup, then set it down. Caiaphas licked the purple liquid from his fingers. "It irritates me. Joseph is a stubborn man but a smart one. He could have been an asset, a useful tool, but your incessant pride turned him against us. So much so that he went and placed the Nazarene's body in his own tomb. I'm betting he had a plan for moving the body even then. And now he plays this game, keeping us off balance. He understands well that even dead, Yeshua threatens our power. And a martyr's voice is often the strongest of all. Joseph will use it. Yeshua's followers will do the same."

"Not if they're identified, located, rooted out, and crushed. That's the way to contain this. No need to make it more complicated than it is."

Caiaphas studied him. "The people won't stand for such aggression. Even from the Sanhedrin."

"The people? What can they say? Anyone who complains will receive the same. They will quiet down. All it will take is a few of the followers made into examples."

"How do you propose to do this without it tainting our office?"

"We simply distance ourselves from the process. Shift focus."

"I repeat. How?"

"A proxy."

"A proxy? You know of such a man?"

"Would I bring it up if I didn't?"

"Who?"

Beryl stood, stepped to the chamber door and opened it. "Send him in." A few seconds later, a man appeared. Short, gaunt, but thick in his shoulders. Oil dripping from his unruly black beard stained the front of his Pharisaical robe. Large, obsidian eyes glinted. The man nodded to Caiaphas and Beryl in turn.

"Wine?" Beryl said.

"No, thank you." The voice was clipped and edged with glass.

"Is this our fear-inspirer then?" Caiaphas said.

"He'll do the job," Beryl said.

Caiaphas studied the man. "I take it you have no love for the Nazarene's followers?"

Muscles tightened around the man's eyes. "I do not."

"Your semblance and accent is strange to me. Where are you from?"

"Cilicia."

"A Cilician… But you reside in Jerusalem?"

The Cilician shrugged. "Jerusalem is the center of the world, is it not? And therefore the center of learning."

"From your robes I take it you're a Pharisee?"

"I am."

Caiaphas slurped his wine and nodded. "Very good. You might do, at that."

Beryl cut in. "Cilician, you understand the problem. Yeshua's influence didn't die with him on the cross. It has to be stopped quickly and efficiently—brutally if need be. There is no other way."

"I understand and agree," the Cilician said.

"You have the authority of the Sanhedrin behind you," Beryl said. "The Levitical Patrol is at your service. Find, expose, destroy anyone who dares speak on behalf of the Nazarene. Force them into the open, then do what needs to be done. By any means necessary. Can you do this?"

"I look forward to it. The Nazarene was a plague on this city."

"Fine," Beryl said. "Find the roaches and step on them, wherever they are and however you see fit. In the beginning, make examples. The rest will deny Yeshua quickly enough. How you do this is up to you. We don't need to know details. You may go."

The man nodded, turned, and made his exit without word or backward glance.

Caiaphas sipped. "Where did you find him?"

"A student. And a very vocal one. I heard him in the synagogue preaching vehemently against Yeshua, and I recognized his possibilities immediately."

"I don't know, Beryl. I have the uncomfortable feeling we may be grabbing the tail of an animal that will turn and bite us."

"The man is intelligent and has the ruthless drive of a zealot. You said you wanted tools? The man is a tool."

"There's still the Joseph problem. As long as the body is missing, the rumor of resurrection will continue."

"The body will be found."

"How can you be sure?"

Beryl set down his cup and struggled to his feet. "You heard me tell the Cilician to make examples? Joseph of Arimathea will be the first."

4

Black…

The very black that had terrified now became a harbor—a place of respite. Black meant the beatings had stopped, at least for the moment. The small cave was no longer a cell but an inky womb Joseph, bloody and shaking, crawled into. He now understood the man who had first come to him had not a shred of mercy in his body. The guards would drag Joseph out, shackle his wrists, lift him by the chains until his toes no longer touched the floor, then, at a nod from the man, the beating would start. No greeting, no question first, always the beating. Then, finally, after a lifetime of agony, and always in the same, brittle voice, "Joseph, where is the body?"

But what could he say? A million lies came to his mind. Anything to stop the pain, if even for a minute, a few seconds. But when he opened his mouth to speak, only the truth came. Because, when it came down to it, truth was all he had left.

And so it would go.

"Joseph, where is the body?"

"I don't know."

"Where is the body?"

"Yeshua said he would rise."

"The tomb belongs to you, and the body is gone. What did you do with it?"

"I had nothing to do with it."

And the beatings would commence again. An ugly pattern of pain that became every waking moment. Alive and dead at the same time.

And now, here in the black again. He curled into a fetal position, face to the wall, and attempted the only escape possible to him—sleep.

The cell door opened.

Joseph spoke without turning. "Please, not again. I told you a hundred times, I know nothing."

"I doubt you have another hundred in you. You've already lasted longer than expected."

Joseph rolled, holding up a hand against the light coming through the doorway. "Beryl... Of course you're behind this madness."

The fat priest moved into the room and lifted a torch. "I must say, son-in-law, you look awful."

"Where is Ariella?"

Beryl lowered his bulk to a heavy wooden bench against the wall. "Ah yes, that's better. I find my joints don't like the damp these days." He waved the torch. "Look at this place! Carved from solid rock. Amazing, isn't it?"

"Where is she?"

Beryl rubbed at his knee with thick fingers. "That daughter of mine, yes. What can I tell you? What happens to her is really up to you, isn't it?"

Joseph shifted and fought a wave of pain-driven nausea. "I don't know anything about the body. Neither does she. Leave her alone."

"Let me be clear, Joseph. Either you cough up some useful information or Ariella will suffer worse than you have."

"She's your daughter, Beryl."

"She's nothing. You're nothing. Not down here. Your world has become very small. How could you possibly have thought you could challenge me?"

"Where is down here? Where am I?"

"Depressing, isn't it? So much stone and dark and damp." Beryl smiled. "This is nice, our having time to chat. You chose wrong, son-in-law. That Galilean goat over the Great Sanhedrin of Israel? Really, how could you have been so stupid?"

"Yeshua is the Son of God. I'm not the one who made the wrong decision. You will answer. All of you. Your arrogance and position can't hide you from God."

The torch bounced slightly as Beryl chuckled. "Son of God… How long will you cling to your fantasy? Death came to the Galilean like it does to any other mortal man. In the end he was a piece of meat hanging on a stick, nothing more."

"You're a fool."

"Says the beaten, bloody pauper in a forgotten hole."

"My circumstances change nothing. This is not about me, my life is nothing. It's about God. Truth is truth."

Beryl started to laugh again but wheezed a cough instead. "Your circumstances? Your circumstances are you might as well be in Hades. You're at least near it." He waved the torch in a slow arch. "So strange to think Jerusalem is up there somewhere. Everyone going about their business with no thought of you at all. And to think, you'll never see it again. At least alive."

"We're under the city?"

"Do you know this place is older than you or me? Older than our fathers even. Maybe older than King David. But very few know about it. And no one will help you here, be assured of that."

Joseph finally managed to sit up. "Beryl, listen, do what you will to me. But Ariella is with child."

The torch became very still. "You're lying. That's impossible. The cow is barren."

Joseph tried to rise, but the pain might as well have been chains. "I'm not a liar. My words are true."

"Everyone is a liar sometimes. You're only trying to worm a way out of here."

"I know my chances of leaving this place alive are nothing. She's with child. I'm not lying. Don't hurt her."

"Are you begging? The great Joseph of Arimathea?"

"If that's what it takes, yes."

Beryl scratched at his beard. "It's interesting, isn't it? Here you are, dead, while God smiles on me. Maybe you speak truth. If you do, a child holds real possibilities."

Joseph laid his head back against the stone floor. "Just don't hurt them. Please."

Beryl groaned to his feet and brushed at his robes. "Again, that's up to you. I'm tired now and we're wasting time. Mine, not yours. I'll be blunt, you will die down here. That's a given. And after you die, your body will be found in a public place outside the walls. Your corpse will send a clear message to the city. They'll understand that this is what happens to the followers of the Galilean. So, tell me where the body is and be done with it. You will die quickly, and your wife will not suffer. Or, you can keep up this stubborn charade and they can take you apart bit by bit."

"Three days. He said he would rise again in three days. Have you even considered?"

Beryl lifted the torch and studied Joseph for a long second. "For the life of me, I don't understand you. Even after the Nazarene is crucified, you continue to make trouble. Why? What do you have to gain but more pain for yourself and your household? Tell me and save your wife!"

"Three days…"

Beryl shook his head, an edge to his voice now. "Fine. The beatings continue. Enjoy."

"I took him from the cross and put him in my tomb, that's it. Nothing more."

"Do you think my patience is endless? It was your tomb! On your property! I'm not an imbecile!"

"There was almost nothing left of the man after what you and the Romans did to him."

"He was a traitor. He deserved every blow."

"He deserved nothing. He was innocent."

"He was a problem. And the problem is solved. Except for your pathetic residual games."

"Is it? I think, for you, the problem of Yeshua has grown exponentially. I think it's just getting started. You say you're not an imbecile? Then think. How could I have taken him? The Romans rolled the stone across the mouth of the grave and sealed it with iron. They placed a guard. How on earth could I have removed the body?"

"You've had business dealings with Pilate before. A word. A bribe. It was your property. You had opportunity and motive. Who else?"

"You're a sad fool, Beryl. But one day you will fall to your face. You will face God for what you've done."

"Goodbye, Joseph. We won't talk again." Beryl turned for the door.

"Have you thought?" Joseph said. "What if it's true? If Yeshua has actually risen, what will you do then?"

"Goodbye, Joseph. Die knowing this: If it's true what you say about the child, then at least Ariella will have a few months reprieve before she comes here. But she will see this place eventually. She will suffer greatly. And I will raise your son."

"God will protect them both."

"Like He's protecting you? God is on the side of the righteous. And I think we both can see where His favor lies."

"You're the devil's son."

Beryl waddled close and stood above Joseph. He hacked deep in his throat and released a long string of spittle onto Joseph's face. "Goodbye, son-in-law. I'll see you on the street. But you won't see me."

5

The beatings continued, though the question came less and less. By Beryl's instruction, surely. Fists, clubs… They weren't choosy. Joseph tried to ignore the blows, focusing his mind on prayer, begging God to protect Ariella and their unborn child. The guards would beat him until he passed out. Time and time again he woke on the cold floor of the cell, wracked with pain and loss. "Curse God and die." Wasn't that what Job's friends had advised? Like Job, Joseph wouldn't curse his Maker, but there were certainly times he prayed for death's release. Anything to end this torture that did nothing but soothe Beryl's wounded ego.

Black…

Black and empty…

Aside from Beryl's single visit and the guard coming for him, the time Joseph spent in his cell was completely solitary.

Until it wasn't…

The beating had been particularly vicious, and Joseph had only a vague recollection of being dragged back to the cell. A long time later he woke with a start, sensing immediately something was different. No voice came to him through the ink. Not even a breath. But as sure as he knew his own name, he knew he wasn't alone. "Who are you?"

The reply came low, neither young nor old, friendly nor unfriendly, with a hint of accent he couldn't quite place. "Good question, brother. Who is anyone down here? Do we still have names? Faces? Who knows? Does it even matter, if everyone up there has forgotten us?"

"I'm remembered."

"Yes. Of course you think that. We all do at first. And you've not been here long enough to doubt. But you'll learn. We're ghosts, nothing more. Who I was I'll never be again. You, though, I know, Joseph of Arimathea. Recently of the Great Sanhedrin but now a creature of the earth's belly like me. Just another worm. I've heard them beat on you. Heard your screams. Why don't you just tell them what they want you to know? You'll never see the sun again anyway. What's the difference?"

"You know me, but I don't know you. Who are you? Why are you in my cell? I've been alone until now."

"I'm called Gershom. Or I used to be. And why am I in here with you? Who knows how the brutes think? They needed my hole in the rock for some other miserable creature, maybe. They tell us nothing, and it saves you a clout on the ear not to ask. All I know is that they grabbed me and threw me in here. You might as well be grateful for the company."

"Why are you down here in the first place?"

"Why are any of us? We offended someone above our station. Everything else is semantics."

"Who did you offend?"

"It's a long story. And it breaks my heart to think of it. My wife, my sons…I think they have no idea what happened to me. For all they know, I've left them to starve."

"How long have you been here?"

"A month? A year? How do you measure time down here? It's impossible. I was a sandal maker when I could find work. Not a wealthy man. My family has nothing now. It's my youngest I worry about most. Only four years old and my constant shadow. He must be crushed that I'm gone. How could he possibly understand?"

"But what happened? What did you do?"

"I told you it was a long story."

"We have time."

"Maybe I do, but not you. I heard them talking. They say with the next beating they won't hold back. Either you tell them where the body of Yeshua is or they'll beat you to death. You have family as well, I suspect?"

"I do. A wife… She's with child."

"Then why not just tell the scum what they want to know? Yeshua is dead anyway, what does it matter?"

"What do you know of Yeshua?"

Cloth brushed stone as the man shifted position. "Only what I've heard. A homeless rabbi who challenged the Council and paid for it with his life. Now the body is missing, and the powers-that-be are afraid that some kind of messiah myth will perpetuate among the people."

"You've got the bones of it. Yeshua claimed in life that he would rise in death."

"They say that you're a Sadducee. Yet you talk of a man rising from the dead? Surely you don't believe such things."

"Much has changed for me in the last months. All I know is what I know."

"And what is that?"

"Yeshua is the Promised One the prophets spoke of. He is the Messiah."

A dry laugh. "Pardon my skepticism, brother, but these are lofty thoughts coming from a man in your current position. Yeshua died on a Roman cross. What kind of messiah is that?"

"My position means nothing. Yeshua means everything. Truth is everything."

"Truth? No, there is no truth. And if there was, what would it matter to ghosts?"

"God is truth. Truth matters to God."

"God, yes. But, look around, God has left us to rot. I've had a beating or two myself down here. What I don't understand is why you don't just save yourself. Tell them something. Anything." The voice dropped low. "Listen to me, Joseph, no one is listening. I'll level with you. I've developed a connection with one of the guards. One who carries some authority. I believe that if I can offer him a little information, just a scrap, it might go well for me. And I may be able to speak for you, too.

You might see your wife again. And me…please, brother, think of my son."

"I will never leave here alive."

"But you're a righteous man. You can help a brother in need. My family! Please."

"I'm sorry, friend. I can't tell what I don't know."

A sigh. "I'm sorry to hear it, brother." Another scrape of cloth on stone. "I—"

A sudden rattle sounded, and the thick door slammed open with a boom. A torch arched and landed in the center of the room. Sucking a breath against the pain in his wrecked body, Joseph rolled away from the sudden burst of light, catching a glimpse of dark robe and flash of steel as he did so. A struggle. The clash of metal on metal. Then the sickening sound of sword striking bone accompanied by a strangled cry.

Joseph shuffled until he hit wall, then rolled, blocking the torchlight with his hands. With the torch on the floor, he could only make out the lower half of a man. Studded sandals beneath a coarse robe. A hand gripping a bloody sword. Behind the man, the crumpled form of the poor creature who must have been his cell mate, a puddle of thick, black blood quickly forming around him. Joseph raised a hand, meager defense against the coming thrust that would finally do him in. Finally, after all the agony, Beryl had decided to end it. *God, protect my wife! Be with our child!*

"You're a hard man to find, Winemaker."

The room focused again. *Winemaker?*

"Longinus?" Joseph rasped.

"Who else? Rescuing you is getting to be a habit. Arimathea the last time. From that murdering mother of a goat, Barabbas. And now I have to descend to the bowels of the underworld. I expect a lifetime supply of your best for this one. Get up. Quickly. We have to go."

"I don't understand. Where is your uniform?"

"There are some places in this city a Roman uniform, even that of a centurion, is a detriment rather than an asset. We walk those paths now. Please, get up, time isn't on our side here.

With the centurion's help, Joseph managed to get to his feet. His legs immediately buckled, but Longinus' strong arm around his back pulled him upright.

Joseph stared, dazed, at the crumpled figure on the stone floor. "You killed him."

"I did. Walk now."

"But why? The man had a family. A wife. Sons. Why would you…"

Longinus reached out a studded sandal and rolled the body until the man lay face up. A deep gash across the throat. Longinus rummaged through the dead man's cloak until he came up with a wicked looking dagger.

Joseph stared, stupefied. "He said he was a prisoner. That he'd been here a long time. Been beaten…"

The centurion shook his head. "A lie, Winemaker. They say he was a master at it. A chameleon in his trickery."

"But…"

"This man had no family. He loved no one and no thing except himself and the gold in his purse."

"I don't understand. He said—"

"If his mouth was open, he was lying. He was a killer, pure and simple. A merchant-mercenary who traded blood for gold." Longinus lifted the knife. "Here is his only family. If he couldn't get you to tell him what they wanted to know with smooth talk, his instructions were to cut you apart, piece by piece, to kill you slowly and in the most painful way possible. And if there was one thing the man could do better than lie, it was inflict pain. Now, no more time. We go."

Joseph tried a step but stumbled, even with Longinus' arm around him. Longinus swung Joseph's arm over his own shoulder to better support the burden. "They've gone hard on you, Winemaker. But you have to try. Even if it kills you, you have to move. Lean on me. I hate to say it, but we've a ways to go."

Joseph stumbled again but forced his feet one in front of the other. Pain in his ribs raged where Longinus held him. The centurion held his sword low but in front of them as they moved. Joseph could feel the coiled tension in the man's body.

"How did you find me?" Joseph said.

"Later. I know you've suffered, Joseph. I know you hurt badly. But keep moving. That pig of a guard will be waking with a headache shortly and no doubt sound an alarm. I won't be able to hold off all of them on my own."

A steep set of stairs loomed before them. "How will we get past him?" Joseph said.

"We won't. I know another way."

Longinus swung left around a support column and into a passageway so low the two had to duck to make forward progress. Bent at the waist, Joseph forced himself to keep pace. He coughed, the metallic taste of blood in his mouth. He soon lost track of how many times they wound and turned. For a bit they waded through water up to their knees, then their waists, the torch throwing ghoulish shadows on walls of earth and stone.

"I don't think I can go on. Can we rest?" Joseph said, after ages of walking.

Longinus pushed on. "No time. Don't think about it. Just keep moving your feet."

"Where are we going, Longinus? To Ariella? Is she all right?"

It was several steps farther before the centurion answered. "Trust God, Winemaker."

Joseph coughed blood again.

"You've some broken ribs, I think," Longinus said. "And who knows how much other damage. You need time to heal. But to do that, first you need to live through the day. Think only of that for now."

"You didn't answer me. Do you have news of Ariella?"

"As far as I know, she's still at your home. But so is your father-in-law. Save your breath for now. You won't do her any good if you die on me. If you live, I'll get word to her."

"I'll live. We have to—"

"Winemaker, if you don't shut your mouth and walk, I may kill you myself."

A fresh wave of pain shot light through Joseph's vision. He coughed and slowed. "How much farther?"

"As far as needed. You're a man, Winemaker, I'll say that for you. The beatings they gave you would kill most."

Joseph closed his eyes, clung to Longinus. He no longer felt his legs, but he was still moving. "I'll live. If for no other reason than to make Beryl pay for what he's done.

"Fine. Revenge has kept many a man alive before you. Focus your anger. Let it push your body." What seemed like a lifetime later, Longinus slowed, lowered his torch, and hooded it with a careful hand.

"What is it?" Joseph said.

The centurion answered in whisper. "Quiet. We're nearly to the end. Not far now." He gave a low whistle. Someone returned it. The hard face relaxed, but only by a fraction. "It's clear. Come now. Quickly."

They rounded a corner moving at a jarring trot. Light flickered up ahead. Then Joseph made out the figure of a man. Longinus shoved his torch head into a deep puddle, dousing it with a hiss. "What word, Calvus?"

The waiting man had the bearing of a soldier but, like Longinus, none of the usual trappings. His sandy hair Roman-cropped, his narrow face wind-burned and beardless. He wore a colorless robe over a ratty tunic. "They're searching, but closer to the Temple Mount. You're as safe here as anywhere, which isn't very."

"And a cart?"

"Yes, though you'd do better to wait for darkness."

"Maybe, but they'll have expanded the search by then. They don't want this one talking."

Calvus shrugged. "It's a gamble either way, I'm afraid."

They ascended a narrow flight of steps, then an even narrower wooden ladder. Calvus first, Joseph next, Longinus supporting much of Joseph's weight from behind. A few seconds later, Joseph found himself in a low-ceilinged, dirt-floored room. The walls were dingy with old smoke. The air close and heavy, reeking of alcohol and sweat. Muted conversation could be heard through one wall, accompanied by sporadic shouts of muffled laughter.

"Where are we?" Joseph said.

A corner of Longinus' mouth lifted. Deep lines in his cheek. A tall, dark, rangy man, whip-quick and battle-hard.

"Somewhere foreign to you, I think. The Lower City. But the

man who owns this tavern is discreet. He has to be or he'll answer to me, and he knows what that means. You're safe for the moment."

Joseph glanced around, taking in the racks of clay amphoras and crates stacked against the walls. A wide cot with a filthy blanket stood in one corner. Longinus pulled one of the amphoras and broke the seal. He drank, wiped his mouth, then passed the container to Joseph. Joseph followed suit, the liquor burning his throat on the way down. Wincing, he handed it back to Longinus. "Does this pass for wine in this place?"

"You're complaining?"

"I'm grateful. No."

"It will ease the pain if nothing else."

"We're in a storeroom?"

"It's used for storage, yes, among other things."

"Does 'other things' explain the cot?" Joseph said.

Longinus grunted a laugh. "Again, don't ask. But you use it now to get some rest. We'll have to move again soon."

Joseph pushed the blanket away and sank onto the dank, straw mattress. He leaned back against the wall and closed his eyes. "How did you find me, Longinus?"

"A few days ago I received an early morning report that Yeshua's body had disappeared and that the Sanhedrin believed you were behind it. And then you disappeared. The rumor was that you'd run, but I knew there wasn't a running bone in your body, so I poked around. Over a dice game and a camel-load of fig liquor, one of the Patrol slipped and mumbled something about your abduction. I pressed and, though I doubt he remembers doing it, he bragged about the butcher your loving father-in-law was planning to stick in your cell. A few more drinks and I got the location out of him. I'd heard of the place. I found you, just in time, it seems. You know the rest."

"It's only been a few days?"

"Four."

"Four days… The last thing I remember was leaving the Council meeting. But I woke up with a pounding head. They must have hit me from behind. I thank you, Longinus."

"Don't thank me yet. You may have been better off if I'd let the man kill you."

"No. I have to get to Ariella."

"We'll do our best. You have my word."

"She's with child."

Longinus drank again and gave a satisfied exhale. "A child. Well, one thing at a time, Winemaker. Get ahead of yourself now and you may not live to see tomorrow. What good will you be to a child then?" He whispered something to Calvus. The man nodded and ducked through the low doorway. Longinus dropped onto the cot next to Joseph and passed the wine jug.

Joseph drank. "Yeshua's body is really gone?"

"I've seen the tomb myself."

Joseph handed the jug back. "There were guards. Your men, correct? What do they say?"

Longinus drank again and studied the wall opposite. "They swear on their lives his disciples stole the body while they were sleeping."

"His disciples? Not me?"

"You own the tomb. It's been an assumption…"

"You think I had a part in it?"

"Not if you say you didn't."

"I say I didn't."

"Then you didn't. But the Sanhedrin doesn't care to complicate a good story with facts."

"The Sanhedrin's position is driven by Beryl's pride. And Caiaphas' fear of losing his tenuous hold over the people. They prefer his father-in-law, Annas, over him."

"They've convinced most of Jerusalem that the Eleven took the body with your help. It's the accepted story."

"I didn't even know Yeshua was missing until the Council called me for questioning."

Longinus passed the jug. "Drink."

Joseph did. "What if he did it, Longinus? What if he really rose from the dead?"

"I've come too far to question anything now, Winemaker. After the things I've seen, I'd say anything is possible, though it boggles my mind to the point of a headache. I once thought I had a fairly good handle on the world. I thought you people lived in a fog of superstition and meaningless tradition. But when I saw him on that cross. When the earth shook and the sun disappeared…"

"Prophecy is clear. He's the Son of God. There's no doubt."

"I believe it. What more can I say? It doesn't change the fact the city has been turned on its ear. Or that your people are on the verge of civil war. Or that Pilate is furious, though he doesn't know who to be furious with."

"The governor is involved?"

"He's looking into the matter like the rest of them. Trying to get to the bottom of who moved the body and locate it before the city explodes."

"Does he keep an open mind?"

"Of course not."

"And if Yeshua has risen?"

"That's not a reality Pilate is prepared to accept."

"The truth is unacceptable?"

"The truth is rarely acceptable to any man unless it's convenient. Pilate would be perfectly happy making his own reality as long as his reality serves Pilate."

"Truth is truth. Either a thing is or it isn't."

"That's where you rub against the rest of the world, Winemaker. Try telling that to them. Everyone is convinced they're the center of the story, and that skews everything. For most, it's much easier to invent their own truth and play the righteous hero, facts be hanged." He drank again and wiped his mouth with his sleeve. "Tell me. Does your father-in-law know your wife is with child?"

"He does. I was hoping that by telling him I might protect Ariella. I think I may have only made things worse."

"It may yet protect her. Regardless, one way or the other, I'll get word to her that you're alive."

Joseph took the jug, started to drink, but set it on his lap. His head spun with pain and weariness. "You're a good friend, Longinus."

"For a Gentile?"

"For anyone. You know, I should have taken her to Arimathea as soon as they'd killed Yeshua. I should have gone and not looked back."

Longinus drank again. "You can't live backwards, my friend. What is, is. What will be, will be."

Joseph tried to reply, but the room slid into a slow tilt and turned dark around the edges. His chin found his chest.

Longinus' voice barely reached him through the rapidly narrowing tunnel. "Yes, Winemaker, rest. You're going to need it."

6

The storeroom door cracked and Calvus stuck his head in. "Longinus, they come…"

"Delay them if you can. Start a fire, a revolution, I don't care. Just get me a little time."

The soldier nodded and ducked back out.

Longinus stood and paced. He felt no fear. He'd seen too many battles for that. But he had to fight to push down rising frustration. He glanced at Joseph. The winemaker's face was so swollen and bruised he was hardly recognizable. Both ears were smashed, puffed, and bloody. Two black eyes and a deep gash testified his nose was broken. And then there was the fact he'd had to practically carry the man through the tunnels like a bag of loose bones. How the Sadducee had anything left in him at all was a mystery. And now the Levitical Patrol at the door… He sighed. "All right, up, Winemaker. I'd hoped for longer, but we have to go. I'm sorry."

Joseph, on his side on the dirty cot, only groaned in reply.

How much time can Calvus possibly buy us?

The door slammed open sending Longinus' hand to his sword. But it wasn't the Patrol. Instead, a short, impossibly fat man wedged himself through the opening, his shiny bald head topping a face that would make a toad's mother blush. The man's heavily lidded eyes narrowed and he wagged a finger when he saw Longinus. "Centurion! I should have known it would be you. The stinking Patrol is everywhere out there! It's you they're looking for, isn't it? What have you done?"

"Is it my fault there's a tunnel opening into your storeroom, Fishel? Tell me now, how do I get out with cover?"

"Simple. Go back the way you came and leave me alone."

"Impossible. By now they'll be down there as well. It would be suicide."

The toad shrugged. "So? Your problems are my problems now? If it would be suicide, then die. What's it to me?"

Longinus indicated the unconscious Joseph with a jerk of his thumb. "Look at him. Help us."

The fat man shuffled forward and nudged Joseph with a toe. "He looks like he's been drug behind a camel through a stone quarry. Who is he?"

"Better you don't know."

"Well, if they're looking for him, he must be important, eh? Which means if they find him here they'll burn me to the ground, you know that."

"You're a crafty badger, Fishel. Get us out, you owe me."

"I owe you a week's worth of watered down drink over a bad dice roll. I don't owe you risking my life and business."

"I'll tell you what. At this moment, I'm choosing not to put my hand around your fat neck and squeeze the life out of you. There, now you owe me more. This man's done nothing wrong, but if they find him, he'll be dead before sundown. Help us. You've no love for the Patrol."

"I've no love for Romans, either."

Longinus put a hand on his sword hilt. "Fine. Then go. Tell them I'm here. I'll stand, but I won't guarantee there'll be much left of your tavern. One thing I do promise, if I'm alive when it's done I'll tear this place down stone by stone myself and leave your fat carcass in the alley for the rats."

Fishel's eyes rolled. Rolls of fat jiggled on his neck as he shook his head. "Longinus, Longinus. I said I didn't love you. I didn't say I wouldn't help you. He moved behind a wine rack and thumped on a wall-board. Another board beneath it dropped open, revealing a space large enough for a man to slide into. "Climb in, Roman. Time to disappear."

"Two won't fit in that hole. You think I would leave him out here to be found? I'd die first."

"We all die sometime. But have a little trust." The innkeeper pulled a blanket from a shelf and tossed it over Joseph's form. "See? Problem solved."

Longinus' fists clenched.

"Have faith, Roman! Get in the hole. There's a latch there on the inside, see? So you can pull the board in behind you."

"You throw a blanket over him and tell me to hide in a hole like a mouse? This is your idea of help? You take me for an idiot?"

"Do you want to live or not? Now get in. I'll be right back." Fishel hiked his robe and scooted out of the room.

A full minute passed. Sure the fat innkeeper had sold them out, Longinus drew his sword, ready for the worst. But when the door opened again, it was Fishel, pulling a woman along behind him. Her black hair curly and wild. Lips red against her pale skin. Her eyes were dark and made darker by black eyeliner. She sized Longinus up with a glance and dismissed him just as quickly.

"She's my sister. Don't get any ideas," Fishel said. "Unless you have coin, that is. Then get all the ideas you want, just come back when we're not in imminent danger of losing our heads."

Longinus studied the woman, then Fishel. "This is your sister? You really *must* think I'm an idiot."

"Just get in the wall!" Fishel directed the woman to the cot with a stubby finger. "You know what to do."

The girl shrugged and climbed under the blanket, pulling it up over Joseph's head.

Shouts sounded from outside and Fishel made a hasty retreat. "Hole!" He hissed as the door swung shut behind him.

Longinus looked at the woman.

"Do as he says. I won't betray you," she said.

She was truly lovely. "I don't believe it."

"You call me a liar, Roman? I said I wouldn't betray you and I won't."

"No, not that... Are you really his sister?"

She pointed. "In!"

"And then what?"

"And then I climb under the blanket with him and tell whoever's looking for him he's a worthless passed-out drunk. And that if they don't leave, I'll scream."

"You think they'll care? They want this man."

"It's worked before once or twice. You have a better idea?"

Shouts sounded from the other side of the wall.

The woman pointed. "In!"

7

The Patrolman cursed under his breath. His feet hurt and his head throbbed. His feet from the march-run across Jerusalem and his head from far too much wine the night before. And now this fool's errand. After all, the Sadducee had escaped half a city away from here. Still, he did as he was told. Patrolmen who kept their heads down and tongues still tended to last longer. And he planned to climb through the ranks. As it went, another year or two and he'd be the one giving orders. Not this idiot Chaggai, a man who wore the Captain's uniform because he had an uncle on the Council.

His fellow patrolmen moved through the tavern, examining faces, shouting, threatening, searching… Someone smacked him on the arm and he turned.

Chaggai, his captain, pointed toward a door in the back of the place. "Looks like a back room. Check it. And be quick."

The Patrolman took a deep breath, making a concerted, mental effort not to put a fist through the Captain's face. A thought came. What if he actually found the man? Him, a lowly foot soldier? Now a thing like that would shoot him to the top quickly. Maybe even a higher rank than Captain. First thing he'd do would be to send that blithering Chaggai off on some hot and dusty pointless march into the Negev.

At the door, he rattled the wooden handle. Locked. No matter, he reared back his foot and kicked.

And that was when the screaming started.

He stepped into a little storeroom. The screamer proved to be a woman, dark hair askew and shoulders bare, sitting up on a cot, clutching a ratty blanket in front of her. Her screams shoved daggers into his already throbbing head. He put his hands over his ears. "Woman! Quiet!"

The woman stopped screaming but glared. "What do you want? An eyeful? Shame on you!"

The Patrolman squared himself. "Watch your tongue! I'm Levitical Patrol. Holy before God."

No mistaking the mock in the woman's laugh. "You wouldn't be the first wearing that uniform to grace this cot."

He let the comment pass. After all, she spoke truth. "We're looking for a man…"

She indicated with a jut of her chin. "There's a tavern full of them. Take your pick. Although I'll warn you, one is about as worthless as another." She removed a bare arm from under the blanket and slapped a still, covered form next to her. "This one, for example. He comes in this morning, drinks all day, makes me an offer, and passes out. But just you watch, I'll have my money out of him one way or another."

The Patrolman stepped forward. "Let me see him."

The girl yanked the blanket to her neck. "I know what you want to see. Do you take me for a fool? One more step and I'll start screaming again. And believe me, all of Jerusalem will hear exactly how holy you're *not*."

The Patrolman paused, eyes on the sleeping lump under the blanket. The woman seemed the type to make good on her threat. And any scandal at all could have a negative effect on his career. Still…to find the man… He stepped forward. "I have to look. It's imperative this man be found."

She scooted away slightly. "Who is this man?"

"A Sadducee. A rich man."

"Believe me, this is no Sadducee. Quite the opposite."

"Let me see."

"No! I'll scream, I promise you!"

And she did. But she stopped when the Patrolman pulled the blanket from the form next to her.

"See?" she said. "Does he look like a Sadducee to you?

Disappointed, the Patrolman had to shake his head. "This man is a Roman."

"I told you this wasn't the man."

"A Roman? Have you no shame at all, Woman?"

"Roman coin spends like any other. Better in some places. Now get out."

The Roman groaned, shifted, then let out with an ugly snore.

The Patrolman stepped back. At the door, he paused and took a long last look at the woman.

"Shut the door behind you," she said.

He gave her a mock salute and pulled the door closed.

"Well?" Chaggai called from across the room.

The Patrolman shook his head. "Nothing."

8

As soon as the door swung shut, the woman shoved Longinus off the cot with a strong kick. He hit the floor with a teeth-jarring thud and sat up, rubbing his elbow. "Why did you do that?"

"I told you to hide. Not shove the Sadducee in the hole and climb in bed with me."

"You know it had nothing to do with you or your bed. And good thing I did."

"I would have talked him away."

"It sure didn't seem like that to me. The man was determined. I told you they want my friend badly."

She gave a derisive snort and pushed herself back, knees to her chest, leaning against the wall. "Just stand there and keep your distance. They'll be gone soon enough and you can go."

"Fine. I'm standing."

A minute passed, then another.

"I can't sit?" Longinus said.

"No."

"All right." He stepped over to the wall, thudded the correct board, and checked on Joseph. Breathing deeply, oblivious to the world. He glanced at the woman. "Thanks be to your god he didn't make a sound when that Patrolman was in here."

The woman just shrugged.

Longinus crossed to the door and listened for a few seconds. All quiet. "You didn't answer my question," he said, keeping his voice low.

"That's because you didn't ask one," the woman said.

"Yes I did. When you came in. Are you really the toad's sister?"

"What do you care?"

"Call me curious."

"Yes. I'm the toad's sister, all right? Not that I can see how it matters to you."

"You look nothing like him."

She shrugged a noncommittal shoulder. "They say he took after our father. Me, our mother."

Longinus marveled at the woman's composure after her encounter with the Patrol. "Then your mother must have been a goddess. What do they call you?"

"Are you actually flirting with me while a dozen Patrol are looking for you? You've no need. You want me? Bring coin like everyone else."

"I'm simply asking your name."

"Why?"

"I'm curious."

She sighed and hesitated. Her cheeks reddened. "I don't have a name. They just call me Sister, if it will shut your mouth."

"Sister? How can you not have—"

The storeroom door burst open and Fishel pushed in. "All right! Up you go! Out! Out! You only have seconds. The cart is out back. I'll help you carry him."

9

From the window of her bedchamber, Ariella watched one of the Le-vitical Patrolmen make his rounds in the courtyard below. He remind-ed her of a human crow, robe and cape flapping in the wind. *Joseph, where are you?*

He wasn't dead, she was sure of it. At night, in the dark, she could almost physically feel his heart beat against her own chest, his breath on her face. *No, husband, you can't be dead…*

She'd never dreamt the world could feel so empty. And after they'd come so far. How could it be that not more than a year ago she'd actually looked down on him? Berated, scolded, challenged. What a child she'd been! In her mind, he'd been a hill country farmer, riding her father's influence to a seat on the Sanhedrin. Her father's choice for her, not hers. But her father had seen nothing but Joseph's gold. She knew that now.

My father… Why on earth had she listened to him? Even after a lifetime of nothing but his bitterness and hate. Still, for some reason she couldn't fathom now, she'd wanted to please him. Even once. To hear him say he loved her. But, to her father, Ariella was just another thing. Worse than a thing—a daughter, a disappointment. She'd been such a fool hearing only her father's words and never Joseph's. But Joseph had proved himself to be a thousand times the man her father could ever hope to be. Joseph was hard, yes. Quiet, maybe. But his was a toughness and strength

47

born of making his own way through a hard life. He'd been given nothing and he'd earned everything. And now that inner steel of his was something she had come to rely on. Something she loved. Without a doubt, her heart, once stone-hard and bitter with scorn, had been crushed and re-formed, beating with a love deeper than she'd ever thought possible.

Yeshua had changed everything.

From the first time Joseph had taken her to hear Yeshua speak, the world had been a different place. Bigger, brighter, holding a promise outside herself. Yeshua had loved those society had deemed unlovely. Yeshua had stood up to the elite. Been a voice for the downtrodden. And, even hanging on a Roman cross, defined grace and forgiveness.

Yeshua was love.

It had been four days since Joseph had disappeared. Two days since her father had taken over their home. One day since she'd locked the door of her bedchamber and refused to come out. She'd refused to admit anyone but Yaffa. Her father had bullied and threatened, but Ariella wasn't the little girl he'd run roughshod over anymore. She was a woman now. And she'd found an inner steel of her own.

A movement down in the courtyard caught her eye. Yaffa, carrying a basket. The guard at the gate tried to grab her arm, to stop her, but Yaffa shoved him, talking loudly and waving the basket in his face. The guard shrugged and waved her away. Ariella watched as the older woman, with her since her childhood, made her way across the street to the bread vendor's cart. They talked a while, Yaffa using all the universal hand motions of the expert dickerer, the vendor shaking his head and giving the occasional exaggerated eye roll. At length they both nodded and Yaffa picked out several loaves of brown bread. She entered the courtyard again without the slightest glance at the guard. Five minutes later there was a soft knock on the bedchamber door.

"Neshama Shelli... Open."

Neshama Shelli—My Soul—the pet name Yaffa had used for Ariella for all memory.

Ariella crossed the room and unbolted the thick door. "Don't let him hear you call me that. You know how angry it makes him.

"I know he's nothing but a mangy goat. A big fat mangy goat."

"Yaffa, please, he'll punish you."

Yaffa scooted into the room and shut the door. "I've brought you bread. You have to stay strong for the baby."

"I know, I saw you beating up Tuvia with your dickering. Why do you do that to the poor man?"

"We're Jews, dickering is conversation. It's like talking about the weather. He wouldn't have it any other way. If I didn't argue, he probably wouldn't sell." Her voice dropped. "But listen, Neshama Shelli, this time it wasn't arguing you saw. It was a show for the brute down there."

"You mean the guard?"

"Same thing. Tuvia is a good man. A believer in Yeshua. And therefore a conduit to the outside."

Ariella's gut clenched. She reflexively put a hand on her unborn child. "He has news?"

"From the Roman, the centurion friend of Joseph's. Joseph lives but he's badly hurt. Thank your father for that."

"But he's alive."

"Yes. Alive and in a safe place, at least for now." The woman studied Ariella's face. "Are you hearing me?"

"I hear you."

"Then what's wrong? He's alive!"

"And I'm so grateful. But you know Joseph, there's no give in him. He'll come for me."

"And?"

"My father has all the Levitical Patrol at his disposal! And I know he wants Joseph dead. It's not enough to steal everything he's worked his whole life for. My father won't rest until Joseph has suffered and died. I know him. Maybe you could get word back to him and tell him to stay away?"

"I might as well tell a thunderstorm to turn around and go back to God."

Pounding came from the door. "Daughter! Open!"

"Speaking of mangy goats," Yaffa whispered.

Ariella considered. "Open for him, there is no choice."

"He's not right in the mind, child. I won't leave you alone with him."

"All right. Then stand in the corner. Be seen but not heard. Do you understand?"

Yaffa nodded, pulled the bolt, and opened the heavy door.

For as long as Ariella could remember, it had felt as if her father sucked all the available air out of any room he entered. Pharisee, chief priest, member of the Sanhedrin—larger than life in every way. She'd never noticed the hard lines around his mouth before. Or how too much wine and rich food had left him red-veined and multi-chinned. She did notice now, as he pushed his bulk into the room. She also noticed the bright cruelty in his eyes. His life was a field where the all-consuming vines of ambition choked out any root of tenderness that dared try to grow.

He glared at her. "Well, what a privilege to be allowed into my own daughter's chambers." He crossed to a table against the wall, picked up a goblet, sniffed, and drank. His gulping loud in the quiet room.

"Or prison cell," Ariella said.

Her father wiped his mouth with the back of his hand. "Your choice, not mine. I've given you free access to the house."

"Access to my house? Who are you to give me anything?"

"When your husband chose to blaspheme God, he forfeited his rights to property. And you're a woman, you never had any to begin with."

"Things are changing. The Romans allow women to own."

"Not in this case."

"You use the word woman as if it were some sort of profanity."

"No, not profanity. Simply inconsequential. You have no right to anything in this house, that's not my fault. The Council, in its wisdom and grace, allowed me to take over my son-in-law's holdings since he's either dead or fled Jerusalem in shame."

"Joseph would never run. And he has never blasphemed God."

"He spoke against me, he spoke against the High Priest, he stood against the entire Sanhedrin."

"Is that considered blasphemy then? To be strong? To seek truth?"

"The priesthood is truth. We are God's representatives. His voice to men. And, as in this case, his hard hand of judgment. No one has the right to question. Joseph knows this. He either ran or he committed suicide."

"You know better. He would do neither."

Her father scratched one of his chins. "And yet he's gone. So the subject seems to have closed itself." He slurped from the cup again.

"I was drinking that," Ariella said.

"What is it?"

"Goat's milk and pomegranate juice. Yaffa says it's good for the child."

He made a face and set the cup down. He pointed to the edge of the bed. "Sit down, Ariella."

"Why?"

"Because I told you to."

"I prefer to stand."

"Sit!" The boom of his voice made her jump. "Your husband has spoiled you, I will not. Now sit."

When she did, he pulled up a stool and sat opposite, close enough for her to smell the milk on his breath. "Give me your hand."

She clenched them together in her lap.

He reached and took her hand in his, squeezing hard enough to bring tears to her eyes. "Listen to me closely, daughter. You and your husband openly took a stand for the Nazarene. A very, very foolish thing to do. It would be within reason and our rights for us to take your life for it. But I'm nothing if not merciful. I'm giving you a second chance. You and our child."

"Our?"

"You no longer have a husband. You're my daughter. You are my property. So is the child. Just like this house and all that's in it. And as soon as I can get there to settle things and take ownership, the vineyards in Arimathea as well. I'm offering you a choice. You have friends among the followers, and you can find them for me. Yeshua is dead, so is their hope. And their stubborn existence is a thorn in the paw of true Judaism. To all of Israel. They must be stopped for the good of the nation. They must be silenced."

"You would have me betray friends?"

"I would. For their benefit as well as yours. It would go easier on them if they would quietly stand down"

"What do you mean by easier?"

"Caiaphas has turned loose a man. And not a normal man. He'll torture and kill if he feels it necessary. Maybe even if it's not. Personally, I think he relishes the opportunity to spill the blood of Yeshua's people."

"This man would kill?"

"Absolutely. So, is it really betrayal, or are you saving their lives?"

"And you'd show them mercy…"

"Absolutely."

"And my child? You would show my child mercy? And me?"

"If you help, and if your help has any value, you can continue to live here in comfort. If you refuse, you'll be confined until you give birth, then you'll never see the child again."

"You would separate a mother from her child?"

"To please God? Without hesitation."

"Then your God is not my God."

His slap spun her, almost knocking her off the bed. Yaffa jumped forward, but Ariella stopped her with a quick shake of her head.

Her father rubbed his hand. "You see the things you make me do? But maybe now you've heard me. One way or another, you will obey. In the meantime, you can live here, or you won't ever see the light of day again. Choose."

Ariella made a sidelong glance at Yaffa. The woman's eyes were wide. "I don't want to be locked in a cell."

Beryl stood, smiling. "Good. You're doing the right thing." He picked up the goblet again. "Milk and juice, good for the child—I never would have thought." He took it with him as he walked out.

Yaffa closed the door after him, hurried to wet a cloth in the wash basin, and pressed it to Ariella's face. Ariella put her hand over the woman's. "I'll survive. It's not the first time and it's not the hardest he's ever hit me."

"The man is evil."

"God will protect us. We have to hold on. Joseph will come for us. Please, God, don't let him die trying."

10

Sister sat on the low wall bordering one of Joseph of Arimathea's wine presses. The place was beautiful. Just as a rich man's garden should be. Perfectly kept, and far enough outside the walls of the city to offer solitude and peace.

A fitting place to bury a man like Yeshua.

A gust of wind pulled her hair into her eyes, a dark and curly mass that momentarily blocked out the world.

Fine with her.

Still, she pushed what she could behind her ears, knowing it wouldn't last, the next gust would only undo the effort. A sparrow dropped to the grass with a fluttering whisper. Only a cubit away, he hopped and plucked at the ground paying Sister no mind. She didn't blame him. It had been that way all her life. She was only the sister. Nothing. Something to be ignored.

But that wasn't entirely true, was it? Not everyone ignored her. Men didn't ignore her. Men had never ignored her. Since she was a child, men had pinched, prodded and pawed. And eventually it had been easier to simply become what they wanted her to be.

So, that's what she was. And that's how the world saw her. A million pairs of eyes laughing, mocking, judging... A million pairs of eyes lusting. Well, let them lust. And let them laugh. A person did what they had to do to get along. The world was a hard place where no one was allowed to stay young. As far as she knew, not one human living under the sky had ever remained untainted. This was her lot, so be it. Life could make a person numb. She didn't even feel shame anymore.

At least she hadn't, until Yeshua…

The sparrow flitted off with a whir of wings as a shadow appeared. Pushing her hair back again, she looked up. A Roman stood above her outlined in the sun, his shadowed face framed by the steel helmet of a soldier. His voice was clipped and stern. "This is a private tract of land. Who are you and what are you doing here?"

She stood and met his stare. "Looking for a little solitude. Is that a crime now?"

"It is if you're looking for it on private property."

"A Jew owns this land. Not Caesar."

"The Jew you refer to is under investigation. We're here to search the grounds. Back off, woman, if you know what's good for you."

She knew men. This one had a cruel streak. She took a step back, eyes darting to his clenched fist then back to his face. "I was only looking for a quiet place."

He looked her up and down, that familiar glint in his eye. "A Jewess without a head covering? Are you sure that's all you were looking for?"

She forced her voice neutral. "I'll leave."

The soldier put a hand on her arm, his grip a vice. "No, woman. What you're going to do is come with me and answer some questions."

"Why? I know nothing of the man who owns this place. Or his business."

"Because I said so. You need no more reason than that."

She yanked her arm back. "I know what you're after, and it isn't answers."

He grabbed her again, this time hard enough to bruise. "Be that as it may, what's wrong with one stone for two birds?"

"Decimus!" The hard-edged growl came from behind her and she turned. Another soldier approached with long strides. "What's going on here?"

The man called Decimus stepped back, his manner markedly less confident. "Just a woman. A prostitute by the look of her.

Trespassing. I thought to take her for questioning."

"You thought? Since when do you think?" The newcomer said. "Go with the others and search the area like you were supposed to do in the first place. Be quick and be thorough."

"Yes, sir." Decimus, eyes lowered, moved off toward his compatriots.

She steeled herself, pushed back her hair again and faced the order giver. "I was just leaving."

She expected a reprimand. Or worse, a blow. But smile lines formed at the corner of the man's eyes. "My apologies for his tongue. You can trust me when I tell you Decimus will be reprimanded." He shook his head. "May Apollo strike me, I still can't believe you're that toad's sister."

11

Sister stared as recognition dawned. "You look different in uniform. What is your rank, then?"

"Centurion."

"You'll arrest me?"

"Have you broken Roman law?"

"The other man wanted to take me for questioning."

"The other man is an idiot and will be standing double guard duty and scrubbing latrine troughs for daring to voice an idea without my consent."

She couldn't help the slightest of smiles. "You're so important then?"

"Let's just say, in his world, I'm God. Come, sit with me a moment. I won't take you to the Fortress, but I do have questions."

She followed as he led her down a stone-lined path. She stopped when they passed a wall, and she realized they were no longer within sight of the other men.

He glanced back at her. "Come."

"Where?"

"You're a delicate flower in fear of your virtue? Are we really playing that game?"

"I may not be either delicate or virtuous, but I still have a shred of pride. Do you need to insult me?"

His eyes softened. "Again, my apologies. I'm no righteous judge, believe me. But I only want to talk with you."

"I'm listening."

"Some place we can't be heard."

She squared herself. "Why should I believe you?"

A muscle clenched in his jaw. A quick temper, this one. "Believe me or not. That's your choice. But follow."

She stiffened. "If I refuse?"

He moved quickly for a large man. A step, a flash of arm, the next thing she knew she was slung across his shoulder and they were once again moving down the path. She kicked a few times, slapped his back, cursed a blue streak, but the man was made of sinew and stone. At length he flopped her onto a patch of grass and lowered himself onto a stone bench, looking down at her.

"Can I get up?" she said.

"I'm not sure yet. I have the feeling you might bite."

"You didn't have to carry me like a child."

"You were acting like a child."

She started to rise, but he put her back down with a simple, two-fingered push. He sat back and studied her, expression thoughtful.

She thought of him under the blanket on the cot and sighed. "How is your friend? Alive?"

"Thanks to you. You have steel in you."

"I was only trying to save my brother's business. The fool is always in debt, so I do a lot of that. Mostly on my back."

"Are you trying to shock me?"

"Did it work?"

"Not at all. Fishel takes all the money you earn?"

"He thinks it's his right. But I manage to keep my share. I have to eat. What do you want with me? Let's get it over with."

"To start with, your name."

She felt blood climb to her neck and cheeks. "I told you, my brothers only call me Sister."

"You spoke truly? Surely you have a name."

"I may have had one once. If so, I don't remember it. Our parents either died or left. I was a very small child. I don't remember them."

"Sister… All right. I'm Longinus."

"Good for you."

Shaking his head, he held out a hand. "Off the ground. Come on."

She hesitated, then took it. He helped her to her feet and guided her to the bench.

"What do you know of Joseph of Arimathea?" he said.

She looked away. "Nothing at all. Only his name and that he owns this place and buried the Galilean here. I've never met the man."

"No, not officially, I suppose. But you helped hide him yesterday."

She stared at him. "The man you were helping? I never got a real look at him. Why were you helping a Jew?"

"Jew, Roman, Barbarian—an honorable man is an honorable man. And Joseph of Arimathea is an honorable man. He stands up for what he believes and doesn't back down. I respect him for it."

"Are you an honorable man then? Someone that crawls the city's secret tunnels in old rags and gambles with my brother?"

"I am what I am. I make no excuses. In battle I would call myself honorable. And I hope those who've fought at my side would say the same. In life, you do what you have to do."

"At least on that point we agree. What did you do with him? The Arimathean?"

"He's in a safe place. At least as safe a place as I could find with my back to the wall."

"The Sanhedrin thinks he's involved with the disappearance of the body?"

"They grasp at straws. It's his property. But they hold no good will toward him regardless. He backed the Nazarene publicly."

"And what would happen to me if it was found out I helped him?"

"With the Jews? I imagine they would go hard on you. This man, Yeshua, has the city in an uproar even after his death."

"It would go hard on you as well? If they found out you helped?"

"It would. With both the Jews and Rome. That's why I wanted to talk with you alone. Most of my men are loyal to me, a few only to themselves. Caiaphas, the Sanhedrin, Pilate—they all believe Joseph of Arimathea took Yeshua's body. Or at least aided Yeshua's disciples in the theft."

"But you don't?"

"The Winemaker's word is good enough for me."

"Did you know Yeshua claimed he would rise on the third day?"

"Yes, so his disciples claim. And that particular spark of rumor is what the Sanhedrin wants to stamp out most. After all, they requested the man's death."

"I heard Yeshua predict it myself."

"You believe he rose?"

"There was much talk in the tavern about the man Lazarus, from Bethany. They say Yeshua brought him back from the grave. But talk is talk. People love a good story with their liquor."

"I've met Lazarus. He looked very alive to me."

"But did he really die? Who knows?"

"You say you heard Yeshua speak. Did you know him?"

"In a sense." Her throat tightened and she looked away.

Longinus must have noticed. "He meant something to you, then?"

She shrugged, pushing grief to the back of her mind. A skill she'd learned the hard way and long leaned on. "All I know is, if he were to be alive somehow, he would have good reason to hate me. If he thought about me at all."

"Why? I understand there were others of your profession among his followers. And he bore them no ill will. He welcomed all."

She shook her head. "If there were, they're not like me. I don't want to talk about it."

The sparrow was back, picking at the grass. A breeze rustled the foliage.

"Where did you encounter him? On the Temple Mount?" Longinus said.

She squared. "Why would I want to rub elbows with the pious and pretenders?"

He arched a brow. "You've never been?"

She watched the bird for a moment. "I don't even have a name. What could a woman like me hope to find on God's mountain?"

"It seems to me your lack of a name has nothing to do with you and everything to do with your toad of a brother."

She had no answer for that.

"Speak. Why are you in this place? Clearly Yeshua meant something to you," he said.

"Why do you want to know?"

"I need all the information I can gather. If I can somehow locate the body, I might be able to help Joseph. Believe me, he needs it if he wants to survive."

"What I know can't help you. And it's a long story."

"I have time," he said.

She looked at him, debating. "You know what I am."

"I've already told you, I hold no judgment."

"You might not judge me, but Yeshua was a good man. He would judge me and be right to do it."

"What happened? Tell me."

She wiped a firm hand across her eyes.

"It won't help you find his body."

"Let me decide that. Tell me."

She sighed. "Three years ago, that was the first time I saw him…"

12

Longinus nodded. "Three years ago… Go on."

For some reason, this woman moved him. There was a river of pain beneath her tough exterior, though she hid it well. She'd seen the hard side of life and was still standing. In her world, that was saying something. She was blunt in her approach. He knew, even as she started, her story would offer no sanitized whitewash. She would be seen for what she was, nothing more, nothing less. She would ask no pity and make no excuses.

She pushed her hair out of her eyes. "I was drunk that night. Drunk and very angry."

Longinus frowned. "Two partners that should never dance but never seem to be able to keep their hands off each other."

"I was in the tavern, sitting on the lap of a fat, sweaty, pig of a young man. His clothes and rings said Upper City. His breath smelled like old meat. But I could also smell the gold in his purse."

"This was three years ago? You have a good memory."

"No, not always. But I remember every second about that night, even through the haze of the wine. The fat fool kept sputtering on endlessly about nothing, the whole time trying to work up the nerve to voice his true desire."

"You could read his thoughts?"

She shrugged "Why would I need to? I've been an actress in the same boring play a thousand times. The players change around me but the story never does."

"Go on."

"Fatty was with friends. Real men of the world, those. Nervous and laughing and trying to impress each other. Each one talking cruder and louder than the last. They undressed me with their eyes and words. I hated them all but they kept the wine coming. And, like I said, Fatty had a heavy purse. I was just waiting for him to work up his nerve for an actual proposition and I'd leave him with a smile and a story he could brag about."

"And poorer for it."

"His own fault. I would have stripped him of every coin he had and been glad to do it. As it turned out, I never got the chance because my idiot brother showed up."

"Fishel?"

"No, Yoram, my younger brother."

"Two brothers that call you Sister."

"Yes."

"And what happened then?"

"Yoram stumbled into them, a cup in one hand and a wineskin in the other, singing some Roman sea shanty about a red-haired woman in Crete he'd heard from one of you."

Longinus chuckled. "Ah yes, I've been to Crete."

"I don't wonder. The next thing I knew, Yoram had spilled his cup all over my payday. Fatty jumped up shouting curses and dumped me onto the floor like a sack of grain. Yoram was beyond drunk. He slurred out some kind of apology and tried to clean the wine off Fatty's very white tunic with a smelly bar rag."

"But Fatty wasn't satisfied?"

"Fatty's friends threw Yoram through the back door of the tavern into the alley."

"And what did you do?"

"Followed, of course. The idiot Yoram owed me. My payday was gone. Fatty already had another woman on his lap. I doubt he even knew the difference. And I wasn't about to go fight over him. Yoram went stumbling down the alley toward the street and

I followed, yelling at him. I was drunk and mad. He'd cost me and I wanted to kill the fool. Finish the job the Upper City weaklings didn't have the stomach for."

"I'm hoping this story ends with your brother alive?"

"Unfortunately, yes. I shouted for him to stop. He turned, grinning like a moron. Looking at me with those same eyes he gets every time he drinks, all vacant and glassy."

"What did he do?"

"What else? He vomited. I asked him if he had any idea what he'd cost me that night. And told him I'd have it out of his hide. He didn't even bother to wipe his chin. Didn't say a word, slurred or otherwise, just turned and continued stumbling down the alley. I yelled again, but he crossed the street, crashed into a wall, and thumped over on his side, cradling his stupid wineskin like a baby. Idiot." She drifted in her memory.

"Is all this vomiting and passing out going to lead to Yeshua?" Longinus said.

"I told you it was a long story. Now be quiet and listen if you want to hear it."

The woman really did have beautiful eyes...

"Go on then," Longinus said.

"I kept after him, probably not walking too straight a line myself. He'd cost me, and I figured I'd do what would hurt him the most—steal his liquor. So I went over, bent down and took it from him. He never even twitched. Which is when I saw the little Pharisee."

This stopped Longinus. "What little Pharisee?"

"I found out later that his name was Nicodemus."

"Nicodemus. I know the man. What happened next?"

"He was headed somewhere, but he'd stopped and was just standing there staring at me like I had two heads. Or maybe like I was a cockroach. Looking back, he was probably just shocked I was stealing a wineskin from a helpless man."

"It might also have been the fact your eyes were painted and your hair was unbound. The man is a Pharisee, and a member of the Sanhedrin, after all."

"Trust me, Centurion, there are Pharisees and even Sanhedrin as familiar with the Lower City taverns as anyone else."

"Nicodemus is a family man. A dedicated one."

"Even so."

"Point taken."

"Still, you may be right about him. You should have seen the poor man's eyes. Wide as shekels. 'Woman?' He says to me. Like I said, I was intoxicated. And mad. And here was this stub of a Pharisee standing there in his pious robes judging me. Who was he to judge? I figured there was only one reason a man like him would be lurking around the Lower City that time of night. I took a long drink of the wine and looked him right in his shocked eyes. I wanted to hurt someone and he happened to be there. I remember my words exactly. 'Well…what do we have here?' I said. 'Another Pharisee out looking for some Lower City feminine comfort? Do you have the coin to pay, Rabbi?' When I propositioned him, I thought he'd pass out, I really did. But he pulled himself together and scurried off like a little gopher. He definitely had a destination in mind. He walked with purpose. The wine I took from Yoram was sweet and strong and it made me even more reckless. And who was the Pharisee to snub me? In my addled state, I somehow figured it must be another woman he had in mind."

"Yes. Probably his wife."

"You know what I mean. I followed him, thinking to make some kind of trouble. When I passed the open front door of the tavern, Fatty still had the second woman and still hadn't made his move. I almost forgot the Pharisee and went back in, but what was the point? More filthy talk? More sweaty hands? The night was cool and felt good so I followed the Pharisee instead. He had quick little feet. He'd walk on, then stop, like he was considering, then move on again. His actions made sense to me. I was convinced he was sneaking down to see a woman of the night, and he was as nervous as old Fatty had been. He finally stopped at a door. I'd seen it before but didn't know who lived there. It was blue, I remember vividly. I began to wonder if maybe I was wrong about a prostitute at that point. Most of us know each other, at least in the Lower City, and, as far as I knew, none of them lived or worked behind that blue door. Still, what else could it have been? The way he was acting? It took a full minute before he finally pulled enough guts together to lift a hand and clack the knocker. I watched him. I made no attempt to hide, but he was so wrapped up in his own thoughts he never even noticed me. The door opened. A man, not a woman. A large man. He and the Pharisee spoke for a while. I thought then the man might be a procurer. Maybe this was a brand new brothel I hadn't yet heard of. I was curious so I walked closer to hear them talking. But then another man came and the Pharisee followed him into the house. I went and tried to find a way to see inside. I found a narrow break in the wall and a path leading to the back. I heard voices back there so I followed them. The path circled around. There was a fence made of branches. Inside, a large courtyard. I could see parts of it through the fence but not all of it. I smelled bread baking. I remember wishing I could have some to slow the spin in my head. I climbed up into the branches of a tree and peeked over. It wasn't a brothel at all. Just a bunch of people. Men, women, young and old. Even some children. But there was one man…"

"Yeshua."

"Yes, but I didn't know it at the time. He was nothing remarkable. You know that if you've seen him. His back was to me. but even so something about him pulled me. I couldn't account for it. He looked like just another working class Jew. Hair cropped short, worn clothes. He wasn't tall, wasn't short— everything about him was just totally…ordinary."

"Ordinary." Longinus said. "He was far from that, I think."

"Yes. I couldn't explain it then and I can't now. I was curious. I remember Yeshua turning and looking right at me. I was deep in shadow. Hidden behind branches and the fence. There was no way he could have known I was there. No way he could see me. Still, I knew he had. And those eyes. Those eyes of his reflected a million stars. I'm telling you they pinned me and I couldn't move or even look away. It was like he saw through that fence and my skin and my bones and looked into my soul. And…"

"And what?"

Her eyes flashed. "And I wanted no one looking at my soul. Not after the things I've done. In that moment, I felt shame. More shame than I thought possible. And it made me angry."

"You were angry with Yeshua for looking at you?"

"You didn't see those eyes! Yes. I was mad at Yeshua, mad at myself, mad at God, mad a Fishel, Yoram, Fatty… I was mad at the universe and everyone in it. I was mad all the way through."

Longinus could hear his men calling to one another as their search moved closer.

"Then Nicodemus came," she said. "They brought him to Yeshua. I moved a little higher for a better view. They talked for a while. Not long. I was surprised at Yeshua's voice. Quiet but also strong. There was so much in it…"

"In his voice?"

"I don't know how to describe it. Joy, love…and a sadness that brought tears to my eyes. I'm not used to crying, believe me, but I did that night. And I didn't even know why. I blamed it on the wine but it wasn't. I couldn't understand what was happening to me. I tried to focus on the things they talked about, but after a while they might as well have been speaking another language. But my heart heard Yeshua. Not his words maybe, but him. None of it made sense to me. It still doesn't even as I sit here telling you. And then Nicodemus left. I knew I should leave too—Yeshua knew I was there. But I didn't leave. I couldn't. I just sat there, wine-soaked and with a branch cutting into my thighs, paralyzed by his presence. A man I didn't even know." She bent her head down, thick hair falling around her face. A single tear fell on her folded hands.

Longinus touched her leg with a gentle hand and she flinched a little.

"This is why you're here? You think the Nazarene looked into your soul?" Longinus said.

She looked up, her cheeks red, and he wondered at it. Here was a woman who had seen much.

"That wasn't the end of it," she said. "I wish it were—I'd give anything—but it wasn't. A few nights later he came into the tavern. I still didn't know his name. He was just the man with the eyes to me. The *seer*. But I hadn't been able to think about anything else. I was dancing when he came in." She met Longinus' eyes. "I'm a very good dancer."

"I believe it," he said.

"I wanted to know him. So I danced for him. Or at least I tried to. Everyone in the place watches when I dance. And I wanted his attention. Do you understand?"

"I think I do. It's what you knew. Did he see you?"

"He saw. I made sure of it. But he saw with none of the usual reaction. He only looked…sad."

"So you stopped?'

"It made me angry all over again. I suddenly wanted to break him. In my stupidity I wanted to own him for myself. So I danced harder. I let a little more skin show with every spin."

"And?"

"And nothing. Only those eyes. Worlds or sorrow. Sorrow like I'd never thought possible. Later that night he spoke to the people. Words of love, words of God. Words like I've never heard before. I stood in the back of the room. I felt so ashamed. He spoke of life, but what was that to me? I died inside years ago, the first time I let a man touch me for money. What was life to me? Still, it felt like a tiny spark deep inside me flared a little. Something I didn't even know was there. Then…"

"Then what?"

"As he was leaving, he looked at me again. Only a glance. But that glance was everything. Again, like he saw into my soul. He knew it all. A half second, but that glance lasted forever. After he left, I made an oath with myself. If he came into the tavern again, I wouldn't dance. I wouldn't tempt. I would try to talk with him. Was it too much to ask for me to find a little life? Something small to hold, that's all I wanted, nothing big. I wanted to ask him if there was any way for a harlot. Could there be any hope for someone like me?"

"There is always hope."

"No. Not anymore. He's dead and so am I. And now even his body is gone."

"What did you want to find here?"

"I don't know. A few minutes of peace, maybe? It was stupid to come when I think about it. But see? My being here has nothing to do with your missing body. I can't help you. Or your Arimathean."

"What will you do now?"

She wiped her eyes with a hard hand. "Go back. What else? I have to eat, don't I? I have to have a place to live."

He considered her. Here was a woman who had never had a chance. Not even a name. She'd been considered property, plain and simple. A commodity to be sold and used until her usefulness had faded and gone. He'd seen the same a thousand times in a dozen different countries, but this woman touched him deeply. Buried in hopelessness, she had dared hope. His fingers itched for fat Fishel's throat. He wanted to say something to help her, stir that spark again that she'd felt that night. He struggled with the words. "You are a very beautiful woman. And you need to know your beauty is much deeper than a body and a face."

She looked at him and a tear slipped down her cheek.

Longinus stood. "Get up now and follow me."

13

Sister ignored the leers of the other soldiers as she and the centurion passed. He barked a few orders at them and moved on, not looking back. Obviously a man accustomed to being obeyed. He was very tall, she realized as she followed. His back straight, head high.

They exited the garden property, followed a worn path to a main road, and passed through a guarded gate into the New City. Not as crowded as the Lower City or even the more spacious Upper City, the New City spread its arms and made itself comfortable. Dirt paths connected a wide scattering of dwellings and shops. Livestock lent a pungent stench to the air. They passed a young boy leading a goat by a length of twine. He cast sidelong glances toward Longinus, very careful not to meet the centurion's eyes. The Antonia Fortress loomed ahead on the left, a stark reminder of Rome's oppression. Beyond it, the Temple shone.

It was true what she'd said. In her whole life, she'd never been to the Mount. What would it have been like to hear Yeshua speak up there? Among the crowds? In the shadow of the Temple? She looked at Longinus but he seemed lost in thought. "Where are you taking me?"

He offered nothing in reply, only quickened his pace.

Romans... She'd had her fill of them over the years. Even courser than usual Lower City rabble. Yet this centurion was an enigma. He'd helped the Arimathean, a Jew. He'd moved her away and protected her from his overtly rude subordinate. He didn't seem to be interested in her body. Then what?

They passed through another gate—this one at the North Wall—cut through a narrow alley behind the Governor's residence, and descended into the Valley of the Cheesemakers. The retaining wall of the Temple Mount rose twenty stories on their left. Store owners hawked their wares from doorways with loud voices. Smoke and ash rose from ovens and open fires, filtering the already-limited sunlight and giving the canyon an ethereal feel.

"Are we—"

He shushed her with an upheld hand as they turned down a new and dark alleyway. Quieter here. Cool and dark. With a glance around him, he ducked through a low archway and she followed.

She pulled up and stopped. After all, what did she really know of this man? "What is this place? I won't go further until you tell me what's going on."

"We're almost there," he said, keeping his voice low. "Follow and keep quiet."

"Tell me."

"You'll see soon enough." He took her hand and led her on.

They cut left, through another passage, then right. *I'll never find my way out of here...* How many times in her life had she followed some man she didn't know into the dark? Or led them there herself? She'd been physically hurt many times. Once or twice, seriously. Still, into the dark she continued to go. Once a road is traveled for so many years, exits become impossible to find.

A shaft of sunlight tumbled ahead. The Roman stopped in front of a tiny courtyard, high walls on all sides. In the center of the courtyard, the lone sun-shaft cast its light on a trickling fountain. Plants grew in stone pots. A few well-worn benches stood against one of the walls. A bird flitted. A woman's voice drifted down in lilting melody from some window far above.

Sister had a sudden and unexplainable urge to lie on one of the benches and sleep, such a peace she felt here.

"What is this place? she said. "You have a secret apartment?"

He turned to her, eyes dark. "You saw me help the Arimathean and you told no one. This makes me think I can trust you. Can I?"

She squared her shoulders and lifted her chin. "Of course I can be trusted. But, why the mystery? I need to go home. I don't belong here."

"You don't belong *there*. This life of yours is no life at all. I offer you a new path."

She hesitated. "What new path?"

"Fishel is scum. What I told you is true, there is a beauty in you. I see it in your eyes. I hear it in your story, your voice. Let me help you."

She sighed. "Save the harlot. I've heard it all before, Roman. It's an old song."

"I'm sure you have. But you needn't hear it again. A new path, yes or no?"

A new path? She thought about Fishel's pig eyes. So very different from Yeshua's. Different from this Roman's, for that matter. She bit her bottom lip, listening to the fountain splash and the woman sing. "How can there be another way me?"

"Yeshua sparked hope in you. Fan that spark now. Find in it enough strength to do this."

Her heart thudded in her throat. "What would I have to do?"

"Disappear for a while. Maybe not forever, but definitely for a while. And it may be dangerous."

"Why would it be dangerous? Because of Fishel?"

"No, not Fishel."

She looked around her. Such a peaceful little courtyard, yet she suddenly felt she was standing on the edge of a cliff. "I don't understand. How dangerous?"

"Dangerous enough, but I'll be close by. But decide now. It wouldn't be good to be seen here."

She studied his face for a long moment. A good face, she thought at last. Hard, yes, but good all the same. Some scars, lines, but much life. "You'll know where I am?"

The corner of his mouth turned up. "Yes. Will you trust me then?"

She thought of the tavern. Of the constant, stale stench of liquor, smoke, and sex. Would anyone miss her? Her brothers would miss the money she brought. They would wonder where she'd gone, possibly. But times were hard and they wouldn't wonder long. She wouldn't be the first prostitute to disappear. There were men who would miss her body, but what was that to her? There were a hundred like her to take her place. Still...

"Roman, you could have my body for a few coins. Why all this?"

"You're stalling. You need help. It's enough."

She looked around the courtyard again. Then back at him. "This is madness. Lead on."

He nodded.

Through the little courtyard, up a tall flight of steps, to a thick, wooden door. The Roman gave it a couple hard knocks. Movement within, then just a crack and a narrowed eye.

"Open," the Roman said. He lowered his voice. "I have someone. She needs a place."

"This place?"

"I found her in the garden. By the tomb. She speaks of Yeshua. Open, before someone comes along."

Muffled discussion ensued inside. Then the door swung open and the little Pharisee, Nicodemus, motioned them in.

14

The door swung shut behind them, and there was a finality about the sound. Longinus looked down at the woman. She'd stiffened. Shoulders back, chin high. He could only imagine the life she'd lived among her fellow Jews. Her defenses were so long practiced they had become automatic. He hoped, for her sake, she'd find none of the usual condescension here. And if she did, he would personally put a stop to it.

The room was very large and comfortably furnished. A dozen or so people lingered, every eye on the newcomers. Longinus returned the stares, assessing, daring. Then he looked down at Nicodemus. "You'll help her." A statement rather than a question.

"Of course we will." Nicodemus looked at her. "What is your name, woman?"

Longinus saw her mouth set and stepped in. "*Sister* will do for now."

If Nicodemus found this odd, it didn't show. "Sister. Welcome."

Sister let out a breath. "Thank you."

Worry creased the little Pharisee's face. "Longinus, how is Joseph? It's said that you helped him escape Beryl's torture but that he is badly hurt."

"He's alive. Healing. Worried about his wife."

"Yes, I'm sure he's worried. And Beryl will use it to his own advantage." Nicodemus glanced at Sister. "I'm afraid you take a great risk bringing her here. As much as I'd like to tell you otherwise, we can hardly offer safe harbor."

"We weren't followed. Besides, you and the woman are connected."

Nicodemus studied her with a careful eye. "Woman, do we know each other?"

She shook her head. "I doubt you remember. We saw each other in the Lower City three years ago."

"Three years?"

"You visited Yeshua that night."

"Three years. Yes. A night I'll never forget should I live as long as our father Methuselah. But forgive me if I don't remember you. Were you there? With Yeshua?"

Blood crept up her neck, but her face remained passive. "We saw each other in the street."

"The street?"

"Tell him," Longinus said.

"I was taking a skin of wine from my brother," she said.

"I'm afraid I'm confused. Forgive me," Nicodemus said.

"He was passed out. Dead drunk."

Recognition dawned on Nicodemus' face. "Yes… Yes! You propositioned me."

"And you turned me down cold."

Her eyes widened a bit when Nicodemus let out a laugh. "Ha! Yes. But not for your lack of beauty. It's just that I'm a faithful man. Both to God and to my wife."

Her stiffness receded a little. "Then, in my experience, you'd be the the exception to the rule."

"I wish that weren't true, for your sake. My name is Nicodemus, but I imagine by now you know that. Are you a follower of Yeshua, then?"

"If I'm honest, until recently I followed nothing but coin and a free cup of wine to dull life. I worked for my brother." She glanced up at Longinus. "Then I followed this Roman, not that he left me much choice. Now your door has shut behind me, and I don't know what I'm following or even what I am anymore."

"Yes, yes. You're not alone. I'm afraid none of us know what we are anymore. Which puts us all on equal footing, don't you think?"

Her mouth opened, then closed again. "Equal? A Pharisee and…a woman like me? A harlot?"

Nicodemus smiled. "Is that what we are? Or are we two people with a new and uncharted path ahead? I think yes, we are very equal. Equally lost, equally found. Yeshua will show us the way. Scripture will show us as well."

"You put much trust in a dead man," she said.

Nicodemus smiled. "If Yeshua were dead I would agree with you."

A woman approached, older, dark hair streaked with grey. Kind eyes. She reached for Sister's hand. "Come. Please know you are welcome here. Let's find somewhere to get you settled."

Sister again glanced up at Longinus, and he nodded to her. She followed the woman through a curtained doorway.

"We need to talk, Longinus," Nicodemus said. "Please, come."

Longinus followed the Pharisee through a back doorway and down a long, open hallway. No solid ceiling above, only thick, bare branches laid cross-ways wall to wall. Sunlight filtered down, slats of dancing dust, swirling as Nicodemus passed through them. They came to a walled patio, cool and shaded, heavy brush overhead.

"We're safe to talk here," Nicodemus said.

"But not inside?"

"I think so, but how can I be sure? The world is upside down, and the fewer the ears about the better. We gather here while Jerusalem boils. Tell me, please, what's happening out there? We get a word here and there, but not nearly enough to assess."

"What can I say? Yeshua's murder has opened some deep chasms. The Council is panicked and trying to get ahead of it."

"Get ahead of it how?"

"They've charged the Levitical Patrol with finding and scattering all of Yeshua's followers. A man leads them. I understand he's ruthless in his quest."

"Then it's as we thought. What man?"

"A Cilician. I know nothing more of him except for his mission. And that only second hand."

"What does Pilate say? What is the Roman position?"

Longinus shook his head. "All Pilate wants is for Yeshua's body to be found quickly. He wants to avoid any trouble that might reflect badly on him in Rome"

"Is he working with this Cilician? Are the Romans involved in the hunt for Yeshua's followers?"

"Not yet. But that will come if Pilate gets frustrated enough. If I can find the body before the Patrol finds you, it may save you all."

"I appreciate your help, my friend, I really do. But you won't find Yeshua's body. He is risen."

"I've heard this. The Winemaker believes this as well."

"Of course he does. Joseph knows the prophecies as well as I."

"Tell me, if Yeshua has truly risen, where is he? Why does he not show himself? He could save you all."

"He's shown himself to his closest disciples. Why to no one else, I confess I don't know. I'm searching the scripture constantly for an answer to that."

"I told the Winemaker and I'll tell you as well, I saw and heard things on Golgotha the day we crucified him that I can't account for. But this…a man surviving a Roman cross? It's a lot to accept."

"Not surviving, conquering death. Rising from the grave. He was dead, sure enough. I helped Joseph put him in the tomb. This is God, Longinus, it's as simple as that. An event prophesied to come to pass long before either you or I were born. Yeshua is the Promised One of Israel. No grave can hold him."

"Your prophesies spoke of these things?"

"With such detail it will make your mind spin. Now, tell me about the woman."

"She needs help. What more can I say?"

"Many people need help, my friend. Why this woman?"

Longinus studied his hands for a moment, then explained in detail Sister's help in the tavern storeroom and this morning's encounter at the tomb.

"She means something to you," Nicodemus said.

Longinus considered avoiding the question. It was madness, after all. He hardly knew her. What was there to explain? What words? To put his voice to it seemed ridiculous. Still, he'd brought her here. There was no going back, and, in truth, he wouldn't if there were. He cleared his throat. "What can I say? There's something about her. I can't explain it. I'm no youth to be enamored by a pretty face or glimpse of flesh, yet since I first saw her in that tavern storeroom… And then I find her in front of me again this morning. There is something deeply wounded inside her. But also something precious. I see it in her eyes, her movements, her hands. I don't have time for such things. She is a Jew, I am Roman, but here I am."

"These are strange times, Longinus. Momentous times. I think the world has accelerated in a way, for lack of better words. Unexpected events at every turn and a spiritual wind howls that knows no border or country. What can we do but take what comes? The woman may be part of your story, eh?"

"Sister… She doesn't even have a name. What kind of life is that? Pharisee, if you have the time, I'd like to hear more of these prophecies of yours. Maybe in them I can find answers to some of the questions that plague my mind."

Nicodemus smiled. "Let me get some wine."

15

The sun might as well have been the face of God. Joseph blinked in its relentless light and propped himself up on his elbows, fine sand warming his back and legs, almost burning. He looked right, then left. A perfect beach stretched without end in both directions. Before him a glassy sea, gentle waves lapping the shore. Seabirds dipped and bobbed and screeched. A brilliant-white pelican dropped from the sky and plunged into the water, then burst the surface, diamonds of ocean streaming from his feathers and a meal writhing in his throat pouch.

Joseph stared out at the blue-on-blue horizon line and struggled to pull thoughts together.

The cell…pain…Longinus killed a man…

Far out from the shore a whale breeched, coming down on its side with a mighty splash. What was this place?

He caught a whiff of smoke on the sea breeze. And then cooking fish. Far down the beach he saw a figure. He was sure it had not been there before. He rose shakily to his knees, then his feet, and started walking. He felt no wonder at the sudden apparition of another person where there'd been none before. He knew who and what he would find even as he walked.

And he was right.

"Please help me," Joseph said as he approached the fire. "I need to get to Ariella. Please…"

The old shepherd looked up and smiled…

Hot knives pushed into Joseph's body. He felt a hand on his chest and opened his eyes with a groan. A hard, tough face hovered above him, purple scar stretching mouth to ear.

"So…it lives," Davi said.

"Davi…" Joseph said.

"What a face to wake up to, eh? You are truly blessed, my friend. You're welcome."

"Is there any water?"

"A well outside. I'll be right back. And if you're going to die, do it while I'm gone. I don't want to watch."

Joseph coughed, bringing a fresh and brutal wave of pain. "I'm not planning on it, but I'll try to keep your comfort in mind."

Davi exited and Joseph took in the room. Clean, but small and sparse. A table stood by the wall, a wash basin and towel on it. A colorless rug covered much of a swept, dirt floor. A few scattered straw mats for sitting. The silence was deep, broken only by a distant bleat of a goat and a low, moaning wind. In one corner, smoke had stained the ceiling above an oven made of brick and mud. A pot of something simmered, the aroma sending Joseph's stomach into spasms of hunger.

The door opened. Davi carried a bucket in one hand. The other was pressed to his side.

"What's the matter with you?" Joseph said.

"A long story. Better told after you've had more time to rest."

"Davi, what happened?"

Davi immersed a gourd dipper into the bucket and passed it to Joseph. "Drink. They took the house, Joseph. Beryl along with some of the Levitical Patrol."

"Ariella?"

"I believe she's still there. There's been no report of Beryl moving her."

"You have someone watching?"

"Many eyes. None with a love for the Patrol."

"He took the house? Moved in? Longinus thought as much."

"Beryl tells everyone who will listen that you fled after your meeting with the Sanhedrin. That you were frightened because of the part you played in stealing Yeshua's body. A handy story. Now drink."

Joseph did. Never could he have imagined water tasting so good. He handed the gourd back and Davi refreshed it, obviously trying—and failing—to hide a grimace.

"You're wounded," Joseph said.

Davi shrugged. "A scratch. One of the Patrol."

"You tried to fight them off…"

"And would have done it if they hadn't outnumbered the stars."

Joseph shook his head. "I thank you, my friend."

"For what? Beryl has your home. And your wife."

"He won't hurt her while she's with child. And she may be safer there than anywhere else at the moment. What is this place? Where are we?"

"Bethany."

"Someone's home, obviously. Who lives here?"

"I have no idea. It's been you and me these last two days. And I won't lie, you've been pretty miserable company."

"I've been out two days? How did I get here?"

"The Roman dog friend of yours brought you in a wagon. Buried under a pile of fish."

Joseph sniffed. "That explains the smell. He couldn't have found vegetables? Or straw?"

"He said no one would want to dig through a pile of old fish. Filthy Roman, now we're all suffering."

"That filthy Roman saved my life," Joseph said.

"Well, for that much I'm grateful. I looked everywhere for you. I even went to Caiaphas' home, suspecting the Council had a hand in it. He wouldn't see me, of course. Then the Patrol came. With Beryl behind them barking orders like the coward he is. I met them in the courtyard. Beryl said you'd either run away or were dead. That he was taking over the house and holdings in order to care for his daughter and grandchild. By order of the Council."

"He's been maneuvering for my estate since I married his daughter."

"And as vice president of the Council, who's going to stop him? I would have stuck a sword through his fat throat if I'd had the chance. And I did try, but I caught a Patrol sword in the side instead. They dragged me off and threw me outside the Fish Gate. Next thing I remember, a Roman dumped a bucket of water on my head and told me to come here and wait."

"One of Longinus' circle."

"Your centurion does seem to have a network. I think he has his fingers in every corner of the city."

"At the moment, I'm glad." The room tilted and spun. Joseph pulled in a deep breath, trying to steady it. "I have to get our home back. I have to be sure Ariella is safe."

"I'm with you, always, you know that. But how?

Joseph forced himself to sit up. "God will help us."

"God against the Sanhedrin. What's happened to Israel?"

"Yeshua has happened, I think." Joseph lowered himself back onto his back. The entire universe hurt.

"Look at the two of us." Davi, hand hard against his side, sank to the floor and lay down next to Joseph. "Ready to take on the world."

"We'll heal. We're both too stubborn and stupid to die."

"Or too desperate."

Joseph forced his eyes to focus. "Whose home is this again?"

"I already told you. I have no idea. I was alone here until the centurion brought you."

"A tough man, Longinus. He reminds me of you."

"Not as handsome, I think."

"Ha. I've missed you, my friend." Joseph shook stars from his brain and tried to force himself up, but collapsed again. "But now we have to go."

Davi didn't move at all. "I'm right behind you. One look at us and they'll drop their weapons and run like little girls. They don't stand a chance."

"Just give me a minute."

"Just give me two."

"I'm serious, Davi."

"So am I. We need rest, Joseph." Davi held up a hand, red from the blood leaking through his tunic. "All we could do at the moment is drown them in our blood."

The setting sun slanted through a window, painting the walls of the room gold. Joseph's stomach growled. "What are you cooking?"

"I have no idea. Goat, some onions… Whatever I could find to put in the pot."

"It smells good."

"I'll get us some," Davi said, but didn't move.

"No, you rest. I can…" Joseph's own voice seemed to come from a distance as the world tunneled and finally went black.

When he next woke, the room was bathed in low candlelight. The wind still moaned, stronger now. He tried to bring things into focus but his eyes wouldn't cooperate. He heard someone moving in the room and tried to lift his head. His words came out a raspy croak. "Davi? Is there any water left?"

Footsteps approached and a cool cloth was placed across his forehead.

"I'll get you some, Joseph of Arimathea."

Joseph squinted, and a man came into focus. "Do I know you? You look—"

The man chuckled low in his chest. "We've met but once and it was dark. You were a skeptic then. But now it seems we have a little more in common. Perhaps we've both journeyed to the other side and made it back." He scratched at his chin. "Then again, perhaps it's because we both still have work to do on this earth, eh?"

"Yes, I do remember you. Lazarus…"

The man smiled and handed Joseph the dripping gourd of water. "Lazarus. Yes. Welcome to my home, Joseph."

16

"Where is Davi?" Joseph said.

"You must be hungry." Lazarus rose, crossed the room, and ladled some of Davi's makeshift stew into a wooden bowl. He handed it to Joseph, who slurped gratefully. Davi's concoction tasted as good as it smelled.

Lazarus squatted on his heels. "Your friend is in the back room resting. I insisted. His wound isn't as bad as it could have been, but I think he's been worrying about you when he should have been taking it easy. He'll heal quickly, I think. He strikes me as a very tough man."

"He was trying to protect my wife."

"A loyal friend."

"Is there a physician close by who could attend to him?"

"No closer than Jerusalem. And every road is watched. I might as well climb up on the roof and shout out the fact that you're here. Don't worry. The wound is deep enough but not lethal by any stretch. He'll be fine."

"You take a great risk, hiding us. It wouldn't go well with you if we were found here."

Lazarus nodded. "It would be worse than you know. They say that you've run. There's a heavy bounty on your head. It will be stoning for you if you're caught."

"And the same for you?"

Lazarus smiled. "Probably the same for me, yes. But what do I have to fear? I know what awaits me after this vapor of a life. An end to all this mist and shadow and the beginning of the *real*. I've seen brighter countries, my friend."

"Tell me what you saw."

Lazarus shrugged. "If there were words, I would. But an ass can't recite poetry and an ant can't sing."

"You won't even try?"

"All I can say is this, it's more than you can ever imagine."

They were silent for a while, listening to the wind. Lazarus refilled Joseph's bowl and got one of his own.

"A quiet place, Bethany," Joseph said at length. "I've ridden the outskirts many times."

"Yes, the Horse Jew… You were on a horse when we met, remember? And I've heard hooves out in the night once or twice."

Joseph nodded. "I miss those rides. I can think out there, away from the city and noise. Horse Jew… The name seems to have made the rounds."

"Even here in Bethany. Your rides have been the topic of many a fireside conversation. And now you stand boldly against the Sanhedrin. Some say you're mad, others that you're a prophet. Either way—great fodder for stories."

"Yes, I stood and I spoke. And look what happened, they crucified Yeshua anyway. I accomplished nothing except to get myself tortured and make my wife a prisoner in her own home."

"You've followed God's path. And you're still alive, at least partially, so there's more of it ahead of you. You don't yet know how the story will end."

"Tell me, Yeshua's other followers, how do they fare?"

"Frightened. In hiding for fear of the Sanhedrin. Chased and hunted by the Patrol."

"And Nicodemus?"

"Hiding as well."

"Nicodemus is hiding? I'm surprised he's not shouting his List of Messianic prophecies from the rooftops."

"The List. Yes. I've heard about it. But, to speak publicly now would mean his death. He was able to smuggle his wife and son out with a northbound caravan. But he stayed in Jerusalem. He holds daily meetings with the followers, sharing the List of Messianic scriptures with all. And among Yeshua's followers there are many eager to hear."

"Where is Nicodemus now?"

"A large block of rooms off the Valley of the Cheesemakers. Several of the followers are there. More in other hiding places around the city. It's a good place. Safe for now, I think."

"They hide in the very shadow of the Temple?"

"Where better? But the Patrol is everywhere. They can't hide forever."

"And you. Don't they know where you live? Why aren't you running?"

"I'm an anomaly. What can they do with me? Everyone in Jerusalem and beyond knows my story. I'm Lazarus, the man that was raised from the dead."

"No more than a few weeks ago they spoke of killing you in the Council meetings. I was there. I heard them."

"I think they're afraid. I was touched by a power they don't understand and one they want to stay as far away from as possible."

"And what news of Yeshua?"

The smile on Lazarus' face lit fire in his eyes. "Yeshua! Ah, that's the best part, isn't it? Yeshua is alive, as promised. And he's shown himself."

Joseph's pulse pounded in his throat. "Underground I dared hope it. Has it really come to pass? Has he shown himself in the Temple?"

"No. Only to a few of the women at first. Then to some of the close disciples."

"And you believe it?"

"Who has less reason to doubt than me? Yes, I believe Yeshua is absolutely alive. And he is God's own Son. Ha! What do you think the Sanhedrin will do with that?"

The man's joy was contagious. Joseph found himself grinning as well. "Tell me, though, has he shown himself to anyone else?"

"Not as of yet." Lazarus shrugged. "And who knows? He may not. Yeshua is a wonderful mystery. Better not to question and just be."

"But he must! He must show himself to everyone. They have to see. They have to believe!"

"Let me ask you, Joseph. If Yeshua walked right into a meeting of the Council, would they believe? Because I doubt it. I think they would find excuses. I think they would be happy to crucify him all over again. But I'll tell you this. He's alive, and that fact is a fire that will burn for eternity. A fire no one can quench though the world pour an ocean on it."

The adrenaline coursing through Joseph's body at the news of Yeshua's rising brought him to a sitting position. *Can it be true?* He shook his head. "Alive… I buried him. Or what was left of him. I carried that broken, nothing of a body in my own arms. You should have seen it—blood and bones, that's all there was left."

Lazarus stood. "Is anything too great for God? Certainly not a little thing like death."

"No, Lazarus. It's not little at all. It's everything Nicodemus and I talked about. If what you say is true, then Yeshua conquered death. Defeated it. Not little—huge. Massive. Death is the long shadow the Law has cast over Israel for generations. We watched Yeshua come in the Sheep Gate—present himself as a sacrifice. We wondered at it. And then they killed him. They had no idea what they were doing, but God had planned it all along. I—"

A light rap on the door interrupted. Lazarus put a finger to his lips and moved toward the door. "Who knocks at this hour?" he called.

The voice from without was low but intense. "Open. They come. We have to move them."

Lazarus cracked the door, peeked out, then opened it.

Longinus stepped into the room. Out of uniform, his worn cloak and tunic dark grey and plain. "Ready for another night ride, Horse Jew? Without a horse?"

"It sounds like there's no choice."

"Neither of them is in any shape to travel," Lazarus said.

"Are they in good enough shape to die? Because that's what will happen in about ten minutes. The Patrol is not far behind."

"How can they know they're here?" Lazarus said.

"They don't, but you're associated with the Nazarene. This place is just one in a long string of logical guesses. I'd hoped they'd steer clear, but they're running out of places to look. We'll move further into the wilderness," Longinus said. "I know of a place."

"I don't know if Davi should move," Joseph said.

"I'm fine." Davi stood in the back-room doorway. "I moved myself here, didn't I? I can't sleep anyway, with all the talking going on out here."

"I know a place in the hills where you can hide until we can find something better," Longinus said.

Joseph shook his head. "Not the hills. Jerusalem. I won't have my wife a prisoner in her own home at the mercy of her father any longer. And I need to talk to Nicodemus."

"I won't take you to the city. It's too dangerous," Longinus said.

"Then I'll walk there myself."

Longinus shook his head. "Joseph, listen to me. Ariella is fine, I have it on good authority. If she wasn't in her home, she would probably be with the rest of them. Hiding, running. Be patient, we'll find a way."

"I hate to admit it, but the Roman may be right," Davi said. "Beryl won't hurt her, not because he has an ounce of affection in his rotten bones, but because she's carrying his grandchild. An heir to stroke his ego."

"I know all that," Joseph said. "But she's my wife. I won't have her thinking I've abandoned her."

"She doesn't think that. I've already gotten word to her that you live," Longinus said.

"How?" Joseph said.

"I have avenues."

"Longinus, I'll retrieve her or die trying."

"And she can call you her hero as she watches you die on a cross. Think, Winemaker. Think of your child."

Joseph leaned against the wall. *Ariella...* "Can you at least get me to Nicodemus?"

Longinus sighed. "You've courage, Winemaker, though it may kill us all. Let's go. If it can be done, we will do it."

Davi started for the door. "Just don't tell me we're riding under a pile of dead fish, Roman."

Longinus smiled. "All right, Jew. I won't tell you."

17

Beryl and Caiaphas had charged him with finding and exposing Yeshua's followers. The Cilician took the charge of the Sanhedrin leaders seriously, find them he would. This was God's work. The mission so far had been a failure, and the fact stung. Taking Joseph of Arimathea had been a simple matter. A club to the back of the head by one of the Patrol and off to the pits. The fact Joseph was a fellow Jew had brought only a light pin prick of hesitation. The man's arrogance and stubborn insistence for Yeshua were plenty to condemn. To follow the Nazarene was to turn one's back on the purer faith, an unacceptable sin in the court of the Cilician's mind. And so Joseph had been beaten severely. But the man had proven impossible to break. And then he had escaped. Not without help, but escaped nonetheless. And so Joseph of Arimathea, who was to be the first example to the Followers, had become no example at all, unless it was one to inspire resistance.

That would change tonight.

Tonight examples would be made, and any loyalty the Followers held for the memory of the Nazarene would crumble. Tonight the Cilician would be God's hard fist. Tonight's mission must succeed and success meant there could be no mercy.

The streets lay black and clouded. The Patrol's torches multiplied the Cilician's shadow by ten on the wall beside him. Ten wild beards. Ten robes fluttering in the wind. He wasn't a handsome man. He'd heard it all his life. Features too large for his face. Cheeks scarred with old pock marks. As a child, he'd been considered a runt. Inconsequential at best. But they'd always underestimated his keen mind. His mind was a gift from God and he would use it now. He'd been created for this. Tonight the Cilician was a leader of men. And tonight would be the beginning of the end for a deserving contingency of traitors to righteousness. He smiled. Hard footfalls behind him, ten Levitical Patrolmen in lockstep, studded sandals in perfect cadence on the stone street. Tonight he would be the hand of God.

He didn't belong here, in this time. He would have fit much better in the days of the great prophets. Back when God's strong men would speak and the people would obey. Today's Israel had forgotten God's true voice. The great Jerusalem had become a city of compromise—of sleeping Jews and Gentile Roman dogs, both equally ignorant of scripture.

And into this mix Yeshua had come, one more obscene distraction. Yeshua hadn't spouted and wheedled. He hadn't demanded money or even attention. His had been a quieter game, and a hundred times stronger because of it. Yes, he had been different than the other pretenders; that was the problem. He hadn't come with pomp and fanfare, and that fact had made him wildly popular. He hadn't posed and preened. Instead, he'd come like a midnight ocean tide—powerful and unstoppable.

Except he had been stopped.

And his life had ended the way it should have—tattered and ragged and bloody. The Cilician had seen it all. And he'd rejoiced. Cheered out loud at the glorious sight of the imposter hanging on a Roman cross.

But midnight tides always leave evidence of their passing. And Yeshua's followers still littered Jerusalem like shore debris, though most had sand-crabbed into the cracks and crevices of the city in fear. But now, praise God, those that still dared speak the Nazarenc's name would follow him straight to disgrace.

The Prophet Daniel made the timeline clear—soon the real Messiah would come with a massive army of strength to rule Israel and bring the world to its knees. And the Cilician would prepare the way starting now. He would be all the prophets of old rolled into one. The spear of Saul, the sling of David, the mighty arms of Samson. He would be God's man who would do what needed to be done.

At length the Patrol came to a small home of mud and brick in the heart of the New City. The door was comprised only of branches woven together, a barrier in name only, useless against any real force.

The Cilician turned to the nearest Patrolman. "Kick in the door."

The guard's eyes widened a fraction. "Sir?"

"Was I not clear? I said kick it in. I want all of Jerusalem to hear about what happens in this place tonight." He turned to the rest of the men. "Drag anyone inside out here onto the street. Be quick about it. Now! Don't stand there staring at me. Do it!"

"There may be children inside," the first guard said.

"And? Do as I say or Caiaphas will hear about it."

The men moved. Only the leader at first, but the others fell in. The door smashed to pieces with a single kick. A man shouted. A woman screamed.

Out they came, stumbling, pushed from behind. A husband and wife. The woman, face pale in the torchlight, held a screaming infant in her arms.

The Cilician pointed to the baby. "Quiet the child. Now."

The woman swallowed her own sobs. She shushed and rocked, holding a loose hand over the babe's mouth, her eyes wild with fear.

"What is this? What do you want with us?" the husband said.

The Cilician eyed the man. Large. Strong. "You're Natan? The stone mason?"

"I am. What's the meaning of this?"

"A prophet's name. What a shame."

"What are you talking about? What right do you have to damage my home?"

"In the synagogue, more than once you've been overheard talking of Yeshua," the Cilician said.

The man's eyes narrowed. "The entire city speaks this name. Why do you question me?"

The baby wailed again. The Cilician put his arms out. "Give me the child."

The woman stepped back, shaking her head. "He's only a baby. He's innocent!"

The Cilician frowned. "Do you take me for an animal, woman? Do as I say, now. Give me the child."

The man stepped forward but a Patrolman's spear moved him back again.

"Give me the child, woman," the Cilician repeated.

Trembling, the woman handed over the infant. "Please…"

"Please what?" He shushed and bounced and the baby began to quiet. "See? All is well."

The woman shook violently now. She put out her hands. "Thank you, sir. Give him back now. Please."

The Cilician lifted the child in front of him and studied it's face. "Are you of the opinion I would hurt a child?"

"I honestly don't know," the woman said. "Please."

"Please… You use that word a lot, don't you?" The Cilician flipped the baby upside down and held it by an ankle. He smiled. "Such a light thing, isn't he?"

"Please, you'll drop him," the woman said.

"There's that word again—please A true mother. Just like my own. Tell me, woman, do you follow the teachings of the Nazarene as well?"

"I'll tell you anything you want to know. I'll say anything you want me to say! Just give me back my boy."

"Will you? Then answer my question. Are you a Follower like your husband?"

The child howled.

"He doesn't like it, does he?" The Cilician swung the child slightly. "Quiet now. Be good."

The woman dropped to her knees. "You'll drop him, please…"

"My son is too young to follow anything but his mother's breast," the man said. "Give him back to his mother and I'll tell you what you want to know."

The Cilician studied the dangling child. "Answer my

question.”

“Yes,” the woman gasped. “Yes! we have spoken for Yeshua.”

“Then you blaspheme.”

A door up the street opened and a man stepped out, followed by another man and a woman.

The child’s father stepped forward and shook his clasped hands. “No! We love God. We’re observant Jews! We keep the Law in every way. Observe every feast. We would never blaspheme! Give me my son. You have no right to do this!”

“I represent the Council. I have every right. Was Yeshua the Messiah? It’s a straightforward question.”

“I—” the man said

The wife grabbed her husband’s arm. “No! Say nothing, Natan!” She looked up at the Cilician, agony in her eyes. “Sir, we think anything you tell us to think! We’re your servants! Please!”

The Cilician ignored her and spoke again to the husband. “You look to be a man. Speak as one. Was Yeshua the Messiah?”

More doors had opened. People filtered toward them. The narrow street filling.

The woman sobbed, her pain echoing the night.

“Well?” the Cilician said.

The man sighed. “Yes. I believe Yeshua was the Messiah. I believe it with all my heart.”

The woman’s sobs receded to a guttural moan.

The baby howled. The Cilician gave it a shake. “Shh!” He eyed the child’s father. “An honest man. One who cares for his family. Good. There are other Followers. Where are they?”

“Everywhere,” the man said. “But I swear to you, most of them are hiding. I don’t know specific places. Give the child back now.”

“Give me names.”

“Itamar. He sells olives near the theater.”

The Cilician held the baby higher. “Another.”

“Paltiel. He has a wool shop in the Lower City. Not far from the Pool of Siloam. Now put my son down.”

“Good. Very good. An excellent place to start.” The Cilician looked out across the now crowded street. He pointed at the husband and wife. "Do you see these people? They are your friends! Your neighbors! But they've made a great mistake. They put their faith in a liar and a mocker of God. This will not be tolerated any longer. If any of you know followers of the dead Nazarene, tell me where they are and it will go well with you. You might keep your homes and businesses and seats in the synagogue!"

"Give the child to his mother!" someone called out.

The Cilician held the bawling infant higher. "Do you hear me? These people follow a dead man. Don't make the same mistake."

An older woman pushed through the gathered crowd, her eyes bright fire. "What do you think you're doing? Give me that child. There's no need for this."

The Cilician gazed at her for a long moment. "And who are you?"

"I'm the baby's grandmother. Give him to me."

"His grandmother… And are you also a misguided follower of the Nazarene?"

The woman's face flushed. "I'm a Jew. I follow God. No one else, you included."

The Cilician chuckled. "You're a bold one. A Jew, you say. Well very good. All right." He walked over to her and lowered the infant into her arms. He looked out at the crowd and spoke to be heard "Let it not be said I've shown no mercy here. The child is too young to think for himself. Therefore he carries no guilt. Praise God, he's too young to follow the unfortunate folly of his parents. But let it be known to all in Jerusalem and beyond, allegiance to the Nazarene will not be tolerated. Not anymore." He looked back to the grandmother. "Woman, raise the child as he should be raised. As a Jew. A boy, is a gift from God. Don't waste it."

The woman arched a brow. "Raise him?"

But the Cilician had already turned to the Patrol. "The parents are admitted blasphemers. Take them outside the walls and stone them. Then report back to me."

18

Sister lay, breathing hard, suspended in the dark between reality and dream. She'd been running. Weaving and dodging through the streets of Jerusalem, footsteps pounding behind her. Who, or what, chased her she didn't know, only that she had to get away. Out of the Lower City, then through the wide silent streets of the Upper. The homes and structures so beautiful by day became grotesque and evil things in the dark. On and on until she found herself at a flight of stairs leading up to the Temple Mount. Forward and up, relief surging. Surely she'd be safe on the Mount? But he'd caught her in the Stoa. Hard fingers grabbing her from behind. He'd spun her around and shoved her back against one of the pillars, her head cracking against the cold stone. And then pressed, as she knew he would. Moonlight slanted across the courtyard and caught on his face. He wore the robes of a priest. His face handsome. No, more than handsome—beautiful. But his eyes... His eyes were black and empty sockets... "Woman," he'd said. "You know what you are. A nameless worthless whore." He'd drawn back a clenched fist.

She'd woken with a gasp, face wet with tears in the darkness.

The room, the night, it all felt wrong. And it wasn't only the dream. *It's the quiet,* she told herself. No tavern noise. No drunken brawls in the next room.

They'd been kind to her, these followers of Yeshua. Three days now she had lived and moved among them, all the while holding fast to her secret. Not the fact that she'd been a prostitute—there were others like her here, one she'd even known in the Lower City—but the fact that she'd flaunted herself like an imbicile in front of the man these people revered. When she saw them she saw him. Yeshua. And that sad, hard, wonderful face.

Kindness—a new concept to her, really. These people were afraid, yes, but even in their fear, they seemed to genuinely care about each other. And to care about her. They were Jews, certainly. Observant to a fault and neglecting no religious detail. But there was something more to their lives… Most good Jews would have spat on her. Once, not long ago, a group of Pharisees had threatened to stone her. And a few of them had been some of her best customers. But these people, they were different.

And you don't belong among them. You don't deserve their grace.

She told herself it was the quiet that kept sleep at bay. But that was a lie. And it wasn't the lingering feeling of the dream. No, shame was the reason. Shame that filled her completely. She wondered as she lay there: Could she have been like these people had she given Yeshua a chance that night? If she had stopped her idiotic posturing and listened, really listened, to his words? Could she have been washed clean of that Lower City tavern stink? Replaced it with light? Hope? Even love? Could she have had what these people have?

But it didn't matter now, did it? Even after listening to Yeshua in that back courtyard that night, and later in the tavern, she'd chosen to continue that old familiar path. Now, in the dark, peaceful sounds of sleep all around her, she put her hands over her face. Oh those sad, sad beautiful eyes! Why wouldn't they leave her alone? The shame would kill her.

No, this is no place for you… Out of the shadows of her tortured mind the voice came. Or maybe from the shadows of the room, she couldn't tell. She knew it well. She'd heard it since she was a child. Maybe it was God Himself, reminding her who she was, what she'd done. Whoever it was, the voice was without fail incessant and unwavering in its conviction.

These are good people. What do you think you're doing here among them? A whore! A seducer and defiler of men! You danced for him.

She pressed her hands to her ears. A horrible whisper, it was. But a true one. Yes, what right did she have? The centurion didn't know her. She'd hoped against hope he might be right, that there might be another path for her, but she knew now it was fantasy.

Back to the streets, nameless woman. Back to your back. The centurion won't miss you. No one will miss you.

It was true.

On silent feet she moved. Down the long hallway. Past people dreaming good dreams. Pure dreams.

Too late! Too late for you!

Sadness welled. She would miss these good people. But the voice wouldn't be denied. The voice was true.

A lower door led to a walled patio. A path lay beyond. An alley of sorts. Narrow. Private. She took it. If she could just find a main avenue, she would know the way. Vining bougainvillea laced the walls. The scented air hung cool about her as she padded along. An alcove loomed on the right, black with shadow. Heart pounding, still haunted by her dream, she hugged the left wall as she moved past it.

"Woman…"

Her legs turned to liquid. "Who is it?"

"Don't be frightened. Where are you going at this hour?"

She squinted into the inky recess. "Who are you?"

Flint scratched steel. A spark flared up and a tiny lamp burned, small and dim. A man sat on a bench in the rear of the space. Powerful shoulders and a thin beard. He was young. His hair, what there was of it, was trimmed very short, nearly shaved.

"My name is Peter," he said. "You have fear in your eyes. I wouldn't have it so. Please, I mean you no harm. Why are you out so late? Jerusalem isn't safe these days."

"I could ask you the same."

He shrugged. "I can't sleep, so I sit. And this is a good spot to be alone."

"Until I came along?"

He smiled. "I don't own the path. You're as free as I to use it."

She took a step closer, peering hard into the dark. "I've seen you before. In the Lower City. You were with Yeshua."

A cloud of sorrow passed over his face. "I was. I am one of the Twelve—the Eleven now since Judas hung himself. I was among the first Yeshua called. My wife and family are in Galilee, but I've traveled and lived with him day and night for three years."

"You left your family?"

"I've seen them occasionally. But Yeshua… There are things bigger than us, aren't there? Now tell me, why you are running away?"

"Who says I'm running away?"

"You're just out for a nice walk in the middle of night?"

She lifted her chin. "You have no right to question me."

"True. I've no right to anything. But I meant no offense."

She paused, considering him. "I don't belong here, that's all. Not with these people. *You* people."

"Are we so different from you?"

"You're…good. I'm not."

He lifted the little lamp and studied her face. "Yes. I remember you now, woman. You danced in one of the taverns. Down in the Lower City. Your face is a hard one to forget."

"I told you I wasn't good."

"That's not what I meant. Don't misunderstand me."

"I understand you perfectly. I'm a prostitute. It's a simple fact."

"Then I suppose we have something in common."

"You and I? I doubt that very much."

He held the lamp up a little. "Yes, the Lower City. You danced in front of Yeshua. I remember it."

"I was stupid. And I regret it. But it happened and I can't take it back."

"Let me tell you something about those good people up there, as you call them. You aren't the first among them to trade your flesh for shekels. Not even the second or the third. And many have done much worse. But, in Yeshua, all of them found love. They found a purpose. A rebirth. You can do the same. You say you regret? We all regret. But Yeshua's love won't just heal that pain you cling to so tightly, it will crush it to dust and blow it to the ends of the earth."

The spark deep in her soul glowed as if a warm wind touched it.

Whore! Back to your back! The voice boomed loud she almost covered her ears. *Why do you listen to this man's deceit? You know who you are. Everyone knows who you are!*

"I have to go," she said.

Peter patted the bench. "Come, sit with me for a few minutes."

"I think not."

"We're souls in the night, you and I, yes? We've met now, and there are no accidents with God. Please, you have nothing to fear from me."

He did make her curious, alone out here in the dark. Something about him seemed lost somehow. She didn't sense danger from him. And sensing danger in men was a fine-honed sixth sense her very survival often hinged on. Still, when she sat, she made sure she was as far away from him as the bench would allow.

She watched him. "Why do you say we have something in common?"

"You called yourself a harlot, didn't you? Well, so am I. Maybe you've sold your body, but the truth of the matter is, I've sold something as well. I suppose we all sell, don't we?"

"What have you sold?"

His face remained neutral, but his eyes filled immediately. "I sold my loyalty. The one and only thing I had of any value."

"Loyalty to Yeshua?"

"Yes. And I'd give my life right now to get it back. I'd give it in a heartbeat."

"How did you do this thing?"

"In the courtyard of the High Priest, I denied I knew him. Not once but three times. And up until that moment, I swore to anyone who would listen that I'd die for him."

"And what did you receive in return for this betrayal?"

"A single night of safety. And a burden of shame that crushes me."

"But you did what you did for the sake of survival. I've done the same. We've both done what we've had to do."

"You rationalize for my sake and that's kind. But I heard the way you said the word harlot. You carry your guilt with tired arms. As do I. And as we should."

She gazed out at the darkness. "Until Yeshua, I felt no guilt at all. After all, what choice did I have? I didn't choose my life. Fate, the universe, life—call it what you will—made my choices for me."

"Really? Does fate have a will then? Does the universe have a will? No, God has a will. And so do you and so do I. I chose to betray. You chose to sell your body. That's why you're slinking through the dark back to your old world. It's easier to choose what you know, dark as it is, than face uncertain things."

"You know nothing about me."

"Don't I? Your story isn't new. Far from it. Your life has been hard, yes, but you've also made choices. And you're making another tonight, right now. Just like I chose to lie about knowing Yeshua."

"Did Yeshua know you did this thing?"

His eyes reflected the lamp's flame. "Not only did he know, he told me I would do it. 'Three times, before the cock crows,' he said, and I scoffed at the idea. I swore the opposite and I believed it. But he knew, he always knows. Three times they asked me if I was one of his, and three times I denied him. As the first cock crowed, he looked at me. Into me. The way only he can."

She thought of the night she'd hidden in the tree. "I've felt that very thing. I remember his eyes most of all."

"I wish he would have been angry, but all he looked was broken-hearted. My own heart shattered. I wanted to die. I still pray for death. I was praying for that very thing when I saw you walking by. I deserve Hades, nothing less. So, you see, if you call yourself a harlot, well, I'm the greater one."

"You saw. I danced for him… I was horrible."

"I remember it well. But you only wanted him to love you. You went about it the only way you knew. But the thing you didn't realize was that he already loved you. Because Love is who he is."

"Love… They say he's alive. Do you believe it?"

"Of course he's alive. I've seen him. Not more than a few hours ago. He is, without a doubt, more alive than anyone I've ever known. He told us to travel north and to meet him in Galilee. We leave before dawn. That's why I came here tonight, to say goodbye to some friends. Or maybe it was to meet you. Only God knows. Tell me, will you stay?"

"I don't belong."

"If you doubt, why are you here in the first place?"

"A centurion brought me."

"A good man?"

"He's a Roman."

"That doesn't answer my question."

"He… He was kind enough to me. I thought at first he wanted to use my body, but he brought me here instead."

Peter thought for a minute. "Let me tell you something. One day I was fishing, just like every other day of my life for as long as I could remember. Then Yeshua came. He called me to follow. He said I would be a fisher of men. I've not looked back. I tell you from experience you can change direction."

"It's different for me. You belong here. You belong with him. He called you. He didn't call me."

"There is no one he doesn't call. You're here because God wills it. It's simple. You must stay."

"Did God call? Or did a Roman feel sorry for a no-named prostitute? Maybe he thought he could reform me, I don't know. But I'm not one of you."

"Drop your weapons, woman. There is a better way." He stood and held out a hand. "Come, please. Let me take you back before I go meet the others. You do belong here. All belong."

She looked up at him, then down at her hands. "My road may lead nowhere, but my feet know it too well."

"Don't be a coward. Come."

"Coward? I wasn't the one who pretended to be something I wasn't."

"You're right, of course. And I'll live with that. But in this moment I only think of you."

In the night a cricket sang. Sister stared into the tiny lamp-flame. Such a small thing to stand against so much black. "Everyone seems to think of me all of a sudden."

"Or God has thought of you your whole life and you're only now realizing it."

She stood. "All right. I'll come. But I don't promise to stay."

He blew out the lamp. "Good. Quietly now. And follow close."

With the lamp gone, the darkness became once again complete. She slowed as they started out, lagging behind until she could no longer hear his footsteps. Lamp smoke still lingered in the black. She hadn't wanted to lie to the man, but the voice left her no alternative.

Back to your back...

She stood, listening to the night.

"Are you coming, woman?" The man called Peter whispered from up the path.

She turned in the opposite direction and padded away on silent feet. Away from the broken man called Peter. Away from those good people upstairs. Away from a hope she never should have entertained. Back toward the Lower City. Back to the tavern.

Back to her back.

19

Three things alerted Joseph that dawn had passed and the sun was climbing—the rising heat, the rank stench of the fish covering the blanket above them getting stronger, and Davi's constant, whispered curses about the first two, as well as how much he hated all Romans and all mothers of Romans.

"This centurion of yours is doing his best to find every rock in the road," Davi muttered after a particularly jarring bump.

"He's risking his life to save ours. Be grateful."

"No, saving our lives would have been taking us out to whatever desert cave he mentioned in the first place. As it is, we're not headed away from the bees, we're bouncing right toward the hive. And, hear me, we will get stung."

"He takes us to Jerusalem at my request. So if you want to blame someone, blame me."

Davi chuckled low. "Oh, I do blame you, don't worry about that."

"Shush," Longinus hissed from the wagon seat. "We're approaching the gate."

"Will you be recognized?" Joseph said.

"The sentry is a man I can trust."

"Of course he is. You—" Davi's next word was cut in half as his teeth smashed together, thanks to a deep hole in the road.

"That one was for you, Jew," Longinus said. "A little gift from Rome. Stop your babbling."

They passed through the gate without incident. The roads smoothed. Joseph dozed but came to when the wagon stopped. He heard hushed conversation but couldn't make out what was being said. Finally, fish were shuffled and the tarp lifted.

Longinus looked down on them. "We made it in one piece, Winemaker, one more thing to thank your God for."

Joseph hurt head to toe. He tried his best to hide his grimace as he sat up but knew he failed. Longinus, a man used to wounds and pain, did him the courtesy of not mentioning it.

The wagon had come to a stop in what looked like a wide cavern. The air was damp and cool.

"What is this place?" Davi said.

"An unused cistern with a side wall caved in enough to allow entrance," Longinus said. "And a convenient place to hide a wagon full of dead fish and two Jews who smell like dead fish. Now come." He handed the two of them hooded cloaks. "Put these on. We'll be on the street, albeit briefly."

There were crude and ancient stairs cut into the side of the cistern. They climbed them and entered a narrow corridor. Then up a ladder and into an unoccupied goat shed.

"Hoods on. Follow." Longinus didn't look back as he ducked through the sun-filled doorway.

Joseph didn't recognize the street, but behind them Herod's Temple retaining wall rose. They worked through a maze of walkways and narrow alleys.

At length, Longinus stopped and indicated a stairway at the back of a small courtyard. "Up you go. Knock softly, and when questioned, announce yourself quietly. Every wall in Jerusalem has ears right now."

"Where are you going?" Joseph said.

"Believe it or not, I have things to do besides constantly saving your battered carcass."

Joseph extended his hand. "I thank you."

Longinus took it. He glanced at Davi. "Try to keep him alive, Jew." Three steps, a sharp corner, and he was gone.

"Romans…" Davi said.

A woman passed them pushing a cart. She sniffed the air and cast a quizzical look their way.

"He had to use the fish," Davi muttered.

They passed quickly through the courtyard and up the steps. Davi swayed a little and put a hand on Joseph's shoulder for support. Joseph gave a light rap on the door.

"Who?" came a quiet reply.

"Joseph of Arimathea. Along with a friend."

Words were passed on the other side of the door. Latches rattled, the door opened, and Nicodemus smiled and clasped Joseph's arms. He motioned them in and shut the door behind them. "I knew you'd come, Joseph. Longinus says it has gone hard for you."

"I don't kill easy, it seems. Though it hasn't been for a lack of trying on the part of my father-in-law."

"The Sanhedrin is desperate."

"No doubt. Davi is wounded and we are hunted. We need a new place to rest, Nicodemus. But I would talk to you first."

"Of course. You are both welcome, my friends." Nicodemus motioned a woman over and explained briefly. Her face a picture of concern, she beckoned Davi to follow. With a glance toward Joseph, who nodded, he did so gratefully.

The room was large. Nicodemus led Joseph to a table surrounded by cushions. A young man brought a pitcher of wine and a wooden platter of bread and cheese. Nicodemus poured.

Joseph eyed a group of a dozen or more people gathered in a rough circle around an unrolled scroll at the other end of the room. "They search for prophecies?"

"It's a confusing time, Joseph. Yeshua has been seen alive, but only by a select few. This brings up more questions than answers. Why has he not made himself known to the masses? Why not manifest himself on the Temple Mount where the Sanhedrin would have no choice but to admit their error? Why has he not taken his rightful position as King? Now he goes to Galilee and we're here, fearing for our lives, hunted. So many things don't make sense on the surface, I'm convinced the answers must be in the scriptures.

"You've not seen Yeshua yourself?"

"Not personally. But Peter, one of the Eleven, was here last night. He's both seen and spoken to him. Yeshua instructed them to meet him in Galilee. They left Jerusalem before dawn this morning."

"Yeshua must have a reason. Though what it is, I can't imagine."

Other things are happening as well. Incredible things. When the earthquake happened, they say graves were opened. Saints, some of them very long dead, have been seen alive all over the city. They speak of Yeshua continually, testifying that he is indeed the Son of God."

"Resurrected? You're sure?"

"I've seen some of them myself. Tremendous things, Joseph! Even death is no longer sure."

"Tremendous things…" Joseph shook his head. "The world is turning upside down. I can hardly consider it without losing my mind."

"There's an element of that with all of us. It's like a dream that continues after one wakes. Many Followers gather here, and I teach practically nonstop. I find there is much comfort for them in the words of the scriptures. And the List grows every day. Scripture coming to life. *For dogs have surrounded me; A band of evildoers has encompassed me; They pierced my hands and my feet.* Picture him there, Joseph, up on that cross surrounded by Roman soldiers, the crowd cheering and celebrating his suffering. Innocent! Good! And he hung there, *pierced through for our transgressions,* just as Isaiah said he would be. And then he breathed his last. Listen to Amos: '*It will come about in that day,' declares the Lord GOD, 'That I will make the sun go down at noon and make the earth dark in broad daylight.'* It all happened exactly as prophesied."

"How many prophecies have you added to the List?"

"Dozens. Even this miracle of the resurrected dead walking the city. Daniel said that many who sleep in the dust of the earth shall awake and arise. A circular prophecy, perhaps. I believe he spoke what we're seeing now in Jerusalem as well as what will come during the earth's final days."

"These people who come from the graves, what do they say about the afterlife?"

Nicodemus shook his head. "It's as if they don't have the words to describe it, but they have an all-consuming joy. And Yeshua is much on their lips."

"It brings Lazarus to mind. He said much the same."

"A different circumstance but the same experience, I think. And yet another thread leading back to Daniel. And doesn't God have the power over life and death? Perhaps this is not like a dream at all, but waking from one, to a new reality."

"But not everyone wakes. Many bury their faces rather than face the dawn," Joseph said.

"The Sanhedrin? How can they confront what they've done? Can you imagine? And in the end, all it really takes for a man to deny a truth that's staring him in the face is a turn of the head. And so theories circulate and are believed in desperation. The Sanhedrin, of course, publicly says disciples stole the body. Others say Yeshua survived the cross and wasn't really dead."

Joseph tore off a piece of bread and shook his head. "Has anyone ever survived a Roman cross? It would be impossible. The body we buried was just that, a body. You saw."

"Of course I saw. Everyone saw. And I know he now lives, just as the prophets said. Just as Yeshua prophesied himself: *Jonah was three days in the belly of the sea monster, so will the Son of Man be three days in the belly of the earth.* Mocked, spat on, scourged, killed, he predicted it all. And, most importantly, he knew he would rise on the third day. This List, Joseph, it doesn't belong to you and me, it belongs to the world. I pray that soon, even the most stubborn in their pride will have to admit the truth. Listen, one we just found today: *For You will not abandon my soul to Sheol; Nor will You allow Your Holy One to undergo decay.* So perfect. So exact! I feel it's never ending. God reaching down to us."

"And Lila and Jonathan? Longinus tells me they've left the city. Are they well? Do you have word?"

"None. But I trust God. What choice do I have? It eases my mind to have them outside the reach of the Patrol."

Joseph nodded. "I must get to Ariella. I can't bear the thought of her being under Beryl's thumb."

"The good news is, your home isn't as secure as Beryl likes to think. The servants have gotten several messages out. She's well, but worried about you. She goes along with his madness for the sake of the child."

"I need to let her know I'm coming for her."

Nicodemus smiled. "She knows you live. Longinus saw to that. So she also knows you won't rest until you make things right. Of that I'm sure. Now, tell me what happened to you. Everything."

Joseph recounted his missing days, starting with the Sanhedrin meeting and everything else he could remember to the present.

Nicodemus sipped his wine. "That explains one mystery."

"And what's that?"

"Why you smell like the summer bilge of a Galilean fishing boat."

Joseph tore another piece of bread. "Yes, the fish. Is there somewhere I can clean up?" He glanced across the room toward the scroll readers and lowered his voice. "I wonder why they keep looking at me. Is it because I'm a stranger? Please tell them I mean them no harm."

Nicodemus chuckled. "Oh, they know who you are, Joseph. We were just studying about you this morning. Your timing couldn't be better."

"Studying? What do you mean studying?"

"The prophet Isaiah—*His grave was assigned with wicked men, Yet He was with a rich man in His death.* You buried him in your own grave, Joseph. And to think, after all our debate and study, all your reluctance, you made The List.

20

Pontius Pilate's residence was open and airy, Roman to the core. Pillars lined the wide reception hall. Frescos of gods and battles covered the walls. High above, a bird fluttered against the blue ceiling looking for a way out. Longinus' cleated sandals clacked on the marble floor as he paced.

Hinges creaked and a tall door swung open. A soldier stepped out. "You can go in now, sir." The man stood at attention as Longinus swept past.

The decor of Pilate's inner chamber was an extension of the great hall—pillared and frescoed. Soldiers stood at attention every six cubits along the walls. Animal skins covered the floor. Longinus recognized a few species from his time in Ethiopia, others were a mystery. A very pale, very thin woman sat in a far corner, working a needle back and forth through a piece of cloth. Sunlight played in her thick, red hair. She glanced up with colorless eyes, assessed him, then went back to her work.

Pilate stood in the center of the room. Tall and thin, sandy hair short and pushed forward in Roman style. His robes rich in color and tailored to hang close to his form. He was smooth and freshly shaved. He gave a curt dip of his head, keen eyes taking in Longinus head to toe. "We've kept you waiting long,

Longinus. We've been debating in here. I hope you can help us navigate what I find to be very muddy water."

Longinus nodded. "I'll help any way I can." He turned to a second man standing with Pilate and bowed. "King Herod, I wasn't aware you'd be here. I would have worn dress white."

Pilate's voice was clipped as he answered for the king. "Antipas has a vested interest in the matter. I asked him to come at the last minute. You're fine as you are."

Herod Antipas was a small man working hard not to be. He gave the impression of a boy trying on his father's clothes. And indeed, if your father had been Herod the Great, those clothes would be hard to fill. His robes were oversized and hung loosely on padded shoulders. His curled hair hung long. He stroked his small beard into a point, taking in Longinus with narrowed eyes. "Pilate tells me you're a man that has an ear to the ground in Jerusalem."

"I'm a soldier. Knowing the terrain and the people that inhabit it are the first rule of survival. Jerusalem is no different."

"This problem of Yeshua's missing body, what have you heard?" Herod said.

Longinus formed his words carefully. "It's not easy to say. Jerusalem is a very delicate balance. Especially now. People are tight-lipped."

"Do you believe the Sanhedrin when they say Yeshua's followers stole the body? The guards confirm it. What do you say?"

"Anything I say would be one man's opinion. And even at that, I'm not sure I have enough facts to form one."

"Your opinion then. Are they telling the truth? Did the disciples steal the body?"

"Respectfully, sir, I can only speak to what I know."

"And what is that?" Herod said.

"The tomb is empty."

Pilate waved a hand and began to pace, studying the floor. "Longinus, you're wasted as a soldier. With answers like this, you should be in Rome running the Senate. Look, I happen to know you're an octopus with many tentacles. And that's fine, I respect it. I'd be the same way in your position. Right now I need those tentacles, do you understand? Jerusalem is about to come apart. And it's on my watch. I refuse to let this happen. I need you to turn over every stone. Look behind every wall, every bush. Find me an answer. Find me a body. Find me a guilty party. Find me something!"

"It's difficult, sir. Most of Yeshua's followers are in hiding for fear of the Sanhedrin. Especially since they've turned loose this Cilician."

Pilate shook his head. "Caiaphas is a fool. He never should have asked us to crucify the Nazarene. But he's also High Priest."

"And now it's all of our problem," Herod said.

"The Sanhedrin is drunk with power," Longinus said. "And it invokes the name of its god to hold it. The people are afraid. This Cilician had a Jewish couple killed in his quest to crush the support for Yeshua. They had done nothing illegal."

Herod waved a hand. "And Romans haven't done the same on the frontier? A brutal move, granted. But I understand it was meant as a message. To instill fear and close mouths. If it works, it was worth the blood."

Pilate nodded his agreement. "Will it work, do you think, Longinus? Will this be an end to it?"

"To tell you the truth, I doubt it. The Followers are committed to their God."

Pilate glanced toward the pale woman sewing in the corner. "Some say the Nazarene lives. My wife feels there might be substance behind the story. What say you?"

Longinus paused a beat. He too glanced at the woman, then at Herod. The king's face was unreadable.

"Speak freely, Longinus," Pilate said.

Longinus rubbed the back of his neck, considering, then met Pilate's eye. "I've never been a spiritual man. But I have to admit I've seen things since I've been in this city I can't explain. I know this, if Yeshua lives, then he does so at the hand of a great god. He was, without a doubt, dead when he came off that cross."

Herod laughed. "The Nazarene died just like every other flesh-and-blood being. These Followers claim he was the Jewish Messiah. I ask you, would a true messiah submit himself to death on a cross? Pure rot. This is a simple issue. The man made claims, those claims threatened the hierarchy, so he died. And, in my opinion, he should have."

"Messiah or not, his people loved him. And they grieve," Longinus said. "Grief is a powerful thing."

Pilate struck fist to palm. "You're right. It's a tenuous situation and emotion is beyond high. Personally, I think the Sanhedrin would gain more by diplomacy. Let these people communicate their grief without threat. It might yet blow over. This Cilician only makes things worse."

Herod brushed imaginary dust from his robe. "No, Caiaphas is right. Squash an uprising with a hard hand before it gets out of control. Rumors must not trump reason. Or the established priesthood. Order is order."

"You don't think it's already out of control?" Pilate said. "I *talked* with Yeshua. I looked into his eyes, and I'm telling you there was something there I still don't understand. But this much I know, he was innocent of the Sanhedrin's charges. None of this had to happen."

Herod waved a hand. "Leave the ghost stories to children, Pilate. I looked into his eyes as well, and all I saw was a broken Galilean waiting to die. He was nothing. And we're allowing these people to lift him up as a martyr."

"Not a martyr," Longinus said. "They claim he is the Son of God. They believe he lives."

"The Jews believe the Messiah will break Rome's hold on Judea," Herod said. "Let me ask you, Longinus, do you sleep well in your fortress at night? Are you afraid for your life? Do you see an army of God breaking down your gates? This man is as dead as the stone we stand on. Someone knows where the body is. We simply need to find that someone and find the body."

"What of the soldiers who guarded the tomb?" Pilate said. "You've questioned them?"

Longinus nodded. "Of course."

"They must have seen something. Does nothing in their statements help to identify the thieves?"

"No. And in my opinion their story is false."

"False how?" Herod said.

"These men claimed to have fallen asleep and that Yeshua's disciples stole his body."

"And?"

"If this is true, they're worthless as soldiers. And the law is clear, their punishment should be death." Longinus fixed his gaze on Pilate. "Yet you stayed my hand in that respect. Why?"

"Caiaphas wanted to show mercy. I granted his request."

"Mercy like he showed Yeshua? Or anyone for that matter? Why show mercy to Romans he claims to hate when he wouldn't do the same for his own countrymen? No, I believe Caiaphas bribed them to his own purpose."

"Ridiculous. Of course the disciples stole the body," Herod said. "Most probably with the help of Joseph of Arimathea. It's the only plausible explanation."

"Go on, Longinus. What else fuels your suspicion?" Pilate said.

Longinus glanced at Herod.

The king waved a hand. "Oh all right, go on. Let's hear it."

"One of the men assigned to guard the grave has been gambling and losing a lot of money," Longinus said. "Money he never had before. The Sanhedrin paid them to lie. They have to crush the rumor that Yeshua rose."

"Bah!" Herod said. "The city is filling up with children's stories."

Longinus shrugged a shoulder. "Yeshua claimed he would rise after three days. He said it more than once. Darkness, earthquakes, can you deny them? You must admit this has been a strange time."

"Strange indeed, but natural phenomena. Easily explained," Herod said. "And a perfect opportunity for someone to steal the body and perpetuate the myth."

"To what end?" Longinus said. "If Yeshua is indeed dead, what do they gain except what they're getting now— persecution?"

"You act like you believe the Nazarene is up and coming to dinner," Herod said.

"Of course he doesn't," Pilate interjected. "He's a Roman. We don't play these Jewish games."

Herod sank into a chair and sighed. "Well, even if the Sanhedrin did invent the story, it's not working. At least not on the scale it needs to."

"No. So they send out this Cilician as insurance against loose lips," Longinus said. "Making it worse than ever."

"Maybe, maybe not," Herod said.

"Longinus, how sure are you these soldiers are lying?" Pilate said.

"Very sure," Longinus said.

"Kill them."

Longinus nodded. "Consider it done."

Pilate paced. "That will be all. Keep your ears open. I may call you again in a few days for another report."

Longinus gave a stiff bow. "I'll do what I can." The great hall was still empty as the chamber door swung shut behind him. His footsteps echoed off the marble walls. He'd traversed half the hall when he heard the voice.

"I once saw a troupe of acrobats in Rome…" Pilate's wife stepped from behind one of the heavy tapestries.

Longinus paused his stride. "I'm sorry?"

The woman stepped closer. "A man walked across a rope suspended high above the ground. Can you imagine? A fall from that height would have meant certain death."

Longinus had the sudden impression he was looking at something unworldly. More spirit than flesh. She was bone thin. Her skin fine as parchment, tiny blue veins tracing a map across it. The only vital thing about her, red hair so bright it seemed the sunlight had followed her into the shadow. She extended a delicate hand. "We haven't met. You're Longinus. I'm Procula, Pilate's wife."

"Yes, I know who you are. I'm at your service."

"Yet you wonder—do I listen to all of my husband's meetings? Am I right?"

"You read minds then?"

"Your face betrays you. The answer is no, I don't listen to all the meetings, but some do interest me. And I like to think my husband values my opinion."

"And well he should. You strike me as particularly astute."

"Flattery…" She fixed on his face. "It doesn't suit you. Tell me, have you ever seen a man walk across a rope?"

"Once. In Germania, I think it was."

"I was very close. I could see his face. Like I could see your face today. I divine you're walking a rope of your own."

"I don't know what you mean."

"You know exactly what I mean. You believe in him. Did you know I had a dream the night before they crucified Yeshua? Oh yes, I've had dreams since I was a child. I've learned to trust them. That particular dream told me that an innocent man would die. And that the result would be both glorious and terrible. I warned Pilate, but his hands were tied. I understood his position, though I cared for it not."

"Why are you telling me this?"

"Because I had another dream, just last night. Yeshua is alive. I know this as sure as I'm standing here talking with you. He has risen from the grave, and the world will change forever because of it. You know what I'm saying is true, but you balance up there on your rope."

Longinus prided himself on being able to read people. He looked deep into the woman's eyes, trying to decide if she was genuine. After all, she was Pilate's wife. And the governor would stop at nothing to collect every scrap of information he could. In Jerusalem, like every city since the dawn of time, knowledge was power. And it was always the safest tack to hold one's own collected knowledge, and often even loyalties, close. "I know nothing for certain. The last I saw of the Nazarene, he hung on a cross. Very much dead."

The opaque eyes narrowed a fraction. "It's hard, isn't it? When your mind won't accept the things your soul knows? But heed me, Longinus. Caiaphas, Beryl, the lot of them, they have no idea the path they walk. I've seen. I know. And so do you whether you admit it to me or not. When the Nazarene breathed his last, bright daylight turned dark. The earth shook. There has been a shift in the heavens. The world must choose. And the stakes are high."

"I'm a soldier. I deal in tangibles."

"Do you?"

"Yes."

"I think you're much more than a soldier. And who defines what is tangible and what isn't? Is the wind tangible? Is love tangible? Are dreams? I say yes."

"I respect your thoughts, Procula. And who am I to say your dreams are not real? But I must deal in the things I know. Nothing more."

"You think I ply you for information. For my husband. Or for Herod. I'm loyal to my husband, yes. I love him, and at heart he is a decent man. But Yeshua is bigger than any of us. Do you see? We are really inconsequential when it comes down to what will happen. But I've seen you in the dreams, Longinus. And I've seen the people you help. And these people, they need you."

"These people…"

"There is one who needs you in particular."

The woman had a way of breaking through defenses, no matter how carefully constructed. Longinus smiled. "I feel sorry for your husband if he often comes under your scrutiny."

"Oh, he survives. But you change the subject. There is one who needs you most assuredly. You must not fail in this.

"You speak of Joseph of Arimathea. I'm afraid the Winemaker is very much his own man. He'll stand or fall on his own, though I have much respect for him and will do what I can."

"No, Longinus. Not the Arimathean. The dream showed me a woman."

"A woman? What woman?"

"Procula?" Pilate's voice boomed from his chamber. "Come! Where are you?"

Procula put a hand on Longinus' arm. "There is a wind coming, Longinus. A great, great wind! It will give you life or blow you out. "

"This woman—"

But she was gone.

Later that night in his bunk in the fortress, he walked back through her words. A mysterious soul, Procula. He tried to picture her face. The wild red hair, the colorless eyes.

But, as he drifted into dreams of his own, it was Sister's face that came to him.

21

Music rattled the tavern. The heat tonight was oppressive, the room thick with the press of bodies. The walls dripped. Spice, scented oil, sweat, and the din of patrons talking over one another in their attempt to be heard.

And through the haze of smoke and hopelessness, the sister, the woman without a name, danced.

Men handed her coins that she slipped into a small bag tied to her wrist. Every night she danced. Every night she took the coins. Every night she drank enough to blur the things that would go on later in the back room. But Yeshua's sad eyes, Peter's admonition, the Roman—these things she shoved into a closet in the back of her mind, shut the door and locked it.

And always the *voice*.

Louder than the music, louder than the patrons, louder than her own thoughts, the voice refused to give her a moment's peace. It pressed and accused and berated. Always the same.

Whore... Nameless, nothing, whore.

The musicians paused and she moved to the rear of the room, hoping for a cool breeze from the back door. Fishel met her there, holding out a cup of wine. "You outdo yourself tonight, Sister."

She took the cup and drank deep. "One night is the same as any other. It makes no difference."

He reached over and jiggled the sack of coins on her wrist. "The way you're dancing, you could name your price from any man in this room."

"Most of them should be home with their wives."

"Good for us they're not. They can't spend their shekels from home."

She drank again and lifted the back of her hair, letting the breeze cool her neck. "I'm tired, Fishel. I want to go to bed."

"You'll go to bed later. But right now, there's no time for tired. You've got them clamoring out there. Keep their coin coming."

"I don't only mean tonight. I mean I'm tired. How long can I do this? Does life hold nothing more?"

"What are you talking about? We depend on you to keep this family afloat, you know that."

"There are men in this world who put food on the table without selling their own flesh and blood. Figure it out."

"Maybe, yes, but figuring takes time. And we need food on the table now."

"It doesn't look like you're missing any meals to me."

Fishel's fat neck bulged. He took a cloth out of his tunic and mopped at the sweat streaming off his bald pate. "I don't know where you disappeared to those days or what you did. I didn't ask and I don't care. But you're back now. And…"

Something in his pig eyes, she felt a creeping dread. "And what? What did you do, brother?"

He wiped his head again. "I find myself in a little trouble. But nothing that can't be handled."

"You've been gambling again."

"I couldn't lose. If I've ever seen a sure thing, this was it."

"*Sure thing.* That phrase doesn't apply when you lose, you idiot. How much do you owe?"

His pig eyes turned mean. "You know nothing. It was stacked against me from the start. A rigged game. There was no way I could know."

"It's always stacked, Fishel! And you *never* know. How much?"

His chins jiggled. "Everything. The tavern, the stock, everything."

She sighed. "Good. I told you I was tired. Maybe now I can rest."

"No. Now you help."

She indicated the room. "If we emptied the purses of every one of these sweaty cows tonight, it wouldn't help. Not if you bet everything."

"The situation isn't hopeless. The man who holds my marker, he's been here before and he's seen you dance. He's, how should I put it? Enamored."

"What man?"

Fishel hesitated.

"What man, Fishel?"

"His name is Larcon."

She stared. "Larcon? *The* Larcon?"

"Is there more than one Larcon?"

"When was he here?"

"I have no idea, but that's his claim. And Larcon is not a man to take issue with."

"Larcon heads the biggest criminal network in Jerusalem. And now you owe him?"

"We owe him."

She laughed out loud. "No, brother—you. I owe Larcon nothing."

"Sister, if you go to him, he'll forgive the debt. All of it. It's simple. You have to do this thing. There is no other choice."

"Ridiculous. Why would he forgive such a large sum for one night with a prostitute? The city is full of women. Ten shekels on any corner in the Lower City would buy him heaven."

Fishel looked at her for long seconds.

"Fishel?"

"It might be a little more than just a night."

"Fishel, what's going on?"

"You have to understand, a man like Larcon won't just take the tavern, Sister. He'll kill us. Yoram and I both. And we're your brothers. If he's in a bad mood, maybe he'll kill you too."

"If it's not a night he wants, what is it?"

"I'm telling you, he'll kill us…"

"What does he want, Fishel?"

"I already told you. He wants you…"

"What did you agree to, you fat imbecile? What did you commit my body to? A week? A month?"

"You. Just you."

"What?"

"There's no time period. He will take you and that will be the end of it. We'll be free."

A roar started in her ears. She grabbed two fistfuls of Fishel's tunic and shoved him back against the wall. "You mean you'll be free! You think you can sell me? Sell a human being to save your own sorry skin? You're pathetic! I hope he does kill you. I'll have none of this."

"And Yoram? You'd sentence him to death as well?"

"I hate you, Fishel."

His eyes set. "Listen to me, woman. Because that's what you are, a woman. I'm the head of this family and I make the decisions. It's not as if I haven't thought this through. A man like Larcon will tire of you quickly. I'm sure his appetites are constantly shifting. You'll be home in a week. A month at the outside."

"A month?"

"All right, maybe two months. But it is what it is. You don't have a choice. You will do this thing."

She threw the wine cup into his fat middle. It shattered into clay pieces on the floor between them. "You're a monster." Turning, she stormed through the open back door.

"Woman!" He called after her. "Fine, go cool down. But he's expecting you tonight."

She paused in the darkness, breathing hard.

Why are you complaining? You know what you are. And it's all you're good for.

"I don't want this anymore!" she hissed back at the voice. Her heart jumped at her own words. It was the first time in her life she'd dared question the voice. But Yeshua's eyes… The first sentence emboldened her. "I'm so tired! Leave me alone!"

Then why did you leave the Followers? I'll tell you why, because you're a worthless harlot through and through.

"No, because I listened to you. I saw a better way. But I still listened to you."

You listened because you knew I was right. And you still know it.

"I don't want—"

What you want doesn't matter. It's what you are that counts. And that will never change.

"Are you talking to yourself, woman?" A different voice now. Brittle like dry clay.

She hadn't seen the man leaning against the wall. Straightening, he stepped toward her.

"If I was, I don't see how it's any of your business," she said.

"No. Of course it isn't."

"I'd like to be alone."

"It's just that I couldn't help but hear your conversation inside. The door was open."

"I think you could have helped it easily."

The man smiled. "This Larcon sounds like an evil man."

"And how is this your business?"

"Maybe I could help you."

"Help how?"

"Do you know who I am?"

She considered him. "I have no idea who you are. Why would I?"

"Some call me the Cilician."

22

"You're the Cilician?" Sister said.

"Cilicia is a beautiful country, though not nearly as splendid as Jerusalem."

"I heard about the couple you killed in the New City. All Jerusalem has."

"Which was the point, wasn't it? The Followers wage a war against Judaism, do you understand? And in a war, there are casualties, sometimes many of them. The casualties that night in the New City sent a message across Jerusalem and beyond. Perpetuating the Nazarene's myth will not be tolerated."

"Why are you here?"

"The Nazarene spent time in the Lower City. What better place to seek information than a drinking establishment? People talk. But, woman, I look for you in particular. And here you are. God smiles on me."

"You look for a woman? There are many. I'm tired tonight. Leave me alone."

"Don't be crude. I'm a Pharisee. My wife waits at home for me even now. I look for you because I have questions and you have answers."

"What answers could I possibly have that you would want?"

"You stayed with a group of Followers for a few days. I want you to take me to them."

This gave her pause. "Why would I be with Followers? You see what I am. Leave me alone."

The Cilician picked something from under one of his fingernails, studied it, and flicked it away. "The thing is, if you lie to me, I have the authority to have you buried to your waist and stoned and I'll do it without hesitation. You were gone for a few days. When you came back, you were tightlipped about where you'd been. Except last night, after copious amounts of wine, you decided to get things off your chest and talked to your brother, Yoram. Yoram, it turns out, is greedy. And all Jerusalem knows there is a reward available for anyone who has information leading to the location of the Followers. So here I am."

She did a quick, mental search. It had been a hard night. And there had been quite a lot of wine, it was true. She had no recollection of speaking with Yoram, but she couldn't be sure it hadn't happened.

"It may be," said the Cilician, "that you and I have gotten off on the wrong foot. I can help you. You've been sold by your brother into servitude to a man named Larcon. I know nothing of him, but I have the entire Levitical Patrol at my service. Larcon can easily be stepped on and you can continue on with your life. Simply tell me what I want to know. We seek a man named Nicodemus."

"I want to go inside now."

"This man, Larcon…I hear that criminals like these tend to have violent appetites. Even sadistic. You never know."

"You killed law-abiding Jews. They had a child. And you talk to me about being sadistic?"

"It's expedient to hit enemies where they are the most vulnerable. In the long run, this may save men from Hades. Much different than evil for the sake of evil."

"You lie to yourself."

"You're not afraid of me, are you? I find that interesting and not a little foolish. What are the Followers to you? After all, you're here, so you left them. You're a known prostitute and clearly don't have any interest in following the Nazarene's ghost. I just want to know where to find Nicodemus, that's all."

"Why is this Nicodemus special to you?"

The Cilician shrugged. "He's one of the worst of the lot. An educated man. A student of scripture. But he distorts everything to his own purpose. Nicodemus is a blasphemer, and gullible people are pulled into his lies. He will stand trial and either be imprisoned or die."

"I know nothing of this man."

"Yet you mentioned his name to your brother? How strange."

"I had too much wine. It must have been rambling nonsense, that's all. Maybe I heard the man's name somewhere. Then again, Yoram would say anything for a shekel."

The Cilician tugged at his beard, his black eyes glinting. He smiled. "Woman, woman, we don't have to do it like this." He reached out and stroked her upper arm with a rough hand. She wanted to move, but something in his manner kept her frozen in place. She swallowed. "Don't touch me."

He continued to caress. "Where were you those three days?"

"I was with a man. You're misinformed."

"Where is he hiding? What part of the city?"

"Leave me alone."

His fingers found purchase on the bare skin of the back of her arm. He squeezed lightly. Then harder.

She tried to pull away but couldn't. "Stop it. You're hurting me."

His grip tightened. "Tell me where you were."

"With a man. I don't even know his name."

His fingers became steel. Light burst behind her eyes at the sudden increase of pain. She clawed at his hand. The agony took her to her knees. Tears streamed down her face. "Stop it!"

"Tell me."

"Let her up." A hard voice barked the order.

The pain subsided and she scrambled to her feet holding her arm.

A large man with a brute of a face and small, rotten teeth stood in the tavern doorway. "This woman is mine."

"Ah. Are you Larcon, then?" the Cilician said.

"Come here, woman," the big man said.

"The woman comes with me." The Cilician reached for her again, but she dodged his hand with a back step.

The big man pulled a long, curved knife from his belt. "Wrong. She comes with me."

"I can have a dozen Levitical Patrolmen here within an hour. You'll find yourself on a Roman cross," the Cilician said.

"An hour is a long time. Her brother owes a debt. A legal debt. I came for the woman and I'll leave with the woman."

The Cilician lunged for her again, and again she avoided him.

"Look at him, woman" the Cilician said. "You can see what awaits you. I'm offering you a way out. Tell me what I want to know and avoid hell."

She looked into the Cilician's murky, bits-of-glass eyes and felt cold in the sticky heat of the night. She turned to the big man. "Let me get my things."

23

Joseph read the note Longinus had handed him for the second time and silently thanked God for Ariella's insistence he teach her to read and write.

"She's well?" Nicodemus said.

"The woman is a survivor," Longinus said. "You should be proud, Winemaker."

Joseph nodded. "Beryl keeps her locked in the house and holds our unborn child over her head. She placates him with feigned meekness, hoping she may be of use to us."

"She may be right," Nicodemus said.

Joseph set the note on the table. "Beryl has been the aggressor long enough. I'll tolerate it no longer."

Nicodemus looked up from the scroll he'd been working on. "You have a plan?"

"Yes, not to sit here like an old woman. The effects of the beatings are fading. I still hurt, but I'm feeling stronger every day. And I may be an abomination to the Sanhedrin, but I'm not without resources."

"What resources?" Nicodemus said. "They've taken everything. Mordechai the moneychanger was the highest bidder for my shop. Can you imagine? That crook will run it into the ground in less than a year, mark my words. With his big mouth, he'll burn every bridge it took me half a lifetime to build."

"Would you go back if you could?" Joseph said.

"I would have my shop, yes. But if it meant turning my back on Yeshua? I'd rather die."

"You may yet," Longinus said

"Then so be it," Nicodemus said.

"I have no intention of turning my back on Yeshua," Joseph said. "But I also have no intention of turning my family and holdings over to an evil man without a fight."

Nicodemus nodded. "I understand. It's easier for me, I think, with Lila and Jonathan safely away."

"I wish I'd been so wise," Joseph said.

They sat on the tiny secluded patio behind the apartments, a pitcher of chilled wine between them. Nicodemus dipped a quill and began scratching on the parchment again. A sparrow dipped through the space and fluttered up into the vines above.

Nicodemus glanced up from his work. "She's been working on that nest for days. She'll lay soon, I expect."

"A good, secure place," Longinus said. "Safe from predators above or below."

"Spoken like a soldier," Nicodemus said.

"We're the same as the bird," Joseph said. "Hiding here from the Council."

"Yeshua will come," Nicodemus said. "He's been seen in Galilee by many witnesses. He's not hiding."

"If you haven't seen Yeshua living with your own eyes, then how do you know the story isn't fabricated? Or an impersonator?" Longinus said.

"Scripture is clear. The Messiah will come, suffer, die, and rise from the grave. Yeshua is alive." Nicodemus scratched with the quill again.

"What are you writing?" Joseph said.

"Notes. Things I've heard from the Eleven and others."

"What things?"

Nicodemus set the quill down, lifted his cup and drank. "I've been thinking, Joseph. We've made a list of pertinent prophecies from the Tanakh. And it continues to grow. But if Yeshua is truly the Son of God, what about the things he said himself?"

"For instance?" Joseph said.

"Look here." Nicodemus turned the scroll. "*I am the way, and the truth, and the life; no one comes to the Father but through Me.* Yeshua said this publicly. Yeshua is Truth. Therefore, I submit that the teachings he leaves us in the memory of his disciples should be equal to scripture."

"Be careful, Nicodemus. All scripture is given by God," Joseph said.

"This is exactly my point. If these words come from Yeshua's mouth, they must ring true throughout the universe. And the story is nowhere close to being finished. He made a multitude of promises to those who love and follow him."

Longinus leaned in. "So? What else did he say? You have me curious."

Nicodemus scanned his writings. "For one thing, he talked much about love for one's fellow man. Look: *This is My commandment, that you love one another, just as I have loved you. Greater love has no one than this, that one lay down his life for his friends. You are My friends if you do what I command you. No longer do I call you slaves, for the slave does not know what his master is doing; but I have called you friends, for all things that I have heard from My Father I have made known to you. You did not choose Me but I chose you, and appointed you that you would go and bear fruit, and that your fruit would remain, so that whatever you ask of the Father in My name He may give to you. This I command you, that you love one another.* A radical teaching. But he clearly means there is work for us to do. Work for the very Kingdom of God. Imagine."

"A dangerous work, then," Longinus said.

"A very dangerous work." Nicodemus scanned again. "Later, during the same teaching: *"These things I have spoken to you so that you may be kept from stumbling. They will make you outcasts from the synagogue, but an hour is coming for everyone who kills you to think that he is offering service to God."*

"You speak of the Cilician," Longinus said.

"And others. Caiaphas, Beryl, the lot of them. They have no idea what they do."

Joseph studied his hands. "Yeshua talked of love. And of a gentle spirit. But does God expect a man to hide here like that sparrow while others with evil intent steal his home and threaten his wife and child?"

Nicodemus set down his quill. "We're all different, Joseph. All have a part to play. But what can one man do against the Patrol?"

Joseph drank, then set his cup down. "Nicodemus, you teach, it's your calling. You expound on the scriptures, interpret and order them, and your effort brings much knowledge and comfort to many. Myself included. But what have I done these last days other than been beaten half to death? It's time to act."

"Well and good, my friend, but I repeat, what can you do? All the power of Israel is against us."

"No. All the power of Israel is against God. We're on the side of God, Nicodemus. There is nothing stronger than that." Joseph looked at Longinus. "Longinus, you've done much for me already, and I'll be forever grateful. But tell me, can you get Davi and me outside the city walls once more without being seen? And can you get horses?"

Longinus drank, deep lines around his eyes. He set his cup down and sighed. "That's the Winemaker I know. No end of entertainment. I'll do you one better. I'll get you your own stock."

"Beryl won't have them guarded?"

Longinus refilled his cup from the pitcher. "Animals have been known to wander off."

"Good. Then one more thing. I need you to go to Pilate."

Joseph leaned in, taking time to outline his plan. When he'd finished, Longinus stood, shaking his head. "You don't ask for much, do you?"

24

The big man hadn't spoken again when he'd taken Sister. Just dumped her and her few belongings into the back of a donkey cart and disappeared. A wiry handler holding the donkey's lead rope looked her over, then started off.

"He's not coming?" she said.

The handler said nothing.

"I guess you're about as talkative as your boss," she said.

The handler shrugged and plodded on.

She looked back at the fading tavern lights. Neither Fishel or Yoram had had the courage to look at her when she'd left.

"They can both rot in Hades…" she said.

The little donkey's head dipped and bobbed as it worked to pull the cart up through the Lower City streets. A swirl of breeze sent dust circles whirling across the worn stone beneath the wheels. Lamplight shone in windows. Through an open door, a father sat hunched over a scroll with his son.

"Who?" The thin man's voice was surprisingly deep.

"Who, what?" she said.

"Who can rot in Hades?"

"My brothers. Though I'm ashamed to call them that."

"Family can be that way."

"Yes. Some more than others. Do you have family?"

"Worse than yours, I imagine. And already rotting in Hades. It's hard to believe you're related to fat Fishel."

She looked up at the sky as they rolled along. The stars were heavy tonight, like summer fruit hanging just out of reach. "Someone else said that to me recently."

"I don't doubt it. You probably hear it every day."

They climbed out of the Lower City with its narrow, smoke-choked streets and pathways and through an arch into the Upper City. The change was marked. Here, large oil lamps burned along the street throwing flickering light across white Jerusalem stone. Water bubbled and pooled in the fountains lining the center of the boulevard. Vine-covered trees grew behind high courtyard walls, and Sister wondered, as she often had, what delights lay beneath them. A lute offered a plucked melody accompanying the sweet voice of a child. The air was cool and spiced and clean.

"Can I ask you a question?" Sister said.

"If you must."

"Will he use me roughly?"

"Who?"

"Larcon."

The cart rattled on.

"Can you at least tell me where we're going?" she asked.

"It won't be long."

Almost completely through the Upper City now. Down one particularly wide and grand avenue on her left, she caught a glimpse of the white marble wall surrounding Herod's palace. She'd heard much of the place. Stories of wide, magnificent porticoes and constantly flowing fountains. Of jungled gardens where exotic animals roamed. Of dozens of gold-gilded bedchambers that could sleep a hundred people at a time. Each room of the palace was reportedly filled with furniture of gold and silver. Herod the Great had been a man with a great appetite for opulence, and his son, Herod Antipas, was said to carry the tradition forward in grand fashion.

Another block and the monolithic Zion Bridge blocked the stars as the little cart passed under, wheels rattling echoes. Just beyond the bridge, the handler tugged the donkey left, heading into a part of the city Sister was unfamiliar with. They passed under another low bridge and took a sharp turn down a long, sloping ramp. Well below street level, the handler pulled the cart into a large subterranean stable and closed the door behind them. Stalls lined the walls here, most of them occupied. A boy stepped from the end stall, hay stuck in his curls, rubbing sleep from his eyes. The handler handed him the donkey's lead. "A little grain with his dinner, I think."

The boy nodded and the handler turned to Sister. "This way." He started toward the back of the cave.

"I wondered what an animal like Larcon's lodgings would look like, but I never expected an actual stable," she said.

"Antagonism isn't an attractive trait in a woman. I'd highly suggest you lose it," the handler replied.

"Why? It's not my personality Larcon is interested in, I think."

The back of the stable narrowed, and the handler paused and took a burning torch from an iron holder pounded into the rock.

Sister paused. "I don't like caves."

The handler turned and raised an eyebrow. "You want to disappoint Larcon? It's not a good idea."

"What is this place? What's happening?"

"Just follow, woman. It might not be as bad as you think."

She didn't move. "He must have wealth. Why here? Am I not worth a mattress at least?"

"You talk too much. Come."

He swung open a thick wooden door set into the wall and moved through it. Peering in, she was surprised to see a flight of white stone steps leading upward.

"Come," the handler repeated.

Up they went, passing three or four landings, each having hallways branching in several different directions.

"We must be well above ground by now," she said.

"Must we?"

"Why are there no windows?"

He made no reply.

"Can't you answer a simple question? What's wrong with you?"

"Nothing that a little quiet won't cure. Which is what I'm going to have as soon as I deposit you."

"Deposit me where?"

They came to another landing. This time the handler turned right and started down a hallway. They passed several closed doors. At the end of the hall he stopped and opened one. "Here we are."

She stepped in and stopped short. The single room was as big as Fishel's whole tavern. The floor and walls were white Jerusalem stone. The ceiling was domed, supported with huge carved cedar beams. Thick rugs covered the floor, giving the space a hushed stillness. A fire burned in a fireplace at one end, low couches and tables spaced around it. A large bed sat in an elevated alcove. Opposite her, several doors stood open to the night and beyond them a wide patio invited. She walked out onto it and stared in stunned silence at a Jerusalem view she could never have imagined. To her right and at least two floors below her, the Zion Bridge spanned the city. On the other side of it, Herod's torchlit palace and towers rose, shining in the night. Ahead and right, the Upper City sprawled. Ahead and left, the dark and smokey expanse of the New City. And straight ahead of her, though distant, the Temple topped Mount Zion, so splendid it seemed it had been set there by the very hand of God. Beyond the Temple, a handful of faded stars as the sun readied itself for another day of giving.

The handler appeared at her elbow. "Finally you stop talking?"

"It's unbelievable. I've never seen anything like it," she said.

"Not bad as far as caves go."

"Not bad at all." She thought of Larcon's brute features and rotten teeth-nubs. "Will he come tonight?"

The handler lifted a shoulder. "He's Larcon. Who knows?" He clapped twice and a woman appeared through an inner doorway Sister hadn't noticed at first. "Amaris, would you please see the woman is cared for. Bring her anything she needs. I leave her in your hands."

The woman nodded. "Gladly."

The handler fingered the thin fabric of Sister's dress. "You might want to clean her up. She reeks of Lower City tavern."

"I think we can manage that very well," the woman said.

The handler gave Sister an almost imperceptible smile and was gone.

Sister turned to the woman and examined her. She had a wide, triangular face and high forehead and would have been plain were it not for her smile. Her smile was inexact…and crooked…and so happy it lit the room like a thousand lamps. She used it to meet Sister's hard-eyed scrutiny. "There is a basin of water in the next room," she said. "And towels for drying. And scented oil for after. There are clothes as well. I'm sure we can find something to fit you."

"I don't smell as bad as he says, you know."

The woman stepped forward and sniffed. Still smiling, she said, "I'll show you the basin."

25

The lonely copse of trees sat hidden, far away from any regularly traveled road in the Jerusalem hills. The night was cool. The moon high and full, filtering its light through the thick branches of the jujube trees.

Joseph breathed deep, alive for the first time in days. A rush of wings passed, then a muted cry as a nocturnal bird of prey went about its business. "He hunts."

Davi looked in the direction of the cry. "Let me ask you, Joseph, are we owl or mouse tonight? Hunters or hunted?"

"I'm afraid our game is a bit more complicated."

"You're sure this is where he said to wait?" Davi said.

"I am," Joseph said.

Davi looked around. "The place makes me uneasy."

"Better here than out in the open."

"He may have trouble getting the horses out."

"He may. But he'll be here."

"If you say so."

A low whistle sounded somewhere out in the darkness. Davi returned the signal. "The Roman continues to surprise."

Longinus loomed out of the darkness, two horses behind him. One of the animals nickered and stretched his head toward Joseph. Joseph reached out a hand and stroked the beast's neck.

"He's happy to see you," Longinus said.

Joseph adjusted the animal's bridle. "And I him. We've seen some miles together. And we'll see some more tonight."

"Arimathea is a long ride." Longinus began removing sound-softening leather pads from the horse's hooves. Davi leaned to help. The two made quick work of it.

"What word from Pilate?" Joseph said.

"He's been entertaining dignitaries in from Lycia," Longinus said. "I've not been able to get to him."

Joseph swung into the saddle. "It has to happen by sundown tomorrow."

"And if it doesn't?" Longinus said.

"Then may God help us, because I'm not backing down."

Longinus stepped back. "If I can't get to Pilate, God will be the only reason you live to see another sunset." He patted the horse's neck. "You're a bold man, Winemaker. I think you would do well on the frontier."

"Don't tempt him," Davi said. "He'd drag me with him."

"I think you would do well too," Longinus said.

Davi mounted, pulling back on the reins as his horse tried to sidestep. "To fight for the glory of Rome? No thank you."

Longinus shrugged. "Rome is a glorious place, like no other on earth. And the Empire is changing. Africa, the Near East, Germania…Rome is ever expanding. I hear of lands to the far north filled with barbarians so fierce and full of fight they still gnash their teeth and swing their swords while they die, a hundred arrows in them. Your Messiah, if that's what he is, chooses a turbulent time to make his appearance in the world."

"What better? Men are in need of God," Joseph said. "Even my own race, it seems, has turned its back on the prophets."

"But not you," Longinus said.

"I'm a simple man. I want truth and I'll stand with God."

"Though it kill you?"

"Even so."

"And what of your child? You'd let him grow up without a father?"

"That's a hard thing to contemplate, I'll admit. But better the legacy of a man who died a righteous and honorable death than one who compromised his principles simply to save his skin. I'll trust God. What other choice do I have?"

"You could hide with the rest of them. That's certainly a choice. Keep your truth and your head attached to your body as well."

"Is that what you would do in my place? You're out here with me now, so I think not," Joseph said.

"I'm a fool who likes the fight, and I've never pretended to be anything else. If this God of yours allows me to keep drawing breath, I'll continue to stand with you."

"Thank you, my friend. For everything."

"Are you sure about this, Winemaker? Pounding across the countryside on a horse will torture those ribs of yours. Possibly damage any healing you've already managed."

"I have no choice. This must be done. They're wrapped as well as possible."

"Then you'd better ride. I'll do what I can here."

"I know you will. Go with God."

"And you as well."

Joseph put heel to flank. The reins in his hands, the powerful mount moving beneath him, the feeling of finally doing… He gave the stallion its head, welcoming the familiar surge of adrenaline and praying it would serve to ease his aching body if even slightly. Eager for the run, the horse leapt. Davi's mount did the same. Forty miles, give or take, to Arimathea and back, they wouldn't run the animals long. No more than a mile or two. But, now, in this moment, even in pain Joseph needed the speed. He pushed the stallion faster until wind-tears formed at the corners of his eyes and began to stream back toward his ears. They topped a rise and the land fell away before them, beautiful and broken, baptized in silver light.

He pushed the horse faster… *Ariella, only a bit longer…*

Stars stretched horizon to horizon, a heavenly chorus, and the Shepherd's song rose on the wind and tumbled across the plains, filling Joseph's pounding heart and vibrating his soul like a bowstring. His muscles stretched and moved with the horse's long stride. The Romans called him the Horse Jew, and Horse Jew he was. His fellow countrymen had long considered the horse a symbol of war and some disapproved of his riding. Well, wasn't this war? Not one of his choosing but war nonetheless. A war for truth. A war for good. A war for God.

He pulled back on the reins. Dead run to gallop, then gallop to lope that he held. A pace that would spare the horses and still eat up the miles quickly. Davi pulled alongside and they rode abreast, horses blowing, saddle leather creaking.

"You're smiling. It's good to see," Davi said.

"It feels good to be riding toward something rather than running away from it."

The horses reeled in the miles, and it wasn't many hours until the outskirts of Arimathea loomed. Smoke from bread ovens stretched lazy, waking fingers into the breaking dawn. Joseph made no attempt at subtlety of approach. The village people would hear the hooves and know exactly who it was that came their way.

A woman pulling a water bucket from a well paused and watched them ride by, wind whipping her skirt above dust-covered bare feet. She lifted a hand in greeting and Joseph nodded. Vineyards, heavy with buds, stretched away over the surrounding hills. They passed through the village, hooves loud on the packed dirt and stone. Several people stepped out of their homes to watch them go by and offer greetings.

Joseph returned the acknowledgments. These were his people. People of the earth. Many of them work in his vineyards. And he'd done his best to be good to them.

The village soon fell behind them, and they climbed a low rise to Joseph and Ariella's sprawling country estate. In the wide courtyard they swung down from their saddles.

Joseph passed his reins to Davi. "I won't be long."

"You would go alone?"

"I'll be fine. Check on the staff. Make sure all is well and they haven't had any trouble from Jerusalem, although I think there hasn't been time for that yet."

Davi nodded. "Be careful, Joseph." He led the horses off toward the stables.

Joseph left the courtyard on foot and headed with long, fast strides up a narrow path through the grapes. Past the vineyard, the path wound over a hill, then cut down into a canyon, at times descending so steep he had to turn around and work himself down the rock hand over hand. At length, breathing hard, he made the canyon floor. A wide, sandy wash curved back into the hills. A mile or so up the canyon, he took a faint path angling up the slope through the rocks. Strains of woodsmoke touched the breeze. As he rounded a low cliff, a camp appeared—a small clearing backed by a low cave. A man squatted before a fire. Thin, naked to the waist, wisps of gray hair moving on the light wind and reflecting morning sun. He turned as Joseph approached and regarded him with milk-white eyes. "I wondered when you'd come. It's been a long while, Joseph."

"You see well for a blind man," Joseph said.

The man chuckled. "I could hear you even when you were coming down the other side of the canyon. You're about as subtle as a herd of goats."

"All is well?" Joseph said.

"Why not? Nothing happens here. Who wants to bother an old man? Will you sit? Breakfast with me?"

"I wish I could, Meshulam. I ride for Jerusalem as soon as I get what I came for."

The old man lifted his boney shoulders. "I assumed as much. You're in trouble of some kind or you wouldn't be here." He indicated the cave with the stick he held. "You know where it is. But I think you've not been well. It would do you good to rest, even for a few minutes. What's happened to you?"

Even as the old man spoke, Joseph realized how tired he was. The first adrenaline burst of the ride had long since faded. And even though he felt his body healing, fatigue clung to him. He lowered himself onto a rock. "You're right, as always, old man. It's been a rough time but I'm healing. I'll sit, but only a few minutes. Time is of the essence."

"Isn't that the way with time? So self-important. Always demanding something of us." The old man passed Joseph a worn wineskin. "A bit stronger than your vintage, but it will put a little strength back into your bones. You've far to go still, unless I miss my guess."

Joseph sipped and made a face. "Either it will strengthen or kill me."

"Don't be a snob, boy."

"Not a boy anymore. Though there are times I long for those days again."

Meshulam chuckled. "You and Davi slaying your imaginary lions. No more than nine or ten when you first came out here. I remember it like yesterday. He's with you, I suppose?"

"Back at the house. There are things to check on and—"

"Time presses. Yes, I know."

"The lions are real this time, Meshulam."

"And what form do these lions take?"

"The Great Sanhedrin."

"You're no longer of them?"

"I stood for someone they were against."

"You speak of Yeshua, of course. If so, these lions must be very angry indeed."

"You've heard of Yeshua?"

Meshulam poked at his fire. "Who in Israel hasn't heard of Yeshua? I'm not a complete recluse, boy. I go into town once in a while. And I still have ears." He waved the stick around his head. "And the time I spend out here? God and I have long talks."

"Yes? And what does God say to you?"

The old man set down the stick and, as if he could see as well as any man, his milky eyes found Joseph's. "That this path you walk—there will be blood and grief in abundance."

"You only have to look where I've already been to know that."

"There is more to come."

Joseph stood. "Still, walk it I will."

"I would expect no less from you."

"I won't be long."

"Of course not. Time won't let you."

The cave was dark and dank and more than what it looked from without. In fact, the little scooped-out hollow in the cliff face where Meshulam kept his few belongings opened into a much larger system of caverns, a place Joseph and Davi had explored much of as boys. Room after room of stalactites and stalagmites, silent and imposing sentinels guarding passages to the underworld. It was to one of these caverns, torch in hand, Joseph now went, his path marked by carefully placed scratches long ago etched into the stone. Here and there, water flowed and dripped. Silence pressed and unbidden thoughts of his cell under Jerusalem sent a shudder through his body. An hour later he emerged back into the sunlight with a heavy leather sack slung around his shoulder.

Meshulam hadn't moved from his spot. "I've been talking with God about you, Joseph."

"And has He talked back?"

The old man's milky eyes stared nowhere in particular. "You have many friends here. And a thousand ways to disappear for as long as is needed. These caves alone could hide you for years."

"They've taken Ariella. There's no hiding for me. The only path is forward."

"Into the lion's den."

"If need be."

"They have your child as well."

Joseph stared at the old man. "How did you know about the child?"

"When I say I talk with God, you don't believe me?"

"I thought you meant you were just praying."

"Just praying? What is just praying? You think we babble at an empty sky? The greater part of praying is listening. A teacher of Israel should know this."

"And you hear God?"

"Of course I hear God. So do you. You hear the song, don't you?"

Joseph kneeled, crossing his arms across his bent leg. "I've not said a word to anyone about the song. God told you about this?"

The little fire caught a twig and blazed up. "The sheep know their Shepherd's voice, Joseph. You know the Shepherd's voice. Otherwise you wouldn't be here."

"This blood and grief you spoke of… Will it be the child?"

"The child is in God's hands. Blood and grief, yes, but where the Shepherd leads, joy always outweighs the pain. You ride with the God of the universe, Joseph. The Sanhedrin, Israel, the world for that matter—all a speck of sand against the infinity of God. Even the time that presses you so hard is nothing but a whisper of breeze, a plaything, to Him."

"Joy…"

"Of course! There will always be Joy."

Joseph stood and hitched the sack to a more comfortable position.

Milky eyes stared up. "Have they killed Yeshua then?"

"Crucified on a Roman cross. I took him down myself and buried him in my own tomb outside the city."

Meshulam gave a slight nod. "But the story continues?"

"He rose three days later."

"You're sure? You've seen him?"

"Not personally. But there are those who have."

"But the Sanhedrin doesn't believe?"

"Some do, I think, but they're afraid to speak for fear of Caiaphas and Beryl."

"But you weren't afraid to speak. Because you know in your soul Yeshua is the Messiah." A statement, not a question.

"The scriptures are clear. And his miracles speak for themselves. For three years now the Council, the entire Priesthood, has refused to recognize what's right in front of their faces."

"Of course they do," the old man said. "Power is a hard cup to set down once it's touched one's lips."

"You're right, I'm afraid." Joseph reached down for the old man's hand and placed a gold coin into it. "If I don't return, you know what to do."

The old man smiled. "I always know what to do, Joseph. So do you. May God be with your every step."

"Yours as well, Meshulam."

The sun was high as Joseph and Davi left Arimathea behind them at a quick trot. To their left, great pillars of cloud converged above the mountains. To the right, far away across a land green with spring, the vast, pale sea faded to sky beneath a daylight moon.

"You're sure about this?" Davi said. "At this pace we'll arrive long before dark."

"Davi, listen to me. You're a good friend, and I know you would be by my side though I stormed the gates of Hades. But this…this I can't ask of you."

"Nor could you dissuade me."

"I mean it. The odds are we won't survive the day."

"You're wasting your breath, Joseph, you should know that. We've been through too much."

"There'll be no sneaking, no hiding, no carts loaded with fish," Joseph said. "I'll ride openly into the city."

"Right beneath the noses of the Sanhedrin. Well, if we're going to do it, why not?"

"There's every chance in the world Longinus wasn't able to talk with Pilate."

Davi sighed and scratched his cheek. "So, in the end, your Roman holds my life in his hands."

"Both of our lives are in the hands of God."

"Your lips to God's ears." Davi grinned and put heels to his mount.

They rode the sun across the sky and made Jerusalem by early evening beneath piles of pink, lightning-laced clouds and the smell of ozone and new rain.

26

Jerusalem, a city in search of itself. Herod the Great's affinity for all things Roman had bled into his monumental building projects across Judea. Palaces, citadels, viaducts, fountains, monuments—Herod had embarked on a single-minded campaign to increase Judea's importance in the eyes of Rome. His many residences, from Jerusalem to Caesarea Maritima to the remote and inhospitable desert mountaintop of Masada, dripped with opulence. Roads criss-crossed the land, well cared for and wide spread. Complicated systems of aqueducts carried fresh water to previously arid parts of the country. Not since before the devastation of Nebuchadnezzar had the words of the Lamentations rung so true: Jerusalem, once again *the perfection of beauty* and *a joy to all the world.*

The Romans had been a prominent part of civilization for centuries, but with the rise to power of Augustus Caesar in the last century, the polity had strapped on its studded sandals, taken up sword and shield in earnest, and pressed toward the frontier in an Empire-building effort unparalleled in human history. Israel, who had long benefited economically through Roman interaction, found itself on a balance scale between an independent spirit and desire for trade and profit. Eventually the scale tipped. In 6 A.D. the nation came under direct Roman rule as the southern part of the province of Judea. Twenty-seven years ago now and Jerusalem was still a roiling whirlpool of unrest. Because when it came right down to it, Jews were Jews and Romans were Romans. Mosaic Law collided with polytheistic licentiousness with a mighty boom. Armed resistance rose and fell. Robber-rebels like Barabbas operated and thrived. The Priesthood bellowed and lifted a clenched fist to their oppressors. The Romans answered as they always did—with hard boot and sword.

Still, through it all, in the melting-pot culture that was now Judea, trade boomed and the economy soared. And even though class disparity still ruled the day, for those bold enough to seek it out, opportunity abounded. Many got rich and Joseph was a good example. His extensive vineyards supplied most of the wine in Judea and beyond.

And wealth in the right hands can be a powerful weapon, Joseph thought as he rode tall past the Pool of Israel and along the base of the northern Temple Mount wall. In a few minutes he might die, but in this moment his horse moved solid and sturdy beneath him and the Shepherd's song moved quiet on his soul.

Davi glanced up at the Temple guards posted in intervals along the retaining wall of the Mount. "How long before Caiaphas and the others know we're here, do you think?"

"I'd guess minutes if they don't already."

"And not hide nor hair of our Roman."

"He's our Roman now? Not just mine?"

"If the man comes through, I claim him absolutely."

"With or without him, we ride on."

Davi looked up again, shielding his eyes. "It's hard to ride punched full of arrows. I've tried it. I didn't do well. I leaked."

"That was only one arrow."

"It was enough."

"I know Beryl. He'll want us alive. At least for a little while."

"So he can make us suffer longer."

They skirted the city wall without incident and rode on until they intersected the heavily traveled Damascus Road. As they passed through the wall, Roman guards watched them with curious eyes but made no challenge. Inside, the street bustled with shops and shoppers. Fish, cloth, oil, weapons of all types…this was one of Jerusalem's centers of commerce, anything and everything could be purchased here.

Horses weren't unheard of in Israel; still, the sight of Davi and Joseph mounted was enough to turn faces their way and cause heads to poke out of shop doors and the windows above. Children stared, wide-eyed. A washerwoman set down her work and watched them pass.

"Still alive," Joseph said.

"I just wish the Patrol would come. At least that way we'd know where the fight is."

No place in Jerusalem exemplified the friction between Israel and Rome like the Roman Antonia Fortress butting up to the Northern Wall of the Temple Mount. And it was toward the Fortress they now rode. It rose ahead, a four-towered monolith blocking the evening sky. Smoke lifted from inside, mixing with early stars.

Joseph reined his horse onto the boulevard leading to the Governor's residence. "Almost there, my friend. We may make it after all."

Davi shook his head. "No, we'll have to fight. I feel it in my bones."

No sooner had he said the words than shouts rang out from a side alley. Swords rattled and spears clacked, accompanied by the heavy thunder of feet.

Joseph glanced at Davi. "You asked how long for word to reach Caiaphas? Here's your answer."

"And no Roman."

Joseph drew his sword. "I'm sure he tried."

Within seconds, several heavily armed soldiers filled the road ahead.

"There must be twenty of them," Davi said.

"Caiaphas likes a show." Joseph turned and looked back. "There are more behind. They'll take us here."

"Joseph of Arimathea!" The voice boomed off the stone.

Joseph ignored the call and simply rode forward, directly toward the waiting men.

Davi drew his sword. "The Roman's failure may have cost us our lives, but there will be more blood than ours staining the street, I promise that much."

Joseph's mount sidestepped and whinnied as the body of men closed and surrounded them, a tight circle of pointed spears. Along the street, people stopped what they were doing and watched.

The Guard captain stepped forward and reached for Joseph's bridle, but the horse jerked his head, snorted, and bared his teeth and the man stepped back.

"I'd be careful, Yachiel," Joseph said, "if you want to keep your hand."

Yachiel stared daggers. "Control the animal."

"He doesn't like your smell. What can I do?" Joseph said.

The man squared himself. Business head to toe. "Joseph of Arimathea, you're under arrest. You'll surrender your weapons and come with us immediately."

"No," Joseph said.

"What?"

"I said no. I will not."

"But you're under arrest!"

"Arrest for what?" Joseph spoke loud enough for his words to ring off the surrounding buildings and echo up and down the street.

"By order of the Sanhedrin." Yachiel turned to his men. "Take them." None of them seemed eager to make a move toward the agitated horses.

Joseph pushed his mount a step toward Yachiel, forcing the captain to give ground. "What did I do, Yachiel, other than speak up for an innocent man? A man the Council murdered?"

A murmur rippled through the gathering crowd.

"You accuse the Sanhedrin of breaking God's commandments?" Yachiel said.

"I merely point out the truth. Was it God's command for the Cilician to murder?"

Yachiel's left eye narrowed. "I know nothing of the incident. Dismount and come with us. Right now. No more of this."

"I won't, Yachiel. Kill me if you're going to. But I'll not bow to that brood of Sanhedrin vipers again."

"You use the Nazarene's words."

"The Nazarene spoke truth. They killed him for it."

Yachiel lowered his voice. "Hear me, Joseph, you're a brave man, I'll give you that. And I don't necessarily condone the actions of the Cilician. But if you don't do as I say, your blood will flow here and now. Your man will die as well. I have no choice."

Joseph drew his sword from his scabbard. "So be it." He stood high in his stirrups and looked down the crowded street. "Let it be known today that we die, innocent men, in the name of God and in the name of Yeshua!"

Yachiel shook his head. "Take them! Now!"

Forty spears moved in. Davi pushed his mount sideways, engaging.

"Hold! Hold on the order of Rome!"

Yachiel's head swiveled. "Who speaks?"

"I speak! And I say hold!" Longinus appeared pushing his way through the crowd, several of his Romans behind him.

"You?" Yachiel said. "What do you have to do with this? This is Jewish business."

"That it may be, but Pilate would speak to Joseph of Arimathea. I'm here to escort him to the Governor's residence."

Yachiel shook his head. "As I said, it's Jewish business. And your men are outnumbered here."

Longinus shrugged. "Be that as it may, you have my word my sword will split you chin to crotch before you can blink. If you want to try me, go ahead. But you know who I am. And you know I'm serious. Are you really that eager to stir the ire of Rome?"

Yachiel lowered his spear slowly. "Stand down." He looked at Longinus. "For now."

27

Longinus watched the man back down. Truth be told, he was a little disappointed Yachiel hadn't responded to his challenge. He'd never liked the pompous guard and would have felt no qualms at all over spilling the man's intestines into the street. He took Joseph's horse's bridle and led the animal forward, forcing the Levitical Patrol to part. After they'd traveled a small distance, he glanced up. "I'm sorry, Winemaker. I couldn't get to the Governor until minutes ago. From the look of things, I was almost too late."

"It was close," Joseph agreed. "But you came. And we thank you."

Longinus chuckled. "I doubt our good friend Davi the Jew thanks me."

Davi didn't smile. "Roman, I would have died if not for you. Which I suppose wouldn't have mattered all that much in the larger scheme of things. But Joseph has a child coming. So it's possible my opinion of Romans is softening somewhat."

Longinus nodded his salute. "You're welcome."

At the wide steps leading up to Pilate's residence, Joseph and Davi dismounted. Longinus passed the mounts to a waiting soldier. "Grass, grain, water, and a comfortable stable."

The man nodded and led the animals toward the side of the Fortress.

Joseph walked tall as he took the steps and, for the hundredth time, Longinus was impressed with the man's fortitude. He'd come within a second of dying, yet he moved with confidence and authority. Not an easy feat and a rare trait.

Joseph glanced at him, black eyes hard above that hawk nose of his. "How much did you tell Pilate?"

"Not much that he doesn't already know. He knows the Council wants you, and he knows why. What he believes, I couldn't tell you. But he says he'll hear you out."

"And send us straight to the Sanhedrin?" Davi said.

"I don't know, Pilate is a strange one. It's certainly a chance you take," Longinus said.

The wide reception hall sprawled. A couple of dignitaries Longinus recognized from Cyprus paused in their conversation to watch them pass. The winemaker paid them no mind. The door to Pilate's offices opened as they approached and a guard waved them through. "He's expecting you."

Longinus nodded and followed Joseph and Davi into the room. Pilate stood as they entered, uncoiling his long body from the cushion he'd been sitting on behind his low table. Procula sat in her corner, this time beneath the light of an oil lamp, working her needle and cloth. Her pale eyes met Longinus' for a brief second, and she nodded. Pilate beckoned Joseph forward and studied him for a few long seconds before speaking. "Joseph... I must say I was very surprised to hear from you."

"We've known each other a long while. I don't see why you should have been," Joseph said.

"The last time you were here, you asked for the body of the Nazarene."

"Not long ago. That's right."

Pilate stepped closer, eyes fixed on Joseph's face. "Not long ago, no. But much has happened since."

Joseph said nothing, his expression unwavering.

At length, the governor threw up his hands. "Bah! Let's not play games, Joseph, it's just us." He waved a hand in the general direction of the Temple. "Not Caiaphas. Not the rest of the lot.

Just us. Joseph, tell me the truth. Did you take that wretched body? If you did, simply say so. It's caused no end of grief."

"I did not."

"It's between us, Joseph, you have my word. You're saying you have no knowledge of what happened?"

"No, I'm not saying that. I'm saying I didn't take the body. No one took the body. Yeshua rose from the grave of his own accord."

Pilate glanced over at his wife. "Procula says the same. And I've heard the rumors. But really, Joseph, we're intelligent men! And you're a Sadducee! You don't even believe in angels, how can you believe this? How can you expect me to believe it?"

"I expect nothing," Joseph said. "Truth is truth, whether you, I, the Sanhedrin, or the goatherd down the street denies or accepts it. I say what I know. That's all."

"The Sanhedrin tells me you and his disciples took it."

"I did not."

"His disciples then."

"His disciples have been in fear for their lives. Not even daring to show their faces. Do you think they had the fortitude to go up against Rome? Your own soldiers guarded the tomb. Your own soldiers sealed it with iron."

"Yes, at the Sanhedrin's request because they feared this very thing."

"Think, Pilate. What did his followers have to gain? More persecution? This Cilician? The Council is covering, pure and simple."

Pilate shook his head. "A man rising from the dead? After a Roman beating and crucifixion? I stood beside him! The man was scourged to shreds. It's impossible."

"It's God, Pilate."

"Your god, not mine."

"There is but one God."

"Do you have any idea what kind of pressure this puts on me, Joseph? From the Priesthood? From Herod? All of them? I should be back in Maritima watching the sun set over the water and sipping a cup of your wine. But no, now Caiaphas and Beryl are terrorizing the streets of the city with their Cilician puppet. I can't stop him for fear of upsetting the Temple hierarchy, and, at the same time, I can't let him continue for fear of an uprising from the people." He clasped his hands behind his back and turned, pacing. "It really would be so much easier all around if someone would simply turn up a body for me. Just a body! I'd hoped it would be you. That's really the only reason I even agreed to see you, even though I know it will invoke the Council's displeasure." He stopped, lifted a cup off his desk, and gave a rueful smile. "You know, Joseph, your being wrapped up in all this very well might sabotage the one thing that makes this godforsaken outpost the slightest bit bearable—your wine. The Sanhedrin wants you dead. If they succeed in their desire, who's going to supply as fine a vintage?"

Joseph lifted a shoulder. "I think as long as there are both humans and grapes, there will be wine."

"Yes, but not your wine. I tell you, they talk about it even in Rome."

"I've heard that. I'm honored."

"So tell me, then, if you don't bring me a body to solve my problems, why do you come? I can't hold them off forever. Even now I suspect the Levitical Patrol are waiting at the door."

"I'm sure they are. And they'll kill me as soon as I walk out. But remember, all I did was stand up for an innocent man. You yourself said you could find no fault in Yeshua."

"I couldn't. But what was I supposed to do? I have one job, Joseph. One job! Keep the peace—can you imagine? They throw you into an ant pile of Jews and then add a garrison of Roman soldiers? How do you keep the peace with a recipe like that? Rebels in every crack in the hills… Incessant bickering over some coming messiah… And then Yeshua has to show up. I don't even care if it's his body! Just give me some poor bag of flesh that has generally the same size and shape. Anything! If the Sanhedrin wants to keep everyone playing guessing games, maybe I should too."

"I have no body to give you, Pilate. I'm telling you, Yeshua lives. But the wine? Maybe we can work something out about that."

Pilate paused his pacing. "At last, a drop of water on the brushfire. What might we be able to do about the wine?"

"It might be more than a drop."

"You have my attention."

"You just said yourself my wine's reputation has traveled all the way to Rome. I can get them as much as they like. Should the endeavor look promising enough, I'll even purchase the ships to transfer the product. And I'll sell at a more than reasonable price. Would this please your superiors?"

"It would. If it were possible."

"It's not only possible, I'm willing to offer you, personally, ten percent of the profits."

Pilate's eyes narrowed. "Ten percent? And what do you get out of this?"

"I get protection. I need a few good men."

"Protection from the Sanhedrin."

"Yes. I need enough time to get the wheels turning. That's all."

"I understand the Av Beit Din has taken control of all your holdings."

"Beryl is a squatter. He holds my wife and unborn child there and I'll stand for it no longer."

"You'd go up against the leaders of Israel over this?"

"Wouldn't any man?"

"No. Some, possibly. But they would also die."

Longinus hadn't noticed her move, but Procula was suddenly at her husband's side. She put a bone-white hand on his arm. "Do this thing, husband. It's as it should be."

Pilate looked down at her, his face a tangle. Then back at Joseph. "I'd be taking a great risk if I were to back you with the resources of Rome. But, then again, the grape harvest has been poor the last few years in the west. If I were to procure a regular supply of wine—especially wine like yours—it's the kind of thing that could make a man's career."

"Then we have a deal?" Joseph said.

"I ask you, Joseph, what guarantee do you give me you won't simply take your pregnant wife and fade into the hills? It seems to me, all the risk is mine."

Joseph pulled the leather satchel from his shoulder and dropped it to the floor with a metallic clunk. "Is gold a good enough guarantee? There are a few jewels as well. More than enough to pay for what I ask a hundred times over. Consider this collateral. If I fail to deliver what I promise, it's yours to keep. If you help me and I do deliver, you return it to me minus ten percent for your trouble."

"Plus the wine agreement in perpetuity."

"Of course."

Pilate knelt and examined the contents of the bag. "I suppose you know how much is here?"

"I do. Exactly."

Pilate looked again at his wife. He nodded. "All right, Joseph of Arimathea, you have your protection for as long as I can manage it. That's the best I can do."

"That's all I ask."

Pilate glanced at Longinus. "Longinus, you'll arrange this? As of now, I suspect all of the Council's venom regarding the empty grave will be directed at the grave's owner, who, with a bag of gold at my feet, presents a convincing argument that he is innocent of the accusations. I'll not have another death on my hands if I can help it. I have enough nightmares as it is. So try to keep him alive in as peaceful a fashion as you can."

Longinus threw Procula a glance. "It will be like walking on a high rope, but I'll do my best."

Pilate held up ten fingers. "Ten men—you have ten men at your disposal. No more. I don't want a war. It's simply a peace-keeping effort, understood?"

"I pick the men?" Longinus said.

"What do I care? Take who you want."

"Consider it done, Governor."

"Joseph," Pilate said, "may the God of Israel help you. And may he help me while he's at it."

"God will triumph," Joseph said. "But you have the gold. Either way, you win."

Pilate sighed and pursed his lips. "I understand how you would think that. Believe it or not, I have no desire to see you die at the hand of the Jews." He held out his hand.

Joseph clasped it with his own. "Thank you, Pilate."

In the main hall of the residence, Longinus told Joseph and Davi to wait while he made arrangements. He started for the Fortress. Even ten men would take a bit of time when they needed to be hand picked. If it came down to a fight, the

Levitical Patrol would probably outnumber them at least three to one, though he certainly didn't mind the math if he had the right men at his side.

Darkness blanketed the city by the time he returned. Joseph stepped out into the night, surveying the small contingency of Roman soldiers, one of them holding the two horses.

"No Levitical Patrol?" Joseph said.

Longinus lifted a shoulder. "We gave them the night off. I understand Caiaphas and Beryl tried to force their way into the meeting while we were in with Pilate."

Joseph nodded. "I expected as much. I'm glad they weren't successful. Where did Beryl go afterwards?"

"Home, I understand."

"My home."

"A very debated subject, I think," Longinus said.

Joseph pulled himself into the saddle. "Well, let's go end the debate."

28

Ariella watched her father from across the room. He sat there in Joseph's chair, his fat body hunched over one of Joseph's scrolls, a cup of Joseph's wine in his hand. She bit her tongue. Pointing out the obvious would only earn her a hard cuff on the ear or a backhand across the mouth. Her father had simply moved in and picked up where they'd left off before she'd married—treating her as he had when she was a child. All those years she'd both idolized and feared him, and now she found herself wishing he would die.

She rubbed her aching head. Her whole body hurt, down to her bones. She'd been having a hard time keeping food down. Yaffa assured her it was the pregnancy, completely normal, but Ariella knew it was more. She worried constantly about Joseph. Prayed for him without stopping. Even when her hands were busy with other tasks, her heart prayed all on its own. A life was growing within her, but another life had been cut away. And she felt the loss as acutely as if it had been an arm or a leg.

Her boredom finally got the best of her. "What are you reading?"

He looked up, eyes glassy with drink. "You wouldn't understand."

Her indignation overcame her fear of his fists. "And why wouldn't I? Because I'm a woman?"

"This is the written scripture. God breathed."

"I know what it is. You read the Prophet Jonah. I've read it myself many times."

His eyes glinted. "You've read? Don't be insolent. You're a woman. Maybe your husband tried to explain it, maybe you've heard the story in synagogue, but don't try to bait me."

"Joseph taught me to read."

"Did he? Did he also teach a pig to dance?" He turned back to the scroll with a shake of his head.

"What does the story of Jonah say to you?" Ariella said.

He drank from his cup and set it on the table. "It says that daughters should learn to keep their silence or be swallowed by a fish."

"Or be slapped or hit by one?"

"Why must you insist on provoking me?"

"Jonah is both a prophecy and a call to repentance."

He snorted a laugh. "You know nothing."

"*An evil and adulterous generation craves for a sign; and yet no sign will be given to it but the sign of Jonah the prophet…*"

His head came up. "What did you say?"

"Don't you remember the words? You were there when Yeshua spoke them, I believe."

"You speak nonsense."

"*For just as Jonah was three days and three nights in the belly of the sea monster, so will the Son of Man be three days and three nights in the heart of the earth. The men of Nineveh will stand up with this generation at the judgment, and will condemn it because they repented at the preaching of Jonah; and behold, something greater than Jonah is here.* You see, I do understand the prophet. And I understand Yeshua. Your pride blinds you."

He struggled to his feet, fists clenched.

She stood and faced him. "And so it continues. You attack truth with violence. You did it with Yeshua. You do it now. It's the only way you know. Well, go ahead. But know this, you will face the judgment of God!"

Her words stopped him. He stood there, mouth half open. "How do you know these words of Yeshua?"

"How do you not? You claim to study the Tanakh. You stare at scroll after scroll of scripture, but do you really read it? I think not. If you did, you would know the truth."

He shook his head. "You've been listening to Nicodemus' nonsense. I should have guessed."

"The prophets of God spoke nonsense?"

"Nicodemus pulls words out of context and fits them together to suit his purpose, nothing more."

"And what purpose is that? To be hunted like a rat in a cellar? To lose everything he has? To fear daily for the life of his wife and son, not to mention himself? Is that the glorious purpose you speak of?"

"Nicodemus always thought he knew more than everyone else. Now he's paying for his pride."

"No, father, you've turned your back on God."

He crossed the room toward her, raising his hand as he came. "I'm a Chief Priest, woman! How dare—"

It was then Ariella heard the marching.

Her father, distracted by the sound, lowered his hand. His mouth turned down. "Where are the Romans going at this hour? Don't they ever rest?" He fixed his glassy eyes on her again. "Go to your room. You sicken me."

"I'm not a child, and I won't be sent out of my own hall. Finish what you started if you've the stomach for it. But I'm not moving."

The marching stopped. Then a shout of challenge from one of her father's guards.

Then the sound of hooves!

Ariella rushed to the window in time to see her father's men backing away from five or six well-armed Romans. The hoofbeats sped up and Joseph and Davi clattered into the courtyard. Ariella turned to her father. "It's Joseph."

His eyes narrowed. "Good. He can die while you watch. Guards!"

"I believe they're preoccupied with the Romans at the moment," Ariella said.

"What on earth do the Romans have to do with it?"

"I suspect you might soon find out."

Even as she said it, the sound of the great entry door slamming open boomed through the house.

"Ariella?" Joseph's voice.

"Here!"

And then he was there. And she was in his arms. She sobbed, breathing him in. "Joseph…"

"I'm here."

"You have nerve, Joseph," her father said.

Joseph released her and turned to him.

"I should have killed you down in the hole and been done with it," her father said.

Joseph started for him, speaking not a word.

Her father backed up, lifting his hands as if to push his attacker away. "Guards!" His voice rose in pitch. "Joseph of Arimathea, you're under arrest by the order of the Av Beit Din! I demand—"

But then Joseph was on him. A sight Ariella would never forget for all eternity. With a quick hand, Joseph spun her father around. He grabbed two fistfuls of robe and half carried, half shoved her father toward the entry door. Her father tried to speak but only managed a desperate sputtering sound. Joseph passed into the entry hall, Ariella following. Avner stood at the door and smiled as he opened it. Down the wide steps and through the courtyard they went.

"Guards!" her father finally managed to shout.

Davi stood with the Romans at the courtyard gate, grinning. "Your men have been sent home, Beryl. If you can call them men. They were running last time we saw them."

Her father's wild eyes found the Romans. "Arrest this man! He's—"

But then they were at the gate. Joseph gave a mighty lift and shove, followed by a kick to the backside. Ariella put a hand over her mouth as her father sprawled on his belly in the middle of the street. He rolled over, a great pile of robes and fat and spit and hate. "You—"

"No, Beryl—you!" Joseph said. "Beryl of the Sanhedrin. Beryl, Chief Priest and Av Beit Din, you are a hypocrite and a liar and a mocker of the living God. You came to my home like a king. But you leave like what you actually are—a coward hiding behind his title, abusing his position for selfish gain. You'll never darken this door again, do you understand?"

Her father glared at the small group of onlookers who had gathered, then looked back at Joseph. "You're trespassing and assaulting a Chief Priest. You'll pay with your blood. I'll make sure of it. I'll see you on a cross!"

"May God judge between us, Beryl."

"The Sanhedrin will come for you. You will die and I'll be there to watch."

Joseph took a step back. "You tell them I'll be here. Now get up off the street, Av Beit Din, you're embarrassing yourself."

With that he reached up and swung the courtyard gate closed.

29

Though Sister paced the suite much of the night, Larcon never came. Nor had he come in the morning.

Or the afternoon.

Or the evening.

The woman, Amaris, ghosted in and out, ever attentive to Sister's smallest need, not that they were many.

What am I doing here?

Then again, why not here? Maybe Larcon would be a brute but hadn't she encountered brutes before? It was part of the life. And—she looked around the lavish room—when had she ever in her life lived like this? When had anyone she had ever known lived like this? She rose from the divan and walked out onto the long patio. The night was warm, the breeze a caress against her bare arms.

Amaris appeared, moving on those silent feet of hers. "Should I turn down the bed?"

She looked the woman up and down. "Why doesn't he come? Why did he bring me here if he's not going to come?"

"He'll come."

"When?"

"I don't know. No one really knows. He comes and goes."

"I don't understand. I'm not good enough now? Is that it?"

Amaris opened her mouth to speak, then shut it again.

"What is it?" Sister said.

"I know who you are…"

"Of course you know. I'm the woman Larcon won in a bet with my idiot brother."

"That's not what I meant."

"Then what did you mean?"

"I mean you were with the Followers."

Sister paused a beat. "What Followers?'

"Your secret is safe. I won't tell anyone."

"What do you know of the Followers?"

"I know you were with them for a few days. And I know you left in the night."

"Maybe I did. Why do you want to know about it?"

"You talked with Peter, then you left in the night. Why did you leave?"

Sister turned fully to the woman. "How in the world do you know this?"

That smile again. "Because I'm a Follower as well."

This stopped her. "You?"

"Yeshua's words changed my life. I heard him speak many, many times. Sometimes even just the two of us."

A twinge of unreasonable jealousy tugged. "You talked with him?"

"Yes. Did you do the same?"

"I heard him in the tavern. And a time or two on the streets in the Lower City. But never one on one. Unless…"

"Unless what?"

"Never mind. It's nothing."

The happy eyes clouded. "You're troubled. You can talk to me. It goes no further."

Sister started to turn away but found her feet rooted. This woman disarmed her and it was an uncomfortable feeling. Why should she talk about Yeshua? Even as the thought came into her mind, so did Yeshua's face. Not sad this time. But hopeful, beckoning.

She took a breath. "I never talked with him one on one, unless you count dancing for him."

It surprised Sister when the woman responded with a little burst of laughter. "You danced for him? What do you mean?"

A sharp retort formed on Sister's tongue. But looking at the woman's face, she knew no slight had been intended. Anger receded as quickly as it had come. Sister smiled herself. "I was a fool, I admit it. But my whole life, when I desired the attention of a man, I sought it with my body. Why wouldn't I think Yeshua would be the same? Now, thinking back, I can hear his words. He spoke gentleness and honor and goodness to the people in that room that night. What in the world was I thinking?"

Amaris' crooked smile was so infectious. "You weren't. But he spoke those things to you, as well."

"No. He spoke them *in spite* of me."

"It will be okay, Sister. Just talk to him when you see him."

"You do know Yeshua is dead, don't you?"

"No, he rose. He's alive."

"You can't really believe that. It's impossible."

"Is it? Weren't his miracles also impossible? And others were raised by him. Is the earth impossible? The stars and moon? Yet God spoke them into existence. To me, Yeshua rotting in a grave, that would be the impossible thing. God is Love, and he's chosen to love us through Yeshua. Yeshua is the Messiah of Israel."

"God is Love? I'm a Jew, just like you, and all I've ever seen of God is hypocritical men raising their hands to pray in the street and then using my body behind closed doors."

"But not all men."

"Enough of them."

"Still, you talk of men, not of God. You might as well talk of a stone rather than the stars."

"Why didn't God stop them then?"

"Are you mad at God? You had a choice to stay with the Followers, didn't you? They welcomed you. Yet you went back to your old life. And those same men you complain about. Is that God's fault?"

"I know what I am. So does God if he thinks of me at all. I don't blame him for anything, but I can't change what is."

"Of course you can. And he thinks of everyone. He thinks of us with love. I've heard Yeshua speak of this many times."

"I don't understand. You're a Follower. Why are you not in hiding with the rest?"

"I live with Larcon. It's a different kind of hiding. Not many would dare bother him. Now you're here too."

"It's not the same. I'm here because I'm a harlot, not a Follower."

"Your body has been safe enough in this place. Wouldn't you agree?"

"A temporary state only. The beast may walk through that door any minute."

"What if you went back to the Followers?"

"I could never really be with the Followers, no matter what the Roman thinks."

The happy eyes stilled. "The Roman?"

"A fool of a centurion. He's the one who took me to the Followers in the first place. To rescue me from my debauchery, I suppose. At first I thought he wanted what every other man wants, but he left me there."

"Then he doesn't sound like a fool to me."

Sister looked out over the city. "He's…a Roman."

"It sounds like he tried to do you a kindness. Kindness knows no nationality."

"He was kind, I suppose…in a quiet, irritating sort of way. He carried me over his shoulder, can you imagine?"

Amaris laughed. "From the tone of your voice just now, it sounds to me like your feelings for this man might not be limited only to irritation."

"I… No! None of it matters anyway. He dropped me with the Followers and I've not seen him again."

"Maybe you will."

"No. I belong to Larcon now. I'm here. I left the Followers. And even had I not, and if, as you say, Yeshua is alive, he would never want me with them. Not after what I did."

"Don't ever try to put your rationality onto Yeshua. Let me tell you something. Some time ago some of the scribes and Pharisees brought a woman to him. They wanted to trap him. She was an adulteress, caught in the act. They pushed the matter, demanded he condemn her. They wouldn't relent and they wouldn't retreat. They would have stoned her, *wanted* to stone her. But Yeshua looked at them and said, *He who is without sin, let him be the first to throw a stone at her*. What could they say? Which of us is innocent? I tell you, one by one they slunk away. By the Law of Moses they would have been justified in killing her. But Yeshua *embodies* forgiveness. Even on the cross—I was there and heard him with my own ears—*Father, forgive them, for they don't know what they're doing*. He said this about the very ones who were killing his body!"

"Killing his body…"

Amaris nodded. "His body, yes, not his spirit. And three days later, just as he said, body and spirit met again. A grave could never hold the Son of God."

"You really believe he's alive."

"Peter saw and talked with him. So did many others."

Sister knew the tiny hope-spark smoldering deep in her to be a dangerous thing. Even as a child, she'd learned to snuff it when it flared. If she allowed it to get too bright, it would burn her. It would scar and cause pain. She snuffed it now. "A woman like you can't possibly understand. You're kind. Good."

"Am I? Yeshua's words have been passed around among us. I love to remember them. Repeat them to myself. Once, he said, *Come to Me all who are weary and heavy-laden and I will give you rest. Take My yoke upon you and learn from Me, for I am gentle and humble in heart, and you will find rest for your souls. For My yoke is easy and My burden is light.* You don't have to worry about what Yeshua will think, no matter what you've done. I promise, Yeshua will love you because God loves you."

"He can't possibly."

"He's God's son. And God is Love. What's simpler?"

"No. God is Judge."

Amaris thought. "Yes, he is that as well. And yes, we're all guilty. But don't you see? Yeshua took our punishment. Yeshua paid our debt."

Sister looked out over the city, the smell of rain on the wind. Clouds filled with moonlight hung over the Temple. "You almost convince me, you know that? But hope will only hurt me. I know this."

Amaris leaned a hip against the low wall. "Sister, if you haven't already guessed, I was the woman pulled from a married man's bed by the Pharisees that day. And that man wasn't the first, far from it. They threw me into the dirt at Yeshua's feet like a piece of garbage. He could have turned his back, but he lifted me out of the dust and out of myself. I'll never go back. So I don't speak to you in hypotheticals. I speak from experience. Yeshua rescued me not only from those men but from myself. And he will rescue you, too, if you will only reach out your hand."

30

Beryl pulled the hooded robe tighter as he moved through the black Jerusalem streets. No priestly clothes now, just a colorless, shabby robe kept expressly for occasions such as this. He'd stopped at his small home only long enough to change. The place had smelled dusty and unused. By the time he'd left, it also smelled of the oil running down the wall from the clay lamp he'd smashed.

Joseph…

He limped into the night, favoring his left knee, bruised from Joseph's treatment. South through the Valley of the Cheesemakers and beneath the Zion Bridge. It was late and the streets were dark and empty. Most people slept. *Good.* He wanted no chance of being recognized. And a robe, no matter how old and shabby, could never disguise his bulk in daylight. Forward he shuffled, white anger fueling his tired muscles. There would be no rest tonight. Not until he accomplished what he set out to do.

He pushed on, past the grand theater and its surrounding shops and stands and down a narrow flight of steps, one of many time-worn routes descending into the Lower City from the Upper. A little farther and the stench of open sewer struck him. He covered his mouth and nose with his sleeve. Something moved across the street in front of him, cat or rat—it was too dark to tell. He kicked at it, missed, and almost fell. Light spilled through the open door of a tavern. A man spoke and another laughed. He avoided the place, turning left and skirting a small corral populated by a handful of donkeys and a smaller shadow that might have been a goat.

The path dropped and twisted and he hoped he wasn't lost. A few minutes later he caught an unmistakable whiff of moisture on the breeze. The Pool of Siloam must be close. It was said Yeshua had restored a blind man's sight there. *Isn't there anywhere or anyone in this city the Nazarene hasn't left his stink upon?*

He paused and leaned against a wall, catching his breath. What had happened to his city? What happened to order? With the coming of Yeshua, everything had descended into madness. Just off in the darkness was the tunnel King Hezekiah had built, over seven hundred years ago now, to bring water to the Pool of Siloam from the Gihon spring outside the walls in the Kidron Valley. Beryl had often explored it as a boy, sometimes pretending to be Joab out to decimate the dreaded Jebusites. Or sometimes he was King David arriving in triumph and fortifying the city against all who dared come against God's chosen people. The tunnel was still there, but childhood fantasy was gone. Now the battle was real, along with the blood.

And battle there would be. Joseph would finally die. Hopefully before the sun rose. At the very least, within days.

Joseph... The man had taken what rightly belonged to Beryl. Then thrown him into the street like a bucket of used dishwater. And people had seen it! Yes, Joseph would die a painful and slow death, and Beryl would soon be back in the luxury where he belonged. And maybe Ariella would actually bear a son. A boy that would be Beryl's own blood. Who would learn from his wisdom and follow in his footsteps.

But first Beryl would spit on his son-in-law's body. As surely as the sun would rise, Joseph of Arimathea would die.

Ten minutes later, the city wall loomed in the darkness. Beryl turned right and began to count windows and doors. When he reached the number he'd been told, he stopped and rapped lightly. A full minute passed before a light appeared in an upper window.

"What?" A man's voice came down.

"Open, I'm expected," Beryl said.

"Who are you?" the voice repeated.

"If I wanted to give you my name, I wouldn't be here, would I? Open, you imbecile!" Beryl hissed.

Another minute. Then two. Beryl was lifting his hand to knock again when a bolt slid and the door cracked.

"You have money?"

"I do," Beryl said. "Open, time is of the essence."

"Show me."

"Look at me. Do you know who I am?"

"Don't be stupid. If I did, would I have asked? Do you have money or not?"

Beryl rolled his eyes and fished into his purse. He came out with a handful of coins, counted, then poured them into the hand poking through the crack in the door. The hand receded, the coins jangled, then the hand appeared again.

"Double it."

"Double it?" Beryl said. "That was the price I was told."

"The price you were told didn't take into account the fact you weigh as much as a pregnant camel. Double it or be gone with you, I'm tired."

"I was told—"

"I don't care. The sun comes. Make up your mind."

With a sigh, Beryl fished again and dumped coins into the hand. The door opened.

"Come in if you can fit through the doorway." The man was scrawny and dirty. His thin, mouse-colored hair had receded to ebb tide, and the visible beach of skin scaly and scabbed. He waved a hand. "Follow then."

They passed through a filthy room and climbed a flight of stairs to another. Squalor everywhere. The odor of rotten food and feces overpowering. Two more men stood in the room, one large enough to make even Beryl feel dwarfed.

"I had to wake reinforcements," the scrawny man said, teeth shiny black nubs in the dim lamplight. "It's not often we have to lower an expecting camel."

"If you knew who I—"

"I know exactly who you are, Av Beit Din. But you're in our world now. The rules are different here. Now listen to me. The dawn comes in less than two hours. If you haven't finished your business by then, find a hole and hide in it until full darkness. Either that or enter through one of the gates. Although if you're here now, I don't suppose that's an option you want to explore. Now," he pointed at a window, "out you go."

Beryl bit his tongue. He needed these cretins for the moment, but their time would come. He would make sure of it. With the help of the bigger man, he climbed through the window and lowered himself into a waiting, suspended basket.

"Shalom," the scrawny man said. "And keep your purse handy for the return trip."

The basket began to descend down the outside of the city wall in stomach-lurching drops and jerks. At last the thing hit the ground, but at an uneven angle that spilled Beryl onto his back. Muted laughter rained down.

"Before dawn," Scrawny's voice said, and the basket disappeared up the wall.

Following a route long committed to memory , Beryl limped into the hills. In time he came to a narrow valley where broad piles of refuse smoldered in the starlight. The place reeked of garbage and death, but tonight the effect fit."

"Stop or die." The quiet and calm voice came from the darkness above. "Arrows are notched and ready."

"He knows me," Beryl said.

"So you say."

"Tell him the Av Beit Din is here."

This statement was answered with a long pause, then, "Tell him yourself, Sanhedrin."

From behind a large pile of refuse a monster emerged. He was massive. A giant worthy of David's sling. Long hair wild and matted, a tangle of knotted beard falling to his waist.

"Barabbas," Beryl said. "It's time to repay your debt."

31

Ariella opened her eyes, the bedchamber window a dark rectangle of predawn sky. For the hundredth time that night, she reached over and placed a hand on Joseph's slow-breathing form. She eased out of bed so she wouldn't wake him and moved to the window, the stone cool beneath her feet.

He's home and he's alive. Thank you, God, it wasn't a dream.

Below, she could just make out two Roman guards standing at attention on either side of the courtyard gate. She slipped through the door and made her way down the stairs to the first floor kitchen. The servants were still asleep and would be for a while. The room lay in deep quiet. Stoking the coals still glowing in the brick oven, she added a handful of fuel from the woodbox. When the flame burned high enough, she poured thin yogurt from a clay jar into a smaller cooking pot. She added a liberal amount of honey and a few mint leaves. When the liquid came to a simmer, she pulled it from the flame, poured it into two cups and carried them outside. The Romans looked surprised but not at all unhappy to see her and took the drinks with hesitant thanks. A Jewish woman offering a smile, let alone a cup, an unusual happening in the soldiers' lives.

She was headed back across the courtyard when a low voice stopped her. "You'll spoil them, you know." A man stepped down off the columned side-porch. He was at least as tall as Joseph. Very hard and wore the uniform of a centurion. "It's been a long time, Ariella."

Her memory sparked. "Longinus!"

"I'm surprised you remember my name."

"How could I forget?"

"He's had a bad time. And I'm afraid it will only get worse. He's home now, talk to him, keep him here. He's a stubborn man."

"I wouldn't have him any other way."

"He's lucky to be loved like that."

Something in the tough face pulled Ariella's heart. "Tell me, Longinus, is there a woman waiting for you somewhere?"

The weathered cheeks reddened, a strangely touching sight. "I've carried the Roman sword for almost fourteen years now. I've fought everywhere from Germania to Syria to lands without names. There have been many women. I doubt any of them wait. The life of a soldier is transitory."

"I suppose it would be."

"Your husband has been a friend. He talked to the governor and secured an early and honorable release for me. I'd be back in Corsica where I spent my boyhood by now, sitting on the porch of my own home and watching sea wind blow the grass. There would be a woman too, I think. At least there is when I dream of it."

"If he secured the release, why aren't you there?"

He shrugged. "Someone up the ladder got the idea into his head I'd been flirting with his wife. Instead of Corsica and the sea, I got a long trip leading a patrol of new recruits into the Negev."

"Was the man right? About his wife?"

A soft chuckle. "On that subject I make no comment except to say that perception often carries more weight than reality."

"And now you're still here in Jerusalem. How long?"

"Until my term is up, most likely. Two more years."

Ariella smiled, liking the man. "I know what you did for my husband. He would be dead but for you. More than once, I think."

"He's an exasperating man with a knack for putting himself in the middle of trouble. Which is probably why I like him."

"Tell me, what do you think will happen now?"

"Your Sanhedrin wants him dead. He's an embarrassment to them at this point. But they have no legal authority to kill him. Of course, if he was a person of little or no consequence, they'd simply take him outside the city walls and have him stoned. Rome usually turns a blind eye to these things. But Joseph being Joseph, to be safe they'd have to make the request of Pilate. And your husband has already circumvented them on that front."

"He embarrassed my father. And my father isn't one to take a slight. You'll continue to help him?"

"As much as I can. You Followers are an interesting conundrum. Odds are you'll all be in prison or killed before this is over. But I've fought on the wrong side of the odds many times."

"Followers… They give us this name as if we're no longer Jews. As if we're outsiders."

"There are a handful of Romans in the garrison who believe in Yeshua as well, though they'd probably not admit it out loud. Your Nazarene has made quite an impact not only in Jerusalem but beyond."

"And will continue to," Joseph said, approaching. "Longinus, my wife is beautiful and off limits."

Longinus smiled. "Of course she is, Winemaker. Though you'd better appreciate this woman, or I just may drag her off to Corsica."

"Joseph, your best robes?" Ariella said. "Where are you going? You know it's not safe for you anywhere in the city."

Joseph nodded in the direction of the Temple Mount. "They'll arrest me as soon as they have the chance. I know this time we have is borrowed. But I won't sit here and wait while this Cilician terrifies Jerusalem. I'm going to them."

"To what purpose?" Ariella said.

"To try and stop the bloodshed."

"It's not wise, Winemaker," Longinus said.

"Not wise, maybe, but I think it's right."
"You're acting the fool," Longinus said.
"But fools love company, don't they?"
Longinus sighed. "All right. Let's go."

32

Longinus left six men to stand guard over Joseph's home and took four along. The Temple Guard would be on the Mount, of course, and Levitical Patrol in numbers as well, but with Pilate holding things at bay, Longinus was betting on the hope that any Roman presence at all would be respected enough to keep peace.

The rest was up to Joseph.

"You know, it's interesting," Longinus said. "Not many days ago there was a Jew claiming to be the Messiah on every corner in Jerusalem. Not a single one to be seen now. Funny what one old-fashioned crucifixion will do."

"They'll be back," Joseph said. "The lure of power is too strong to resist for long."

"Not to mention shekels they strip from the people," Davi said.

"One provides the other," Joseph said.

Longinus scratched his face. He needed a shave. "There are similar games played in Rome. And any place else in the world where people gather and live. So it has always been, and so it will always be."

"What I don't understand is what you hope to accomplish by accosting the Council today, Joseph," Davi said. "Protect what's yours, yes, I'll stand with you all the way. But to walk into trouble makes no sense."

"The Followers can't show their faces for fear of the Cilician and the Patrol," Joseph said. "These are good Jews who don't deserve such treatment. It's wrong. If the Council won't call off their wolf, then at least I can show them for the cowards they are before the people. With the possibility of upsetting Pilate and Rome, the Sanhedrin may keep its claws in."

"You have more faith in Rome than I do," Davi said.

They crossed the Zion Bridge and entered Solomon's Porch without incident. It wasn't until they passed from Porch to Stoa that a shout rang out and several of the Temple Guard rushed forward, spears leveled. Longinus pushed Joseph to the side and drew his sword as he moved forward to meet the threat. At the sight of the Roman, the guards slowed, then stopped just outside the range of Longinus' weapon.

"This man is under the protection of the Governor," Longinus said. "Stand down."

One of the Guard, a thick man with a wide, blunt face glowered. "You have no jurisdiction here. This man is wanted by the Council."

"The Governor represents Tiberius Caesar, and Tiberius Caesar has jurisdiction anywhere he says he has jurisdiction. I'm charged with protecting this man. Do you want blood spilled on your holy hill? Because spill it I will."

"No, they don't." Joseph strode past Longinus, pushed the spears away like they were no more than curtains and walked on.

Longinus smiled at the guard. "I suppose that answers that."

"You defile this place," the blunt-featured man said.

"If I were a lesser man, I might take offense at your rudeness. And trust me, brother, that would not end well for you."

"Maybe one day soon we'll see," the man said. "You'll not always have power here. Rome's bravado is nothing but political talk."

Longinus tapped the man's spear with his sword. "I think there are a million corpses on battlefields across much of this earth that would argue with you if they still had tongues." He pushed the spear aside and followed Joseph. As they approached the gathered Council, he stopped and held up a hand for his men to do the same. He turned to Davi. "We let Winemaker do what he must but stay close enough to step in if needed."

"Agreed," Davi said. "But I don't trust Beryl no matter what comes out of that grave he calls a mouth. I'll keep sword in hand."

"I'll do the same. If we fight, we fight together."

The tough little Jew nodded.

"Aside!" Joseph boomed up ahead. "Aside and let me through!"

Council members grumbled and turned. Eyes widened when they saw who approached. A roar went up.

"Aside!" Joseph repeated.

The group of men parted like he carried a disease.

Joseph didn't stop until he was five feet from Caiaphas and Beryl. A few of the Temple Guard moved quickly to form a line behind the High Priest, hands on sword hilts.

"Do you fear harm from me, Caiaphas? "Joseph said.

Caiaphas, sitting, considered Joseph with practiced condescension. After a long pause, he said, "Desperate times tend to bring out desperate actions in desperate men. I'm the leader of Israel, am I not? Concern for my safety comes with the territory. I presume you've come to turn yourself in?"

"You presume wrong."

"I see your Romans back there. And I've heard from Pilate that you're under his protection. The reason for your boldness today, I imagine."

"Imagine what you like. I come to deal in truth, not imagination," Joseph said.

"I'd call it stupidity before I'd call it boldness," Caiaphas said. "You come to die."

Joseph ignored the High Priest and turned to the Council. He spoke loud enough for his voice to carry through the busy Stoa and across the Court of the Gentiles below. "I tell you all today, in the presence of witnesses, what you already know. Yeshua, who you have called a wicked man, who you have claimed posed a threat to good Jews, was, in fact, the very best Jew. How many of the sick did he heal? And what did he ever ask in return? Did any one of you ever hear Yeshua teach hate? No, he taught love at every turn, even love toward those who persecute you. He called hypocrites to repentance and the broken to peace. He loved everyone who came to him without exception. He kept the Law of Moses to perfection!" He waved a hand. "I ask you, has any man here done the same? Has any man here even come close? Was putting Yeshua to death an act of love? Or was it the epitome of hate, jealousy, and fear? Are these the traits of righteous men? I tell you, when you murdered Yeshua the Nazarene, you not only killed a man innocent of any wrongdoing, you put to death the promised Messiah of Israel."

Out beyond the group, the curious gathered.

"The Romans crucified the Galilean," one Sanhedrin member said. "Take it up with Pilate."

"*His blood shall be on us and on our children...* I was there, Shabtai. Do you forget? You stood not ten feet away from me and I heard you say this myself. You were shouting as if you'd lost control of your senses. And maybe you had. How else can you account for this action?"

"It's done. The matter has been discussed and put to rest," Caiaphas said.

Joseph shook his head. "What exactly have you discussed? Have you discussed the earth shaking beneath our feet at the moment the Son of God took his last breath?"

"As I've said before, a natural phenomenon."

"Was it? How about midday turning to night at the same time? And how often is the Temple veil torn from *top to bottom*? When in the history of Israel have the graves opened and people walked out of them?"

"Rumors and rantings," Caiaphas said. "All things have an explanation if one chooses to see."

"No. Death could not hold him, Caiaphas. Yeshua himself quoted the psalm of our father David who prophesied of that very hour: Surrounded by Gentiles! Hands and feet pierced! Crucified! Right down to lots being cast for his clothes. You can't deny the Word of God. Nicodemus tried over and over to warn you! Prophecy after prophecy he brought to you as God opened his eyes and spirit through the Tanakh until he could actually tell you in advance what would happen next. But you wouldn't listen. Try as we might, you ignored the truth! And now—"

"And now his disciples have stolen the body!" Caiaphas shouted. "Enough of your games! You only confuse the issue."

Joseph glanced out and estimated at least a few hundred people gathered in the court below. "Is it a game when your Cilician and the Levitical Patrol slaughter good Jews?"

Caiaphas looked uncomfortable at the mention of the Cilician. The first crack in the stoic shell Joseph had seen.

"What good Jews?" the High Priest said. "Apostates. Enemies of the Temple!"

"No," Joseph said. "Lovers of God. Lovers of our fathers. Lovers of Israel. Keepers of the feasts and the Law. Good Jews who recognized God's gift with joy and gladness. Faithful people who want nothing but to live in peace and love their neighbors. Every day this body is guilty of persecuting good, practicing Jews."

Caiaphas stood. "If Yeshua was truly the Messiah, and if he walked out of the grave after a Roman crucifixion, then where is he? Everyone knows the true Messiah will crush the Romans. Yeshua is gone and Rome is still here."

Joseph took a half step forward. "If you would read the list of prophecies Nicodemus and I compiled, you would—"

"You both had your chance to convince us and you failed to do so. You're still fools following a fool's fantasy."

"It wasn't our responsibility to convince you. The scriptures were given to all of us. You're the leaders of Israel, yet you use God's word only for your own gain. Have you no fear?"

"We know the scriptures," Caiaphas said.

"If that were true, you would have known God's Son!" Joseph turned a slow circle. "There are those of you here today who know this! You believed in Yeshua as well. Was it easier to turn your back on truth to save yourselves? Shame on you! I call on all of you now to stop this shameful persecution of your own brothers and sisters. If you refuse, may God judge you!"

"No!" Caiaphas said. "We will judge you, Joseph. Because that is our duty and our right. Are we children to be frightened by your tales of open graves and walking corpses? You're as insane as the Nazarene was. And you will suffer his same fate."

"Possibly. That's up to God. But though He slay me, I will hope in Him."

"You quote our father Job? Even now?" Caiaphas said.

"Whether I die in the near or distant future, that's yet to be seen. But when I do, I'll stand before God, knowing that I fought for truth. Will you do the same?"

"We serve God. You do not. Without Pilate's protection, you would be dead even now. But it won't last long, be assured."

"I ask you one last time. Will you call off the Cilician?" Joseph said.

"And I'll tell you one last time, until every one of the Followers either recants, bleeds, or rots in prison, the Cilician will not rest."

33

To live in Jerusalem was to understand contrast. From the gleaming white-gold of the Temple to the dusty grime of the Lower City alleyways. The horrible heat when the late summer winds whipped off the Arabian deserts and tumbled across Judea, to the cold hand of winter turning Zion's streets slick with ice. A city of peaks and valleys, both figuratively and literally. Past Moriah and the Temple, the Mount of Olives climbed, the little village of Bethany just out of sight on the other side. And even farther east, across the Judean Mountains, the Dead Sea and the deserts. To the west, across the rolling hills and cut canyons, a vast and very living sea, the gateway to the world the Romans called *Mare Nostrum—Our Sea*.

Sister had never laid eyes on a sea herself, dead or living, in her life. In fact, before Larcon had sent for her, she could have counted on her fingers the number of times her whole body had been immersed in water. But now that had changed. Deep in the bowels of Larcon's home—if that's what this was, she was starting to wonder—Amaris had shown her a deep and apparently forgotten *mikveh*.

"No one comes here, and the water runs fresh all the time," the woman had said.

For Sister, the sensation of weightless suspension seemed a miracle. The first day she'd come, she'd spent an hour slipping under the water and stretching her body out flat until she thought her lungs would burst. She'd rise, pull in great gulps of air, then do it over again, the water cold silk against her skin. Amaris bobbed and floated as well, delighted to have introduced something novel and new. It was a secret, torchlit place of private dreams, the tinkle and splash of water echoing like laughter off the stone.

The women had talked much over the days and a wondrous question began to form in Sister's mind.

Do I have a friend?

Still, a constant and hard warning sounded within her. Trust didn't come easy, but something about Amaris disarmed, and bit by bit she found herself opening to the woman. Amaris talked constantly of Yeshua, the things he'd taught, or even just said in passing. About how the children would gather to him and how he'd spend hours laughing and playing with them. How he had stood up against the priests and scribes and, with bold authority, called them out for their hypocrisy. How he'd driven the vendors and moneychangers from the Temple Mount with a leather scourge and then risen early in the morning with his disciples just to sit in silence to watch God paint the eastern sky with color and light. Through Amaris' stories, Yeshua's words washed over Sister, cool and clean as the mikveh water. But later, alone in the darkness waiting for the elusive Larcon, the voice would find her, taunting, whining, accusing. She would remember Yeshua's sad eyes as she'd danced in the tavern and the anger she'd felt when she couldn't break through to him.

Yeshua...

"Sister..." Amaris sat next to her on the mikveh step, water streaming from her hair.

"Yes?"

"Open your heart."

Sister looked at her. "What?"

"Everything is changing. The world is changing. Open your heart. This voice you tell me you hear in the darkness is a liar. Why do you think it comes to you in the dark? Come to the light. Open your heart."

Something in her face. Sister couldn't bear to disappoint the woman who had become a possible first and only friend. "I'll try, I will."

That smile. "Good. Let's go up."

"Already?" But the woman had already robed and was headed up the stairs.

Sister paused when she saw the door to her quarters was ajar. Amaris glanced back, still smiling, before entering. Sister followed. A man stood on the balcony overlooking the city. He turned as the women entered. The wiry little handler who had brought Sister the first night.

"Oh, it's you," she said.

The handler glanced at Amaris. "Such a warm welcome. Tell me, did she ever run out of words?"

Amaris smiled. "Don't be so cranky."

The man turned his attention back to Sister. "Who did you expect? King Herod?"

"Larcon, of course. Don't be dense."

"Then you expected right."

"What is that supposed to mean?"

"I'm not the one being dense. You expected Larcon," he put his hands out, "and Larcon is here."

"Please. I saw Larcon at the tavern. He wasn't you."

"No, you saw Dov. He works for me. A very handy person."

"You expect me to believe you're the great Larcon who sends fear into Jerusalem hearts?"

"What you believe or don't believe is of no concern to me."

"But you said—"

"No. *You* said. All you did was say, if I remember right. From the time we left your brother's little hovel until I dropped you here with Amaris, you talked." He cupped a hand to his mouth. "Dov!"

The side door opened and the big man with the bad teeth from behind the tavern stuck his head in. "Yes?"

"Are you Larcon?"

The man's eyes narrowed in confusion. "No, I don't think so."

"Who are you then?"

"Dov?"

"Correct, now shut the door." He turned to Sister. "Not the brightest star in the night, but he's consistent."

Sister crossed her arms in front of her. "All right, so the dreaded Larcon finally comes to claim his property."

Larcon straightened his tunic and put his hands behind his back. "Sister, this isn't what you think it is."

"Then why are you here?" she said.

"For me."

Sister had almost forgotten Amaris was still in the room. "What?"

Amaris walked over and took Larcon's arm in hers. "He's here for me. Larcon is my husband."

Sister stared at the two. "I don't understand. Then why am I here?"

"Because he wants you here," Larcon said.

"What? Who is this *he*? Are you telling me you have a boss?"

Larcon smiled. "I wouldn't call him a boss. More of an acquaintance. But when he asks a favor, one does it. It's generally the safer path."

"What interest could anyone possibly have in me?" She lifted her chin. "I'd like to go home now. Will you arrange it, please?"

"No, he won't…"

She turned. The Roman stood in the apartment doorway.

34

"You?" Sister said.

"Me." He strode into the room.

"Are you a criminal as well then?"

"He's simply a man with influence in many arenas," Larcon said. "So mind your tongue. You'd do well to stay on his good side."

She shook her head, eyeing the Roman. "Why am I here? Why didn't you simply come to the tavern?"

The Roman shook his head. "I took you to the Followers and you snuck off. If you won't choose what's best for you on your own, then someone needs to do it for you."

"What business is it of yours?"

"I've made it my business."

"You don't know me. So you can't know what's best for me."

"I know enough."

Sister felt the blood coming to her face. "What right do you have to manipulate my life?"

He shrugged. "None. Except for the fact I can. And am. And I'll continue to do so."

She didn't even realize she'd slapped him until she felt the sting in her palm. She cringed, waiting for the return blow.

Instead, his laugh sent her anger level even higher. "Roman dog! You have no right to my life. I ask you again, why am I here?"

Longinus ran his fingers through his hair and sank into a chair, stretched and crossed his legs in front of him. "Amaris, have you any wine?"

"Of course." Amaris retrieved a pitcher and cups from a long sideboard. She poured for Longinus and Larcon both.

Longinus drank long and sighed. "You know, Sister, I'm always amazed at how quick you Jews are to use the word dog, the greatest of insults to you, I think."

"I may be a harlot, but I'm still a Jew," she said.

"No," Longinus said, allowing Amaris to refill his cup.

"What do you mean, no?" Sister said.

"You're no longer a harlot, and I'll not have you use the word again. When I took you to the Followers, you had a chance to choose. You ended up choosing wrongly. Now I'm choosing for you. Your body belongs to you and your God. Your past is now exactly that—the past."

She turned to Amaris. "And you! Why did you say nothing of this? And why are you smiling? Do you find this amusing?"

"I'm smiling because I love you. And because Longinus is right. You deserve better than the scrap of a life your brother let you have."

"I deserve… You knew this all along? You pretended to be my friend!"

"I never pretended anything. I am your friend. They told me not to speak of any of this."

"But why?"

"Would you have stayed if you knew? Or would you have run back?"

Sister hesitated. "I don't know," she admitted. "But a Gentile? A Roman? You take his orders?"

"I did," Amaris said. "Because it was the right thing to do. And he's a man, not a dog. Shame on you. Did you know Yeshua himself healed the servant of a centurion just like Longinus in Capernaum? And Yeshua called him a man of great faith."

"Fabianus. I know the man," Longinus said.

"Yeshua again…" Sister looked at Larcon. "Did you know this wife of yours was a Follower?"

"As am I," he said

"You? You're the worst criminal in Jerusalem! How can you say this?"

"What can I say? I've lived a wicked life. There was a time I would kill a man with no more tug of conscience than swatting a fly. But Yeshua is Yeshua. He saw past it all and welcomed me with open arms. And I'll serve him with my dying breath."

"It may come to that," Longinus said. "This Cilician is dangerous. Five men and a woman were stoned last night outside the Damascus gate. Many others have been dragged off to prison."

Larcon set his wine cup down. "There was a time not long ago when even the Sanhedrin would have stayed clear of me. And maybe they still will, but should anyone look behind the veil, they'll quickly see that other than a faithful few, my men are gone. Those that are left are Followers themselves." He glanced at Amaris. "My position is weakening. I've not paid expected bribes in over a year and unwelcome eyes are starting to look my way. It may be time for us to get out of the city."

"You're my husband," she said. "Where you go, I go."

"I'll arrange it. I have connections in Caesarea Maritima. And there are Followers there."

Sister stared at Longinus. "You're a Roman. If you people didn't invent licentiousness, you at least perfected it. I don't understand this. Why do you care what I do?"

"Because I do."

"Are you a Follower too, then?"

"As you seem to love to point out, I'm Roman. I'm sure the God of the Jews has little concern for me."

"You're wrong about that," Amaris said.

Longinus gave a slight shake of his head. "The Jewish Messiah is for the Jews. All say so."

Amaris put a hand on Larcon's arm. "What will happen to Sister if we go to Caesarea Maritima?"

"I'll go home," Sister said.

"She'll stay with me." Longinus' eyes were blue ice. She hadn't noticed the color before.

"Do I not have any say in this at all?" she said.

"Even if you wanted to go back, there's no place there for you now," Longinus said.

"What's that supposed to mean?"

He lifted a shoulder. "Your brothers are enjoying retirement. They no longer own the tavern."

She stared at him. "What retirement? What are you talking about?"

"They've a little gold now. Not that they deserve it. Maybe they'll be smart and find a nice place by the sea. More likely they'll drink and gamble it away. It's up to them. I care not."

"Whose gold?"

"Mine."

"You bought them out?"

"Not really. Fishel lost the tavern on a single dice roll. And they happened to be my dice."

"Honest dice?"

Longinus smiled. "Fishel could have checked them. Even so, I still gave the toad a pocketful of gold. Not that he deserved it, mind you. But they're your brothers, after all, and family is family."

"My family, not yours!"

That hard smile. "That will change soon enough. I still can't explain it, even to myself, but once you calm down, I have every confidence you'll make a fine wife. God help me."

35

Joseph watched the shadow of the Temple grow across the Kidron and up the Mount of Olives. One by one, it overtook the burial caves scattered across the slope, light to shadow as the sun dropped in the west. From the Arimathea house, brilliant sunsets could be seen far away over the water, but here in Jerusalem all the best views centered on the Temple. And the panorama from Joseph's Jerusalem balcony was one of the best. He'd missed it.

Joseph turned from the balcony edge and walked back beneath the vine-covered pergola that covered much of the rooftop. Nicodemus sat at a wide table, several open scrolls in front of him. "I'm glad your collection wasn't damaged, Joseph. It really is impressive."

"I imagine the safest place for a scroll would be in the same room as Beryl. I can't picture him working up the mental energy to unroll one."

"If only he would. Look." Nicodemus leaned far over the table and pointed to a passage. *I gave My back to those who strike Me, and My cheeks to those who pluck out the beard. I did not cover My face from humiliation and spitting.*

"Isaiah," Joseph said.

e List was conclusive enough before to prove Yeshua was the Sent One. But look how many more prophecies were fulfilled through the last week of his life. And then his resurrection. If only we had understood long ago. We could have spoken up so much sooner."

"They wouldn't have heard, I'm convinced. You should have seen their faces when I went to them about the Cilician. Unyielding as stone. They were like bodies without souls. God's plan is a great and powerful river. Who are we to think we could have diverted its course?"

"Yes, but still… Possibly more would have believed. We could have done something."

"It's in the past now. It's the future that matters."

"I just don't understand how any reasonable being couldn't see."

Joseph sank onto a cushion, wincing slightly over his still-sore ribs. He picked up a cup and swirled the liquid in it without drinking.

"What bothers you, my friend?" Nicodemus said.

Joseph set the cup down. "I don't understand what Yeshua is doing. People are dying. Others in prison. Still others beaten. Why isn't he here? What is he waiting for? Why did he have the disciples meet him in Galilee at all? Why not take his rightful place on the throne as the King of Israel? Honestly, when Caiaphas asked this very same question at Council, I had no answer. Yeshua's absence only adds veracity to the stolen-body story. The grave is empty yet darkness still wins! What's going on?"

"God is going on, Joseph. I confess it confuses me as well. All of us. But there must be a purpose. We have to wait and see what it is."

Joseph leaned on an elbow, stretching his feet to the side. "What choice do we have?"

"Ah, Joseph, my friend. It's good to study together again. You do spur me."

"It's good for me too. Though I worry about you walking about the city."

"I've not been noticed, and I'll continue to trust. There are
many who need to hear the scripture. They're confused and
afraid."

Joseph waved a hand. "Well, thanks to Pilate, this house is
safe for the moment. Why don't you just stay here?"

"I'm needed in the valley. Many gather there. Yeshua said
he would send a comforter, but no one knows who that is. And
so far the scriptures are silent. For now, The List helps them.
They are good people, Joseph. Good Jews. Faithful both to
Yeshua and the Torah."

"There will be more suffering, I'm afraid."

"Yes."

"He has to come soon."

Nicodemus frowned down at his folded hands.

Avner appeared in the doorway at the top of the stairwell.
"Longinus to see you, sir."

"Of course."

Longinus swept past Avner, the red cape of rank swinging
behind him. Ariella followed him, along with another woman.
He approached the low table, pulled his *pugio*—the long,
straight, dagger favored by the Romans—from its sheath, leaned
down and speared a peach and a piece of hard cheese. He bit into
the peach without removing it from the knife and wiped his chin
with the back of his hand.

"Help yourself," Joseph said.

"Thank you, I will." He sank to a cushion and poured a cup
of wine. "I wanted to let you know, you have a new house guest.
I need her safe and with my men here, this is the best place for
now."

Joseph nodded, eyes shifting to the woman "You're more
than welcome. I'm Joseph, my wife is Ariella, who it looks like
you've already met, and this is—"

"Sister and I are acquainted," Nicodemus said. "It's good to
see you again."

Whether the curve of the woman's lips spoke trouble or
simply mischief was hard to tell. "I'm surprised you don't
remember me, Joseph of Arimathea. After all, we shared a bed.
At least for a moment."

"Joseph?" Ariella said, looking back and forth between the two.

The scene crept into Joseph's consciousness, although the edges were hazy. "You're the woman from the tavern… The one who hid me. I'm sorry, I don't remember much of it."

Ariella took the woman's arm. "That was you? Longinus told me the story. It seems we owe you a great debt of gratitude. Thank you for saving my husband."

The woman leaned slightly away from Ariella's touch. "It's the Roman you should thank. I did nothing, really."

"Longinus knows my gratitude," Ariella said. "You shall as well. Our home is your home for as long as you like."

"But you don't even know me."

"Of course I know you. You're Sister and I'm Ariella. You helped save my husband and I'm forever in your debt."

Joseph glanced at Nicodemus, then back to the woman. "Are you a Follower then?"

Sister sighed and offered a ghost of a smile. "The only person I seem to follow is this Roman to every corner of Jerusalem. But you speak of Yeshua. I hear much, but at the moment I don't see him anywhere, so how can I follow him?"

"You will," Nicodemus said.

Ariella suggested taking Sister down and having a room prepared for her. Though hesitant, Sister followed. When they were gone, Longinus poured a second cup of wine and emptied half of it in a drink. He eyed Joseph and Nicodemus. "She's had a hard time of it."

"That much is obvious," Joseph said. "She's broken, and you hope to mend her."

Longinus' let out a slow breath and leaned back. "I don't know what I hope. But somehow I understand it's a task that's been put before me. Life has crushed her, yet she still has spirit. Her strength is remarkable. *She's* remarkable."

"She's more than welcome here for as long as you deem prudent," Joseph said. "My home is your home, my friend."

"Thank you, Winemaker." Longinus bit into the peach and chewed. "Joseph, I need you to be careful."

"Is this about Sister?" Joseph said. "Why do you say this?"

"Not Sister. My men have seen Barabbas several times now. He walks by the gate in broad daylight. He doesn't even bother to hide himself."

Joseph considered. "Then he moves with the authority of the Council."

"I doubt that," Nicodemus said. "At least not all of the Council. But I certainly don't put it past Beryl."

Joseph nodded. "The two have history. Beryl wants me dead and Barabbas would love to do the job. The perfect pair."

Longinus emptied his cup. "Not just dead, Winemaker. I know much of Barabbas. What he would do to you would make killing look like a mercy."

36

When the night had come in full and the Upper City windows had all gone dark, Longinus stood in the black shadow of a doorway across the boulevard from Joseph's home. He was good at waiting. He'd honed his watch skills on battlefields all across the frontier. An old general had once said patience could very well save a man's life as often as a sword. That bit of offhand advice had served well over the years, and Longinus held to it now. He leaned against a wall, not moving a muscle except for his eyes which, try as he might to tame them, kept glancing up at the only lamplit window in Joseph's home. Sister's room. He knew this because he'd checked in on her before he'd left, not that she'd seemed to appreciate it. He mentally cursed himself. *What's the matter with you? You know better than this.*

It was true. While patience could save a soldier's life, getting distracted by a woman could get him killed. He no longer had only himself or his men to worry about. Not that there hadn't been women, but this woman… There was strength in her, true strength. But there was deep damage too. And it hurt him to see it.

You're getting old and sentimental.

But not so old. He'd joined the army at twenty, out of necessity. A middle son from the middle class, the army was the expected path. He'd thought of trying to make a go of it on his home island of Corsica, but fishing, farming, it all seemed so small. Now, almost fourteen years later, he'd seen war on more fronts than he cared to remember. The sword at his side had parted a hundred souls from as many bodies. Maybe the fact should bother him like it did many in his position. Some soldiers claimed they dreamed of the dead. Longinus never did.

At least he hadn't until Yeshua had come.

He'd been present at the beating and a tremendous beating it had been. The kind only the Romans could inflict. By the end, there'd been hardly anything left of the man. And man he was! He'd taken the punishment with stoic strength that stirred deep respect in Longinus. And deep regret.

And now he dreamed.

At night on his mat he saw those eyes. Eyes nearly swollen shut and so blood infused they were the color of raw meat. Eyes forced to gaze out from that cross over the crowd of tormentors and mockers and heartsick disciples. *It is finished*… the man had said. What did it mean? A finalized life, yes, but there had been something much deeper in Yeshua's tone. And now Longinus heard the words in his dreams.

The night passed. Only starlight now. He smelled the giant before he heard him. Old sweat and rotten food, just the faintest touch on the air. His hand went to his sword hilt.

"You might as well step out, Roman. As good a time to die as any other, don't you think?"

So much for surprising the beast. Longinus stepped out of the doorway. Moonlight played across the alley. Barabbas was every bit as large as Longinus remembered. The man was a tree. His hair long and matted. His knotted beard hung nearly to his waist. The sword he held was meant to be used two-handed, but he seemed more than comfortable using one.

"The house is guarded," Longinus said.

The giant squinted in that direction. "How long will you Romans trample our country? The time for retribution is coming, Gentile."

Longinus laughed. "Your country? You kill these people for pleasure. You take what you want at will, from Gentile or Jew. Our being here simply gives you an excuse to be who you really are. A killer of women and children."

Barabbas scratched at his beard and shrugged. "I've killed my share of them. But I've killed men too. And not a few Romans."

"And now you're here to kill Joseph of Arimathea."

"He killed my nephew. I owe him a blade. He should have been split long ago."

"If he killed your kin, it was only trying to escape your attack. You kidnapped *him*, if you'll take the time to remember. You have a warped sense of justice, I think. Like the grin on your face when you walked free and an innocent man took your place on a cross."

The big man shrugged. "What can I say? Only that God's will was done."

"A word of advice. Leave the winemaker alone and go find another hole in the hills. Faraway hills. This will not end well for you."

Barabbas took a quick step forward. He grinned when Longinus did the same. "You meet my charge? You've courage, Centurion. I'm glad, you'll die well." He swung a wide loop with his sword and Longinus parried, the clang of steel on steel ringing into the night.

Heavy footsteps sounded from across the street, heading their way.

Barabbas cast a glance into the darkness. "Your men?"

"I told you the house was guarded."

"Maybe you get to live through the night then. But soon you'll bleed. So much to look forward to, isn't there? You, the Arimathean, and best of all, that pretty wife of his. The woman walks through my dreams."

"I'll tell you what, stand and I'll have my men hold back. It will be just the two of us. You can dream in your grave."

"I'd take the word of a Gentile?" The spit on Barabbas' rotten teeth glistened in the moonlight. He backed away, sword still pointed. "Tell me, who was the woman you brought here today? Maybe tonight I'll dream of her instead."

Longinus started forward but the giant was several feet away now.

"Stand and fight," Longinus said.

"Soon enough, don't worry."

Longinus pressed on but the giant was gone. Only shadow where his body had been, vanished into the alley ink like a ghost.

37

Caiaphas' palace in the Upper City wasn't a long walk. Still Joseph felt grateful to be flanked by Longinus and five of his men, leaving the other five to guard the house. People on the street stared as the contingency passed. A few nodded at Joseph but most avoided his gaze.

He hadn't been in Caiaphas' courtyard since Yeshua's trial, and as they entered and climbed the wide steps, his stomach churned at the memory. Several of the Levitical Patrol stood on the landing beside the tall double-entry door. They bristled visibly at the sight of the Romans.

"I'll go in alone," Joseph said. "I think you and your men might be better positioned for trouble out here."

"My men, yes. But I go in with you. I trust none of the the wolves waiting inside," Longinus said.

Caiaphas met them in the great room. Wide and pillared, painted shades of pale blue and white, the hall offered a bright and cheery feel Joseph knew to be, much like Caiaphas himself, a peacocked illusion. Beneath these floors were cells designed for the poor souls unlucky enough to be tried and judged by the High Priest. And farther down, below the cells, was something Joseph had only heard about—a pit of horror. Carved down into solid stone, the pit was said to be accessible only through a narrow round opening at the top. The accused would be lowered down into the black by a rope. Many never came out again. Imagining that black hole of rotting death made Joseph sick.

And that's where they kept Yeshua... These men will answer.

Caiaphas and Beryl sat on heavy, wooden chairs. Caiaphas wore all the splendor of the High Priest he was. Rich robes and high hat. Beryl's chins gathered above the humbler dress of a Pharisee. His expression was passive. Pilate, to Joseph's surprise, stood off to one side of them.

Caiaphas cleared his throat. "You put me in a very difficult position, Joseph. You run to Rome and strike a deal. You do this behind my back."

"I do what I have to do." Joseph pointed at Beryl. "Should I stand by and let this man take my home? My family?"

Caiaphas frowned. "You were a member of the Sanhedrin, yet you went against us. Publicly. You ceaselessly confront us with accusations. You make a mockery of God's system."

Joseph shook his head. "No, you twist and manipulate to your own advantage, not to honor God. I did nothing wrong. It's easy enough to take a man's world away when he's being beaten in a cell, but I'm in that cell no longer."

"All of that is history," Beryl said.

"Is it? The bruises are fresh enough," Joseph said.

Caiaphas lifted a hand. "Be that as it may. Joseph, I'm choosing against my better judgment to ignore your disrespect, but only because I believe the time has come for us to come to an agreement. You put me in an awkward position. Until now, the Council has been able to foster a somewhat peaceable and mutually beneficial relationship with the Romans. Much of that is thanks to our friend Pilate here." Caiaphas waited for Pilate's nod before continuing. "You claim you didn't take Yeshua's body. Fine. All well and good. The Council is willing to let the matter drop. Most of Jerusalem thinks his close disciples were responsible anyway. And now they're gone, which lends credence to the story. As for you, we'll officially restore your property and offer safety for you and your household. You're free to continue to conduct business and attend the synagogue. We'll be happy and Rome will be happy. As I understand it, there are important people there who will be very pleased to have a consistent flow of your wine. You'll have no more need for your personal army, either."

"And for all this, what do you get from me in return?" Joseph said.

"You publicly denounce Yeshua and apologize to the Council. You admit before all that you were wrong to support him."

"No."

Beryl threw up his hands. "Stubborn man!" He turned to Caiaphas. "I told you he would answer such."

Caiaphas leaned forward in his chair. "Joseph, do you understand I'm offering you your life back?"

"I understand perfectly. And the answer is no."

Caiaphas put his hands on his knees. "Joseph, the man is dead! No matter what you think of us, what good can possibly come of refusing?"

"As I told you before, I don't believe he's dead."

The High Priest looked around him, eyes wide, and lifted his hands in mock question. "Then where is he? Don't be a fool, Joseph."

"He will return. And even if he doesn't, the answer will still be no."

Pilate stepped forward. "Caiaphas, a word with Joseph if I may?"

Caiaphas made a shooing motion with his hand. "Please! Talk some sense into him."

Pilate led Joseph to the opposite end of the hall and spoke in quiet whisper. "My friend, I'd advise you to do this thing. It will be easiest for all."

"Are you saying you will no longer honor our agreement? You'll remove your protection?"

"No, I'm not saying that. But I can't continue to allow Rome to protect you forever. From the start it's been temporary at best, you know that. You're back in your home now. Your wife is safe. Agree to Caiaphas' terms and all stays that way. I'm telling you, it's best for everyone."

"It's a matter of honor, Pilate. It's a matter of truth."

Pilate dropped his head and sighed, then met Joseph's eye again. "As I asked the Nazarene, what is truth? Look, he's gone but you're here. Your wife is here. And your unborn child! Make your own truth, Joseph. I speak from experience, sometimes it's the best way."

"No. It's never the best way. I'll stand with God and I'll stand with Yeshua."

"Even if it means your death? Your family's death?"

"Yes. So be it."

"I have to tell you, your father-in-law has already approached me privately, promising to keep and honor the wine agreement should I pull protection from you and he retake possession of your holdings. He's a very determined man. I win either way, you see. Even so, I respect you, Joseph. I'd see you safe and well."

"I would have expected no less from him. But I'm asking you to stand by your word."

"I hope to, I really do. But in my heart I fear I'm a selfish man. I tend towards the path that bodes the least resistance and promises the most profit. I'm a Roman, Joseph. In my world it's a matter of survival. In this situation, you need to do the same."

"Pilate, you looked into Yeshua's eyes. You saw. I know you did."

Pilate internally drifted for a second. He ran a hand through his hair. "There are things, my friend, it's best to unsee. Please, I ask you to think about what I've said."

"Well?" Caiaphas called from the other end of the hall. "I have other things press—"

A shout from outside interrupted him. Then another. Longinus headed for the door and then through it. Joseph followed, holding a hand up against the sun as he exited. In the courtyard the Levitical Patrol stood in a wide semicircle, spears at half mast. Longinus' men faced them, swords drawn. A Roman was on his knees on the stone, not one of those who'd come with them but one who had been left behind to guard the house. He held a blood-covered hand against his neck.

"What's happened here?" Longinus barked.

One of the Levitical Patrol turned. "We had nothing to do with it. This man stumbled in and started yelling for you."

"Stand down, all of you." Longinus' tone left no room for argument. Both sides lowered weapons, though the Patrol did so with slow reluctance. Longinus knelt in front of the wounded man and pulled his hand from his neck. "An ugly wound, but you'll see another sunrise."

The man nodded, face a mask of pain.

"Report," Longinus said.

The soldier coughed blood, then swallowed. "We were attacked. They wore no uniforms. A dozen men at least, heavily armed."

"Barabbas," Longinus said. "It could only be him. And the women?"

The soldier coughed again. If he answered, Joseph never heard him—he was already halfway down the street at a dead run.

38

So much blood…

Joseph saw it in the gutter before he made it to the courtyard.

Inside, four Romans soldiers and at least ten men Joseph didn't recognize lay sprawled on the stone. A quick look told him all were dead. Only during Passover sacrifice had he seen so much blood. One of the men had been nearly decapitated, the lifeless form lying just inside the gate. Beyond, a long trail of blood followed another man who had crawled several cubits before succumbing to death. Joseph ran toward the great door, feet struggling for purchase. "Ariella!"

A Roman sat propped in the doorway breathing shallow gasps, eyes glassy, still gripping a sword with an arm that had been all but removed from his body. Joseph leapt over him and ran into the great hall. "Ariella!" He returned to the doorway, knelt, and took the soldier's face in his hands. "My wife! Did you see my wife?"

The man, past hearing, shuddered, let out a breath, and didn't take another. Joseph crossed the great hall and made his way to the first-floor kitchen at the rear of the residence. An unassuming door stood open a crack in the rear of the room. *Please, please, please…* He shoved it open and took a downward flight of stairs three at a time. At the base he lit a waiting candle with the flint and steel sitting next to it. The small flame revealed a storeroom much bigger than most Upper City homes contained, even the most wealthy. Thanks to Yaffa's oversight, the place was usually immaculate in its tidiness. But now wine barrels were on their sides, bags of milled flour had been sliced open, casks of olives and oil dumped. The bunches of figs usually hanging from the cedar rafters were gone, along with the meat from the drying racks. Fine flour dust hung in the air. Joseph paused, listening. Nothing. Confident he was alone, he moved with quick purpose around a pile of toppled shelves and approached a wall covered with bins of spices. He pulled and the bins swung away from the wall on oiled hinges revealing a darkened recess behind. Joseph spoke quietly into the shadow. "Ariella?"

A whispered reply. "Joseph?"

Relief flooded his body. And then she was in his arms, sobbing. "Joseph! They came so fast! We barely had time to get down here. They were here only minutes ago! Even now we thought you might be one of them."

"I'm here, Ariella. Are you all right?"

"I'm fine now."

After Ariella, Avner and his family exited the space. Joseph glanced at the darkened hole. "And Davi? Where is Davi?"

Ariella shook her head. "The last I saw, he was in the thick of the fight and holding his own. The rest of us ran here, like you've always told us. We heard them search the cellar, but they never found the hiding place, praise God."

"Yes…praise God." Even as Joseph said the words, dread consumed him at the thought of Davi. Good and loyal Davi… Was he dead? His body hadn't been in the courtyard, of that Joseph was certain. No, he couldn't imagine it. Not Davi. The man had been part of Joseph's life for as long as he could remember. But, after the kidnapping in Arimathea, if this had indeed been Barabbas, Joseph knew all too well what the man was capable of. The only thing the giant enjoyed as much as killing was inflicting as much pain as possible leading up to the event.

"Come upstairs, it's safe now," Joseph said.

Longinus was in the great room when they entered. "A few of my men are searching for any survivors or lingerers. I've sent to the fortress for wagons and men to move the bodies. It will be done shortly." He glanced at Ariella and the servants. "They're all right?"

"I had a hiding place built and stocked long ago for such emergencies. Everyone in my household knows what to do should danger come."

Longinus turned to Ariella, his face a neutral blank that failed to hide the storm behind it. "Sister?"

Ariella's eyes filled. "I'm sorry, Longinus. I called for her and looked as we ran, but there was just no time. They were at the door."

Longinus nodded and glanced toward the entry door, a blood stain now the only evidence a man had died there only minutes ago. "I'm sorry this happened, Winemaker. I failed you."

"No! It's not your fault. How could you know? We all thought we had sufficient protection here."

"Barabbas is a murdering pig. He must have had a large force. It wouldn't have been easy. I hand-picked these men and they were brutal fighters, every one. I can't imagine any less than four to one could have possibly been successful. Even at that, they would have had to have been a tough, seasoned lot. And somehow they knew we would be divided today."

"They may have simply waited for an opportunity."

Longinus shook his head. "That many couldn't have just loitered and watched. Not without drawing attention. They knew we would be gone and they knew the house would be vulnerable. This was planned in advance with the benefit of inside knowledge."

"Who could have told them we'd be gone? One of yours?"

"My men are loyal to the core. And some of them paid for it with their lives today."

"Yes, and my deepest apologies, Longinus. But I trust my household as well. Completely."

"Then who?"

"Sister?"

The Roman's face darkened. "I hope not."

"I know you're fond of her, Longinus, but I also understand she left the last time you tried to help."

"Still, I don't think she would betray a family who helped her."

"I hope you're right."

Longinus looked out at the courtyard for a long second, then sighed. "So do I, Winemaker, so do I. And I'll know soon enough."

"You're going after her?"

"Immediately."

"Good. I go as well."

"No. You're a brave man, and I mean no disrespect, but this is a task for soldiers, not a merchant."

"Davi is either dead or soon to be. He's a brother to me. I'm going after him, whether you take me with you or not."

Longinus looked at Ariella. "Talk to your husband. Tell him his son will need a father."

"My husband is his own man. If I wasn't with child, I'd be beside him. We owe Davi this much. A hundred prisons couldn't hold Davi if the roles were reversed."

Longinus shook his head. "All right, then. Winemaker, I'll need to borrow some clothes. This uniform will only attract attention."

"Done." Joseph motioned to Avner, who hurried away.

"We leave now," Longinus said.

Joseph nodded. "Good."

Two minutes later, Avner returned with a colorless tunic and robe. He handed the bundle to Longinus.

"Thank you." Longinus said. "All right. Then let's go."

Joseph hugged Ariella, whispered encouragement into her ear, then broke their embrace and followed the centurion out and into the courtyard. "What about your men? They aren't assembling?"

"Barabbas knows every nook and cranny of every canyon within a hundred miles. If we traipse into the wilderness with even a small force, he'll vanish like leaves in a wind and we'll never find him."

"You have a plan to find them, then?"

"I have recent information about where they've been camped."

"And you think they'll still be there?"

"Barabbas spoils for a fight. Especially with me. He knows I'll come, and he'll want to be there to meet me."

Longinus changed clothes quickly in the stables. Joseph fell into step as he exited the courtyard at a jog and headed in the direction of the Lower City.

A thought brought Joseph up short. "Longinus, it must have been Beryl…"

Longinus glanced back. "Beryl?"

"It had to be him. He's behind all of this. I don't know why I didn't think of it before."

"But Beryl was with Caiaphas. He was willing to make peace."

"Yes, and I wondered about it at the time. It was a ruse. He used Caiaphas. He talked him into the meeting only to divide our forces and provide an opportunity for Barabbas' men to attack. He wanted Ariella because he knows it would hurt me most. The more I consider it, the more sense it makes."

"Not Sister…"

"No, not Sister."

"But they still have her. And your man, Davi, if they haven't killed them."

"Beryl may keep Davi alive to strengthen his bargaining position. That's my hope."

"You know this is a long shot, Winemaker. We'll both likely be dead by sundown."

"That seems to be the norm these days. God's will be done."

"God's will. But we'll keep our hands on our swords."

39

Sister gathered her saliva and spat, watching as the wad slid down the giant's face and into his beard.

He smiled, rocked back a fist, then the world went black.

Stars swirled as her vision cleared. On her back in the dirt, left side of her face and head throbbing.

"Pig." She sat up and spat again.

He laughed.

"Kill me now. Be done with it," she said.

"The Roman will come. He'll kill you." This from Davi, the Arimathean's man. He was on his knees beneath the full force of the sun. His hands were tied behind him and attached to his also-bound ankles with another short length of rope.

"Of course he'll come," the giant said. "I'm counting on it. And he'll die. And he'll take his last breath knowing I now own his woman."

Blood dripped from Davi's crushed nose into the dust in front of him. "And to think they released you instead of Yeshua."

The giant grinned. "Yes. And to think."

"I'm not the Roman's woman," Sister said. "Please, just kill me."

"You're right. You're my woman now."

Davi cleared his throat and spat blood. "The Roman won't die easily. And I think you know it. If you're smart, you'll let the woman go back to the city."

They were in a narrow canyon, steep walls of rock rising on two sides. Sister had counted eleven men on the short march, though only eight were present now. The others must be keeping watch.

A low whistle sounded from the mouth of the canyon. The giant turned toward the sound. "Well?"

"The fat priest," came the reply.

"He's expected, let him pass."

A minute later a fat man trudged into the canyon, breathing hard and mopping his brow with a cloth. "Barabbas, you couldn't find anywhere closer?"

"If you weren't so fat, it wouldn't seem so far," the giant said.

The fat man looked at Davi and smiled. "Ah, a familiar face. And my daughter?"

"She wasn't there," Barabbas said.

The fat man's smile vanished. "Of course she was there."

"We searched every room. I'm telling you, she wasn't there."

The fat man walked over to Davi. "Where is my daughter?"

Davi met the man's eye but said nothing.

The priest cuffed Davi on the ear. "Answer when the Av Beit Din speaks."

Davi smiled, showing bloody, broken teeth. "The Av Beit Din needs to learn to hit harder."

Barabbas took a long stride toward Davi and swung a fist, the crack so loud it echoed off the rock and stopped Sister's heart. Davi slammed into the dirt face first.

The priest's mouth dropped open, shut, then opened again. "You killed him?"

Barabbas shrugged. "He wanted to be hit harder so I hit him harder."

She breathed relief when Davi's leg stirred and he rolled over with a moan.

"He's tough, that one," Barabbas said, grudging admiration playing across his face. He turned to the fat man. "You have the gold?"

"What do you mean, do I have the gold? I told you I'd pay you to secure my daughter."

"Your daughter wasn't there. You said she would be. Your fault. I lost ten good men to the Roman scum. I'll have my money now."

The fat man shook his head. "I explained it to you. My son-in-law would come for his wife, you would kill him, and I would send out a patrol to rescue my daughter. Then everything is mine. Without Joseph's holdings, I don't have the gold."

"You've no gold of your own?"

"Of course not. Where would I get gold?"

"You think you wouldn't be suspected? Your hate for him is well known."

"Why would I be suspected? I was in a meeting doing my best to restore him to his old life when you attacked. I was the driving force in trying to keep peace between the Sanhedrin and Rome. I was magnanimous in word and deed."

"How do you know he has gold?"

"He bought Pilate's protection with gold. There has to be more where it came from. But I tell you, we needed my cow of a daughter!"

Barabbas pointed. "I brought the Roman's harlot."

"No one cares about a harlot ."

"The Roman cares. He'll come."

"The Roman is nothing in this, either. Trouble is all he contributes."

Barabbas eyed Davi. "We have him."

This stopped the fat man. "Yes… The servant is close to Joseph. He very well might be worth something."

"We'll know soon enough," Barabbas said.

"You left a trail? As agreed?"

"And the Romans have spies in the hills. Longinus knows where we are. He'll come. And the Arimathean as well. That one has a backbone, I think."

The fat man threw Sister a glum look. "If she means as much to the Roman as you think, they may show up with half of Rome."

"I don't think so. The Roman wants the woman. He knows if he brings men, we'll be gone before he gets within a mile of us. He'll come alone."

The fat man lowered his bulk onto a rock. "You're very sure they'll find us?"

"A child could follow our trail. And the Roman is no child."

"You fear him?"

Barabbas showed his rotten teeth. "No, but I understand him. There are some men who won't stop coming until they're dead. The Roman is one of them. So am I. We've met, we've looked into each other's eyes, and one of us will die. Fortunately for me, it will be him." He walked over to Sister and fingered her hair, his breath putrid in her nostrils. "Before I'm done, he'll beg for death's release." In a quick motion he knotted her hair into his fist, pulled her to him and pressed his thick lips against hers. She gagged and the giant, laughing, shoved her away.

The fat man stood. "I'm a priest. You do this in my presence? What's the matter with you?"

Barabbas shrugged. "Then why are you looking at her? Are priests not men as well? Did not God make Eve for Adam?" His pig eyes glinted. "Look at his creation. An even better choice than the Arimathean's wife, I think."

"My daughter, you mean."

"Daughter, wife, what's the difference? She's a woman." A whistle sounded up the canyon and Barabbas turned.

40

Joseph scanned the top of the canyon cliff for the sound's origin. "A guard?"

"Yes. They know we're coming now," Longinus said.

More whistles followed by replies.

"They're communicating," Joseph said.

"Barabbas knows by now that it's only two of us. He will be pleased."

"They may kill us before we even get to them."

"I doubt it. Barabbas wants me himself. I saw it in his eyes last night."

Joseph studied the cliff face again. "I can feel them watching."

A dove cooed, low and sad. Brush on the cliff face stirred in the breeze.

"It strikes me," Joseph said. "that a man in your position couldn't possibly live very long if he's in the habit of charging toward death without a plan. The woman has turned your head so much?"

"You're here as well, aren't you?"

"Davi is a brother to me. I have no choice."

"You had a choice. But we do what we have to do."

"I suppose so."

"Still, Winemaker, I never said I had no plan…"

"Would you care to let me in on it?"

"In good time. If we live long enough."

The canyon narrowed, then widened again. The faint odor of wood smoke hung in the air.

"We're close," Longinus said.

"May the God of Israel be with us."

"We'll need Him."

Joseph spun at the sound of footsteps. Two heavily-armed men followed, several cubits behind them.

Longinus smiled. "They've been there a while, Winemaker. Ignore them. It only gives them satisfaction if they think they're intimidating you."

Joseph kept his eyes forward, a struggle given the skin crawling on the back of his neck. Then the canyon took a sharp turn… And they were in the camp.

Five or six men faced them, Barabbas in the front. Beryl stood off to the side, grinning.

Longinus approached them like an honored guest, hard planes of his face darkening at the sight of Sister standing against the cliff face clutching her tunic to the front of her body.

"Are you hurt?" he said to her

A tear rolled down her cheek.

"Of course she's not hurt," Barabbas said. "She can take a punch, that one."

"You will rot in Hades," Sister said.

"Probably," Barabbas said, "But we'll rot together. Not a bad thought, eh?"

Davi, eyes glassy, hands and feet bound, struggled to get to his knees. Joseph started for him but Barabbas cut him off with a sweep of his blade. Barabbas looked at Beryl. "Priest, you wanted the Arimathean, here he is."

Beryl smiled. "You're surprised to see me, Joseph?"

"Of course I'm not surprised. Who else would be behind something as desperate as this?" Joseph said.

"Desperate? I don't think so. I only take what's been given to me by God for my good service. Barabbas' involvement shields me from unwanted questions."

"Your bitterness against me drives you. You will be judged, Beryl," Joseph said.

Beryl folded his hands in front of him. "Nothing drives me but my faith in God."

"Then Satan is your God. You're a killer of the innocent."

Beryl crimsoned. "No man is innocent! If you—"

"Enough!" Barabbas barked. "Enough, Priest! You bicker like an old woman. Your son-in-law is here, kill him and be done with it. If you want, I'll even hold him for you so he won't squirm."

Longinus drew his sword.

Barabbas grinned at this. "Good! You're eager, Roman."

"Surrender to Rome," Longinus said. "You and your men will stand trial but at least you'll live through the day."

Barabbas barked a laugh. "It's actually hard not to like you. I'm almost sorry to see you die. Still…" He waved a hand and his men fanned into a wide circle around Joseph and Longinus, swords leveled. Joseph drew his own.

Barabbas strolled over to Sister and grabbed a fistful of her hair. "Not a bad thing to fight for, eh, Roman? We'll cross swords, you and I, but maybe there's no hurry?"

The circle of Barabbas' men tightened, giving Longinus and Joseph no room to maneuver.

"Leave her be," Longinus said. "Surrender now."

Barabbas chuckled. "You stand in the center of a circle of drawn swords and still you bluster. Roman, you—"

At that moment, Longinus lifted his hand skyward. There was a hiss, then a thunk. One of the rebels, a knot of a man with a red beard and eyes like slate, grunted and grasped at an arrow protruding from his throat. Coughing blood, he sank to his knees and toppled. The remaining men took a step back, all of them searching the cliffs for the archer.

Longinus' voice was calm. "The next man that moves gets the same."

One man broke for cover, but another hiss sounded and he went down with a scream. The rest stood as if they'd suddenly grown roots.

Barabbas had pulled Sister back into the shadow of the recessed cliff face, shielding himself from attack from above. "I wondered, Roman. It's what I would have done. Your archer must be good to have gotten by my guards. But they'll find him. It's only a matter of waiting."

"No, your guards are dead," Longinus said.

"You think he's that good?"

"He's better."

"Do something, Barabbas!" Beryl said.

Barabbas eyed his men. "It occurs to me, Roman. Your man couldn't possibly get all of them. If I have them rush? What then?"

"It's a gamble you'll have to take to find out."

Barabbas shrugged. "I've never minded a gamble." He eyed his men. "He has but one man up there. Take them. Kill the Arimathean but keep the Roman alive, he's for me."

Not a man moved.

"Obey me!" Barabbas said. "His archer has time for a shot at the most."

A tall, sallow man's Adam's apple bobbed. "And which one of us will die? It's easy for you to gamble when it's our lives that are at stake."

"One will die, yes. But if you continue to stand there, I'll bury all of you to your necks and let the birds and ants have at your eyes before I cut your tongues out with your own teeth. You'll beg for a Roman arrow then."

Joseph could see the men turning it over until, one by one, resolve came to their faces. A four-out-of-five chance of life against the sure and proven cruelty of their leader? There could only be one outcome.

It was the sallow speaker that broke the tide. He lifted his sword and shouted. "Go!"

They all broke.

And they all died.

The still canyon air hissed as the rebels tumbled in a hail of arrows. Then it was over, the afternoon returned to silence and sunshine. A fly buzzed. A man moaned, got to his hands and knees, and started to crawl. Another hiss-thunk and he dropped into the dirt with a thud.

Barabbas shook his head. "Really, Roman? You said there was only one."

"No, you said there was only one."

Barabbas grunted a laugh. "What now? I step out and they kill me too? I go down with an arrow in my back?"

"You'll die on my sword and my sword alone. And it won't be in your back. You have my word on that."

Barabbas looked out at the canyon floor. "Judging by my men, I'm not sure your word is one I trust."

Davi was on his knees now, obviously dazed but shaking his head and trying to focus. "Joseph…"

Joseph pulled a knife from his belt and moved to cut his friend loose, but shouts came from above. A cascade of small rocks and dirt fell. More shouts, then a long whistle.

Barabbas stepped out from the wall, arm tight around Sister's neck. "Stand, Arimathean. Leave your pup where he is. Quite the round of Dogs and Jackals we play, isn't it, Roman? You brought men, good in the brush, too, but I had a dozen waiting in the hills just in case you were as crafty as I thought you'd be. A good thing."

Longinus lifted his sword and stepped forward. "A round to me and a round to you. But it will take them a while to get down here. You may be dead by then."

Barabbas shoved the woman to the side and lifted his own sword. His tangled beard swinging, his eyes bright. "One of us will be. Now we see, don't we?"

"We do." Longinus circled slowly left.

"Barabbas, tell your archers to kill my son-in-law," Beryl said, "and you'll have your gold."

Barabbas' eyes never left Longinus. "Kill him yourself, priest. I'm busy." He thrust. Longinus parried. The two circled.

Beryl glared at Joseph. "Barabbas should have skewered you when he had you in Arimathea."

Joseph stepped forward. "You have it to do yourself now, Beryl. Only one of us leaves this place today."

"God will strike you down, Joseph. I'll have what's mine."

Joseph started for him but Beryl shuffled to the right, a surprisingly quick move given his girth. He stopped behind Davi, pulling a knife from the recesses of his robes.

Joseph froze in place. "Don't, Beryl."

"You've been nothing but grief since the day you married my daughter."

The crash of steel and bodies sounded, broke, then sounded again as Longinus and Barabbas fought, but Joseph didn't shift his eyes from Beryl. Beryl grabbed Davi's hair and yanked his head back. The knife's point winked in the sun.

"Joseph," Davi slurred, "are you there? I can't see."

"Back off and leave him alone," Joseph said.

Beryl's eyes flattened.

"You'll die today, Beryl," Joseph said. "Do you want murder to be the last act you take before God? Above all, you're a Pharisee."

Sweat dripped down Beryl's forehead and into his beard. "You are all blasphemers. I'm within the law and my rights."

"No. He's done nothing to you."

"But you've done everything."

"You've done it all to yourself."

A scramble in the brush pulled Joseph's attention. Men emerged, swords drawn.

"Take them but leave the Roman!" Barabbas barked. He swung a great arch. Sparks flew as Longinus blocked and returned the blow.

The men swarmed Joseph. He slashed with his sword but hands caught him from behind and pulled his weapon from his hands. Sister tried to run but was quickly caught and dragged back, cursing and scratching.

Beryl's face morphed to ecstasy, his laugh to an aberration. Davi had slumped to the side, bleeding from one ear, but Beryl, still clutching his hair, managed to hold him upright. "God has judged between us, son-in-law. I only hope you'll be able to watch from Hades as I raise my child."

"Don't, Beryl, please," Joseph said.

"You beg now? Too late." Beryl lifted his knife.

"No!" Joseph shouted.

But the knife swung down.

The world darkened, blood roared so loudly in Joseph's ears he couldn't hear his own scream. He jerked and writhed so hard he managed to break free of his captors and lunged forward as Davi rolled onto his side. A hard blow from behind and Joseph was down in the dirt, face to face with the man who had been by his side as long as he could remember. Those laughing, familiar eyes that had looked at him over a thousand campfires now stared, open and empty.

The clang of metal against metal. Curses and oaths from Longinus and Barabbas. A curse from the woman. A silent scream from Joseph's own mouth.

Heavily shod feet appeared before him, blocking Davi's empty eyes. One foot rocked back and, in an instant, the afternoon became night, wild and star-filled. As Joseph floated up into the darkness, the Shepherd's song came to him. And out beyond the song, bouncing through shimmering sky—Davi's ever-familiar, joyous laugh.

41

The Romans had come with a rush. On horseback, no less. Beryl had listened from inside the cave as the centurion shouted orders. Of Barabbas there was no sign. The rebel had entered the cave first, and though Beryl tried to follow the broad back into the darkness, he'd soon given up. Afraid to go any farther on his own and with no escape route, he'd simply dropped to his rump and shimmied backwards into a wide crack between two boulders until he bumped hard stone and could go no more. Barabbas' little army of insurgents had been slaughtered, of that he was certain. Barabbas would be alone now, and hunted, at least until he could gather more mercenaries. The Zealot now had nothing to offer so Beryl dismissed him from his mind. The dark pressed. He fisted his shaking hands. They were slick with blood. *I killed the man… I shoved my blade through his throat and killed him while Joseph watched.*

Killed… But the man had been associated with Joseph. A blasphemer. Beryl was the Av Beit Din! God's chosen! The only regret he had was that he'd been robbed of the opportunity to sink his blade into Joseph's heart as well. Another time. He let his back slide along the wall till he was on his side in the dirt. He felt both elated and sick. The Romans would think he'd gone on into the cave with Barabbas. He closed his eyes and tried to sleep but his thoughts rioted. Once he rolled forward and vomited. Finally, after what seemed to him years in the darkness, completely spent, he fell into an uneasy, dream-filled slumber.

Thirst brought him fully conscious. It took him some time to remember where he was. Pitch black now when before there had been the faintest tinge of gray light from the direction of the cave mouth. He lay perfectly still for several minutes, listening. It was as if the world had stopped. It would be all right, he was the Av Beit Din. He repeated the fact over and over in his mind as he scooted forward in the dry dust. He found the cave wall and felt his way. He knew the direction he'd come. Before long a patch of silvery moonlight formed ahead. Night then. He stepped out of the cave and into a buzzing tumble of half-moon light. Since when did moonlight buzz? Moving forward on tentative feet, it came to him with a start that the moon wasn't buzzing at all. The noise came from the masses of desert flies covering things that had once been men strewn across the canyon floor. Turning and supporting himself against the cliff face, he vomited again.

"Beryl…" The voice came from everywhere and nowhere.

He clutched at his heart. "Who's there?"

"Beryl…"

Turning, he lurched and lumbered, moving as fast as his heft would allow the direction of the canyon mouth. Something caught at his feet and he crashed forward. A vibrating roar consumed him and blackened the stars. He realized with horror he was in the midst of a great storm of flies. Then the insects dissipated, leaving a gape-mouthed corpse inches from his face. He screamed and rolled over several times, an attempt to put distance between himself and the abomination. *God of Israel! Please!*

"Beryl…" A woman's voice.

He rose to his hands and knees, heaving great breaths. "What! Who are you?" Grunting to his feet again, he shuffle-stumbled into the darkness.

"Beryl…stop." A woman, yes, but a woman speaking with authority.

He whirled, searching the canyon, eyes darting through shadow and silver light. "Harlot? Is that you?"

"Beryl...is that any way to speak?" It came from his right this time and he searched the shadows for its source.

"If not the prostitute, who? How do you know me?"

A shadow moved, he was sure of it. He squinted into the gloom.

"Here, Beryl." To his left now.

He spun a slow circle. "Show yourself! I'm the Av Beit Din. I command it."

A laugh, soft as tinkling glass. "Av Beit Din…. The title is mist and shadow. I'm sad for you. What happened to you through these years?"

"Wait. Your voice! I know it. Who—"

She stepped from the night then, moonlight catching her form.

He tried to swallow but couldn't. "A… A… Abigail? What's happening to me? You're dead! I watched you die! I held your *body*! Abigail?"

"Yes, husband. You watched me die. And now you watch me live."

The buzzing grew louder. Then louder until Beryl thought his ears would burst. Not the flies, but a great rush of blood to his head. He leaned forward, hands on his knees, struggling for breath. He looked up again, blinking at the woman. Yes, there was no doubt it was Abigail, his wife. Alive though she'd died in his arms almost three decades ago. Same clear, pale skin. Same soft, black hair he'd loved to bury his face in when he'd held her all those years ago. And her eyes! Those amber gold eyes. When she'd died, every woman had died, because no other woman could ever compare to Abigail.

He fought nausea again. *This can't be real! It's a dream… Of course it's a dream…* He sucked in a great breath. "Abigail, my heart is going to burst. Or has it already? Am I dead then?"

She studied him for a long time before smiling. "Having been on both sides, I'd have to say the answer to that is as tricky as the question. In the physical sense, at the moment at least, you're alive, I suppose. At least as alive as this type of alive can be, which isn't very. Otherwise? We'll have to talk about that."

"I don't understand."

"And yet you pretend to be the teacher of Israel? Shame, husband."

"Abigail, please… What's happening to me? Why am I seeing you? Are you a ghost?"

She moved toward him and he backed away.

"I'm not going to hurt you, Beryl." She held out a hand. "Here, touch me. I'm flesh and blood, like you."

His hand shook violently as he reached out. Her skin was solid and warm. Her hand took his and he surprised himself by sobbing. "Abigail… Why am I seeing you? What's happening to me?"

"You're seeing me because you have eyes, husband. As for what's happening to you, that's the problem, isn't it? In your foolish heart, everything in this world revolves around you when, in reality, you're a speck of dust in a desert wind storm. In other words, you're nothing, husband. Nothing but puffed up words that are blown away and forgotten as soon as they've been spoken." She smiled. "Isn't that a wonderful release?"

"I'm the Av Beit Din."

"So you keep saying. Are the words sounding hollow yet?"

Beryl pulled in the deepest breath he could. He straightened. "How are you possibly here, Abigail?"

"I'm sure you heard. All Jerusalem has heard. When Yeshua pushed death aside, other graves were opened. Many of us revived to walk this shadow world. As a testimony to God's great love."

"But Yeshua is dead."

"Oh Beryl, you foolish man. Yeshua is never dead." She looked up at the star-blaze. "Who do you think rolled out the scroll of the heavens? Who do you think shouted with joy as the first morning stars sang? Yeshua is never dead, Beryl, Yeshua is Life!"

"No… This can't be. Yeshua was only a Galilean con artist. He was a threat to the priesthood!"

"Really, husband? You use the words Yeshua and only in the same sentence?… Then the sun is *only* a dim flicker. The sea is *only* a drop of water. When did you become so blind, husband? So completely consumed with *you*? You should have seen long ago—Yeshua was, is, and always will be the Son of God. He will judge the living and the dead. And that includes—most definitely and especially—the Av Beit Din of the great Sanhedrin of Jerusalem."

"No one will judge me but God Himself."

Her face lit. "Good! Very good! You're finally listening."

He raised himself to his full height. "You're a woman! You intend to teach me?"

Her laugh surprised him. "Oh Beryl, you really do miss so much joy."

Yeshua... Beryl's legs weakened until he found it impossible to stand any longer. He sank to the ground. "But Yeshua..."

"Yes. Yeshua. All is and all will be Yeshua. I'm your proof, Beryl. That's why I'm here. I died giving birth to our daughter, you were there, yet I stand before you alive. Because of Yeshua."

Beryl stared down at his hands shaking in his lap. Fat, pompous, ugly hands—he'd never noticed it before. Rings gleamed. Symbols of status he suddenly wanted to hide. Tears began to splash on them. A wail echoed off the cliffs, stirring the wind, rattling the flies. He realized it came from his own mouth. No, it came from someplace deeper, his own soul. His wretched, shattered soul. How could he have been so wrong? He tried to stand but felt sick again. *Yeshua? How can this be? But she's here!* He looked up at her, his eyes blurred with tears, body wracked with the knowledge of sudden truth. The world stretched and tipped. Everything was wrong. All the things he'd done had been nothing but chasing wind! "Abigail..."

"Get up, husband, it's time for us to go. This is a place of death, not life."

"But, Abigail, we killed Yeshua. We—I—put him on a Roman cross! If he was the..." The words stuck in his throat.

"The Promised One of Israel?"

"Yes."

"He was. And is."

"And we—"

"You crucified him, Beryl, yes. You and your stubborn, foolish pride. All of you did. But, you see, neither your pride, nor even death, can thwart the plans of God. You, in all your pomp and self-applied glory, are nothing. Isn't that a relief?"

"You don't understand. I planned. I worked. I debated and maneuvered. Don't you see? *I* killed Yeshua! Not them, *me*. And now I've killed another man. With my own hands!" His palms burned and he wrung them together. "I thought—"

"*Many plans are in a man's heart, but the counsel of the Lord will stand...* You can do nothing, Beryl. God is all. Now get up."

"But I was God's man! I... Why didn't he make himself known?"

"Didn't he? And aren't the scriptures very clear?"

"There are many interpretations. He should have been plainer in his speech."

"You can't justify your wickedness, Beryl. No one can, though all try. A man so sure of his own righteousness is surely wrong. Some of you must have recognized the words of the prophets?"

Joseph... Nicodemus... And there were others. They all tried.

He looked at her. He'd forgotten how absolutely beautiful she was. Her family had called her plain. *Can you imagine?* They'd been wrong. Idiots, every one of them. They couldn't marry her off fast enough. *So beautiful...* Unexpectedly, all the grief of her passing flooded again. The canyon breeze turning the tears on his face cold. "Abigail, you're really here..."

"I am, Beryl."

"For how long?"

"How long are any of us here? We're like the grass, husband. We fade in a season."

"What must I do, Abigail? Is there any hope for me?"

Her smile had always set worlds on fire, spun the stars like a child's playthings. That much hadn't changed. "Simple. Repent, Beryl. Come home to the Father who waits for you. You are loved, after all."

"Loved?"

"Oh yes! Magnificently loved."

"If all you say is true, then I am the wickedest man on earth."

"It is, and you are. Exactly like every other man on earth."

"Then I am beyond hope."

"To say you are beyond hope is to say you are beyond God. And that, Beryl, is foolish pride at its very root. Turn from it and come."

"But a man so magnificently wicked must also be magnificently hated."

"The Psalmist wrote: *God is a righteous judge. And a God who has indignation every day. If a man does not repent, He will sharpen His sword; He has bent His bow and made it ready...*"

"I don't understand..."

"*Yeshua* has made a path, husband. Repent. Run to him."

"I've killed a man with my own hands. And he'd done nothing but offer his loyalty to someone I hated."

"Yes, you did. Repent."

"How, Abigail? I am a Chief Priest!"

"You are a man, that's all. Everything else is smoke and air."

His mind flooded with remembered word and action. All he had done and said. And in the name of God? He had spat on Yeshua. Struck him. Drawn blood. It had thrilled him at the time, the feeling of power, of superiority. Driving him further and further into his dark heart until he had actually taken his knife and shoved it through a man's body. And he'd wanted to do it! Longed to do it! Thrilled to it. He'd wondered for years what it might feel like... He'd killed. He'd ordered killings. The Cilician... All that innocent blood on his hands. He sobbed again. "No, Abigail... I have to die. Hades waits for me. There can be no other way. I have to die!"

"Yes, Beryl, Hades waits with open arms. But so does Yeshua."

"But how? How can that be?"

She held her hand out. "Come, husband, I suspect you'll ask him yourself in good time."

She was so confident...and different...and real. And that realness crushed any argument stirring in his brain with hands of steel and love. He struggled to his feet, his carefully constructed world in pieces on the ground around him. And, not knowing what else to do, took Abigail's hand and let her lead him out of that valley of death.

42

Beryl slept a dreamless sleep. But, indeed, all the world now seemed a dream. He woke to find her sitting by a window in a slant of sunlight sipping from a cup, her unbound hair spilling over her shoulders, her gold eyes upon him. She was even more beautiful in the daylight.

"Get dressed, Beryl. There isn't much time," she said.

He coughed and brought himself to a sitting position. "Abigail, is this real? Am I dreaming it all?"

Her eyes never wavered. "In a way, you are. Yes, I suppose. This world can be like that. But you will wake one day, I promise."

"You speak of the afterlife…"

"I speak of the presence of God, husband. I've come back to the shadow for now, but I'll see The Light again one day."

"Abraham's Bosom? That's where you've been? Tell me, please, what have you seen?"

She smiled. "One day you'll know how impossible your request is and laugh at the thought of it. I'm here now, that's all. For you. And for her."

"Her? You mean Ariella…"

"Our daughter. Ariella. Yes."

"I've…"

She sipped from the cup. "You've what?"

"Things have changed, Abigail. It's not like it was once. That was long ago."

"Why not just speak the truth? Truth is truth, Beryl. All the wishing and imagining and altered remembering in the world can't change truth. And the truth is, those many years ago, instead of letting your grief for me soften you towards our daughter, you let it fester and harden and rot you from the inside out until you became a mean, self-obsessed brute rather than a man."

He stared at her. "You do speak plainly, don't you? But through it all, I became—"

"You became the Av Beit Din, I know. A nice title to prop up your meaningless shell of an existence."

"Your words wound, Abigail. You never talked to me like this before."

"I never needed to. But the man you were has been long neglected. Now you seem to need an earful."

Beryl stood, moved to the water basin and began his daily ritual cleansing. "The man I was… It was a long time ago, Abigail. And now look at the things I've done. There is nothing for me now but to die. And Hades after that."

She studied him. "Maybe. But, if that's true, why do you cleanse?"

He paused, turning to her. "Excuse me?"

"Why do you cleanse? What's the point?"

"I'm—" He walked back and sat on the bed and stared down at his hands. *She's right. How much ritual cleansing, how much water, will it take to wash so much blood from these hands?*

"The Law is all I know. What am I supposed to do, Abigail?"

"Yeshua."

"Yeshua?"

"You asked a question. And *Yeshua* is the answer to every question. Now stand and dress, we'll be late."

"Late for what?"

"Get dressed, husband, if you have something big enough to cover that carcass of yours. Stop asking questions."

"I have to be at Council. I'm—"

"No, you have to be where God wants you." She clapped her hands a few times. "Now hurry up. Do as I say."

"Where God wants me? I'm right hand to Caiaphas. And Caiaphas is second to God! The Sanhedrin—"

"Oh do stop your incessant mewling, Beryl. You sound like a child. No one is second to God. God is all. There is no first. There is no second. There is only Him! He's not yours to control or direct. How can you not know this? Now get dressed!"

Beryl pulled his pharisaical robe from a hook on the wall.

"No," Abigail said. "Not that ridiculous thing. No more posturing. How did you possibly get by these years without me? It's no wonder you've made such a mess of yourself."

Beryl rifled through a chest and pulled out an old tunic. He picked his turban cloth, but Abigail shook her head so he tossed it on the bed and flattened his thin hair with a damp hand. "All right, Abigail. Whether you're dream or flesh, you're here. Where are we going?"

"The day you quit asking that question is the day all eternity will open itself to you," she said.

He followed her out of the bedchamber, through the combined living-cooking space, the small courtyard, and out onto the street. His stomach growled. "Will there at least be food?"

"I hope not. You could afford to miss a few meals. Or a few hundred."

"Were you always so sharp-tongued? I don't remember it so."

"Were you always the size of a hippopotamus? I don't remember that either."

He dropped the subject and they walked in silence for a long while. She was here, and it looked like she was going to stay. She also looked the same age as the day she'd died, which made him feel even older and fatter than he was. His heart began to race again with the enormous press of it all. He forced himself calm and rolled along with the dream.

"When will you see Ariella?" he said at length.

"When it's time."

"When will it be time?"

She would say no more so he let the subject drop. He followed, grunting, down a series of steep steps deep into the Valley of the Cheesemakers. Business in the Valley was loud and brisk. Crowds pressed. But, minus his priestly attire, not one of them offered the accustomed differential nod or respectful look. His emotions became a confusing jumble of irritation and embarrassment. But, he realized with no little curiosity, everything he felt was topped by a sense of overwhelming freedom. A relief he couldn't account for. He turned his face to the sun momentarily and closed his eyes.

"It's wonderful, isn't it?" Abigail said.

"He opened his eyes and looked at her. "What's wonderful?"

"To shed yourself of yourself. All the ridiculous nonsense we carry around for so long. Like we wouldn't be able to breathe without it. Or we would cease to exist. I imagine that robe and turban hanging in your bedchamber must weigh a thousand pounds." She walked on, the towering retaining wall of the Temple Mount on their right. Only yesterday, he would have thought of the structure with massive pride. Now he shrank from it, as if from the very face of God. At length, Abigail turned left, threading the narrow passageways through the shops and businesses, and they began climbing again, though not nearly as steep as the descent. Still, Beryl's leg muscles and knees complained loudly. Abigail moved lightly through a maze of streets and alleys until they were in a part of the city Beryl had never seen.

"Where are we?" he said.

"The depths of the city," she said, smiling. "The heart of Jerusalem."

Children played underfoot as they walked. A woman hung clothes on a line. A little farther on, a group of men passed around a wineskin and argued good-naturedly.

"I've spent my life in this city and I've never been here."

"You've lived your life in the Upper City, why come mingle with the commoners? Although, a real Av Beit Din probably would, wouldn't he?"

"I—"

"Oh, don't get worked up, husband. I'm only teasing. Well, a little of me isn't, but still. Jerusalem is a huge city. Do you think you can know them all?"

"But how do you know this place?"

"You asked last night where I'd been these weeks? I've been here. With the others. Not all the others but a good many."

"Others?"

They'd passed a small communal courtyard and climbed a flight of steps. Abigail stopped before an unassuming, colorless door and knocked quietly. A long pause, then the door cracked. An eye widened, then the door opened a bit more.

Nicodemus stood in the doorway.

43

Nicodemus' face clouded. "Abigail, you actually brought him."

"I did," Abigail said.

"You know, with him here, we either run or we die."

"A third option exists," Abigail said.

"And what is that?"

"Speak with him. Show him. Teach him."

Beryl felt the blood rush to his face. "Teach *me*?"

Nicodemus eyed Abigail. "You see what I mean? I'm telling you, he can't be convinced."

"His old pride dies hard and slow. But it does die, even as we speak. I know him better than you. Take him in, Nicodemus. Show him. Yeshua walks the earth. I'm here as well. These are things that can't be argued with."

"Abigail, this man is responsible for—"

"We all know what he's responsible for. Show him truth."

"Why are you here, Beryl?" Nicodemus said.

"Because she brought me. I'm still not convinced I'm not dreaming."

"That's the only reason? Then we have nothing left but to vacate this place before you get word to the Cilician."

Beryl's mouth worked but no words came. "Her…" he finally managed to say. "Abigail. She's alive… I'm trying to understand." His eyes began to sting. "No Cilician, Nicodemus. I just want to know how Abigail is alive. Or if I'm dead. Or dreaming. Or if… I just want to know. If you have answers, I would listen."

Nicodemus considered for a long moment. He glanced at Abigail, then back. "Yes, the line between this world and the next does tend to blur these days."

"She didn't tell me where she was bringing me. I didn't know. I've enough blood on my hands already. I tell you, the Cilician is no part of this."

"He's willing to listen," Abigail said. "Aren't you, husband?"

"I'm willing," Beryl said.

Nicodemus considered, mouth turned down and forehead furrowed. Then he stepped aside and beckoned. Beryl followed Abigail inside. The room was spacious and well appointed and, to Beryl's surprise, a large group of people were gathered. They sat on every available piece of furniture, in the windows, and on the floor. Men, women, children. They quieted as Beryl and Abigail entered. Beryl instinctively lifted his chin, then realized it wasn't he who had stilled them, but the sight of Abigail.

"Follow, please," Nicodemus said.

They passed through a doorway down a long hall and out onto a vine-covered patio. A pile of scrolls covered a low table and Nicodemus lowered himself onto one of the pillows next to it. He motioned Beryl and Abigail to do the same. Beryl did so. Abigail, smiling, said she preferred to stand and moved to a corner.

For a minute or so, Nicodemus sat unmoving, head bowed.

Uncomfortable with the long silence, Beryl shifted on his seat. "Are you praying?"

Nicodemus looked up. "Yes, Beryl, I'm praying."

"Praying why?"

Nicodemus arched an eyebrow. "I take my life in my hands just opening the door for you. The life of all these people. And you ask why I seek God's wisdom before I open my life's work to you?"

"The others, they are Followers?"

"Of course they are. And you would see them bleeding in the street. The Cilician has abused many. Some from this very house. Abigail is one of the Risen or the room would have been abandoned even now, just at the rumor you might come. As it is, they await my word."

Beryl nodded and looked down. "I know you won't believe this, but I told you these hands have enough blood on them. I think they'll never come clean. I know what awaits me in the next world. And…" Beryl steeled himself. "And I accept it. I deserve it."

Nicodemus met his gaze. "I search my heart for sympathy and, to my shame, I find none. You are a butcher, Beryl. Still, you are here, and I promised my God I would share truth with all comers no matter the circumstance. And so I will, though I won't pretend my heart doesn't argue."

Beryl sighed. "So it should, Nicodemus, so it should."

Nicodemus began to arrange the scrolls in thoughtful order.

Beryl rubbed his chins. "You said Abigail is *one* of the Risen?"

"I am," Abigail said. "When Yeshua conquered death, the graves opened and many of us rose."

"She speaks truth. Supported by many witnesses," Nicodemus said.

"How can these things be?" Beryl said.

"How could anything our human minds could ever imagine not be if God were to speak them? Or even think them when it comes to that. You've seen Abigail with your own eyes because God wishes it so."

Beryl sighed. "Who is this man, Yeshua, that he holds power over life and death?"

"Oh, that you would have asked that question months ago."

"Nicodemus, I've been a wicked man. The most wicked. Seeing Abigail… I'm beginning to ask myself if I ever believed in God at all. I believed in religion, in the greatness of the Temple, certainly. I believed in our history and our fathers. But to think that God exists outside of me? Outside my will? That His will is different than mine? I can't say definitively that I've ever even considered it. I don't know why, but I haven't. And you tried to warn us all those times. Nicodemus, Abigail is right—you must teach me. I will die for my transgressions, but before I leave this world, teach me."

Nicodemus looked long into Beryl's eyes. Finally, he nodded. "May God help me." He selected a scroll and unrolled it. "It started here. With this List."

"This is the List you spoke of at Council? The one you and Joseph developed? The one you tried to show?"

"And the one you slapped out of my hands as you prepared for Yeshua's slaughter."

"Yes, I remember."

Nicodemus pointed to the first entry.

1. *So you are to know and discern that from the issuing of a decree to restore and rebuild Jerusalem until Messiah the Prince there will be seven weeks and sixty-two weeks; it will be built again, with plaza and moat, even in times of distress. Then after the sixty-two weeks the Messiah will be cut off and have nothing, and the people of the prince who is to come will destroy the city and the sanctuary.* - **the Prophet Daniel**

"Daniel's prophecy, yes," Beryl said. "But many know of it. Which explains why there is a would-be messiah on every street corner in Jerusalem."

"Not so many since most of them saw Yeshua murdered."

Beryl winced a little. "Yes…"

Nicodemus indicated the scroll. "We followed, not without some debate, with this."

2. *Then the eyes of the blind will be opened and the ears of the deaf will be unstopped. Then the lame will leap like a deer, and the tongue of the mute will shout for joy.* - **the Prophet Isaiah**

"Yes, the Messiah will fulfill this someday, but on his immediate coming—"

"Beryl, you're late to this conversation. Many minds have been here before yours and discussed and debated this to death. This does apply to the immediate arrival of the Messiah. And it applies to *his* earthly reign. *Light to heavy*—circular prophecy. There is no doubt. Now, let's continue."

Beryl expected the usual rush of temper that nearly choked him upon receiving any rebuke but was surprised when it didn't come. "All right, go on."

"This…"

3. *He has no stately form or majesty that we should look upon Him, nor appearance that we should be attracted to Him. He was despised and forsaken of men. A man of sorrows and acquainted with grief. And like one from whom men hide their face He was despised and we did not esteem Him.* - **the Prophet Isaiah**

Beryl read, then looked up at the little Pharisee. "Forgive me, I'm not arguing, but I want to understand clearly. Isaiah might not be speaking of the coming Messiah at all, here, correct? Even in the Council, we've debated much on the subject."

"We have. But I've studied this deeply. The Essenes are the greatest scholars of our day, and they believe unequivocally Isaiah is referencing the Messiah." Nicodemus put his hands on the table and leaned in. "And then there's the fact Yeshua rose from the dead! And that Abigail, your long-buried wife, brought you here. Beryl, you're in the student position at the moment and in the privileged position to be able to see with hindsight many of the things we long struggled with. Your job is to simply accept truth right before your eyes."

Beryl held up his palms. "Yes, I know. Old habits."

"Look, you have the benefit of hindsight here, that's all I'm saying. I wish we would have had the same luxury."

"That's true, but it seems these prophecies could apply to others as well."

"I'll ask the same question I always do when someone inevitably makes the same statement. Tell me who? Who else could they apply to? Give me three names. Give me even one name."

"Someone, I'm sure!"

"That's not a name. Read on, Beryl. We call these the first twenty-five. But we add nearly every day. With every passage, you'll find the odds of these combined prophecies pertaining to anyone other than Yeshua increase astronomically. There is no question."

Beryl nodded, put a finger on the scroll and began to read. Nicodemus had added a short heading above each word-for-word passage from the Tanakh.

Through Abraham's lineage...

4. *And I will bless those who bless you. And the one who curses you I will curse. And in you all the families of the earth will be blessed...* - **Moses**

Born of a virgin...

5. *Therefore the Lord Himself will give you a sign: Behold, a virgin will be with child and bear a son, and she will call His name Immanuel...* - **The Prophet Isaiah**

From King David's lineage...

6. *'Behold, the days are coming,' declares the Lord, 'When I will raise up for David a righteous Branch; And He will reign as king and act wisely And do justice and righteousness in the land.'*

"Yeshua was of David's line?" Beryl said.

"Through both his parents' side."

Born in Bethlehem...

7. *But as for you, Bethlehem Ephrathah, Too little to be among the clans of Judah, From you One will go forth for Me to be ruler in Israel. His goings forth are from long ago, From the days of eternity.* - **The Prophet Micah**

"And he was born in—"

"He was. Common knowledge."

Beryl read on.

He will come out of Egypt...

8. *When Israel was a youth I loved him, and out of Egypt called My son..* - **The Prophet Hosea**

"Egypt? I thought he was born in Bethlehem?"

"His parents took him and fled to Egypt when Herod the Great decided to slaughter the young males. Which he did, by the way, because he'd heard a King had been born in Bethlehem. It goes on. A story only God could orchestrate."

He will be preceded by a forerunner. John (son of Zechariah the priest) who baptized in the River Jordan and was killed by Herod Antipas, when he saw Yeshua approach said: *Behold, the Lamb of God Who takes away the sin of the world...*

9. *Behold, I am going to send My messenger, and he will clear the way before Me. And the Lord, whom you seek, will suddenly come to His temple; and the messenger of the covenant, in whom you delight, behold, He is coming,' says the Lord of hosts.* - **The Prophet Malachi**

"John the Baptizer?"

"All know the story of Zechariah the priest and his son, John. John was a cousin of Yeshua. Spoken of in scripture. Absolutely."

The Messiah will suffer before he reigns

10. *Surely our griefs He Himself bore, and our sorrows He carried; Yet we ourselves esteemed Him stricken, smitten of God, and afflicted.* - **The Prophet Isaiah**

"No! The Messiah will drive out the Romans. Not suffer and die."

"Will he? We've said so for as long as any of us can remember. But where does scripture tell us this?"

"It has to! It—"

"Scripture is clear. Will we listen to God or tradition? And has Yeshua suffered?"

Beryl stared at the scroll. "At my hands…"

"Yes. And others."

He will enter Jerusalem publicly on a donkey

11. *Rejoice greatly, O daughter of Zion! Shout in triumph, O daughter of Jerusalem! Behold, your king is coming to you; He is just and endowed with salvation, humble, and mounted on a donkey, even on a colt, the foal of a donkey."* - **the Prophet Zechariah**

"I saw this with my own eyes," Beryl said.

"As did all Jerusalem. Yes."

He will be a stumbling block to the Jews

12. *Then He shall become a sanctuary; But to both the houses of Israel, a stone to strike and a rock to stumble over, and a snare and a trap for the inhabitants of Jerusalem.* - **the Prophet Isaiah**

Beryl's fists clenched on the table.

He will be called Immanuel

13. *"Therefore the Lord Himself will give you a sign: Behold, a virgin will be with child and bear a son, and she will call His name Immanuel."* **the prophet Isaiah**

Beryl read the name over again. "Immanuel… God with us…"

He will be betrayed by a friend…

14. *Even my close friend in whom I trusted, who ate my bread, has lifted up his heel against me* - **the Psalmist**

"The Iscariot," Beryl said.

"And the next prophecy pertains to him as well. Believe it or not, I found it even before it happened. Read on."

Thirty pieces will be thrown on the floor of the Temple…

15. *Then the LORD said to me, 'Throw it to the potter, that magnificent price at which I was valued by them.' So I took the thirty shekels of silver and threw them to the potter in the house of the LORD.* - **the Prophet Zechariah**

Beryl turned cold. "May God have mercy on me… I saw it happen and never realized."

He would be rejected by our Jewish rulers

16. *Thus says the Lord, the Redeemer of Israel and its Holy One, to the despised One, to the One abhorred by the nation, to the Servant of rulers* - **the Prophet Isaiah**

Beryl's eyes filled. Tears splashed the scroll now. Nicodemus pulled the scroll over and read aloud.

He will be crucified, not stoned to death

17. *They pierced my hands and my feet*

He will be struck on the face

18. *Now muster yourselves in troops, daughter of troops; They have laid siege against us; With a rod they will smite the judge of Israel on the cheek.*

He will be buried with the rich

19. *His grave was assigned with wicked men, Yet He was with a rich man in His death* - **the Prophet Isaiah"**

"Joseph…"

"Yes," Nicodemus said. "Joseph."

"What have I done?"

Men will gamble for His clothing

20. *They divide my garments among them, and for my clothing they cast lots* - **the Psalmist**

He will be mocked

21. *All who see me sneer at me; They separate with the lip, they wag the head, saying, 'Commit yourself to the Lord; let Him deliver him; Let Him rescue him, because He delights in him -* **the Psalmist**

Not one of His bones would be broken

22. *He keeps all his bones, not one of them is broken -* **the Psalmist**

He would be resurrected

23. *"For You will not abandon my soul to Sheol, Nor will You allow Your Holy One to undergo decay. -* **the Psalmist**

Beryl rubbed a hand across his face. "You really believe he is alive? These words speak of his physical body?"

"He has been seen. There is no doubt."

He will come into the Temple

24. *And the Lord, whom you seek, will suddenly come to His temple* - **the Prophet Malachai**

"Where is he then?" Beryl said.

"Did he not come and teach? At the appointed time?"

He would be praised by infants and babes

25. *From the mouth of infants and nursing babes You have established strength Because of Your adversaries, to make the enemy and the revengeful cease." -* **the Psalmist**

"I shouted them down. God help me, I shouted them down…"

"These are only the start. As I said before, the List grows daily."

"I am undone, Nicodemus. I have but one consolation in it all."

"What consolation?"

"I know, without a doubt, Joseph of Arimathea will kill me for what I've done. And it's as it should be. I'm ready to die."

Abigail approached and put a hand on Beryl's shoulder. "A glimpse of the man I once knew. These are glad tidings, husband. A man ready to die is a man finally ready to live. Now, Nicodemus, will you take me?"

Beryl looked up at her. "Take you? Where are we going?"

"You're going home, husband. To think and to pray. And I'm going to meet my daughter for the very first time."

44

Joseph woke in his own bed. He moaned and put a hand to his forehead, finding a knot the size of a child's fist. He tried to rise but soft hands pushed him back.

"Easy, Joseph. Slowly. You've had a very rough time."

"Ariella. How did I get here?"

"The Romans. They tell me it was a brutal battle. But Barabbas' men are dead or running."

"And Barabbas?"

"They say he disappeared in the fight. Longinus is furious."

"He and Barabbas fought hard." Joseph swallowed and tried to rise again. "What about Sister? Did she survive?"

"Longinus carried her here in his own arms. She sleeps."

Joseph's heart knotted, a wave of grief filling his eyes. "Ariella, Davi…"

She took his hand, tears flowing freely down her cheeks. "I know, Joseph. Longinus told me what happened. I'm so sorry, husband. For you and for all of us."

Joseph's pulse pounded. "I'll have your father's life, Ariella. With my own hands. I vow I'll look into the man's eyes as he sucks in his last breath."

"Think about it later, Joseph. Please, rest now. You've had a hard blow."

Joseph pushed himself up and slid his feet over the side of the bed. The room spun. He dropped his head and closed his eyes, letting things settle.

"Joseph—"

"No, Ariella. I won't rest. This is no time to play the invalid."

Her voice hardened. "It's not playing, husband. You look like you've been kicked in the face by one of your horses. You need rest."

"Help me up."

"Don't be stubborn!" Still, she helped.

He stood, swaying. "Where is Longinus? I would talk with him."

"Joseph—"

His voice rose. "Where is he, Ariella?"

She took a step back.

"I'm sorry," he said. "Please. I didn't mean to raise my voice to you. I just…" He swallowed the rising sob.

She approached and put her arms around him, holding him tight. "Davi is gone. I wish I could change it. And my father… Oh, Joseph, I'm so sorry. I wish you'd never met me."

He pushed her back, hands on her shoulders. "Don't ever say that, Ariella. You are my life."

"My father—"

"No. He's not your father. He's no relation to us at all. He stopped being that long ago. Fetch me a tunic and robe, help me get dressed. My arms seem to have no strength."

"You really won't lie down?"

"I will not."

She retrieved the desired clothing and helped him as he shrugged into it. "What will you do, Joseph?"

"Beryl murdered Davi. There were witnesses. I will kill him."

"It's against our laws to kill."

"The Law is clear about murder. And Davi will be avenged."

"I can't believe it… Davi… How did…"

He took her hands. "You don't need to hear the details. Now, please, where is Longinus?"

"He was exhausted. He went to rest in the stable. There are still men guarding the gate, though Longinus said it wouldn't be for much longer."

It took a while for Joseph to get down the stairs. At the base he drank a cup of cold water and the spinning abated a bit. He crossed the courtyard, shielding his eyes from a sun ten times its usual intensity. Guards positioned at the gate nodded as he passed.

"Longinus?" he said.

One of them pointed to the stable doors. "Fair warning, sir, he's in no mood for conversation."

"Noted. I'll take my chances."

The interior of the stable was dark and cool. Silent but for the occasional stamp of a hoof. Joseph found the centurion sprawled on a thick bed of hay in one of the stalls. Eyes closed, lightly snoring, but hand still on the hilt of his sword.

The snoring stopped though the eyes didn't open. "I can feel you looking at me, Winemaker."

"Are you hurt?" Joseph said.

Longinus sat up. "Bruised. Sore. Not so much as you, I think. I'm sorry about the Jew. He was a good man."

"You're gracious. He hated Romans, but not you."

"He talked a lot. But we had an understanding, he and I. Besides, who can blame him? There are Romans I hate as well. Jews, too, come to think of it. But Davi was a good man. Loyal to the core and that's rare. I'll miss him."

Joseph swallowed the rising lump and forced calm. "Longinus, what happened to Beryl?"

Longinus narrowed an eye and sighed. "I'd tell you to leave it alone but I'd be talking into the wind."

"Would you leave it alone if you were me?"

Longinus got to his feet with a groan. He brushed hay from his clothes. "I'd have his head on a stake if I had to follow him to the ends of the frontier. But, then again, I'm a Roman."

"Where is he, Longinus?"

"There was a cave. My best guess is both Beryl and Barabbas lost themselves in it. It's the only place they could have gone. I think those two particular rats are especially good at wiggling through cracks."

Joseph leaned against the stable wall, weak to the core. "I'll find him."

"I've no doubt. But rats can be rabid. Don't get bit. The man holds much power. You know that."

"He's a murderer of the worst sort. He is no Jew. No child of God."

"Every father has one or two bad sons. Would it do any good at all if I said you should let Rome handle it?"

"Davi was a brother, Longinus."

Longinus nodded and put a hand on Joseph's shoulder. "Then he will be avenged as a brother should. I'll help any way I can."

"I just need information. Have you heard anything at all?"

"No, but rats have a way of turning up. I suggest you rest now. No doubt the coming time will tax both of us even further."

The stable door pushed inward, throwing a long shaft of light. One of the guards stepped in. "You ordered us to let none pass. Someone is at the gate."

"So? They don't enter, what's so complicated about that?" Longinus said.

"It's the Pharisee Nicodemus, sir. A woman is with him."

Joseph and Longinus followed the soldier into the bright sunlight of the courtyard. As reported, Nicodemus and a woman stood at the gate. The woman vaguely familiar. She had the most extraordinary gold eyes.

"Let them pass," Longinus said.

Joseph clasped Nicodemus' hand.

"You've been hurt again," Nicodemus said. "You don't look like a man who should be on his feet."

"Nicodemus, Davi…"

"I heard, my friend. My heart is broken for all of you."

Joseph looked at the woman.

Nicodemus hesitated, then said, "Joseph, this is—"

"Abigail," the woman broke in. "Joseph of Arimathea. I'm so happy to meet you face to face. I'm here to see my daughter."

"Your daughter?" Joseph said.

She smiled. "Joseph… I'm Ariella's mother."

Of all the things Joseph could have expected, this was the last. He realized his mouth was open. "You're mistaken, I'm afraid. My wife's mother has been dead for thirty years."

The woman's smile was a spring day. "Yes, I know. Isn't it marvelous? I'm your mother-in-law."

"Nicodemus, what's going on?" Joseph said.

"It's true, my friend," Nicodemus said. "I came with Abigail as a testament to her truth. These days death is a fragile parchment. Just look at Lazarus and others. Look at Yeshua himself. This is indeed Abigail. And she is indeed Ariella's mother."

The woman stepped forward and took Joseph's hand in hers. "I went to the next world as Ariella came into this one. But Yeshua, in his grace, has reunited us. Now please, son-in-law, it's time for you to invite me into your home, don't you think? God's mind is not our mind, who knows how much time I have?"

45

They gathered in the great room. Yaffa was present to serve wine, but Joseph suspected all the servants, as protective of Ariella as they were, were within earshot.

Abigail sat with her hands folded in her lap. Nicodemus stood with Joseph a small distance away, giving the women space.

Ariella's face was as pale as Jerusalem stone. "You claim…"

"Ariella, please take a breath," Nicodemus said. "I know this is a shock. But, believe me, reunions like this have happened across the city since Yeshua rose. It's mysterious and unsettling, as is often the case when things bear the fingerprints of Yeshua, but it's happening."

Ariella shook her head. "I confess I've heard this. But it's too fantastic—"

"It's true, daughter," Abigail said. "Please. I ask for nothing. I have no agenda here but to see you. To know you. And, if you'll allow me, to love you."

Ariella studied Abigail for a full minute, silence heavy in the room. A single tear slipped down her cheek. Joseph wanted to go to her, but he sensed the moment was somehow sacred, belonging only to them.

"You're young," Ariella said finally.

Abigail smiled. "As you know, my exit was some time ago."

"My father always said that I killed my mother. He's hated me for it all these years."

"Your father has been a fool. And his foolishness is being attended to."

It was all so impossible. Yet, since Yeshua, impossible had practically become the norm. And the resemblance between the women couldn't be denied. "Abigail," Joseph said. "You are welcome here. But please don't call it simple foolishness that a father would berate and hurt his own daughter all these years. And is it mere foolishness to put a knife through a defenseless man? A good man? A man with his hands tied behind his back?"

The gold eyes shifted to him. "I'm sorry for your pain, Joseph. I really am. My husband knows what he's done. And he knows you have a sword that longs for his blood."

"On that account, at least, he's right," Joseph said.

"I'm not here to stand in the way of what you think you must do, Joseph. God will see to that, as is His way. I'm here for my daughter. But I pray you'll think of her as well."

"Do you imagine I don't? Every second I think of her and our child. A world without Beryl is a far safer place to be born into, believe me."

"I only ask you to listen to God."

"God is just."

Abigail smiled. "Yes, God is. Will you be?"

"What does that mean?

"You've been wronged by my husband. But what about Yeshua? Wasn't he wronged a million times more? What if Yeshua decides to show Beryl mercy? What then?"

"Beryl's death avenges not only Davi, but Yeshua. I will accomplish this."

When Abigail smiled, the joy in her filled the room, leaving Joseph no room for indignation.

"Oh, Joseph!" she said. "Do you imagine the One who guides the stars across the heavens needs your protection? Your revenge? God isn't just, He is *Justice*! Perfect Justice in perfect Love! Oh, the things to come! I can't wait to show you all. And the child… This child will know and do extraordinary things. I can't wait for you all to meet him."

"Him?" Ariella said.

Abigail crossed the room and took Ariella's hands. "Oh, most definitely him." She led Ariella away, down the length of the great room, head leaned in, talking with animation.

Joseph looked at Nicodemus. "You truly believe this? Who's to say she isn't mad? Or simply after money?"

"Money? I've never met a person in my life so disconnected from, and uninterested in, material things. We can hardly make her remember to eat. Yes, I believe her, as I do the others. Several of them came to us. None will talk of where they've been. But all seem to have a purpose here. And, most of all," he lowered his voice, "Joseph, I've never seen such joy. It infects. It saturates everything they come in contact with. It makes a person's heart sing just being around them."

"It's too much, Nicodemus. The dead rise. Yeshua leaves. The Cilician rampages. Now Davi... It's just too much. Where is it going? Why hasn't Yeshua taken his throne? Why the pain? Why the suffering? When Yeshua could end it all with a word?"

"You know I search the scripture day and night. God must have a plan. We have to trust."

Joseph took a deep breath, then exhaled. "I do trust. I know Yeshua is who he is. But Davi..."

"Be patient, Joseph. The path will be shown eventually."

"And in the meantime we hide in our own city as if we're not Jews at all."

"I don't see you hiding."

"I hide. It's just that my walls are made of bought men."

The entry door opened and Longinus stuck his head in. "Joseph."

Joseph excused himself and crossed the room. Longinus motioned him to step outside. "News, Winemaker. My men and I are being called back to the Fortress. Pilate has orders for us."

"What orders? What's going on?"

"They say it's a rebel skirmish in the hills near Ephraim, but something doesn't ring true to me. We already have troops in that area, so why my men?"

"You have a theory?"

"Someone is making a move. Either Caiaphas or Beryl. Once we're gone, you'll be easy prey here. I'd advise you to find somewhere to go. If I'm right, they'll come hard and fast. I have resources, but not enough to protect you from this."

"I have my home back. I won't leave it."

"Listen, Joseph, I'm not a scholar like you, but there are things I know. Yes, you have your home back. Her name is Ariella and she carries your child. She is all that matters. Kingdoms and fortunes rise and fall. They are wind, believe me, I've seen it many times. If you stay here, it won't be the Levitical Patrol that will kill you and yours, it will be your pride. The best generals know when it's time to retreat and live to fight another day. You need to do this now. For your wife and child if not for yourself. I can buy you a half hour, but no more." He held out his hand. "For the child?"

Joseph sighed and the two men clasped forearms. "For the child. But it will not end like this."

"No, I don't think it will, Winemaker, knowing you. I'll do what I can. May God be with you."

46

Ariella watched as the man called Lazarus stirred and added pinches of different spices to the pot. A tall man. Not physically handsome, really, but so very…alive. When he smiled, his dark, narrow face became a thousand crags, a vortex of delight that pulled in all around. It was that expression he turned on Ariella now. "Not what you're used to, I think, but if you don't like it, I'll eat a donkey."

Ariella returned his smile. "If I don't like it, I'll be sure to fib, for the sake of the livestock."

They'd had to move quickly. A few things in a sack, dressed in some of the servant's clothes so they wouldn't draw attention. Joseph in a robe from his farming days and a worn *keffiyeh* draping his head and shoulders. Ariella in one of Yaffa's dresses, a head covering pulled across her face. The servants had gone to the Followers with Abigail. Sister had been escorted away by Longinus and his men, to where, Ariella didn't know. She and Joseph had simply fallen in with a group of traders and walked through the Water Gate unrecognized and unchallenged.

The small village of Bethany rested just beyond the Mount of Olives ridge line, no more than two miles from Jerusalem. So close to the city, yet removed from its view by the mountain and isolated enough to be in another world. No fountains splashed here. No clamor of crowds leaving the theater or heading for the Temple. No shouts or songs of street vendors. Just the occasional bray of a donkey and the lively laughter of some children out playing by the well.

Ariella had expected she and Joseph would garner attention entering the village, but the residents ignored them with practiced focus. These were Yeshua's people, she realized. They were used to strange comings and goings. They asked no questions and made no judgments.

She'd heard much of Lazarus. Both of his resurrection and life since. The Sanhedrin had talked of putting him to death at one point. But somehow he'd continued. And he lived unafraid and unapologetic among the people.

The door opened and his sisters, Mary and Martha, entered, both carrying large skins of water.

"It's about time," Lazarus said, throwing Ariella a wink. "I'm thirsty."

Mary's eyes rolled. "You know where the well is."

Lazarus laughed. "You expect me to do the work of women?"

Martha went to the fire and looked into the pot. "You used cinnamon?"

"Yes," Lazarus said.

"You didn't forget the za'atar?" Mary said.

Lazarus moved behind Martha, put his arms around her waist and swung her, laughing. "Just like you both taught me. Taste it if you have no faith."

Martha beat at his arms and voiced her displeasure, but her eyes laughed.

Lazarus deposited her onto a pillow, dipped a gourd ladle into the pot and poured steaming liquid into a cup. He handed it to Ariella, eyes a bright question. "Now, the moment of truth."

Ariella glanced at the sisters. "Should I trust him?"

"Absolutely not," Martha said.

Ariella sniffed and swirled the thick liquid. She wrinkled her nose. "You might want to hide the donkeys."

Lazarus laughed. "Try it first before you pass any judgment."

Ariella sipped. The drink warmed her throat and spread fingers of comfort through her body. She drank again. "I knew it. It's horrible."

"Liar," Lazarus said.

"All right. I'm a liar. It's delicious. What is it?"

"An old family recipe," Lazarus said. "These cranky sisters of mine would have my head if I told you, but suffice it to say, no donkey has ever given his life."

"Ignore him. I'll teach you to make it tomorrow," Martha said.

Joseph ducked in from the back room where he'd been resting. Lazarus ladled some of the drink into a cup and handed to him. Joseph sipped and nodded. "Thank you." He looked at the women. "Thank you all. I didn't know where else to go. As soon as I can arrange something else, we'll be no more trouble. I won't be long."

"What else can you arrange? The Sanhedrin has a long reach. I think you've discovered that much," Lazarus said.

"Joseph, what about Arimathea?" Ariella said. "If we could get the horses, we'd be there in hours. Maybe we'd be safe."

Joseph's face darkened. "Yes, maybe. Soon. But I have business in Jerusalem first."

"Abigail was adamant it wasn't my father who convinced Pilate to rescind the Roman guard," Ariella said.

Joseph shrugged. "Either way, Beryl's fate hasn't changed."

Lazarus considered Joseph, but said nothing. He held his hand out for Ariella's empty cup. "Shall we save another donkey? They say this makes for strong babies."

"Please," she said.

He refilled her cup and handed it back. She drank deep and let out a satisfied sigh. Outside, the children had stopped laughing. A dove called, answered by another. Then a sound, far in the distance. A voice, then the low rumble of many voices. Lazarus went to the doorway and looked out. His voice softened. "He comes. Finally, he comes."

"Who comes?" Joseph said.

Ariella couldn't account for it, but her pulse began to pound. Lazarus turned to them. "Yeshua. Come, let's meet him."

"Joseph?" Ariella said.

He walked over and stood beside Lazarus, looking in the direction of Jerusalem.

Lazarus put a hand on Joseph's shoulder. "Praise be to God, he comes."

Ariella stood and went to Joseph. "Should we go, Joseph? Is it safe?"

Joseph put his arm around her.

"Of course it isn't safe," Lazarus said. "But it's beautiful. Can you feel it? Something tremendous is about to happen."

"Should we prepare something? Martha said.

"No, sister, come," Lazarus said. He headed out into the street, Mary and Martha following.

"Let's go, Ariella," Joseph said. "The story continues. We go where it goes." Arms around each other, they stepped out.

A small contingent of villagers gathered at the edge of the village, Lazarus and his sisters among them. Ariella watched as a knot of people, still a mile away, crested the hill on the Jerusalem road, passing in rough double and triple file through the tiny, hilltop community of Bethphage. They moved at a brisk clip. No more than ten minutes passed before the first began to arrive, Nicodemus among them. The little Pharisee's eyes lit when he saw them, and he rushed over. "Joseph! Praise God Who makes and keeps appointments. I'd hoped you would still be here. God has heard our prayers, my friend."

"What's happening, Nicodemus? Who are all these people?"

"Followers from across the city. Yeshua bid us come to meet him here. He's been with the Eleven several times, and they say more than five hundred witnessed him in Galilee. Word was sent round this morning."

"And the Sanhedrin? The Levitical Patrol?"

"They took your home, of course. But today they're nowhere to be seen. We left the city en masse without challenge. It's another miracle, I think. As if God blinded them this day."

"Or they wait. Hoping to attack us all together."

"Let them come. This is it, Joseph! Yeshua will restore the Kingdom now. It has to be." Nicodemus turned back toward the Jerusalem Road. He scanned the crowd, then pointed. "There. He comes."

Ariella shielded her eyes. Yes, it was him. Really him.

"Nicodemus," Joseph said, "Have you found anything more in the Tanakh? Why Bethany? Why not Jerusalem? Why not the Temple itself?"

Lazarus turned. "It's Yeshua, Joseph."

Nicodemus shook his head. "I can't account for it, I admit. Perhaps he will gather his army here for entry into the city."

Deep lines again on Lazarus' face. "Be patient and hear what he has to say before you draw your sword, friend. With Yeshua, it's not that you might be surprised, but that you'll always be surprised."

And then he was there. The same Yeshua, yet different. Same brown, wind-scarred face, but brighter, harder…sharper-edged. Same height and build, but larger at the same time. The breeze tugged Ariella's dress, kicked dust and sent a tumbleweed rolling across the packed earth. Ariella felt the thud of her heart.

Yeshua climbed up on a large boulder. He made a slow turn, taking in the group of onlookers. At the base of the rock, his immediate disciples gathered. A couple of them Ariella recognized by sight, others only by description. Peter she'd seen with Yeshua on the Temple Mount. His wide shoulders and red, almost blond, beard she spotted immediately. And the big one they called John; it was said he was never far from Yeshua's side. The Eleven they were called—Twelve before the Iscariot's betrayal and demise. The others gave them deference. A tight knot of men, they'd traveled, slept, eaten and suffered with Yeshua. And, as different as their appearances made them out to be, there was an obvious brother's closeness among them. These were men who'd both fought and loved each other.

A group of women stood a little to the side. One in particular caught Ariella's eye. A little older than the others, slim to the point of being gaunt. A long strand of hair had escaped her head covering, brown with a healthy amount of grey. Her eyes wide set and luminous and filled with enough longing and pain to fill oceans.

"Lazarus," she said. "That woman to the left of the Eleven. The one with the red head covering. She's his mother, isn't she?"

Lazarus nodded. "Mary. She's stayed here with us many times. Think of her, all these years. Following him, loving him. They say she was filled with the Spirit of God while he was still in her womb and I believe it. You will too if you meet her. Think of it, chosen to carry and birth the Savior of Israel. She was practically a child herself."

"I've… I've recently met my own mother."

His face lit. "Ah! Abigail! An adventure, that one. She speaks her mind, doesn't she? And such a runner! None of us could catch her."

"Runner? But when—"

"Hosanna! Blessed is He Who comes in the name of the Lord!" The shout from the crowd cut her thought in two.

"Hosanna!"

As with the other times she'd encountered Yeshua, Ariella found herself filled with a great sense of expectancy. It filled the air, saturated the earth—everyone and everything vibrating with intangible glory. As if an army of angels blew trumpets and pounded drums, their song echoing the halls of heaven, too wonderful for mere human ears but felt nonetheless.

"Hosanna!"

Several picked up the refrain, but it died as soon as it started as Yeshua looked out over the crowd. Gone was the sadness now, replaced instead by fire. This was not the carpenter's son or the wandering Galilean. Before them was the Son of God, to whom all creation answered. Here was the Savior of Israel. Here was God With Man. Here was Yeshua.

As suddenly as it had risen, the breeze died with a sigh and the day turned silent. As if not only the crowd waited for Yeshua's words, but the animals, the fields, all the earth obeying as God the Father raised his hand for quiet. Not a bird flew. Not a bee buzzed. Great billows of white cloud hung in the sky, as motionless as if they'd been painted there. Hair stood up on Ariella's arms. She hugged herself to stop the shiver.

Yeshua looked down at the Eleven and smiled with all the love of a father for his children. "These are My words which I spoke to you while I was still with you…" His gaze shifted, eyes shining, toward Joseph and Nicodemus. "That *all* things which are written about Me in the Law of Moses and the Prophets and the Psalms must be fulfilled."

"The List…" Nicodemus said under his breath.

Yeshua lifted a hand over the crowd. "And so it is written, that the Christ would suffer and rise again from the dead the third day, and that repentance for forgiveness of sins would be proclaimed in His name to all the nations." He swung his arm and pointed in the direction of Jerusalem. "Beginning from Jerusalem! You are witnesses of these things. And behold, I'm sending forth the promise of My Father upon you."

"What promise?" Joseph said quietly. "What about the restoration of the people?"

As if he'd heard, Yeshua turned toward them again. "But you are to stay in the city until you are clothed with power from on high."

Nicodemus practically quivered. He moved forward a few steps, to be heard by all. "What promise? Lord, is it now, at this time, that you're going to restore the kingdom to Israel?"

"Wind, Pharisee," Lazarus said. "Rain and wind. Do you tame a lion? Do you dim the sun? I told you he would surprise you."

"This has to be the time!" Nicodemus said.

A ripple of ascent moved through the crowd.

Yeshua's face displayed patient fondness. He looked at Nicodemus with genuine affection. "It's not for you to know times or epochs which the Father has fixed by His own authority, but you will receive power when the Holy Spirit has come upon you; and you shall be My witnesses both in Jerusalem, and in all Judea and Samaria, and even to the remotest part of the earth."

"But—" Nicodemus started to speak, but stopped, looking around him with furrowed brow. "What is that?"

Ariella had the sudden sense of vibration. As if an intense sound filled the air that she was unable to hear. She turned, observing the people around her. Yes, they felt it too.

But then she did hear something. A low-pitched hum, barely audible but there. And then it grew. Slowly at first, then faster, in seconds becoming so deep and rich she felt it would rattle her back teeth out. Then the hum rose in pitch and became a melody, climbing, dipping, chasing the sun, then crashing back to earth.

Ariella moved closer to Joseph and took his hand. "Joseph…"

He looked down at her, eyes filled with tears. "The Song," he said. "Do you hear it?"

"Oh, Joseph, it's so beautiful! What is it?"

She looked back at Yeshua. "Is he singing?"

"I don't know. I can't tell."

"Joseph, look!" Ariella blinked, glanced away, then looked again. Yeshua's legs and feet blurred slightly. Then wavered, pulsed, as if she were looking at them through ripples in a stream. And then he wasn't on the rock anymore at all, but above it. Then even farther, higher.

"Joseph, what's happening?"

If Joseph answered, his words were swallowed by the Song.

Lazarus raised his hands toward heaven, his smile deep and violent, sheer transport.

Nicodemus grabbed Joseph's arm, pointing heavenward. He was trying to speak, but in the midst of the Song, he was a hummingbird in a hurricane. Still, Ariella understood when he mouthed the word *clouds*. She followed his finger up. Yeshua lifted higher now. And above him, the clouds. No longer the white tufts of Egyptian cotton they had been minutes ago. Instead, the billows had gathered into a mighty, roiling mass. Grey bordering black. Higher and higher Yeshua went, climbing toward the cloud-mass until he became nothing more than a light speck. Above him, the grey-black gathered and began to spin. Faster and faster, an inverted whirlpool of power unlike anything Ariella had ever seen or could have imagined.

And, looking close enough to touch it now, Yeshua. Yeshua, the cloud, and the Song… The three spun together, louder and faster, faster and louder, until all the universe hung on the brink. Ariella pressed her hands to her ears, torn, not wanting to lose the Song but sure she would die of the sheer ecstasy of it if it lasted a second longer.

It didn't.

In a blink it was gone. So was Yeshua. So was the great, heavenly cauldron. Replaced again by billows of peaceful white rolling across the sky.

A breeze tugged Ariella's dress.

A dove called.

She found herself on her knees, face still skyward.

"Gone… He's gone," Nicodemus said. "I don't understand it. What's happened?"

"Wind and rain," Lazarus whispered. "Praise be to God. You are Yeshua. You are Lord of the heavens and all they hold…"

A woman standing close by pointed. "God protect us! Who is that?"

"Angels…" Lazarus whispered.

Ariella spun. Two men stood on the tall boulder, both dressed in the brightest white, turban to toe. One was fair, hair almost as white as his garment, eyes of such aqua brilliance they were bright fire, even across the distance. The other was dark, his skin like polished ebony. Long ropes of muscle rippling his bare arms. It was this one who dropped effortlessly from the boulder and moved into the crowd. His voice, when he spoke, was unlike any Ariella had ever heard. Quiet and low, resonating with melody and restrained power. He was tenderness and war in a single form. Ariella had the sensation she was being offered a glimpse through the veil to another, better, world. That she, being clothed in something as base and temporal as flesh, should avert her eyes. But she couldn't look away.

The man stopped in the midst of the gathering. He made no introduction. "Why do you stand looking into the sky? This Yeshua, who has been taken up from you into heaven, will come in just the same way you have watched Him go."

"Sir," Nicodemus' voice shook. "Can you tell us—"

But the men were gone.

And the breeze tugged Ariella's dress.

And a tumbleweed continued its roll across the packed earth.

47

A Roman. What am I doing?

A Sister sat on the bed in the small room. With the single window and thick door, the place might as well have been a cell.

On a bed… His bed. She sighed and looked around. The room was small and sparse. The bed a simple wood frame and laced leather affair. A battered and scarred shield hung on the wall, testimony to a life of violence. Beneath it, a narrow table with a wash basin. A single straight-backed chair in the corner, a wool blanket neatly folded on it.

He'd slept on the floor that first night. And been gone since.

She rose and washed herself in the basin. She had no color to outline her eyes. No powder for her cheeks. She searched for a comb of some kind but found none. Why should she care what she looked like anyway? This wasn't the tavern. She wasn't fishing for a man with a heavy purse. It was the Roman.

A Roman!

But this Roman had come for her. He had fought for her. Why?

Yes, why, whore? Why would anyone come for you?

She pushed the voice back and went to the small window that looked out onto the massive center square of the Antonia Fortress. Built by Herod the Great and named for his benefactor,

Mark Antony, the Roman had said. He'd told her to stay here. That she would be safe until he returned. Two days ago, now, since he'd marched out at the head of a column of men. And she had stayed. Where else could she go? After all, her world was gone… Then again, though she shoved the thought down again and again, some part of her wanted to stay. Barabbas had hurt and frightened her. And the Roman made her feel safe. Safe, she realized, for the first time in her life.

There was a latrine the Roman had shown her the first day that offered a modicum of privacy. She went there, then returned to the little room. A light knock sounded—a young soldier bringing her breakfast. She thanked him and he left. Back at the window, she ate olives and cheese and watched the soldiers drill. The best part was watching them work out with long wooden training swords, exchanging blows so hard she knew any one of them would kill her.

It had been training like this—years and years of it—that had readied the Roman for war. How many men had he killed? One? Ten? A hundred? She walked over to the battered shield and ran her fingers over the scars. The swords that had caused these hadn't been wooden. Nor had the swords been wooden in the canyon when he'd fought Barabbas. The sight of sparks flying and sound of clanging blows echoing off rock filled her nightly dreams. She shivered at the thought. She'd wanted the pig Barabbas to die. Prayed for it. Yet God had not heard.

Of course not. Why would he answer a harlot?

She tried hard not to listen but the voice was always there. She knew from her dreams what it looked like. Beautiful but eyeless, smiling, mocking, reaching with invisible fingers, dragging her into that abyss from which there was no return.

The Roman had said she would be his wife. She laughed aloud even as her heart tore. She went and sat on the bed again. Her foot bumped something solid and she leaned down to look. A box… She glanced toward the closed door, then leaned down and pulled it. Rising again, she went to the window and examined the box in the light. Burnished wood, old, worn to a smooth polish from much handling.

I shouldn't…

She knew she would.

He's only a Roman. What could it hurt?

Still, it was because he was the Roman that she knew she would open it. His eyes. His hands, his strong, stubborn jaw. She set the thing on the bed and stood over it. It wasn't large. There were no markings on it and only a small clasp to secure the lid.

And no lock.

If it were private, wouldn't it have a lock? And what does he expect, leaving me here like this? Nothing to do but stare out the window at a herd of sweaty Romans beating each other senseless with sticks...

She got down on her knees. Glanced at the closed door again. The clasp sprung easily and she lifted the lid. There wasn't much. A parchment with some writing on it. She couldn't read so she set it aside. A small amphora with a wooded stopper. She pulled the stopper and sniffed—maybe liquor of some sort. A silver ring, a small, carved wooden horse... She picked up the horse and examined it. A toy, a child's plaything. She turned it over in her hands. It had been skillfully carved and brightly painted. Had he had this since he was a boy? The thought struck her as odd. She couldn't imagine the Roman as a boy. He was *the Roman*, a tall wall of man, metal, and red uniform. He was a helmet and breastplate. A machine designed to instill fear. But a boy? Never.

The door swung open and she jumped back, toy horse still in her hand. He stood there in the doorway looking down at her. Her first reaction was anger.

"You startled me! Why didn't you knock?" she said

His eyes went to the box. Then the toy in her hand. "I wondered how long it would take you."

She stood, facing him, chin lifted. "And I suppose you're angry? Will you have me scourged?"

He walked over and sank onto his chair. His face was haggard, his body covered with dust. She realized he was exhausted.

She sat on the bed opposite him. "You went far?"

"And fast...and for nothing, as I expected. Pilate's ruse to get me out of Jerusalem, I'm sure."

"You're not angry then? That I opened the box?"

"Why would I be angry? If you're to be my wife, shouldn't we share things?"

"Why do you keep saying that? What makes you think I'd want you, Roman?"

He rose, moved to the table and poured water into the cup, drank, and let out a long exhale. "Call me Longinus."

"*Roman*. Answer me."

"It's Longinus. Try it."

"Answer *me*! What makes you think I'd ever be married to you?"

He poured the remainder of water in the cup into his hands and splashed his face. "Some things are meant to be, maybe it's as simple as that. He sat again and looked at her. You captured me. From the moment I saw you in your brother's storeroom. I've tried to explain it to myself, but it's really that simple."

"Is there no other woman anywhere you can torture with your affections?"

He stood and walked to the window, looked out over the square. "There was. Once. A long time ago."

"Where?"

"Corsica, where I was raised. She was a fisherman's daughter, as beautiful as the sea."

Why did this bother her? "Well, go find her. A big brute like you, she probably still stares at the moon and dreams of you."

"It's been fourteen years."

"For true love? A year is a minute."

And what do you know of true love, whore?

He turned back to her. "Fourteen years since she died."

Maybe the thought of the girl—*as beautiful as the sea.* Maybe grief for innocence lost and unrecoverable. Maybe the voice and its never-ceasing accusation and taunt. Maybe just a lifetime of wounds. Whatever the source, a wave of anger she couldn't account for washed over her. She lashed out at him with the first thing that came to her mind. "Do you know how many men have professed their love for me? I can't count them. You say you'll marry me? How about protect me? I still feel the effects of Barabbas' fists. I still smell him when I lie down to sleep! You might as well kill me as marry me, Roman. I would be better off and the world would be better place."

"Don't be a child."

"I'm a child? Maybe you should go back to Corsica and find some beautiful-as-the-sea fisherman's brat."

"Barabbas will die. Not you."

"How, Roman? How will he die? You couldn't best him in the canyon. What makes you think you can do it now?"

"*Longinus*. Say it."

"Roman."

"I was a boy back then in Corsica. I thought I knew what love meant. Maybe I did, maybe I didn't. It doesn't matter. That boy is as dead as that girl. He died piece by piece on a thousand battlefields."

She held up the toy horse. "Is that true? Then why does the man keep the boy's toy?"

Muscles knotted in his jaw. He moved to the door. "You keep it. Or burn it. I care not. I need to go check on my men."

She hurled the toy horse at him but missed. It clattered to the floor, one leg broken off. "Then go, Roman."

He looked down at the broken horse, then at her. "I bought it at an Arabian bazaar. A hundred years ago it seems. It was to be my son's one day. The thought of him, and the woman who would bear him, kept me alive through a hundred battles. He turned and the door swung softly shut behind him.

When he'd gone, she stared at the closed door for a long time. Then crossed the room, leaned down, and picked up the broken toy. She turned it over in her hands. The animal's features blurred with her tears. "Then go...Longinus."

48

J oseph woke, Ariella's hand on his chest.

"Hush, husband," she whispered. "Quiet now. You'll wake the others."

He nodded, breathing hard, shifted a bit on the straw pallet.

"Your heart is pounding, Joseph. Are you all right?"

"I dreamed of a black horse. I was riding him across the Negev. A moonless night. Faster than any animal I've ever ridden. Impossibly fast. Then I dreamed of Davi…"

"It's all right, husband. You're here with me. Try to sleep."

The small room was still save for a cricket chirping through the open window. Someone coughed in the darkness and rolled over. They'd gathered at the secret block of apartments off the Valley of the Cheesemakers where Nicodemus and many of the other Followers had been staying, Nicodemus among them. This room was one of many in the deceivingly large complex. The Eleven were somewhere above. Mary Magdalene and Mary the mother of Yeshua as well. Lazarus and his sisters had arrived this morning, making the short journey from Bethany to celebrate Shavuot—or Pentecost—also called the Feast of Weeks since it happened seven weeks after every Passover. By Joseph's assessment, at least a hundred more had followed the Eleven to the rooms, all waiting as Yeshua had given direction.

Several of them had been present at Yeshua's Bethany ascension. The ones who hadn't had certainly heard about it in the greatest detail—especially the promise of his return by the men in white—as the story was passed around, over and over through the group.

Tomorrow would be Pentecost proper, but tonight, as tradition dictated, the entire group had gathered in the spacious upper room to hear and discuss God's word. Nicodemus, sitting beneath an oil lamp, read aloud the story of Ruth the Moabitess. *May the Lord reward your work, and your wages be full from the Lord, the God of Israel, under whose wings you have come to seek refuge.* And as Joseph had looked around the tired and fear-worn group, he'd silently prayed God's promise to Ruth might hold true as well to these bedraggled followers of Yeshua. When Ruth had been read, discussed, and put to bed, Nicodemus had started in on the growing List of Messianic prophecies. The more he'd read, the more the room had thrummed. Memories of Yeshua's travels and life were told and retold, always returning to one theme, one sentence: *He will come in just the same way you have watched Him go into heaven.*

Now, in the dark, Joseph listened to the cricket's song and Ariella's even breathing, off-speed rhythms merging, separating, and coming together again. He tried to sleep but his thoughts wouldn't rest. Memories of Davi as a boy, Davi as a man, Davi as the only real friend Joseph had known through so many hard years. Davi laughing simply because he loved to laugh. His quick temper. His unwavering loyal spirit.

Finally, cursing his restless mind, Joseph rose, making sure Ariella was covered and as comfortable as she could be on the thin straw. He needed air. His body ached to ride out into the empty Judean countryside and, like his dream, push his mount until the speed, bit by bit and hurt by hurt, began to peel away his grief. Out on the small patio he'd at least be able to see sky and stars.

To get there, he had to pass through the long common room. It was very dark, an obstacle course of sleepers, and he stepped carefully to miss their still forms. It was in this room, Nicodemus told him, Yeshua had celebrated his last meal with his close Twelve before the twelve became eleven and Caiaphas and Beryl had their way. In a way, the room had become holy to them all. A place of remembrance and worship. And now waiting as well.

Another short passage, then the double wooden doors leading out to the patio. The doors stood open, and Joseph was surprised to see low, flickering lamplight coming from outside. Stepping out, he found Nicodemus sitting at the low table, several scrolls open in front of him.

Joseph lowered himself to a pillow. "You taught for hours tonight. Do you ever sleep?"

The little Pharisee continued to stare at the passage on the scroll in front of him with focused intent. "I could ask you the same."

"I chased sleep and caught it for a bit but it came with dreams. Too many thoughts of Davi."

Nicodemus looked up now. "He was a good man. I miss him."

"Ariella cries at night. I confess, my grief takes the shape of anger. All I can think of is sinking my blade into Beryl's fat, black heart."

"God will have vengeance, Joseph. You know as well as I it's best to leave it to Him."

"Yes, God will have vengeance. But I'd be lying if I said I didn't pray with everything in me that He will allow me to act as His hard hand in this. I want to watch the life fade from Beryl's eyes as he makes the horrible realization Hades will be his new home."

Nicodemus studied him for a long beat. "I'll pray as well. But my prayer will be that your soul would find peace."

Joseph indicated the scroll that had Nicodemus' attention. "Divert my mind, friend. What trail do you follow that has you here while the rest of the world sleeps?"

Nicodemus lifted a pitcher and eyebrow in silent question.

"Wine?" Joseph said.

"Of course not. It's Pentecost. Milk is the tradition."

Joseph shrugged assent and Nicodemus passed him a cup. He sipped. "Honey and cinnamon, I'm thinking."

Nicodemus smiled. "Milk is tradition, but I see no place in the Tanakh that forbids a little sweet on a long night." He tapped the scroll with a finger. "The men in white said he would return.

But why did he go? What is yet to happen? The answers are here somewhere."

"His return has to be any day. Rome presses ever harder. And even if Rome were to disappear tomorrow, our eyes are now open to the tyranny and corruption of our own leaders."

"Yes…"

"But?"

"It's as we've said before. This is bigger than Rome. Possibly bigger than Israel as well. *Behold the Lamb of God who takes away the sin of the world.* There is much work for us, I think."

Digging deep into scripture, the two talked and debated away the remaining night. In the east the sun stretched beneath the hills and readied for the day, bathing the patio in grainy, purple light. Steps sounded from the hallway and Peter, one of the Eleven, came onto the patio. "A word with you?"

Nicodemus waved him to join. "Of course! Please, sit."

Peter did, and nodded to the scrolls. "You've been at it all night?"

"Like His love, God's words are a bottomless sea. And every day they come to life all around us. We struggle to keep up."

Peter pointed to the pitcher of sweet milk. "May I?"

"Forgive me for not offering," Nicodemus poured a cup for the disciple and handed it to him.

Peter sipped and gave a satisfied sigh. "My mother made the same. It brings back memories. You've heard that the Eleven are again Twelve?"

"I was absent when you drew lots, but yes. Matthias is a good man."

"He's been faithful and there's much to do."

"Of course," Nicodemus said. "Joseph and I were just saying the same."

Peter set his cup on the table. "This waiting around, my flesh fights it but I want to be obedient. We wait for the Spirit promised by Yeshua. I don't pretend to know what it means, but I let him down once. I won't do it again. We'll be ready."

"I fear a hard road ahead," Joseph said.

"As do I. Which brings me to this. Today, as you know, is Pentecost. We've talked it over. Too long we've cowered in the shadows. I propose we send word to all the Followers across Jerusalem. Right now. This morning. Call them to gather with us on Solomon's Porch this day and worship as we should—freely, on our own Temple Mount." He put a hand on the table. "We are Jews! In number, and in such a public forum, it will be difficult for the Sanhedrin to move against us."

"I wouldn't be so sure," Nicodemus said. "The Cilician is as bold as he is ruthless."

"It's Pentecost. What would you have us do?"

Joseph shifted on his cushion, leaning forward. "I, for one, would relish the confrontation. You speak truthfully—we are Jews. And this is a day to give thanks to God for the gift of His word. Without it we would be adrift and rudderless."

Nicodemus nodded soberly. "You're right, of course. Pentecost should be celebrated on the Temple Mount."

Peter stood. "Good. I wanted your opinion as former Sanhedrin members. I praise God you're with us. I'll send word to the others. All Followers who would join us are welcome. The festival of the grain harvest—we take our First Fruits to the Temple like every year." He grinned. "And, since we have little, we'll offer our two loaves as a family. The family of Yeshua. Our offering to God will be small, but like the widow with her two mites, our love and obedience will be great."

49

Sister dreamed of the eyeless man again. Always the same dream. Running, running…hearing his feet pound behind her. Then his hard hands pushing her against the wall, breath like sweet honey against her face. But this time worms writhed in his previously empty eye sockets.

The beautiful mouth smiled. *You will always be mine. We will be together forever and ever. Aren't you glad? I will never leave you. And you will never leave me.*

She tried to call for the Roman, but the beautiful wraith only laughed at her. Over and over she called, harder and harder he laughed. And then, in her dream state, the Roman's name somehow changed and became *Yeshua.* The laughter stopped. Then the strangest thing, she could physically see the words coming from her mouth as she called, gold and shining things, floating into the air. And each one the wraith knocked to the ground until a pile of gold glass lay around them. He clamped a cold hand over her mouth.

That sick, sweet breath. *Always and forever. We will never change…*

But as he spoke, whispering never-ending hopelessness into her ear, another sound began to come. A song? A melody? Faint at first, then louder. The wraith raised his whisper to a voice, then to a shout as the song swelled. And then to a scream, his confident authority wavering for the first time.

Whore! Whore! Whore! Whore! You don't even have a name! You're mine! Forever and ever!

And then she woke, breathing hard, sweating in the thick, stone heat of Longinus' quarters. She looked down at his blanket on the floor, but even in the darkness, she could tell by the stillness in the air he wasn't there.

They'd spoken little since she'd thrown the toy horse at him. Even when she'd asked the young soldier who attended to her needs to bring her some animal hide glue and fixed the little statue, he'd said little. But at night, when he blew out the lamp, it was his steady breathing that helped her sleep, that pushed away thoughts of giants and caves and blood.

She wanted to hear his breath now. Wanted to hear his footsteps in the hall and hear the door creak open with his return. She strained her ears for the sound, but to her stunned surprise, it was another sound she heard.

The song from her dream. It hadn't stopped with her waking.

She blinked in the black. Reached up a hand and touched her own face. No, she wasn't dreaming, she was fully awake. But still the song came to her, faint and distant but there.

Rising, she felt her way to the door and opened it. A little louder in the hall. Only by a fraction, but noticeable. It seemed to be coming from her right. She followed.

The fortress was asleep for the most part. The few guards posted ignored her as she passed. If they heard the song, they gave no evidence of it. She exited the fortress through an arched gate, the song even louder out here in the street. A male voice carrying the melody. Down the street she followed it, at times touching and pinching herself to make sure she was actually still awake. The city was empty this time of night. Except for the singer, wherever he was, she was completely alone. On she walked, realizing with a twinge of trepidation she was getting close to the city wall. Would she follow outside? It wouldn't be safe, she knew, but then again, what was safe about any of this? Who knew what lay ahead? Maybe she was losing her mind. It was the explanation that made the most sense.

But when she reached the city wall, the song seemed to come from above, not without. Very loud now. She wondered how it wasn't waking people. She noticed a narrow stairway to her left leading up and took it. A steep climb later, she found herself stepping out onto the top of the wall itself. Stars winked above her. A partial moon kept itself hidden behind a towering bank of clouds. Jerusalem slept below on her left. On the right, the wilderness rolled away to black horizon, infinite and mysterious.

The song called.

She moved along the top of the wall, her heart racing within her. She wanted the Roman to be here, needed his calm presence. The melody paused, making way for a single, low-spoken word. "Come…" Then the song started again.

The wall widened and the pathway split around a small stone building. An unoccupied watchtower perhaps. She saw it then, a figure sitting on a bench propped against the stone.

The singer.

She pinched herself again.

He halted his song. "Come," he said. "Come, daughter."

She squared and approached. He was old and roughly dressed. His white beard and hair wispy, moving on the breeze. But his eyes were bright as he fixed them on her.

She stopped before him. "Who are you?"

He shrugged. "I'm the Shepherd."

"Why do you call me daughter? I have no father, nor a mother."

"No?"

"No. How could I hear your song all the way from the Fortress? What's happening to me?"

He stood and reached out his hand toward her. "Take my hand."

She backed away. "What's happening to me?"

He smiled. "Everything is happening to you, daughter."

"Don't call me that. I'm no one."

He smiled. "You've been listening to the wrong voice for far too long. I won't have it anymore. Come."

She blinked. "How do you know about the voice?"

"The owner of that voice has been a beautiful liar from the beginning. Take my hand and he'll bother you no more."

"Beautiful… You even know my dreams?"

"He tells you you belong to him, but nothing belongs to him. Not really. Daughter, take my hand."

Her eyes welled and tears she couldn't explain spilled down her cheeks. She choked back a sob. "What's happening? Please."

"I told you—everything."

"I'm a prostitute! I danced for him! I don't even have a name! You don't know!"

"I know everything, *Bityah.*"

"Bityah? Who is Bityah?

"You are."

"Bityah means daughter of God. How can you—"

"And so you are. Bityah has been your name from before the foundations of the earth were formed, and Bityah your name will still be when the stars you see now have faded and disappeared. Now come!Take my hand!"

The old man's form blurred through the flood of her tears. The white beard and hair caught watery starlight and faded, but his eyes still shone.

His eyes…

Those eyes…

She wiped at her tears with the heal of her hand and tried to focus on the old man's face. But the old man was gone. In his place…

"You? I danced for you…" she said. "I was horrible. Yet you stayed, in spite of me."

"Haven't you realized it yet, Bityah? It was you I came for that night. Nothing has ever been in spite of you, but *because* of you. Take my hand. You are wonderfully and perfectly loved. Always.You have been since before time began."

Those eyes… She watched her own hand tremble as she reached out. His was warm and strong. He smiled and his eyes filled her.

"But I danced for you…" she said again.

"Did you? I don't remember."

And then he was gone, nothing where he had been but air and starlight and the whisper of his song.

"Sister," the voice came from behind her and she turned.

The Roman stood, tall and strong against the night. She went to him without hesitation and put her arms around him, unashamedly letting her tears stain the front of his tunic.

"Longinus," she said. "My name is Bityah."

"Bityah? I don't understand."

"Nor do I, completely. But I have a name."

"Bityah…" he said. "I thought I heard singing.

She smiled up at him. "Yes. You did."

50

Longinus kept his arm around her as they started back along the top of the wall. She surprised herself when she leaned in closer.

Bityah—Daughter of God... I have a name.

"How did you find me?" she said.

"I came back to the room and you were gone. One of the men told me which way you'd headed. I followed and heard singing up on top of the wall. What was it? What happened up here?"

"I had a dream. After that I'm still not sure. Maybe it was all a dream."

"And the name?"

"Bityah. He told me..."

"He?"

"You won't believe it. I—"

He stopped with a jolt, pushing her behind him.

She touched his back. "What is it?"

"Stay behind me. Don't move and don't speak." He kept his voice low.

They waited then, hardly breathing, listening intently to the night. Then she caught it, not a sound, but the faintest odor on the breeze. Her knees went weak.

The moon broke the clouds, spilling uncertain light as Barabbas stepped from the shadows, grinning and monstrous, sword already in his hand. "Roman, this is how it should have been in the first place, eh? Just the two of us, and a pretty prize for the one who's still alive when it's over."

Longinus drew his own sword. Bityah backed up several feet and pressed herself against the stone bulwark on the outside edge of the great wall.

"It must have been boring for you, Barabbas, all that waiting outside the fortress," Longinus said.

"You saw me?"

"I knew you were somewhere close."

"The woman left an impression, what can I say? I knew you had her in there. And I knew she had to come out eventually. Boring, yes, but I managed to keep myself entertained imagining different ways I would kill you." The giant leaped forward and swung with such speed it made Bityah flinch thirty feet away. Fury drove him with the strength of a hundred devils. The clang of steel against steel shrieked off the walls. Sparks cascaded to the stone.

And the giant kept coming, driving, grunting with every swing and thrust. Longinus parried over and over, giving ground, struggling for footing.

Cold fingers gripped her. *He's going to die.* She knew it then, watching the two. Barabbas was too huge and too fast. It was like fighting a mountain. Or a lightning storm. Yes, Longinus would die tonight and the idea wrecked her. The Roman had become a presence in her life, one she knew now she didn't want to lose. *I have a name...* But Barabbas was unstoppable. Turning, she scrambled up onto the top of the wall's stone bulwark facing the valley. Below her now, only empty black. How far to the bottom? The thought made her feel sick. Still, the moment Longinus took his last breath she knew she would leap without hesitation. The inevitable reality of Barabbas taking her again wasn't to be endured.

Steel clanged, Longinus cursed. She turned to the fight, dreading what she'd see but not able to help herself. Barabbas still drove forward, Longinus scrambled for balance. Then his foot caught on a raised stone and he stumbled in earnest.

Barabbas wasted no time swinging a wicked backhand with his sword. But Longinus anticipated the move and allowed his body to roll backwards, keeping himself beneath Barabbas' steel. With a lunge he came back to his feet. Barabbas' eyes widened as he found himself off balance and at his first disadvantage. But he instantly recovered and used his body momentum to throw a brutal left-handed fist to Longinus' face. Longinus rocked back but managed to straighten, shaking his head.

"That same blow has killed other men," Barabbas said.

"Then other men were made of parchment and dust."

The giant grunted a laugh. "I wonder, Roman, do you even have blood in your veins? I'm looking forward to finding out." He lunged again, putting everything he had into a brutal attack.

Longinus didn't back up this time. Instead he answered blow for blow, move for move, once making slight contact and drawing blood from Barabbas' chest. On they fought, neither man losing or gaining ground.

"My only regret," Barabbas grunted, "is that you'll die before you get to see what I'm going to do to her. Oh, it will be a sight to see, Roman."

Longinus thrust, barely missing the big man's throat.

"You have nothing to say now?" Barabbas said, breathing hard.

"Only that you talk too much. Fight and die."

Barabbas advanced and Longinus backed up again, making the big man chase him, this time keeping his balance. He switched foot positions often. Moving to one side, then the other. At length, Barabbas took a great step back and lowered his sword a few inches. "Why don't you stand still, Roman?"

"Are you tired, giant?"

For the first time, uncertainty touched Barabbas' eyes. Longinus swung and Barabbas barely got his sword up in time to parry. The giant was tiring. But Longinus' long years of constant training were serving him well. With this apparent realization, renewed fury exploded across Barabbas' face. With a bellowed shout, he rushed with a string of bone-rattling blows. Longinus let him come, parrying time and time again. In the frenzy, one of Barabbas' thrusts got through, catching the edge of Longinus' thigh and drawing blood. Still, the Roman never faltered in his rhythm.

Swing, parry. Swing, parry. Swing… But this time Longinus didn't parry. Instead, he lowered his sword and leapt back, letting Barabbas fall forward in his balance. With a lightning jab, Longinus struck, hitting Barabbas a neck-snapping blow with the fist holding the sword haft. The giant stumbled back and Longinus stepped in, the same blow. Then again. And again. Blood flowed from Barabbas crushed nose and mouth. He sank to his knees, sword in his limp hand before him. Longinus struck him again.

Barabbas started to lift his sword. Blood bubbled on his lips. "You surprise me, Roman. I thought no man could do it."

"You thought wrong."

"Finish it then, and go to your whore."

Longinus hit him again.

Barabbas spat out a tooth. "Kill me and be done!"

Another blow from Longinus.

Barabbas' head rolled back then up again. "You spare the sword? You would show mercy, Roman?" He let his sword slip from his fingers. "Fine. Good. There are other women. She's made you soft, I think. The mighty Longinus, slayer of armies, tamed by a filthy Lower City prostitute who doesn't even have a name." He squinted up, grinning broken teeth and blood.

It happened so fast she almost missed it. Barabbas lunged, scooping up his sword with a flash of moonlight on steel. But even as the rebel's sword rose, Longinus struck. The giant's head parted from his body with a thud. It rolled a few cubits before it stopped against a post.

Longinus cleaned his sword on his tunic, then spat down at the giant's headless neck. "She has a name…it's Bityah."

51

Joseph joined more than a hundred Followers as they walked past the public mikvehs and climbed the southwestern steps from the valley floor to the Temple Mount. They gathered in one place, loosely bunched around the Twelve deep in the shadows of the western portion of Solomon's Porch between the Royal Stoa and the Zion Bridge gate entrance. Peter, true to his promise, carried two loaves of bread for the Pentecost offering. Mary, mother of Yeshua, was there. And also Mary the Magdalene, of whom it was said Yeshua had cast out seven demons. Lazarus and his sisters stood talking with Mathias, the recently chosen twelfth apostle.

In front of the Porch, the Temple Mount platform sprawled, a sun-drenched maelstrom of color and chaos and noise. Different dialects rose and fell as Jews from around the known world pressed into Jerusalem to celebrate God's gift of the Scripture to His people. Laughter and shouts. Prayers went up. Up and down the porch, rabbis recited scripture, their voices tumbling over one another in raucous competition.

"Will there be trouble, Joseph?" Ariella held his arm close.

"I honestly don't know, but I suspect the Council will be reluctant to move against such a large group on the Mount."

Nicodemus nodded in the direction of the Royal Stoa. "There they are."

Joseph looked out across the top of the crowd and scanned the group of Sanhedrin gathered on the Stoa steps. "Beryl isn't with them," he said.

"My sense is Beryl's change is real, Joseph. He did seem sincere," Nicodemus said.

Joseph shook his head. "Impossible. I watched him kill Davi. I saw his face when he did it. He's lying."

"Impossible? Is that a word you really want to use after all we've been through and seen? Lying to what end? He kept his word about not giving the Cilician our location."

"Maybe… I don't know, but with Beryl there's always a reason. And his reasons always benefit Beryl. He deserves to die."

Nicodemus arched a brow. "Well, I suspect we'll know soon enough. Here he comes."

Joseph turned and spotted Beryl's large form and Abigail's smaller one at his side, moving along the Porch toward them from the Northern end of the Mount.

Joseph started for them, but at that moment Peter called out, summoning the group to gather and pray. Followers began moving toward the disciple, including Ariella and Nicodemus. Joseph let them go and hung back, his focus trained on Beryl.

Peter's voice rose in prayer. Others as well. Abigail drifted from Beryl's side and found Ariella. But Beryl edged away, an expression on his face Joseph had never seen before and found difficult to read. Sorrow? Regret?

Good. Whatever it is, let him die in it.

To Joseph's surprise, Beryl locked eyes with him and gave a slight nod. Then, slowly, the priest turned and started back up the porch. Joseph followed. Beryl picked up his pace a little, lacing a path through the harvest pilgrims. Joseph pushed after him. People became a blur of color and noise. Someone recognized Joseph and called his name. Joseph ignored it. A rabbi clutched at Joseph's coat, demanded alms. Joseph shoved the man's hand away, allowing nothing to pull his attention from Beryl's form.

At the northern end of the Porch, the crowd thinned. Beryl turned and met Joseph's eyes, that same broken countenance, then stepped behind a wide pillar.

Joseph found him there, waiting, back pressed up against the marble.

"A private place, Joseph. I thought we should be alone, away from the others."

Joseph shrugged. "Alone or in a crowd, I'd kill you either way."

"I know. I don't hope for my life, but I don't suppose it would help your soul to tell you I do regret what I've done?"

"None at all."

"I suspected as much. I'm a murderer. I will die at your hand. It's as it should be."

"You are an evil man, Beryl, wicked to the core. You've tortured Ariella with your pride and selfishness her whole life. You put an innocent man on a cross."

"Yes. And I killed your friend with my own hands."

Joseph's entire body trembled with rage.

"You're right, Joseph. I am wicked. I know it. I see it. You were right all along about Yeshua. It's too late for me now, I know that. And your man…"

"His name was Davi. A thousand times the man you ever were."

A tear slid down Beryl's face. "Davi…yes. Do you remember that Passover meal? When you told me to leave your home? Davi stood up for you that night. I hated him for it. He wounded my pride deeply. But he was right to do it. I know it was a good man I killed. Yes, much better than I."

Joseph reached beneath his tunic and pulled out a short, curved dagger.

Beryl nodded at the sight. "I was hoping it would be now."

Joseph studied the man's face. "You're convincing, Beryl, I'll admit. But then again, you always have been."

"Don't misunderstand me. This is no game or subterfuge. I'm not asking for mercy. Not from you, not from God. You'll push that blade into my heart and I'll step into Hades. I'll burn. I know it as sure as I'm standing here. But I'm ready to die. I need to die. I *have* to die. I would have taken my own life these last days, but I knew you deserved the satisfaction. It's all I can offer you after what I've done. I won't take it away. Kill me now. Do it. And live in peace."

Blood pounded in Joseph's temples. He took a fast step forward and pressed his forearm into the priest's throat, shoving Beryl's heavy head against the stone. He lifted the knife.

"Yes…do it, Joseph," Beryl croaked. "I only ask you one thing. My grandchild—please don't tell him about me. I'm not asking you to lie. Just say nothing. No child should live with the knowledge of a heritage like me."

Joseph's hand shook, his knuckles turned white around the haft of the blade. He leaned his body closer, smelling the sweat on Beryl's skin. "Rot in Hades, Beryl. Rot with the knowledge I've made no promises to you. He pressed the knife tip to Beryl's chest.

A gentle hand touched his arm. "Don't, Joseph."

He'd been so focused on his enemy he'd not seen Abigail approach.

"Don't," she said. "Don't let it be this way."

Joseph ground his teeth. "Leave, Abigail. You don't want to see this."

"No. I won't leave, son-in-law. Think. This isn't the way. You will live with this your whole life."

"And gladly. It will allow me to finally sleep at night. Do you have any idea what this man has done?"

"I have every idea what he's done. I know exactly. And I know, in his heart, there is great sorrow. Great repentance. Believe me, this is not the way."

"Please, Abigail," Beryl gasped. "Go away. He must do this. Joseph needs it and I need it."

Abigail shook her head. "Oh you foolish, foolish men. Do you really think your emotional needs are what's important today? Of all days? Joseph, put away the knife."

"He will die," Joseph said.

"Yes, he will. But not at your hand."

Joseph glanced at the woman but kept the knife in place. "I know you mean well, Abigail, but go back to Ariella."

"We all deserve to die," she said. "And we all will. But the time? That is for God and God alone to decide."

Joseph looked deep into Beryl's eyes. "Maybe God makes an exception once in a while."

The priest nodded imperceptibly. "Yes, Joseph, do it."

Joseph tightened his grip and leaned in.

And the world exploded.

A sound. Like nothing else Joseph had ever heard. It was as if all the winds of the earth blasted from the four points of the compass to howl their fury with one deafening voice. The cacophony roared through the Porch and across the Mount, so loud it threatened to shake the heavens apart and crumble the earth beneath its immense weight. Joseph fell back and sank to his knees, covering his ears with his hands. Beryl dropped as well. Only Abigail remained standing.

And then, as suddenly as it had come, the air went silent. Joseph felt his heartbeat, heard his own breath. His hands shook. "What was that?"

Abigail beamed down at him, her face the perfect picture of joy. "*Everything*, Joseph. That was *everything*."

52

For long seconds, silence reigned on the Mount.

Then Joseph was up and running, a single thought in his mind—*Ariella*. He flew down the Porch, weaving his way through pillars and crowd. All around him people rose to their feet, eyes wide. Questions hung in the air.

He saw the group of Followers ahead, still bunched. Relief flooded him when he saw Ariella a bit off to the side scanning the crowd with confused concern.

"Ariella!"

She turned at the sound of his shout and rushed toward him. He pulled her into his arms. She clung to him. "Joseph! Where did you go? It was so loud! Did you see it? It was like fire! What was it, husband?"

"Fire? No, I didn't see fire. Only heard the sound."

"Yes! Streams of fire in the air. And the noise! The wind!"

Gone were the stunned and whispered questions now. A great din rose from the Mount as people called out to each other, wondered aloud, argued over what had transpired. The Sanhedrin, still on the Stoa steps, milled in confusion as worshipers called out to them, demanding an explanation.

Then a voice lifted above the rest. John, one of the Twelve, hands held high, calling out toward the heavens. The intensity and confidence in his tone turned heads and the crowd roar subsided noticeably.

"What is he saying?" Ariella said.

"I don't know," Joseph said, confusion filling his mind. "I don't recognize the language."

Nicodemus approached. "Joseph, do you understand any of this?"

"No. None of it," Joseph said.

Another of the Twelve began to speak over the crowd. Another language. Then another, a man named James, followed. Then more of them, until all twelve were speaking, none of their words decipherable.

"Fire, wind, unknown languages. This is the hand of God," Nicodemus said.

"I agree. But what does it mean?"

"The Spirit," Ariella said. "Yeshua told us to wait in Jerusalem. This must be what we've been waiting for."

"Are they all different languages? None of them sound alike." Nicodemus pointed out toward the center courts. "But I think some of them understand."

"You're right," Joseph said. "Look at that group of Libyans. And the Elamites. They're listening."

The tide of people out in the courts had drifted, tightening at the base of the steps beneath the Twelve. More and more came, all eyes on the disciples. A large knot of men dressed in the distinct sleeved coats and trousers of Parthia had gathered beneath the spot where Joseph and Nicodemus stood. One man turned to the others. He pointed up the steps with a long finger. His words were common Aramaic, but halting and formal. "Are not these men Galileans?" He was very tall and very thin, his stooped shoulders giving him the appearance of a scholar rather than a man who worked with his hands. He climbed a few of the Porch stairs and looked back out at the gathering. "How is it that we each hear them in our own language? Look, Parthians and Medes and Elamites. And over there—residents of Mesopotamia and Judea and Cappadocia. I see men from Pontus and Asia, Phrygia and Pamphylia, Egypt and Libya. Romans, both Jews and proselytes. Cretans and Arabs. How do these Galileans speak to us all in our native tongues?"

One of the other Parthians called up to the stoop-shouldered man. "Tell us, what does this mean, Phraates?"

"I confess I don't know. But you hear them. They speak of the mighty deeds of God."

A lantern-jawed man Joseph recognized as a well-known scribe scoffed. "I'll tell you exactly what it means. It means that they're drunk. So full of sweet wine it's flowing from their ears." This brought laughter.

Then Peter, still standing with the other eleven, called out for quiet. The crowd, sensing something in his manner, began to obey. Peter shook his head. Raising his voice to be heard across the Mount, he said, "Men of Judea and all you who live in Jerusalem, listen to me. These men aren't drunk, as you suppose. It's only the third hour of the day. But this is what was spoken of through the prophet Joel: And it shall be in the last days,' God says, 'That I will pour forth of My Spirit on all mankind; And your sons and your daughters shall prophesy. And your young men shall see visions. And your old men shall dream dreams! Even on My bondslaves, both men and women, I will in those days pour forth of My Spirit and they shall prophesy. And I will grant wonders in the sky above, and signs on the earth below, blood, and fire, and vapor of smoke. The sun will be turned into darkness and the moon into blood, before the great and glorious day of the Lord shall come.'" He lifted both his hands out over what had now become an endless mass of people. "'And it shall be that everyone who calls on the name of the Lord will be saved!' Men of Israel, listen to these words! Jesus the Nazarene, a man attested to you by God with miracles and wonders and signs which God performed through him *in your midst*! You all know this! This man, delivered over by the predetermined plan and foreknowledge of God, you *nailed to a cross*!" Peter paused and stared at the gathered group of Sanhedrin for a long moment. "By the hands of *godless men* he was put to death!" Several of the Sanhedrin tried to shout him down, but Peter, having the higher ground, was louder and wouldn't be deterred. Sweat ran down his face and caught in his beard. Eyes wide, his voice boomed. "But God raised him up again! Putting an end to the agony of death, since it was impossible for him to be held in its power! Listen to this! David says of Him, 'I saw the Lord always in my presence; For He is at my right hand, so that I will not be shaken—'"

Caiaphas pushed his way to the front of the crowd. His face purple. "Outrage! Blasphemy! How dare you quote our father David in any sort of connection with that wretched scum of a Nazarene!"

The High Priest's outburst brought complete quiet to the gathering. The Cilician, a contingency of Levitical Patrol behind him, shoved through the crowd along the bottom of the Porch steps from the direction of the Stoa and, hand on his sword, took a stand next to the High Priest.

"They'll kill him outright if he continues," Nicodemus said under his breath.

Ariella grabbed Joseph's arm. "Joseph, is there anything we can do?"

Joseph put his hand over hers. "I don't know."

Peter, ignoring the Cilician, looked down, considering Caiaphas. A pigeon flapped in the rafters above. Someone coughed. Finally, with slow deliberation, Peter began to descend the steps.

"What's he doing?" Nicodemus whispered.

"Look at him. His face. The man is changed," Joseph replied. This is not the man who denied his master. Or the man hiding in the upper room. This is calm strength I've seen only in Yeshua himself.

"God's Spirit fills him," Nicodemus said. "The promise..."

Down Peter went, until he stood within a cubit of the High Priest. Eye to eye they stood. Caiaphas' mouth hung open, such was his surprise at the disciple's boldness.

Then Peter spoke again: "'Therefore my heart was glad and my tongue exulted. Moreover my flesh also will live in hope! Because You will not abandon my soul to Hades, nor allow Your *Holy One to undergo decay*! You have made known to me the ways of life! You will make me full of gladness with Your presence!'" He lifted his voice even louder. "Brethren, I may confidently say to you regarding the patriarch David that he both died and was buried, and his tomb is with us to this day. And so, because he was a prophet and knew that God had sworn to him with an oath to seat one of his descendants on his throne, he looked ahead and spoke of the Resurrection of the Christ, that He was neither abandoned to Hades, nor did His flesh suffer decay. This Yeshua God raised up again, to which *we are all witnesses*! And so, having been exalted to the right hand of God, and having received from the Father the promise of the *Holy Spirit*, He has poured forth this which you both see and hear. For it was not David who ascended into heaven, but he himself says: 'The Lord said to my Lord, sit at My right hand until I make Your enemies a footstool for Your feet.'"

"No!" Caiaphas shouted, visibly gathering himself. "This man is nothing but an ignorant Galilean! He is a breaker of the Law! He is a sinner! He is a blasphemer!"

But Peter stepped even closer to the High Priest. His voice reverberated through the Porch, across the Mount, off the Temple wall, through the very halls of Heaven itself. "Brothers! Let all the house of Israel know for certain that God has made Yeshua both *Lord and Christ*!" Then, the unthinkable. He shoved a stiff finger into the High Priest of Israel's chest. "This same Yeshua, *that you crucified*!"

The crowd erupted at this. Caiaphas slapped at Peter's hand but the sturdy fisherman didn't budge. Only after several seconds did he turn and ascend the steps back to the Porch. The Cilician started after him but paused when the stoop-shouldered Parthian reached Peter first. The man gripped the disciple's tunic. "Brother! I beg you! In light of the words you have spoken today, what shall we do?"

Peter patted the man's hand, then turned to the rest of the crowd. "Repent! And each of you be baptized in the name of Yeshua the Christ for the forgiveness of your sins! You *will* receive the gift of the Holy Spirit! For the promise is for you and your children and for all who are far off, as many as the Lord our God will call to Himself." He looked down at the gathered Sanhedrin again. "I'm telling you, be saved from this perverse generation!"

Caiaphas started to shout again but his words were drowned by the cries and press of bodies.

The Parthian spoke again. Joseph couldn't hear him over the crowd noise but he could read his lips.

"Baptize us! Please!" the man said. "We believe."

Peter nodded, shouted something to the other eleven, and the entire contingency began moving down the Porch toward the Royal Stoa and the Southern Steps.

Nicodemus raised himself up and shouted into Joseph's ear. "They're headed for the public mikvehs to be baptized. I must go as well!"

Joseph nodded. "Ariella and I will be with you."

Ariella took his arm.

With the push to the south, the clamor began to recede.

Then a call. "Joseph…"

Joseph turned, feeling Ariella's grip tighten on his arm. Beryl stood with Abigail several feet away. Abigail smiled, as she always did, but Beryl—never had Joseph seen a man so broken. He'd sunken into himself. Nothing left but a deflated shell. Still, something sparked in his eyes. "Joseph. I remain at your mercy. Neither man nor God could possibly blame you if you push your blade into my heart."

At that moment another shout rang. "Av Beit Din!" Caiaphas strode toward them, his face a purple mask of fury. "What do you think you're doing? Why did you not stand with us? Where are you going?"

Beryl shook his head. "So many questions. My friend, I'm doing what we both should have done that first day the Nazarene faced us on this very mount. I'm bending a knee to the truth of God. And I'm surrendering all I have to His Son."

Caiaphas' reply shot back in a staccato burst. "Then you'll die!"

Beryl's smile was the saddest thing Joseph had ever seen. "Yes, Caiaphas, I will. But don't you see? We both started our dying a long time ago."

Caiaphas took a long step forward and spat on Beryl's face. Beryl made no attempt to wipe it off.

"So be it." Caiaphas said. He turned and with a swish and swirl of robes was gone.

Beryl shifted his gaze back to Joseph. "Son-in-law, I mean what I say. I am dead already. Finish it."

A thousand thoughts flashed through Joseph's mind. Beryl's face, full of condescending hate as he looked at his daughter. Yeshua's bloody and battered face and Beryl's rapture at the sight. And then Davi, precious loyal Davi, the man who had stood at Joseph's side for more than two decades. Davi, blood leaking through his lips and staining the ground, eyes lifeless and vacant to the sky. Joseph could feel the heft of the knife on his belt. His fingers flexed.

But he could feel something else, too.

A glimmer of something. Something down deep. Something tiny but rapidly growing.

Abigail ghosted to his side. "Accept it, Joseph. Open your heart to it. Let it burn away your self."

"What is it?" Joseph said.

She put her arms around him. "I told you before, precious son-in-law. It's *everything*."

And so it was. Sorrow for his lost friend, Joseph still felt. Righteous anger for wrongs done his wife, horror over the injustice done to the Son of God… But looking through Beryl's broken eyes and down into his broken soul, something else began to glow within. Began to fill him. Something unbelievable. Something hard, soft, rich, and beautiful… A dam broke. A river flowed.

Love.

"I don't understand," Joseph said.

"No, you don't," Abigail said. "But isn't it perfect?"

"This can't be," Joseph said.

"Exactly," Abigail said.

Joseph looked at her, then back to Beryl. He sighed. "No, father-in-law. It won't be my hand that sends you from this world. I see the pain in you. I don't pretend to understand it, but it breaks my heart. There it is. We are God's. All of us. That's all."

Tears streaked Beryl's cheeks, mingling with Caiaphas' spittle. "Joseph, I'm so sorry for the things I've done to you and your household. And even more so, Yeshua. If you won't kill me, please, grant me one request."

"Request? What is it you want?"

Beryl stepped forward and put his hand on Joseph's arm directly over Ariella's. "Joseph of Arimathea… Please, will you baptize me?"

53

Beryl walked, not shuffled, as he and Abigail approached their home. He felt lighter, freer, than he had in as long as he could remember. Joseph, fresh from his own baptism, had in turn baptized Beryl in the public mikvehs by the Southern Temple Mount steps. Beryl had emerged to a brighter sky, a brighter world. He was still Av Beit Din, but he determined in his heart at that moment to use his position to persuade for Yeshua. He could never forget his part in the crucifixion of Yeshua, and he could never give Joseph Davi back, but maybe, just maybe, he could try to atone for at least some of the damage he'd caused. Caiaphas would fight him tooth and nail. And Beryl would eventually lose, but what did it matter? He'd gained the world. He had Abigail. He had Joseph and Ariella and his coming grandchild.

What world would the child be born into? The nation was changing. *Everything* was changing. Over three thousand souls had surrendered to the truth of the Messiah today. Would more follow? Surely they would. How could they not? Maybe all of Israel would follow! What a day that would be. Or, then again, and probably more likely, there would be war. After all, wasn't that the way of his people? Wasn't that their stubborn history? The Sanhedrin's pride would force them to press on with persecution against the Followers. And could he blame them? After all, if Abigail hadn't come, he would still be doing the same. Still be shaking his fists and gnashing his teeth. And he hated himself for it. He glanced over at Abigail. So beautiful. So filled with peace and joy and light. *How could I ever have gone so far wrong?*

"What are you thinking, husband?" she said.

"I wonder, Abigail, What will happen to us now?"

"That is for God to know. But the Spirit has come. He will change men. Never has anything like this happened in all history. And you, husband, are the greatest of examples."

"I confess, I feel so different. I don't understand it at all. I wouldn't think it could be possible."

"It's what Peter said—God has poured out His Spirit on all mankind."

"But I'm still a man. I'm a body with a soul. How can everything inside me change so quickly?"

"A body with a soul? No, husband, you are a soul who simply happens to have a body. You are becoming who you were always meant to be. Don't resist it and don't fight it. Seek God and all else will come to you. It's not complicated. The more you trust in Him, the more this world will fade. You will know peace." She smiled and took his arm.

They came then, the Patrol, stepping from an alley. The Cilician was with them. It came to Beryl that he'd half expected it.

"Stay back, Abigail," he said.

"You can listen to him, woman, but it will do little good, I'm afraid," the Cilician said. "This must be."

"What do you want?" Beryl said.

The Cilician shrugged. "Only to follow your own orders, Av Beit Din. What was it you said? Make examples?"

Beryl turned quickly. "Abigail—"

The knife entered his back.

He knew immediately what had happened. Though whether it had been the Cilician's hand or one of the Patrol who had shoved the blade home he couldn't tell. It didn't matter. He sank to his knees, then fell over, landing with his head propped against a wall at an odd angle. He couldn't move. Everything slowed. The strangest part—at the threshold of death, what he encountered was a rush of *life*. He felt the cool sensation of the stone beneath him. He heard a child laughing somewhere far away. He saw the wind whipping the robe around the Cilician's legs…

The Cilician looked down at him. "Hades waits for you, Av Beit Din. Know this—you die a traitor to your nation."

"No," Abigail said. "He does not. He is reborn and redeemed. His life but begins."

The Cilician took a step toward her. "Do you think you won't die this day as well? I know who you claim to be—*what* you claim to be. But I'm not a child to be fooled by your stories like the rest of them."

Abigail only smiled.

The Cilician's face reddened. "Woman! You smile? Do you realize I hold your life in my hand? By the power of the Sanhedrin?"

"No. God alone holds my life. You hold nothing."

The Cilician shook his head. "Have you no fear? Do you know who I am?"

Abigail's smile only brightened. "Oh yes, *Saul of Tarsus*! I know exactly who you are. But even better, I know who you will become. Go away now. And take your men with you. My time here isn't yet finished."

The Cilician's eyes widened a bit. Then he shook his head. "You're mad, woman. Bury your man. I won't waste any more time with this."

"Yes, go, Saul. And know you are loved."

He shook his head again, then turned. At length his footsteps faded into the distance.

The sky darkened a few shades.

"Abigail…" Beryl said.

She knelt by him then, taking his hand in hers, still smiling. "I'm here, Beryl. I'm here."

"I die. It's as it should be," he said.

"No, you but change garments. And, yes, it's always as it should be."

"I'm afraid, Abigail."

"Afraid? No! *Life is a vapor.* You go to the *real.* And soon I'll slip this shadowland of flesh as well. I'll see you there. And we'll run!" Her eyes filled, but her smile remained. "Oh, husband, just wait till you see me run… That's it, close your eyes now. No more pain."

And he did.

And she was right.

There was no more pain.

54

L ight.
The road between Jerusalem and Caesarea Maritima shimmered in the bright afternoon. The summer sun hung high and hot, but an onshore wind from the distant sea carried a cool breath to the little caravan. Joseph and Nicodemus rode horseback. Ariella and Abigail rocked comfortably in the back of a wagon driven by Longinus. Bityah sat on the seat beside him.

A week since Pentecost and Beryl's death. The Followers in Jerusalem, filled with the boldness of God's Spirit, no longer hid but worshipped openly throughout the city. Caiaphas, of course, was furious. He threatened and railed against Yeshua's name daily. The Cilician raged as well, but, for the moment, he and the Patrol were outnumbered by the large number of Pentecost converts still in the city.

The cart wheels rattled and squeaked. Far out over the rippling waves of grass, a hawk rose and dipped as it navigated updrafts watching the ground for an unsuspecting meal.

Joseph nodded toward the road ahead and glanced at Nicodemus. "It will be good for you to be with your family after so long, my friend."

"My arms ache for them," Nicodemus said. "How long will you stay in Maritima?"

Joseph shrugged. "Long enough to line up wine shipments to Rome and let Ariella spend some time with Lila. Thanks to Pilate holding to our deal, the vineyards in Arimathea are well guarded."

The little Pharisee patted his pack. "With the coming of the Spirit, the List will most certainly grow. I'll need your help. Let your overseers take care of the wine. You have bigger things."

Joseph laughed. "It's always The List with you. However, I agree. This is the priority."

"Yeshua commanded his disciples and followers to take his Gospel to the ends of the world. They will need information. Tools."

"I would take a copy of your List with us to Corsica," Longinus said. "Bityah and I will do our best to honor and convey the things that have happened here."

"And God will be with you," Abigail said.

"I'm still getting used to seeing you out of uniform, Longinus," Ariella said.

The Roman clucked at the donkey pulling the cart. "I gave Caesar enough years. And thanks to your husband doubling his efforts for my early release, I'll spend the rest of my life holding my wife instead of a sword."

Bityah laced her arm through his and tucked closer into his side.

"If I know you, Roman, you'll have a network of behind-the-scenes strings you'll be pulling on that island of yours within a week of arriving," Nicodemus said.

Longinus lifted a shoulder and smiled. "You don't know me well enough. I've had a network of people there for years. The strings have already been pulled. But at the moment, all I want is a quiet place where we can sit and watch the sea."

"Where will you stay in Maritima until you sail?" Nicodemus said.

Joseph cut in. "We have plenty of room in our apartments. They'll stay with us. I owe Longinus my life many times over. Anything you need, Longinus, any time, simply name it."

Longinus smiled. "Winemaker, I'll admit you've been entertaining to say the least. If I had it all to do over again—"

"He'd do it exactly the same," Bityah said.

The Roman nodded. "That's probably true. Anyway, thank you for the offer, but we have friends in the city who are expecting us. I've already sent word."

"Followers?" Joseph said.

"Larcon and Amaris," Bityah said.

"Good people," Nicodemus said.

"Larcon the criminal?" Joseph said.

"He was once," Nicodemus said. "And is also loved by Yeshua."

The hawk plunged, rising again with something small and indistinct in its talons. Abigail and Ariella began talking about Maritima and the sea. Bityah listened and asked an occasional question.

Joseph stretched his muscles and looked out over the countryside, liking the feeling of the horse beneath him.

Nicodemus reined his mount close. "All that nothing out there… Will it always be so, do you think?"

Joseph considered. "We watch the clouds for Yeshua. All will change with his return. Even the land. You know the prophecy."

"Yes, but before then."

Joseph looked at the little man. "I hope for him any minute."

"I hope for him as well, you know that. But what if it's a year from now? Or a hundred? Or thousands? What changes then? Will anyone remember our names? Will our story still live? Will they know of the things that happened here? Will the name Yeshua still bring hope?"

"Yeshua's name will always bring hope, Nicodemus. That's one thing we can know."

"Yes. Agreed. But if God should tarry, if this story is only just starting, what roads will cross this place then? Imagine! What cities will rise from this dust? Will Jerusalem still stand? What nations will come against her between now and then? How many times will she be tested? And what new things will man come up with? What new ways to impress his will on others? What all can't we see with our dim eyes?"

"If we can't see it, then it's not for us. We do what we can in our own time, yes? We do what we're called to do. Two hours, two years, two thousand years—God will still be God. His will will be done now and it will be then."

"Amen."

"Amen."

"But I'm still curious."

Joseph chuckled. "You wouldn't be you if you weren't. And I fully expect you to hound me about it until I can't take any more."

"You'll love it."

"While we breathe, we'll keep searching the scriptures for answers, yes?"

Nicodemus nodded "Other writings as well, I think. Did you know the Twelve are already talking of committing the teaching of Yeshua and his story to parchment?"

"Then our road doesn't end, does it?"

"My friend, to tell you the truth, even after all we've seen and experienced, I have a strong feeling our road may be just beginning."

Later that evening, Joseph watched the sun sink into the sea from the rooftop of their Maritima apartments. From behind, Ariella's arms came around him.

"You're a ghost, woman. So quiet," he said.

"I'm not a ghost, husband. I'm very alive. So are you and so is our child."

"I feel him against my back."

"I love you."

"I love you, too." Joseph sighed and put his hands on hers. "Ariella, it won't be an easy world we bring this child into."

She released him and moved to his side, her eyes fixed on the horizon, the dying light illuminating her face. Never had anyone looked so beautiful.

"Our child will have you as a father," she said. "And if I have anything to do with it, Yeshua's name will be on his lips from cradle to grave. We'll be together, Joseph. And the Spirit will be with us always. Yeshua promised. That's all that matters."

As he put his arm around her and pulled her close, the sun slipped below the horizon.

But the Light remained.

The Beginning

If you enjoyed this book, will you consider sharing the message with others?

Tell your friends! Word of mouth is everything. Mention the book in a blog post or through Facebook, Twitter, Instagram, or any of the social media sites you might frequent.

Recommend this book to your pastor, those in your small group, book club, workplace, etc.

Pick up a copy for someone you know who would be challenged and encouraged by this message.

Please write a review online. Your opinion counts!

Want to be first in line for news and info?

Sign up for our email list at BUCKSTORM.COM

APPENDIX 1

NICODEMUS 'ORIGINAL LIST OF 25 OLD TESTAMENT PROPHECIES OF THE COMING MESSIAH

Scholars have identified more than 300 specific prophecies about Yeshua/Jesus in the Old Testament. The mathematical probability of one man fulfilling even a handful of them, let alone all of them, is staggeringly improbable—if not impossible. In our story, Nicodemus continues the search... Will you?

He would bless the world through Abraham's lineage

Gen. 12:3 *"And I will bless those who bless you, And the one who curses you I will curse. And in you all the families of the earth will be blessed."*

The Messiah would be born of a virgin

Is. 7:14 *"Therefore the Lord Himself will give you a sign: Behold, a virgin will be with child and bear a son, and she will call His name Immanuel."*

He would be from King David's lineage

Jer. 23:5 *"Behold, the days are coming, 'declares the Lord, 'When I will raise up for David a righteous Branch; And He will reign as king and act wisely And do justice and righteousness in the land."*

He would be born in Bethlehem

Micah 5:2 *"But as for you, Bethlehem Ephrathah, Too little to be among the clans of Judah, From you One will go forth for Me to be ruler in Israel. His goings forth are from long ago, From the days of eternity."*

He would come out of Egypt

Hosea 11:1 *"When Israel was a child, then I loved him, and called my son out of Egypt."*

He would be preceded by a forerunner

Mal. 3:1 *"'Behold, I am going to send My messenger, and he will clear the way before Me. And the Lord, whom you seek, will suddenly come to His temple; and the messenger of the covenant, in whom you delight, behold, He is coming,' says the Lord of hosts."*

He was not coming as a King with wealth

Is. 53:2 *"... He has no stately form or majesty that we should look upon Him, nor appearance that we should be attracted to Him."*

He was to be a suffering Messiah

Is. 53:4 *"Surely our griefs He Himself bore, and our sorrows He carried; Yet we ourselves esteemed Him stricken, smitten of God, and afflicted."*

He would enter Jerusalem publicly on a donkey

Zech. 9:9 *"Rejoice greatly, O daughter of Zion! Shout in triumph, O daughter of Jerusalem! Behold, your king is coming to you; He is just and endowed with salvation, humble, and mounted on a donkey, even on a colt, the foal of a donkey."*

He would be a stumbling block to the Jews

Is. 8:14 *"Then He shall become a sanctuary; But to both the houses of Israel, a stone to strike and a rock to stumble over, and a snare and a trap for the inhabitants of Jerusalem.*

He would be called "Immanuel"

Is. 7:14 *"Therefore the Lord Himself will give you a sign: Behold, a virgin will be with child and bear a son, and she will call His name Immanuel."*

He would be betrayed by a friend

Psalm 41:9 *"Even my close friend in whom I trusted, who ate my bread, has lifted up his heel against me."*

He would be rejected by the Jewish rulers

Is. 49:7 *"Thus says the Lord, the Redeemer of Israel and its Holy One, to the despised One, to the One abhorred by the nation, to the Servant of rulers,"*

He would be crucified, not stoned to death

Psalm 22:16 *"...They pierced my hands and my feet."*

He would be struck on the face

Micah 5:1 *"Now muster yourselves in troops, daughter of troops; They have laid siege against us; With a rod they will smite the judge of Israel on the cheek."*

He would be buried with the rich

Is. 53:9 *"His grave was assigned with wicked men, Yet He was with a rich man in His death,"*

Men would gamble for His clothing

Psalm 22:18 *"They part my garments among them, and cast lots upon my vesture."*

He would be mocked

Psalm 22:7-8 *"All who see me sneer at me; They separate with the lip, they wag the head, saying, 'Commit yourself to the Lord; let Him deliver him; Let Him rescue him, because He delights in him."*

Not one of His bones would be broken

Psalm 34:20 *"He keeps all his bones, not one of them is broken."*

He would be resurrected

Psalm 16:10 *"For You will not abandon my soul to Sheol, Nor will You allow Your Holy One to undergo decay."*

The exact day of His arrival was predicted

Dan. 9:24 *"Seventy weeks* [heptads, weeks of years = 490 years] *have been decreed for your people and your holy city, to make atonement for iniquity, to bring in everlasting righteousness, to seal up vision and prophecy and to anoint the most holy place."*

Dan. 9:25 *"So you are to know and discern that from the issuing of a decree to restore and rebuild Jerusalem until Messiah the Prince there will be seven weeks and sixty-two weeks* [69 total weeks of years = 483 years or 173,880 days]; *it will be built again, with plaza and moat, even in times of distress."*

Dan. 9:26 *"Then after the sixty-two weeks the Messiah will be* [executed] *and have nothing, and the people of the prince who is to come will destroy the city and the sanctuary."*

He would come into the Temple

Mal. 3:1 *"...And the Lord, whom you seek, will suddenly come to His temple..."*

Thirty pieces would be thrown on the floor of the Temple

Zech. 11:13 *"Then the LORD said to me, 'Throw it to the potter, that magnificent price at which I was valued by them.' So I took the thirty shekels of silver and threw them to the potter in the house of the Lord.'"*

He would be praised by infants and babes

Psalm 8:2 *"From the mouth of infants and nursing babes You have established strength Because of Your adversaries, to make the enemy and the revengeful cease."*

He would heal the blind, deaf and lame

Is. 35:5-6 *"Then the eyes of the blind will be opened and the ears of the deaf will be unstopped. Then the lame will leap like a deer, and the tongue of the mute will shout for joy.*

APPENDIX 2

BIBLICAL VERSES REFERRING TO
JOSEPH OF ARIMATHEA AND NICODEMUS

Joseph of Arimathea

"When it was evening, there came a rich man from Arimathea, named **Joseph,** *who himself had also become a disciple of Jesus. This man went to Pilate and asked for the body of Jesus. Then Pilate ordered it to be given to him. And Joseph took the body and wrapped it in a clean linen cloth, and laid it in his own new tomb, which he had hewn out in the rock; and he rolled a large stone against the entrance of the tomb and went away."* **Matt. 27:57**

"And a man named **Joseph,** *who was a member of the Council, a good and righteous man (he had not consented to their plan and action), a man from Arimathea, a city of the Jews, who was waiting for the kingdom of God; this man went to Pilate and asked for the body of Jesus. And he took it down and wrapped it in a linen cloth, and laid Him in a tomb cut into the rock, where no one had ever lain."* **Luke 23:50-53**

"After these things **Joseph** *of Arimathea, being a disciple of Jesus, but a secret one for fear of the Jews, asked Pilate that he might take away the body of Jesus; and Pilate granted permission. So he came and took away His body.* **Nicodemus,** *who had first come to Him by night, also came, bringing a mixture of myrrh and aloes, about a hundred pounds weight. So they took the body of Jesus and bound it in linen wrappings with the spices, as is the burial custom of the Jews. Now in the place where He was crucified there was a garden, and in the garden a new tomb in which no one had yet been laid. Therefore because of the Jewish day of preparation, since the tomb was nearby, they laid Jesus there."* **John 19:38-42**

Nicodemus

"Now there was a man of the Pharisees, named **Nicodemus,** *a ruler of the Jews; this man came to Jesus by night and said to*

Him, 'Rabbi, we know that You have come from God as a teacher; for no one can do these signs that You do unless God is with him."

"Jesus answered and said to him, 'Truly, truly, I say to you, unless one is born again he cannot see the kingdom of God."

"Nicodemus said to Him, 'How can a man be born when he is old? He cannot enter a second time into his mother's womb and be born, can he?

"Jesus answered, 'Truly, truly, I say to you, unless one is born of water and the Spirit he cannot enter into the kingdom of God. That which is born of the flesh is flesh, and that which is born of the Spirit is spirit. Do not be amazed that I said to you, "You must be born again." The wind blows where it wishes and you hear the sound of it, but do not know where it comes from and where it is going; so is everyone who is born of the Spirit."

*"**Nicodemus** said to Him, 'How can these things be?"*

"Jesus answered and said to him, 'Are you the teacher of Israel and do not understand these things? Truly, truly, I say to you, we speak of what we know and testify of what we have seen, and you do not accept our testimony. If I told you earthly things and you do not believe, how will you believe if I tell you heavenly things? No one has ascended into heaven, but He who descended from heaven: the Son of Man.'"

"As Moses lifted up the serpent in the wilderness, even so must the Son of Man be lifted up; so that whoever believes will in Him have eternal life. For God so loved the world, that He gave His only begotten Son, that whoever believes in Him shall not perish, but have eternal life. For God did not send the Son into the world to judge the world, but that the world might be saved through Him."

"He who believes in Him is not judged; he who does not believe has been judged already, because he has not believed in the name of the only begotten Son of God. This is the judgment, that the Light has come into the world, and men loved the darkness

*rather than the Light, for their deeds were evil. For everyone who does evil hates the Light, and does not come to the Light for fear that his deeds will be exposed. But he who practices the truth comes to the Light, so that his deeds may be manifested as having been wrought in God." **John 3:1-21***

ABOUT THE AUTHOR

Buck Storm is a critically acclaimed author and musician. His books and songs have made friends around the world. Buck and his wife Michelle have been married for thirty years and have two married children.

More Books by Buck Storm

THE LIST
Compass Publishing, 2019

The ancient prophets said he would come. And for centuries the people watched, waited and hoped. He was to be the redeemer of Israel. The all-powerful King of Kings who would finally and decisively deliver the nation from the iron fist of Rome.

Joseph of Arimathea is a wealthy man, but wealth can't buy peace. Nor the affection of the wife he loves. Nicodemus is a leader of Israel who will stop at nothing to find truth. Sadducee and Pharisee—two men, worlds apart, thrown together at the most critical moment in the history of the world.

Set against the spectacle and grandeur of ancient Israel and the brutal violence of the Roman Empire, here is a tale not to be missed. Step into THE LIST and experience the Christ story as you never have before.

THE BEAUTIFUL ASHES OF GOMEZ GOMEZ
Kregel Publications - 2020

When his wife, Angel, is killed in a head-on collision, Gomez Gomez feels he can't go on—so he doesn't. He spends his days in the bushes next to the crash site drinking Thunderbird wine, and his nights cradling a coffee can full of Angel's ashes. Slow, sure suicide, with no one for company but the snakes, Elvis's ghost, and a strange kid named Bones.

Across town, Father Jake Morales plays it safe, haunted by memories of the woman he left behind, hiding his guilt, loss, and love behind a thick wall of cassock and ritual. When a shady business deal threatens the town—and his good friend Gomez Gomez—Father Jake can't just stand by and watch. But what happens when the rescuer is the one in need of saving?
The Beautiful Ashes of Gomez Gomez is heartfelt, and deeply human. Lives and hopes collide in the town of Paradise,

stretching across decades and continents in this epic story of forgiveness, redemption, and love.

THE MIRACLE MAN
Heritage Beacon Fiction, 2015

Welcome to Paradise, a sleepy, backwater town in the mountains of Southeastern Arizona where police chief Luke Hollis is perfectly content to concentrate on nothing but issuing the occasional speeding ticket and figuring out how to get a date with Ruby Brooks, his dispatcher. When an unexplained healing occurs during a service at the Mount Moriah Pentecostal Church of God, Hollis finds his simple belief system challenged and his life forever changed.

TRUCK STOP JESUS
Heritage Beacon Fiction, 2016

Oh, for a simpler time! Struggling actress Paradise Jones dreams of the Hollywood glamour days. Clothes, hair, vintage car—you name it, she's got it. The entertainment rags call Paradise eccentric. The studios rarely call at all. When an altercation with her leering stepfather forces her to flee Los Angeles, Paradise leaves behind everything she loves and longs for.

Throw in a washed-up ball player, couple of oddball bounty hunters, a forgotten movie-star boat captain, and a dashboard Jesus that is more than meets the eye, and the stage is set for this quirky slice of Americana pie. Hop in and buckle up for a road trip you won't soon forget.

FINDING JESUS IN ISRAEL, Through the Holy Land on the Road Less Traveled
Hachette, 2018

We are all shaped and transformed by the oceans we sail, the deserts, mountains, and valleys we wander, and the people we meet along the way. And as any traveler worth his salt knows, the real trip happens within.

Part travel journal but mostly spiritual guide, Finding Jesus in Israel a book for travel veterans, people with wanderlust, or readers who just love a good story.